OF SILK AND STEAM

BEC MCMASTER

sourcebooks
casablanca

Published by Sourcebooks Casablanca, an imprint of Sourcebooks,
Inc.
P.O. Box 4410, Naperville, Illinois 60567-4410
(630) 961-3900
Fax: (630) 961-2168
www.sourcebooks.com

Printed and bound in Canada
MBP 10 9 8 7 6 5 4 3 2 1

To James and Jess

She walks in beauty, like the night
Of cloudless climes and starry skies;
And all that's best of dark and bright
Meet in her aspect and her eyes...

—*"She Walks in Beauty,"* Lord Byron

Prologue

THE FIRST TIME LEO BARRONS SAW HER, SHE'D JUST run a man through with her sword.

Peter Duvall gave a little gasp. Bluish blood dripped down his chest—the color that gave the blue bloods of the Echelon their name.

The young woman stepped back, jerking the tip of her rapier from Duvall's chest. It had gone straight through the heart, one of the few ways to kill a blue blood. The duel had been serious then, or else they'd have used pistols, which were far less lethal in these circumstances. A blue blood could only be killed by decapitation or severe damage to the heart, so a shot had to be true.

Leo Barrons clapped a little as Duvall fell, echoing the rest of the crowd of young bucks, though he could barely take his eyes off her. He'd arrived late at the Field of Blood in Hyde Park, near Constitution Hill, with evening caressing the skyline of London. Just in time to catch the end of the matter.

Who was she?

Tall and slender, the woman had the proud bearing of a queen, but that wasn't what stirred the blood in his veins. The steel manica protecting her sword arm, the long leather leggings, and the head-to-toe black of her tight velvet coat only highlighted the shining garnet red of her hair. It was captured in a chignon at the nape of her neck, although wisps of it clung to her serious face. The setting sun caught her hair on fire. Thick, dark lashes shuttered her eyes as she plucked a handkerchief from her second—a young lad, more boy than man—and with considerable aplomb wiped the blood from her blade.

She might have been standing alone in that clearing, deftly ignoring the excited chatter of the assorted young men congratulating her. There was a sense of aloofness about her, as if she existed outside this world and could never be touched.

And she'd just managed to defeat a blue blood in a duel, which was a talent in itself. Blue bloods were faster and stronger than humans, the craving virus that afflicted them giving them exceptional capabilities. How the devil had she managed it? Duvall was…*had been* no slouch with a blade, though he was hardly a master.

One look. That was all it took. Leo wanted her.

"Who is she?" Leo murmured to the Duke of Malloryn's heir, Auvry Cavill, without taking his eyes off her.

The faintest of smiles touched Auvry's ·mouth. They'd been friends since Eton. "Why don't you ask her? I wouldn't want to ruin the surprise."

A dare. "So I shall."

He strode through the crowd, ignoring the young bucks of the aristocratic Echelon as much as she did. They were unimportant. She was all that mattered, all that he could see.

Some sense of wariness must have alerted her to him, because she looked up, brandy-brown eyes locking on him and piercing him straight through the chest. Or lower.

Handing her second the bloodied rag, she dismissed Leo with a glance and vanished into the grove of trees behind the field of grass.

If she thought that was the end of it, she was wrong. His steps accelerated, and he knew she heard autumn leaves crackling beneath his heels as he followed her. A glance over her shoulder and she stilled, as if realizing he had no intention of giving up.

"You've come to congratulate me?" A mocking tilt of one perfectly defined brow. She wore disdain almost as well as she did aloofness. No doubt she was quite used to men's flattery. With that face and figure, she'd have to be.

"Congratulate you?" he asked. "Perhaps. You were lucky to win that with your form."

Those eyes flashed fire, and shock pierced her expression. Just for a moment. "Lucky?"

He smiled on the inside. If he wanted to capture her attention, he had to be different from all the others who no doubt fawned at her feet. "You drop your shoulder too low on the lunge," he said, gesturing to the offending body part, his gloved fingers brushing the puffed velvet sleeve of her coat. "It creates an opening, if your opponent is aware of it."

She stared at him, then looked down to where his fingers stirred against her sleeve. "Fair warning. I shall take it into consideration if you're ever my opponent."

"I doubt we'll be opponents."

"Do you?" A slight challenge in the soft words.

This was not going the way he'd planned. "Perhaps I should introduce myself. Leo Barrons, the Duke of Caine's heir."

"I know who you are." Cool, expressionless eyes. "Your arrogance precedes you. If you'll excuse me?"

The moment she brushed past him, he turned. "Have I done something to insult you?"

That slim figure froze, her spine stiffening. She glanced over her shoulder at him, one hand resting lightly on the sword at her hip. "You have no idea who I am, do you?"

Evidently. Leo frowned. He rarely paid attention to the young women who formed society. He'd been gifted with two thralls for his eighteenth birthday, and as a man of nineteen, he didn't need any others. Their blood sustained him and he could not afford to keep more. And then, of course: "I've only recently returned from my Grand Tour of the Continent, and I doubt I would have forgotten you."

"I shall take mercy on you this once, my lord," she said, stepping closer and staring him in the eye with a defiance that stirred his blood. "Your father killed mine. You are the last man alive I would ever wish to converse with, let alone…whatever puts that gleam in your eye."

"My father's killed a lot of men." Caine was utterly ruthless when he wished to be. Especially to his wife's bastard son, though few people knew the truth of Leo's birth. "You'll have to be more specific."

The woman leaned forward on her toes, her breath whispering against his skin. "Perhaps this will help?" The irises of her eyes bled to black, heated anger gleaming in their depths.

She was a blue blood. "That's impossible."

Only the sons of certain blue bloods were allowed the blood rites when they turned fifteen. The Council of Dukes would never allow a female to be considered, which made her a rogue blue blood, infected by chance.

"I assure you it's not." She leaned away from him again, smiling. There was no warmth in that smile. "My name is Aramina Duvall."

Another blow; a fist to the abdomen this time. Auvry had known exactly who she was, the bastard.

"I see you know the name," she murmured.

The Duke of Casavian's only daughter. The man had died but a month ago, leaving his affairs in disarray. Leo's gaze shot through the slender trunks of the beech trees to Peter Duvall's bloodied form. No doubt this had been a duel to settle, once and for all, who was heir to the duchy.

"*That* makes me the Duchess of Casavian," she said. "Your father's mortal enemy."

Boldness stole over him. Leo caught her fingers as she turned to leave. "I don't care." Lifting them, he pressed his lips against the inside of her wrist, a shockingly bold deed, signaling his interest in her as a potential thrall.

"You should." She tugged her hand free, furious

heat stealing into her cheeks. Her eyes were black again, revealing the depths of her emotions. She must have been newly made a blue blood; it took years to master one's emotions and control the depth of the predator within. "After all, I'm going to destroy you and your father. And if you ever touch me again, I shall remove the offending limb."

Then she turned on her heel and strode away. Leaving him slightly breathless but no less determined.

PART ONE
THE CHASE

One

There are many facts that we know about that which we call the "craving virus." That it originated in the Orient, used by the Imperial Family of the White Court to make themselves known as gods to their superstitious subjects; that the aristocrats of Spain, France, England, and Russia sought to infect themselves with the virus to promote their longevity, strength, speed, and increased healing rates; that the one unfortunate side effect—apart from the craving for blood—is the inevitable spiral of a blue blood into the Fade—that moment when the virus overwhelms a body, creating a creature obsessed by its obscene hungers: a vampire.

There is one final fact that until this day has been undeniable—that there is no cure for the craving virus. I do not claim otherwise. I believe there is no true cure for the virus, but the rate at which it colonizes a body can be controlled. As such, no longer shall the Fade—and the threat of vampires—be feared by the human populace of London. And it all begins with a vaccination...

—Transcript of journal entries by Sir Artemus Todd, published posthumously by Leopold Barrons in *Philosophical Transactions of the Royal Society,* 1880

Venetian Gardens, London, 1880

LAUGHTER ECHOED THROUGH THE NIGHT, ROUGH, bawdy, and high-pitched. In the distance, automatons played Brahms's most recent string quartet. Cloaks swirled as dancers spun beneath an intricate rotunda carved in the rococo fashion. The enormous clock above the dome struck midnight, and the sky suddenly shattered into violent coruscations of fireworks.

It was time, then.

Lady Aramina slid the hood of her black velvet cape into place and slipped out of the crowd watching the dancing. It was an odd mix of both rich and poor, the brightly clothed and soberly hued, but one thing they all had in common here were masks. The Venetian Gardens were the place to be seen on a warm summer's night, but anonymity was particularly desired during one of the Gardens' notorious weekly masquerades.

Humans mingled with blue bloods, with none the wiser. Of course, she could tell which were which. The scent of blood in a young man's wine betrayed what he was as surely as his pale skin. The pair of young women at his side were dressed in matching ball gowns, one with a collar of pearls and the other with a circlet of rubies around her throat. A blue-blood lord and his thralls, then. The collars indicated that they were under his protection and helped to hide the fine silvery scars at their throats, brought about by his small blood-letting knife. Any sign of scarring was considered vulgar in the world of the Echelon.

A burly man in a homespun cloak staggered into

the pair of girls, reeling with the scent of gin. The blue blood's smile slipped, and within seconds, steel flashed in the night. The man fell, blood staining his shirt from where the lord had run him through. The man's friends, all of them built just as broadly—sailors perhaps, or dockworkers—hurried forward and begged apology, dragging the injured man out of the way. He'd live. Perhaps.

Either way, none of his friends would dare try to claim justice. The Venetian Gardens were on the outskirts of the walled heart of the City, where the blue bloods ruled London from their Ivory Tower, but close enough for fear to rule human hearts. If the same event had occurred outside the walls in the roughened boroughs of London, then perhaps the story would have been a different one.

For years, humans had been considered nothing more than cattle, and mechs—those men or women forced by accident or circumstance to replace limbs with metal—even less so. But recently the tide seemed to be turning. Whispers filled the city, those so-called "humanists" speaking of revolution, of throwing off the yoke of their blue-blood masters. One day those whispers would become shouts, and then the whole city would burn.

Dangerous thoughts to be having these days. The prince consort had ordered dozens of people cut down simply for murmuring such dissidence. There'd been a riot barely a day ago, with dozens of humans crushed beneath the steel Trojan cavalry the prince consort commanded.

Even here the rumble of discontent echoed, with

one of the dockworkers glaring hatred at the lord as he escorted his thralls away. The injured man lay on the grass at his friends' feet.

It's not your concern, Mina told herself, slipping a champagne glass from the tray of a passing servant drone. She had other business to attend to this night. Raising the bloodied liquid to her lips, she glanced around. Nobody was watching her.

An explosion of hot gold sparks rocked the skies, reflecting off the gold lace of her gown and the waters of the nearest canal. Mina walked unhurriedly, her cape fluttering around her and the filigreed gold mask she wore eclipsing half her face. Men glanced at her, but she ignored them, steadily making her way over several bridges toward the back of the pleasure gardens. Here, the trees held no lanterns and the walkways were lined with hedges. Distance blanketed the sound of music, leaving her able to hear crickets chirping in the long grass. A place for secret rendez-vous and scandalous liaisons. A dangerous place for a woman alone.

In most circumstances.

A tall shape formed out of the shadows, his cloak swirling around his leather boots and a sharp-beaked black mask hiding his face. There was no hiding the confidence in his manner or bearing, but nothing of a swagger about his stride. He simply had the air of a man who knew exactly what his worth was.

"You look ravishing, my dear," he murmured, taking Mina's gloved hand and leaning over it. "As a blond."

His lips didn't quite touch her glove.

Mina's gaze slid past his shoulder into the shadows

that clung like dense fog. The wig in question itched like the devil. "Sir, you do me too much honor. I'm not here to be ravished."

"No?" He straightened, a smile twitching behind his neatly groomed beard and moustache. "You're right, my dear. Ravishment wouldn't interest you. My apologies."

Mina arched a cool brow, but his words, as polite as they were, stung a little. She had no choice but to prove herself made of ice. It was one of the few weapons she had at court, but it didn't mean she felt nothing. "You're playing a dangerous game."

"Straight to the point." His smile deepened. "Like a knife. I like that about you."

"Goethe—"

He gave his head a tight little shake and her lips compressed. Too many here knew what that single name represented. The Duke of Goethe was one of the seven dukes who ruled London—or six dukes and one duchess, to be more precise. She knew, though, what the rest of them thought. The House of Casavian was virtually powerless on the Council of Dukes, just one more vote among many.

She wanted them to think that. "Sir—"

"Do you have the note?"

"I do." Their eyes met. "I shouldn't give it to you. I shouldn't encourage this."

"You've hardly been encouraging," he replied blithely, holding out his hand.

And she had her orders. Mina's lips thinned again as she reached into the valley between her breasts and produced a tiny waxed note from a pocket inside her

corset. It was cool from her skin—just another differ-
ence between a human and a blue blood.

Goethe reached for it, but she held on just a fraction
longer. "What you're doing puts you at risk. If the
prince consort finds out—"

"He'll push me into a duel." The pressure increased
and Goethe came away with the note. "Be at peace,
my lady. I know the consequences and I accept them."
He tucked the note somewhere inside his coat and
then, with a faint bow of the head, strode past her.

Bloody arrogant man. Ten years ago this might
have ended in a duel, but she suspected the prince
consort was no longer firmly in command of his
darker nature. Something every blue blood faced
eventually—or would have without the recent dis-
covery of the vaccination for the craving virus and its
effects on a blue blood.

Drinking a vaccinated person's blood could hold
the Fade at bay, though it was too late, in her mind,
for the prince consort. His madness was only escalat-
ing, his thirst dangerously uncontrollable.

No, the prince consort wouldn't challenge Goethe
to a duel if he realized the duke was courting his wife
in secret.

He'd kill him.

Wind whispered through the nearest hedge, and a
prickling sensation rose on the back of her neck. Mina
tugged her velvet hood tighter around her face and
kept walking. The scent of the breeze off the nearest
canal left much to be desired. She took a deep breath
and turned her face just as something blurred out of
the hedges.

An arm wrapped around her throat, a knife coming up sharply. "Don't move, lov—"

Mina caught her attacker's wrist and used his own momentum to flip him over her shoulder. The heel of her slippered foot struck him a glancing blow to the throat, and then she wrenched his shoulder behind him, using her heel to roll him onto his front.

The effort left her breathing hard, warm darkness rolling through her vision as the hunger of the craving urged her to finish the task. He was bleeding. The rich, coppery scent left her a little dizzy and made her swallow.

Mina closed her eyes and let out a slow breath. For years she'd thought herself the only female blue blood in London. The Echelon had long feared a woman's nature too sensitive to deal with such dark hungers, and she *had* to ensure she comported herself with decorum.

It wouldn't do to let the hunger control her. She wouldn't give them the satisfaction of being proven correct. And so she forced the hunger down ruthlessly, deep inside her heart of ice.

"I don't have anything worth stealing," Mina whispered, bending low and locking his shoulder just shy of dislocation. "And unfortunately for you, I am more than capable of defending myself when called upon. However, you didn't know that. You expected to find a pigeon, ripe for the plucking. Now…" Another hard yank on his arm that made him grunt in pain. "If this had been another young woman, she would have been at your mercy. For her sake, should I be merciful?"

The man gathered his fingertips beneath him.

"B-bugger y-you." Then somehow he spun, rolling in the direction of his trapped arm to free it and shoving her out of the way. A boot lashed out at her but Mina darted to avoid it, cursing her skirts. As the man found his knife and rolled to his feet, she triggered the small pistol strapped to her wrist and it slid into her palm.

"Drop it." When his hand clenched on the knife, she took a step forward. "You move too fast to be human, which makes me assume you're a blue blood, though you don't have the look of an aristocrat. A rogue blue blood, then. Which makes you dangerous."

A flash of white teeth. "You have no idea, Duchess."

That was the problem with being one of the two known female blue bloods in London—for she too had moved too fast to be human. "I do wish you hadn't said that. I'll only ask this once more: drop the knife. I'm using firebolt bullets, built to explode on impact, and I assure you, I won't miss."

With the chemical components in the firebolts, Mina wouldn't need to be particularly lucky. She'd seen them take a shark-sized chunk out of a man's chest.

Frustration gleamed in the man's dark eyes, but he dropped the knife. Then his gaze flickered over her shoulder. Something behind her.

Mina wasted no time, bringing the flank of the pistol down sharply across her attacker's forehead. He fell unconscious at her feet, just as she jerked the pistol up and stared through the sights at the newcomer.

A tall man coalesced out of the darkness as if he'd been made for shadows. He moved with a danger-ous, deadly grace that spoke of speed, of strength…

of restrained violence. The predator in her recognized another predator. Her heart stirred, a restless sensation sinking through her skin.

The world faded around her as she focused the pistol directly between the eyes of the black velvet mask he wore. He was tall, but the cloak obscured most of his body. It didn't, however, disguise the broadness of his shoulders or the lean flash of his thighs. A man in his prime.

"Stay back," she warned.

The black-clad stranger held his hands up in a gesture of surrender, a dangerous smile curling over half of his mouth. "I meant only to offer assistance—before I realized you had matters well in hand. I saw him shadowing you from the rotunda."

That smile seemed hauntingly familiar, and his clothes were considerably richer than those on the man at her feet. "Ruffians often work in pairs." Her eyes narrowed. "Why should I trust you?"

The smile widened. He looked almost piratical now as he lifted a hand to the stark velvet mask and slowly removed it, revealing a pair of eyes that were almost black in the night. Eyes she knew only too well and a dangling ruby at his ear.

"Because if I wanted you dead, Mina, I would have done it a long time ago."

❧

Only he dared call her Mina.

The brief hint of shock in her brown eyes was almost worth it as Leo lowered the mask.

Eight years of simmering tension lingered between

them, since he'd made that reckless decision to pursue her. She'd hardly been welcoming, throwing the feud in his face at every chance as though to protect herself, but their encounters fascinated him in a way he'd never experienced with another female.

You just can't help yourself, can you?

"Barrons," she said flatly, her fingers unconsciously clenching the butt of the pistol. "I hardly expected you to play hero."

"Ah, but then you don't know me well enough to predict such a thing."

The filigreed gold mask hid most of her features, but he was certain that he saw a hint of wariness in her eyes. The duchess didn't understand his motives; she never had. And he fully intended to keep it that way.

"I thought you were in Saint Petersburg, cementing the Russian alliance."

"I was. The treaty was signed three days ago. I arrived home by dirigible this morning. Are you going to lower the pistol?"

"Should I?"

The frigidity of her voice made him smile. She didn't like being caught off guard, even for a second. Only when she thought she was in control did she allow herself to soften, just a little. He was curious to find out if there was more softness beneath the steel, having seen just a hint of fire beneath the ice. It was the only thing that had sustained his hope during the long years of coming up against that frost.

That, and the almost-kiss…

That moment when they'd been trapped in a darkened room together and he'd leaned closer, blood thumping through his veins as he realized that what he saw in her dark eyes wasn't denial.

She'd turned away from the kiss, allowing him to make a fool of himself before she took back control, but for a moment there had been something more between them. A lazy, liquid trembling in the air. Need.

She'd wanted to give in. He knew it. He just had to push her to that point again.

Leo stepped forward, and she swiftly thumbed the hammer back. He took another slow step, pressing the muzzle of the pistol directly against his chest. Their eyes met. "If you were going to pull the trigger, you'd have done it years ago."

She'd been his nemesis since the moment they met, but it wasn't hate that existed between them. Not anymore. He couldn't quite define the emotion, but it certainly wasn't hate, no matter how much she tried to pretend it was.

Fascination, on his behalf. A certain dangerous temptation to dip his fingers into the fire to see how hotly it burned, which was foolishness of the worst kind. If he clicked his fingers, a dozen young debutantes would come flocking to his side, offering him everything he desired. Or almost everything... For the one thing he wanted, above all else, was glaring rather fiercely at him over the top of the pistol.

"You shouldn't be so certain," she said.

"But if you shot me, who else would try to seduce you?"

"You think I enjoy your attentions?"

A smile. "I think...that no one else dares. And, yes,

I think that you enjoy every second of them. Who else would argue with you over Council sessions so vociferously? And don't tell me you don't enjoy that, because nothing else fires your blood so." He leaned closer, his breath whispering along her jaw. "It's the only time you get that look in your eye… You enjoy arguing with me, and you like the fact that I chase you. A part of me thinks you *want* to be caught."

A small growl of exasperation sounded in her throat. The pistol wavered. "You drive me insane. You're a hindrance, nothing else."

Leo reached out and brushed a blond curl off her heart-shaped face—it was a wig, he guessed. Mina jerked away from his touch, but the pulse in her throat leaped. It was beating hard; she was not quite as immune to him as she claimed.

Closing a hand over the pistol, he forced it to lower, meeting her eyes again. "You won't shoot me. You'd miss me too much."

"Your arrogance was once amusing, Barrons, but it's becoming decidedly less so."

Ignoring the arctic chill in her tone, he smiled. "*Did* you miss me, Mina? Did you think of me whilst I was gone this past month?"

"I didn't even spare you a thought." Her eyes smoldered.

"*Liar.*"

They stared at each other, at an impasse.

"Why did you follow me?" she asked, tucking the pistol back within her sleeve. It was one of those mechanical-draw ones he'd heard about. "I know it wasn't to protect me."

"Perhaps I was curious. Midnight chimes, and you slip away into the darkness—to Lovers' Lane, of all places." He'd been watching her all night, slipping through the crowd as she sipped her champagne, both of them strolling clockwise around the circle of dancers; only, she had been unaware of the eyes upon her. Content, perhaps, to think her disguise complete enough to fool all watchers.

The only person she would never fool was Leo. Too many years spent dreaming of her, of that slim, upright figure, with her dangerously elegant grace. Nobody should ever mistake her for a human, not with the way she moved, but apparently they did.

"Is that where we are?"

"You know where we are." His voice lowered. "What was in the note?"

Stillness pervaded her body. Another riot of fireworks tore apart the velvet sky. "I don't know what you mean."

"Mina." He stroked her chin. "Don't pretend I'm in any way stupid."

"You have been on occasion." Her eyes flashed fire, and he knew she was thinking of the almost-kiss. Of how she'd lured him in, then proved her point with a knife.

Leo leaned toward her, tipping her painted mouth up to his. Then paused. Her breath wet his lips. "But I'm never foolish twice."

"No?"

He caught her hand as it flipped a jeweled knife toward him. He spun her around, slamming her back against his chest and closing his other hand around her

throat. The press of her bustle against his thighs eased
with a soft shushing noise, a sensuous little whisper
in the night. The pearls at her throat pressed into his
palm, and he could feel the sudden thumping beat of
her pulse against his fingertips. Every inch of her body
was still. Not beaten. Never that. He had no doubt she
was planning her next move, but he'd shocked her for
a moment.

If he could keep her off balance and take his own
measure of revenge for that long-ago not-kiss…

"Perhaps I wanted to see who you were meeting with," he whispered, his lips tracing her throat.
He eased the pressure of his hand and felt her draw
a breath. Leo edged the back of his fingers lower,
brushing over her breasts and the rough gold lace that
contained them. "Perhaps I don't want you meeting
men in the dark of Lovers' Lane." Teeth brushed
against the tender skin where her shoulder met her
neck. "Not unless they're me."

A breathy laugh. "They'll never be you."

"No?" The back of one fingernail rasped over her
tightening nipple. The duchess stiffened in his arms.
"Do you think this cold act scares me away? Like all
the others?"

"What makes you think it's an act?"

He stroked her hardened nipple, and her breath
caught. "That. You're not immune to me."

"Your father killed mine. If you think I shall
ever forget—"

"Who are you trying to remind?"

He could sense the uncertainty vibrating through
her. Gently, he pressed his lips against the delicate skin

behind her ear, touching his tongue to it, just to taste.
Blood and glory, she smelled good. A blue blood had
no personal scent, but her perfume was pure spice,
something direct from the Orient. It went straight to
his head...and other places.

"Let go of me," she demanded.

"Ask me nicely," he replied, trailing his lips down
her neck and onto the sensitive skin of her shoulder. The duchess shivered, and a smile curved over
his mouth.

"Get your hands off me, or I shall—"

Her words broke off as he suckled her skin hard,
bringing the blood to the surface. A good thing he
didn't have his blood-letting knife, or he had a feeling
he'd have it in hand already. His cock hardened at
the thought, the world darkening as the hunger rose
in him.

She felt his hunger rise. She had to. The duchess
stilled in his arms, her fingers curling over his sleeve.
Such a small touch, but it rocked through him, lifting
all the fine hairs along his arm.

She'd never touched him before. Not on purpose.

Leo looked away, breathing hard. Devil take her,
but if her purpose was distraction, then she was winning. Or perhaps he was the one who'd distracted
them both, so intent on tasting her, on touching her...
He looked up at the figure fading into the distance, the
unknown man she'd exchanged a note with. Something
dark flickered to life within him. Rationally, he knew
she wasn't his; instinctively, he wanted to challenge the
bastard to a duel. "Or you shall...what? Usually such
statements are followed with threats."

Fireworks went off again, the sound of laughter and joyful screaming echoing through the night. It sounded so far away. Another crack from the fireworks. This time there were no accompanying lights…

She said something. He wasn't listening. That last exploding crack hadn't sounded like fireworks.

Leo's eyes locked on the figure in the distance, now fallen to his hands and knees. The same man he'd been thinking murderous thoughts about but a second ago. Dark shapes formed out of the shadows around the fellow. Another crack, swallowed up by a lady's delighted squeal. Then a flash of light, like that of a pistol firing in the darkness.

"*Bloody hell.*" His arms tightened around her. "Mina."

"Let me go!" She staggered out of his grasp, clapping a hand to her lips in shock.

Leo snapped up the sword-cane he'd leaned against the hedge when he first arrived. "Stay here," he told her. "I'll see if he's still alive."

One stride and a hand clamped around his wrist, jerking him off balance. "No. He's already dead."

"You don't know that—"

"Yes, I do," she hissed, her fingers tightening on his wrist. "We need to get out of here."

Leo pressed her back into the shadows, using his body to muscle her against the tall hedge as he peered down the dark path. "What do you know?"

What a bloody fool he'd been, thinking the icy duchess had been meeting a stranger for illicit pleasures. She never did anything unplanned. Or for pleasure.

The note. This had something to do with that damned note.

The duchess hesitated.

"What do you *know*?" he repeated in a steely voice that dared her to argue with it.

"Those men aren't thieves or murderers," she replied. "They're Falcons."

The prince consort's elite assassins and spies. Leo searched her gaze. He was right. This hadn't been just a rendezvous, then. "Who was he?"

Her chin tipped up.

"Consider very carefully that I might be the only thing standing between you and them in a minute," he growled under his breath. Her eyes shot toward the fallen man at her feet. "If they're Falcons, Mina, they won't leave witnesses. And if this killing has anything to do with that note—"

"They'll come after me next."

"Yes," he breathed. "You need my help. But I won't give it without answers."

After another tense stalemate, she let out her breath and dropped her gaze. "It was Goethe," she whispered. "The Duke of Goethe."

The blood drained out of his face.

Two

"Is the prince consort mad?" Barrons hissed, tugging her deeper into the shadows of the hedge. He leaned down and tilted the unconscious man's head to the side, gloved fingers sliding through the man's hair, searching for the tattoo all Falcons wore.

"That theory is entirely plausible," Mina replied, keeping an eye on the shadows in the distance. Goethe's death was a bucket of icy water to the face, one she still hadn't quite recovered from. "He hasn't been entirely rational since winter, when word of the vaccination was released."

It had been a challenge to the control the prince consort had wielded over the entire Echelon with his own "cure," a mechanical device that filtered the craving virus from a blue blood's body and lowered the individual's CV percentages for several months. Blue bloods would have given him their souls for the use of it. Only now they didn't have to.

Barrons suddenly swore, and Mina looked down sharply to see that the Falcon—far from being unconscious—had grabbed his shirt collar and was striking up with a knife. Barrons turned it, gritting his teeth and using his weight to slam it down into the man's chest. The Falcon's breath exhaled…then his hand fell to the ground.

Their eyes met. "He recognized you anyway," Barrons murmured. "Best this way."

She nodded slowly.

Light gleamed on a knife in the distance, and Goethe's body jerked as the assassins started cutting out his heart. Bile rose in her throat. Could she have done anything? It had taken seconds; there was no way she could have crossed the space in that time, and her pistol's range was limited, but perhaps…

No, there was nothing she could have done. Useless. Just like she'd been when her father was poisoned.

"Found the tattoo. He's a Falcon. There will be more nearby." Barrons slipped a knife from the man's coat and flung it away. The gaslight nearby shattered, plunging them into complete darkness.

"What are you doing? They'll hear that."

"Do you honestly believe they're not aware of us? You were watched from the moment you left that rotunda. They simply don't consider you a threat at the moment, but I'll hazard a guess that they'll have men watching the gates. It's how they work. They'll take you when you try to leave."

"How do we get out, then? I can hardly climb the walls in this." A twitch of her skirts. She shot a look down the dark lane, her heart leaping into her throat. "They've vanished. The body too."

Barrons looked at her. "Do you trust me?"

"No." His father would have cut her down without

thinking, but Barrons was an enigma. If he were a different man, she would have enjoyed his attentions, but a part of her couldn't help wondering if his pursuit of her was just a way to get closer, to slip the knife in when she least expected it…

Could she trust that he meant her no harm?

His hand tightened around hers, dark heat sweeping through his irises. He focused on her so intently that she could almost feel it on her skin. "Then let us call a temporary truce for tonight. I shall help you escape. In return…"

"Yes?"

His voice roughened. "I want a kiss."

A kiss. Tension slid sinuously along her limbs, each muscle clenching. Those motives she could certainly understand. It didn't mean she had to like them.

Wariness spread through her as he lifted his hand and slowly, carefully brushed the back of his fingers against her lips. She didn't flinch. Instead she tipped her chin up and glared him down. "Help me escape and I shall grant you such a liberty." What harm could a single kiss do? "Until then"—she took a step back, her skirts swishing around her ankles—"I'll thank you to keep your hands to yourself."

His hand dropped but the ghostly sensation of that touch lingered, reminding her that it had been a long time since she'd been touched in any way intimately, and never like this. Never…soft. Full of gentleness, as if the very sensation of her skin beneath his was a pleasure in itself, not merely a step to greater satisfaction.

He was far more dangerous than she'd ever suspected, and she'd known, since the first moment she'd met him, that he was dangerous indeed. He was the only man who had ever managed to make her feel something.

"Agreed." Barrons tilted his head in a nod.

"However, there's something I must do first."

"Oh?"

"I need that note." Her heart hammered a little faster. Not because of Barrons. Of course not. If the prince consort got his hands on that note and decoded it, Goethe wouldn't be the only one who died. She had given in to her queen and delivered the note although she knew how foolish it was. This was as much her fault as the queen's. All along she'd known how dangerous it was to let one's emotions hold sway. From now on, let cold, hard reason be her guide.

"A suicide mission," Barrons said flatly.

"The nail in my coffin if I don't get it back."

For a moment she thought he'd refuse. Then his black eyes narrowed, his voice turning soft and smoky. "*That* is going to cost you considerably more than a kiss."

A part of her was almost tempted to pay his price… But she hadn't clawed her way up through the Echelon and held on to her duchy by giving in to her desires. "And the price?"

For a moment she thought his silence was the answer. It let her conjure up all manner of demands. Let her imagine them in explicit, nipple-hardening detail.

"I want to see your breasts," he said finally.

"I thought you wanted me in your bed."

"I do. But you will come of your own accord—"

Mina let out a rough laugh. "Never," she whispered defiantly. "Now come. We're wasting time."

He caught her upper arm. "I'll have your word first. Let's just say I trust you as much as you trust me."

"But you trust my word?"

"Once given."

Damn him. "If you help me retrieve the note, I'll allow you your intimacies for ten minutes. You will not touch me. Nor will you allow others to see me in such a state."

"Slight amendment. I believe there should be some touching allowed. Agreed?"

She needed him and he knew it. Though a part of her was tempted to slap the smile off his face. "Agreed," she replied through clenched teeth.

❧

Mina played a most excellent damsel in distress.

Sobbing into her hands, she ran through the gardens, crashing directly into a hard chest. Hands came up to steady her.

"What have we here?"

She looked up into the face of a Falcon. There was no mistaking the hard edge in his eyes or the complete lack of empathy there. "Please, sir," she stammered. "It's so awful! I saw a man die!"

"Did you now?" His voice roughened, excitement gleaming in his eyes. "That's a pity—"

Barrons hit him from behind. A slim stiletto to the base of his neck, directly severing a pair of vertebrae. The Falcon went down with a strangled gurgle, his eyes bulging. It was a silent death. No kicking or fighting. Somehow more efficient than anything she'd ever seen before.

Removing his blade, Barrons tucked it back up his sleeve, bending to rifle the man's pockets. This was the second one they'd killed. His hands patted the fellow's waistcoat, then paused, coming up with the waxed note. "Is this—" He saw her expression and smiled grimly. "I'll assume that's a yes."

Mina stepped forward, shedding her submissive persona. Her heart thumped into her throat. "Give it to me."

He yanked it out of reach and stood. "Let's not be hasty. You promised me a kiss."

"Now is not the time." She spared a look around. There was movement nearby.

"No, it's not. And until that time"—the note vanished into the inner pocket of his coat—"I'll keep an eye on it."

"Barrons!"

"Not here." He grabbed her wrist, dragging her behind a hedge. "I count three men," he whispered in her ear. "And I'm not quite good enough to handle three. Run, Mina. And don't argue. I'll draw them away."

She hadn't gotten where she was by foolishness. Mina grabbed her skirts and bolted into the darkness, her slippered feet light on the graveled path. Few had been able to catch her as a girl, and she was no less fleet of foot now.

A stranger materialized out of nowhere. Mina ducked beneath his arm, but some last snatch of his hand caught in her skirts and she found herself ensnared. Arms locked around her chest, and her feet were lifted off the ground. She wasted no time. She cracked her head backward, feeling the impact of his nose at the base of her skull. The man screamed, his arms loosening, and Mina struck with an elbow to the throat, followed by the chop of her hand for good measure as he dropped her. Her pistol sprang into her hand, and she shoved it in his face just as Barrons swung a kick into the back of the bastard's knee.

The Falcon caught Barrons's leg as they went down and Mina cursed, jerking her pistol up as both of the men rolled.

"He was mine," she snapped.

"My apologies." Barrons grunted as a kick struck him in the thigh.

The Falcon spun, blood streaming from his nose as he whipped Mina's feet out from beneath her with an ankle. She hit the ground, hearing several scuffling blows, a grunt, and then…silence. Mina rolled to her feet. Barrons was there, bleeding a little, from the scent of it. Their eyes met and Mina felt the rush of hunger as her mouth dampened.

"Thought you had it in hand," he said with a bland expression.

That roused her ire as she choked back the heat of the hunger, leaving little more than a ragged burn in her throat. No other man ever got beneath her skin like this one. "I thought *you* were creating a diversion."

"I tried. They're not interested in me. It's your perfume," he said, stepping closer and offering her a hand. "They're tracking the scent."

Some cheap concoction she'd worn to complete her disguise. She could barely smell it anymore, but she knew others would be able to. A blue blood's senses were too superior, but she'd never expected to be on the run for her life tonight. "You believe the rumors, then? That the prince consort is infecting his Falcons with the craving virus?" A highly illegal act.

"Obviously. I have an idea of how to counteract the scent, but I don't think you're going to like it."

She didn't trust the sudden gleam in his eyes, but she was hardly a fool. "Do your worst."

Barrons smiled.

Half a minute later, she was shivering from the cold, her mouth opening in shock as water rose over her breasts to her chin. It filled her petticoats, sinking her farther and causing a sudden surge of panic to rise. Clamping her teeth together, Mina dug her fingers into the brickwork under the bridge and drove her whole body beneath the water of the canal.

The bridge above her blocked out even the moon, plunging her into darkness. Slowly she let herself float up, breaking the surface inch by silent inch as she listened.

Barrons had disappeared over the bridge with her dress, leading the perfumed scent away. She could still feel the echo of his fingers on her body as he'd tugged her out of it.

A stealthy footstep landed on the bridge above her. Mina stopped breathing. Could she trust him? Leaving her here would be an excellent distraction if he wanted to escape.

Another slow, almost *listening* step.

"This way," a man murmured. "I can smell her."

The rumors were correct, then. The prince consort had supernaturally strong assassins at his beck and call.

The footsteps died and Mina ducked back under the water, leaving only her face clear of its icy depths.

Something sleek splashed nearby.

She had her knife in hand before she could think. Barrons surfaced in front of her, his dark blond hair wet and dripping, raked back from his forehead. Rivulets of water ran down his skin, hovering in the dip above his darkly smiling mouth.

"You're taking far too much enjoyment from this." Her lips quivered with the cold.

He flashed her another smile, his teeth gleaming in the night.

"Want to have more fun?" she asked.

He swam closer, pressing up against her as his arms trapped her against the wall. She could feel every hard inch of his body locked against hers, leaving her frightfully aware of just how little she wore.

"What kind of fun?"

She wasn't going to be tempted. Not even for a moment. "Lord Matheson arrived in a pleasure dirigible. A grand entrance to awe the masses." Her tone told him what she thought of that. "It's currently moored by the eastern gates, along with two attendants. I could distract them while you cut the tethers. It's the easiest way out of here without going through the gates and risking further interaction with Falcons. No matter what reinforcements they've sent for, they would never be able to capture us."

"You're planning to steal Matheson's airship?"

"You object?" She pressed a hand against his

chest, trying to maintain some sense of distance between them.

"Hell no. I most thoroughly approve."

"Excellent." She glanced sideways, shivering a little as she mentally placed their whereabouts. Perhaps a quarter mile to the dirigible, if the moon and skyline were any indication.

"The question remains: can you fly an airship?"

Mina looked up. His gaze had dipped, reminding her that she wore little more than a gold lace corset and a silk chemise. Sinking a little more beneath the water, she glared at him. "I own stock in Galloway's Aeronautics. Mr. Galloway provided us with an extensive demonstration of his workshop and models, and I've been reading Master Renoir's *Guide to the Skies*."

England might be somewhat behind when it came to air technology, preferring to sink its funds into the infamous steam-powered steel dreadnoughts that lined its coast and patrolled its oceans, but Mina preferred not to be provincial. France's skies were dotted with airships; it was only a matter of time before the staunchly humanist French came north, flying neatly over the dreadnoughts and evading England's best defenses. Even the prince consort had begun to see sense, hiring Galloway's to construct the first fleet of air militia. The perfect time to invest, in her opinion.

"So you only have a theoretical notion of how to fly an airship?"

"I know every cog, bolt, and alignment on the latest engines," she replied haughtily, then added a faint smile. "Perfect bedtime reading."

An eyebrow arched. "So you only have a theoretical notion of how to fly an airship?" he repeated.

"Trust me, Barrons," she practically purred. "I don't invest in anything I don't know the ins and outs of. Besides, where's your sense of adventure?"

"Right next to my desire to live," he shot back.

Mina ducked under his arm, swimming away from him with a taunting splash in the face. "Come, grandmother. Let me show you how to steal an airship."

&

Stealing an airship was the sort of idea that left a burning tingle in the blood. Something he'd have done as a lad for a dare, before he'd grown out of such mischief. That the very cool, rational Duchess of Casavian had come up with the idea was a thought that Leo couldn't stop considering as they stared at the airship from the dark silence of a garden folly.

Another sign that the duchess was not at all what she seemed.

"What sort of distraction do you think would be best?" she asked. Since their truce, she'd grown easier with the idea of working with him. It was surprising how well they'd managed.

He cast a quick glance back at the two uniformed guards standing at the mooring ropes, joined for the moment by the first pilot. One guard lit a cheroot as Leo watched, shaking out the match.

"They're bored, and most importantly, they're men." His hands slid over her shoulders, earning him a wary glance. He teased the clasp of her cloak open. She was shivering wet underneath it, and he was glad he'd left it under a hedge for her. "Why not use the few weapons we have?"

With that, he dragged the cloak off, letting it fall to the folly floor. The duchess wrapped her arms across her chest, her lips trembling.

"Look at you," he whispered, kneeling at her feet. "All wet and cold, with some miscreant having stolen your dress—and dare I say it, your virtue?" Taking hold of her petticoats, he tore them up her thigh, earning a hissed intake of breath. "Trust me. We don't need an extensive diversion."

Mina's lip curled. "One would argue that you're saying men are base fools, to be led by their instincts."

"Have you only just worked that out?"

"I'm going to kill you for this."

"Go." He gave her a gentle shove in the back. "And I would advise you to let your arms drop. You're hiding your best assets."

Giving him a truly evil glare, she dropped her arms, revealing how tightly her stays and chemise clung to her full, rounded breasts as well as the tight puckering of her nipples. "You'll pay for this, Barrons. I promise you that revenge will be excruciating."

He didn't look. There would be time enough for that later. "I shall await your endeavors with great anticipation."

Oh, how those eyes burned him. Leo muffled a laugh as the duchess turned on her heel and strode out of the folly. Hardly the damsel in distress.

She changed, however, when the men caught sight of her, the guard choking on his cheroot.

"Sir, oh sir!" the duchess called. She looked utterly

miserable, bedraggled, and glorious, the flickering gas lamps playing over her gently rounded curves. "Could you please help me?"

Dangerous minx. Leo eased into the shadows, moving around toward the airship. How easily she slipped into the role, as if she'd been fooling people her entire life.

Grabbing hold of one of the mooring ropes, he climbed hand over hand, up toward the deck that lined the edges of the gondola, the muscles in his shoulders burning. Listening for a moment, he stole over the edge and crouched low. The engines were silent, the enormous inflated envelope above keeping the dirigible floating nearly twenty feet off the ground.

What a bloody travesty. The decks were obviously designed for its owner to "take in the air," with a foredeck covered in a daybed and mounded pillows. For the view, no doubt. A floating pleasure palace. Matheson was a modern-day Louis XIV. Leo strode toward the engine room. Its structure reminded him somewhat of the *Valkyrie*, which he'd sailed aboard on his way to Saint Petersburg and back. Only minutely. Captain Alexi Dansk would have sneered at such extravagances, and no amount of frippery would have survived the icy winds as they'd crossed the Baltic Sea.

Jerking open the captain's cabin, Leo found himself face-to-face with a second pilot. The man had his feet kicked up on a stool and was flipping through the *London Tribune*. The moment Leo appeared, the pilot's jaw dropped and he opened his mouth to yell.

"A hundred quid to keep your mouth shut," Leo

said, slipping through the door and examining the control panel. A series of gears and levers greeted him. Hardly incomprehensible, but he preferred to take his time to examine such things before he tried to levitate them off the ground. Stripping out of his wet coat, he tossed it aside.

The pilot was still gaping at him. "Here, sir, you can't be up here."

Leo held up his billfold. It was dripping, along with the rest of him, but the notes within it would dry. He tossed it toward the fellow. "I'm commandeering this vessel. You have two choices. One, I can knock you unconscious and attempt to steer this bloody thing myself, or two, you can take whatever is in that billfold, steer me to my destination, and then return with the airship in one piece to collect Matheson."

"His lordship will have my head," the man replied, hands cupped around the wallet.

"Tell him you saved the vessel from certain destruction," Leo replied, peering through the window. Mina had managed to find herself a man's jacket to cover herself—the first pilot's, by the look of it.

Seconds ticked by. "Aye, sir." The man's shocked expression cleared. "Where would you like to go, sir?"

"What's your name?"

"Whitcomb. Bennett Whitcomb."

"I just need help with one other thing before we get under way."

"Sir?"

He pointed through the glass-plated windows. "That comely lass there is with me."

⤴

"You found a pilot," Mina said flatly, accepting a flute of champagne as Barrons knelt on the edge of the plumply cushioned daybed, the bottle fizzing in his fingers.

"You sound disappointed."

"A little." She ran her fingers along the timber paneling of the daybed at the front of the ship. "It was my only opportunity to fly such a thing."

"Change of plans," he replied, stretching out alongside her as the engines kicked into gear and the propellers on either side of the gondola began to spin faster. A heady rumbling sound vibrated the deck beneath them as all of the boilers lit up. "I'll personally pay for Galloway to provide you with lessons."

"Admit it," she replied, sipping her champagne and shivering. "You didn't like the idea of your fate being in my hands."

"I don't like the idea of my fate residing in anyone's hands." The airship quivered and then gave a faint surging push as it lifted into the air. His gaze returned to hers, the faintest of smiles touching those hard lips. "Least of all yours. You *were* threatening me with all manner of dire retributions, were you not?"

"Please don't think me so limited as to consider dropping you off an airship revenge enough."

A fluid shrug, all sleek muscle and lazy acquiescence now that they were under way. As if he barely felt the cold that was beginning to almost burn beneath her skin. Shouts began to circle up from beneath them. "Here's to retribution." He tapped his glass against hers with a clink, his dark eyes catching glimmer-shine off the gaslights along the rail. "Even if it is merciless."

"You doubt me?"

"Never. I was there when you dueled with your cousin Peter. I know you can be merciless when you need to be."

Cold air streamed over the deck. She couldn't quite reply, the words taking her by surprise. So many years ago now, and yet the memory still lashed her like the cut of a whip, brutal and searing.

Not merciless, a part of her whispered. *Not with Peter.* That had been nothing more than a young girl's survival instinct. Desperation. Him or *her*.

His death was still on her hands, though.

Barrons drained his glass, eyes narrowing as he watched her over the edge of it. Then he reached out and dragged one of the heavy blankets over her.

"I don't know where this has been," she replied through her suddenly dry throat, but she tucked the blanket about her shoulders, trying to create something of a windbreak.

"We could share," Barrons suggested.

What? Her head jerked up. Devil take it! She was so cold that her wits were slowing. And something about the night had softened her focus, made her forget that this man was the enemy. Perhaps the truce. Or perhaps…almost a kind of…camaraderie between them tonight. "I'd rather freeze."

A fingertip traced patterns on the blanket, over her hip. "Something I said?" he murmured, gauging her expression with those dangerous eyes, as if he were searching for answers when she didn't even know what the questions were.

"We've escaped," she replied. "The terms of our truce are finished."

"Not quite." He poured himself more bloodied champagne and sipped at it, resting back on the mound of cushions like some indolent pasha. "The debt has not yet been paid."

Mina sat up, dragging the coat and blanket tightly around herself. "You demand payment tonight?"

"I do."

Of course he did. London glided by, the enormous brick walls that surrounded the heart of the city—and the Echelon's territory—passing directly below them. Lights stretched out for miles, twinkling in the darkness of night. Beautiful.

"Where are you taking me?" she asked.

"Some place safe. Some place nobody knows about."

"And then?"

"Then?" He arched a brow, lying on his side and resting his head on his open palm. "Then we finish this."

Three

"THIS IS A BEDROOM," MINA SAID, HER TEETH chattering.

"Mine, to be precise," Barrons replied, ushering her through the door and then flicking on the gaslights.

"I thought you lived at Waverly Place."

"Officially." He gave nothing away as he crossed toward a decanter and poured blud-wein into a pair of glasses. "Unofficially, I sometimes need a place to stay that nobody knows about."

A small house outside the city walls? Unusual. None of her sources on him had ever turned up anything like this. Why would he need a private sanctuary? That indicated involvement in some mischief. Mina closed the door behind her and tugged the pilot's coat tighter around her in a vain attempt to warm herself.

The bedroom was smaller than expected, with an enormous four-poster bed taking up most of the space and a cold fireplace in the corner. Curiosity bit her, and she found her gaze dwelling on the ormolu clock on the mantel and the heavy damask drapes. She trailed her fingertips over the smooth velvet pane on the bed. *Wonder what that would feel like against my skin.* She jerked her hand away.

Barrons offered her one of the glasses, his fingers brushing against hers. He frowned, then turned her hand palm up. "You're freezing."

"Some idiot pushed me into a canal."

She waited for a sharp response, but instead the line between his brows drew deeper. "If I recall, I suggested it. Come. You need to get out of those clothes and get warm."

He led her toward the connected washroom. At the sight of the enormous bath, Mina balked. "If you think that I'm getting in your bath—"

"Then don't." He flicked the taps, sending a stream of water into the claw-footed tub. "If you won't avail yourself of some scandalously hot water, then I shall." He lifted up a small vial and dropped a generous amount of foaming soap into the machine aerator. It whipped the soap particles into the water, creating a mess of bubbles. "I'll send my manservant, Isaiah, up to set the fire to rights. Hopefully that will warm you instead."

Her gaze flicked toward the water, her skin prickling at the hot steam that began to envelop the bathroom. "This is indecent."

Barrons laughed under his breath. "Not yet, it's not." Shrugging out of his wet jacket, he tossed it aside. "Now, you or me?"

Why not both of us? She lowered her eyes, but the image of him remained. Wet, his sleek shirt clinging like a second skin, delineating the heavy muscle of his shoulders and chest, hinting at the darkness of his nipples behind the fine lawn.

Steam curled up, dancing in the air like a dozen ethereal harem girls. She desperately needed to return home, to set into motion ploys to protect herself, but she was so damned wet and cold. And tired. For the first time in months, she just wished to take a moment for herself. The euphoria and exhilaration of the chase through the Venetian Gardens had vanished, leaving her utterly drained. How the devil was she going to explain all of this? The queen's pale face flickered to mind.

"I cannot remove my corset myself," she replied stiffly, and it was both capitulation and an order.

"Let me play lady's maid then." He stepped closer, the presence of his body behind her sending shivers down her spine. Strong, firm fingers caught her hips and turned her toward the mirror with forceful pressure.

The pilot's crisp white coat buttoned at the front. Mina jerked it open with rough, careless tugs, shivering as the humid air of the washroom met her dimpled skin. The coat slid sinuously down her body until Barrons caught it in his fist. Their eyes met in the mirror, his gaze sliding down over the pale skin of her décolletage to the gold corset and her bedraggled chemise and petticoats. The silk clung wetly, molding over every dip and curve.

Let him look his fill. The promise of their bargain burned within her. So typical of a man to demand such things from her. Men had done so all her life until she'd finally found a way to prevent it by burying her passions so deep that they almost didn't exist anymore. Men did not desire ice. They called it a pity now, such a shame that someone of her beauty should be so untouchable, so untouched, and yet it was the only trait they would have respected in her.

For a moment disappointment flickered. She hadn't hoped that he would be different, had she? For that would mean that a ridiculous girlish part of her still existed.

Hands came up in the periphery of her vision, brushing her wet red hair off her shoulders. She forced herself not to feel it, to watch the reflection of them dispassionately in the mirror over the vanity. Light gleamed off her white-and-gold outfit, but Barrons was only shadow behind her, his hands brushing her hair into smoothness. Surprisingly, he was no longer watching her in the mirror, admiring his prize. Instead he was stroking the knots from her hair, his gaze solely focused on the task. Despite herself, impressions began to leach into her: the rasp of his knuckles against her back, the sharp tug as his callused fingers caught in a knot.

"You needn't bother," she murmured. "I'm only going to wash it."

Those black eyes met hers. So reminiscent of a blue blood when their hunger was roused, but lacking the intensity. Shadows. Eyes of shadows. "You have beautiful hair," he said, and the spell was broken.

Beautiful hair. She stared at herself again and felt nothing.

"*So beautiful,*" the Echelon had breathed, when she made her debut.

She might have damned well been invisible, but she had learned. Beauty could be a curse or it could be used, and she had learned to use it well over the years. "I do believe you were unlacing my corset."

Barrons ignored her, still untangling the knotted lengths that stretched to her waist. "I like the feel of it. It's so very soft." A wry smile touched his mouth. "I keep expecting to feel nothing but sharp edges when I touch you, but it's just a lie. You're as soft as any other woman, aren't you, Mina?"

"No, I'm not." She dragged the heavy weight of her wet hair over her shoulder, curling her hands possessively around it. What he spoke of was weakness, not softness. "My corset, my lord."

"As my lady wishes." The words were gentle, but they made her shiver again—and this time she couldn't blame the cold.

He didn't touch her. Not in any way she'd expected. No lingering caresses down her flanks and hips. No hands curling around her to cup her breasts through her corset. Every inch of her body was on edge. A part of her simply wished for him to make his move.

His touch was not sexual, yet far too intimate. Tender, perhaps? Gentle hands tugging at her wet laces. The only person who ever touched her like this was her maid in the sanctity of her bedchamber, a place where no one wanted to kill her or hurt her, dethrone her or judge her.

The corset gaped open suddenly and she caught it against her breasts, still holding onto her hair with one hand.

"I shall fetch you some blud-wein," he said, looking up then and finding her eyes on him in the mirror.

Startled eyes, she couldn't help but think before she narrowed them.

His own were liquid darkness. Unfathomable. As were his actions.

Mina watched him leave, each step owning the space around him. Far too comfortable in his own skin—comfortable too in this situation, as though he thought he had mastery of it. Leaving her laces undone and her corset sagging, her heart beating just a little too swiftly for comfort.

What the devil was his game here? It felt uncomfortably as though neither of them were Casavian nor Caine at this moment—not enemies but simply two people who found an attraction in each other.

And she'd be a fool if she thought that. She waited, listening to the silence in the room, but there were no answers to the question. He had demanded a kiss from her and more, but he seemed disinclined to take either boon.

And the bath was cooling.

Practicality forced her to examine her options. She had no dry clothes, and no doubt there would be men looking for her, men well equipped to remove her, should the process prove necessary. If she were a Falcon, her first instinct would be to surround her prey's house and wait. People always returned home, seeking what they perceived was safety.

But they wouldn't be looking here, would they? Nobody would ever suspect her erstwhile rescuer to be Leo Barrons, not with the feud between their families. She would be invisible here, and the threat he cast toward her could be…managed, if nothing else.

Wriggling out of her undergarments, she let them fall to the cold tiles and stepped into her bath. Home was no longer safe for the moment, and there was nothing she could do to fix the situation tonight. She needed to think, to find some way to outwit the prince consort, and her first instinct—to run or hide— was hardly suitable.

Scalding water slid over her body as Mina sank into the bath, teeth gritted. Sensible thoughts fragmented, bubbles clinging to the smooth slope of her breasts while her skin turned a pleasant pink. "Oh, goodness," she whispered, sinking farther into the water and leaning her head back against the rim of the claw-footed bath. This was surely divine.

It hurt for a long time, until the heat began to soak into her bones, warming her from within. Mina washed the stink of the canal from her hair, then added more hot water, her foot resting on the rim of the bath and her fingers idly twirling the pearls at her throat.

It was no surprise when the door opened and Barrons returned. She swung cattish eyes on him and stayed silent, not bothering to sink any farther beneath the bubbles that covered her. Let him play his little games; she had her own in place and wouldn't need long to divine his intentions.

Men were so predictable. The thought steeled her will. Barrons was just another man, after all, and she'd been using her feminine wiles to wage war for years.

He'd changed into dry clothes—a black shirt that seemed to absorb all of the darkness in the room and black suspenders riding hard over broad shoulders. At some point he'd rolled the shirtsleeves up, leaving his forearms bare. She'd never seen him in anything other than court clothes. These more informal clothes made him look a little more ruffled, more sensual.

His hair had grown longer in the month since he'd left for Saint Petersburg, and he'd tied it up now with a thin piece of velvet. It highlighted the stark line of his cheekbones and a lower lip that was slightly fuller than it ought to be. She wanted to drag that ribbon from his hair and run her hands through the gilt-colored strands.

Mina sank a little farther into the bath. She wasn't innocent. There'd been two short-lived affairs in her past, but she'd been in complete control of both of them, even when her blood-lust had risen. This sensation left her a little unsettled. The sight of him— perhaps the situation—stirred feelings inside her that she'd never owned.

Lust could be controlled. Always.

"I suppose you've come to claim your prize." She toyed with the pearls.

One tawny eyebrow arched. "I've come to bring you your blud-wein, Your Grace."

There was a tray in his hands. He set it on the vanity, then poured a glass and offered it to her.

Mina accepted, swirling the bloodied wine in her glass. Troubled again. "You make an excellent lady's maid, Barrons."

"Are you hiring?"

She breathed out a laugh. "Hardly."

His fingers trailed over her shoulder as he circled the head of the bath. "We worked well together tonight."

So that was his aim. "You think we could carry this

alliance onto the Council?" He served as the Duke of Caine's proxy, after all.

"It would be the last thing they'd expect. But, no, Mina, I was merely commenting, not offering an alliance."

"Good." She drained her glass and handed it to him. There was no way in hell she'd consider an alliance with the son of the man who'd killed her father. "For the truce is definitely over."

Barrons stared at her wineglass for taut seconds. "A shame." He placed it on the vanity carefully, then turned back to her.

Mina tensed.

Fingertips brushed her cheek. "I have no plans to hurt you," he reminded her, circling around behind her. "You shall never have that to fear, Duchess."

A hand fisted in her wet hair and dragged her head back. His face appeared in her vision, upside down. "Unless I plan on stealing your heart," he whispered. "Then you should be on your guard."

"I'm always on my guard," she breathed.

Barrons's gaze softened, his face lowering. "If I recall, you owe me a kiss."

"You owe me a note," she shot back, her hands clutching the edge of the bath and her heart hammering.

"A kiss," he repeated, "if I managed to get you out of there safely." His face lowered toward hers, candlelight turning his skin a delicious golden hue. "The note was for another payment indeed."

Her whole body burned. The fist in her hair tightened, as if warning her that he had her at his mercy. "I'm already naked," she replied flatly.

"But clothed in bubbles, my dear." That smooth voice turned molten. "Bubbles and candlelight."

The tension between them changed. She could feel it thickening the air around her. The bastard was daring her, a little smile playing around his lips. Knowing that she did not want to pay her dues.

Mina's heart pounded. "So be it." She forced her whole body to relax, her fingers releasing their claw hold on the lip of the bath. "You've earned your kiss. I do hope it's all you imagined."

Reaching up, she slid a hand through his hair, tearing it loose from its velvet thong. Palm flat against his scalp, she dragged his head down, tilting her lips to his.

They were softer than she'd expected, melting over her own and sucking her breath into his lungs. The intimacy of that thought burned between her thighs, a hollow, empty ache that seemed almost alive…waiting for something more. She brushed her mouth against his once. Twice. Licked at his tongue, then sucked it into her mouth as she slid both hands up to cup his cheeks.

Each sensation ignited something dangerous within her: the scrape of his stubble against her chin, the firm pressure on her hair as he held her locked in place and submitting to the mastery of his kiss. It shouldn't have mattered. She shouldn't have felt anything, but something inside her kindled to life at the way he pinned her down. A fever burned beneath her skin. It made her aware of just how large he was, how strong, how easily he held her down…

Want kindled in her. A fierce desire, not unlike the rush of need through her veins when her hunger rose.

She wanted to drag him into the bath with her, to let him put hands and mouth to her body, to fill this unknown void within her. Dangerous things to think, to feel, for she shouldn't be feeling anything at all.

Mina broke the kiss with a gasp.

Barrons's chest rose and fell, his eyes heavy-lidded. His fist in her hair kept her there as they stared at each other, and then those devastating lips curled in a slow, entirely too-pleased smile.

"Was the payment to your satisfaction, my lord?"

"Worth the risk of life and limb?" His gaze dropped to her mouth, dark eyes blistering in their intensity. "Yes." His voice roughened. "Worth dying for."

"No kiss is worth dying for."

"Then you've never had the right kind of kiss."

Her lips tingled, daring her to touch them. *The right kind of kiss…* The kind that could leave her aching and desperate, feeling almost hollow inside as if he'd touched something she never knew had existed there before, touched it and then pulled away, leaving her reeling in the aftermath.

One kiss to devastate her. And more…

I want to see your breasts.

"The note," she demanded, sliding her hand over his and exerting just enough pressure on the tendon so that his fingers jerked open on her hair.

Barrons tugged the small scroll out of his shirt pocket. "Are you going to tell me what's in it?"

"No." She held out her hand and he contemplated her for a moment. "No note, no payment," she reminded him, and his fingers opened, revealing the source of all this excitement.

Mina took the small, waxed piece of paper, still pristine and perfect despite its swim in the canal. Unfurling it, she shoved it directly into the path of a candle flame. A few seconds of nothing and then fire flared up over its length, leaving naught but ashes in its wake.

Success. The tension eased from between her shoulders as the blasted thing vanished, leaving her limp and relaxed.

And bound by a debt owed.

Languidly Mina stirred her legs through the cooling water, the shape of her slender calves clearly visible. Bubbles clung to the hints of smooth alabaster skin that glided through the water, warmed by candlelight. His gaze lowered.

Yes. There were other ways to control a situation. He wanted to see her, did he? Well, she would give him precisely what he wanted. And more.

Bubbles hugged her curves as she moved, prickling slightly where they popped and fizzled against her as the cool air met her skin. Mina slid her knees sinuously beneath her, capturing his hooded eyes as she slowly, slowly unwound herself.

Cool air traced over her bared skin as she stood gloriously nude in front of him, hidden only by the slow, stealthy slide of bubbles. They dripped between her legs and over her sensitive breasts and stomach, a caress that almost made her reach for him. Barrons didn't look down. Instead he stared into her eyes, as if searching for something she wasn't willing to give him.

"And so I pay the second part of my debt. You may look your fill. You may touch me—" Her voice roughened a little. *But you will never own me. You will never touch me here, inside...*

"Do you wish for me to touch you?" he asked in a softer voice than she'd expected.

"What I wish is of little consequence."

Dark eyes flashed and she knew her words had found their target. So he wanted her willing, did he? Melting into his arms, no doubt. Mina had nothing but contempt for such a thought.

Barrons stared at her for a second longer, then stepped back and reached for the towel. Dragging it off the rail, he moved closer, his larger body enveloping hers. Mina tensed a little, but he only draped the towel around her back and bottom, giving a small jerk. She staggered forward a step, her arms held up between them, water dripping down her legs into the bath. Gently he curled the soft towel around her body, hiding her from view, almost as if he were slowly closing a door between them.

"Then I will touch as I desire," he murmured, tucking the edge of the towel between her breasts.

Bending over, he drew her up into his arms, water splashing all over the tiled floor as he lifted her out of the bath and set her down. Another towel appeared in his hand and he knelt at her feet, using it to buff her legs dry. Candlelight gleamed on his dark blond hair, gilding sections of it and turning it gold against the blackness of his shirt.

What was he doing? Mina gasped as he nudged her legs apart and worked his way up each leg, the smooth towel buffing her dry. "You're wasting your opportunity."

"Am I?" Barrons looked up. "You would not know what pleases me. Having you retreat into yourself while I stare at you so rudely doesn't satisfy me, Mina. Not at all." He stood, arm curving around her waist as he directed her into the chair by the mirror. Leaning down behind her, his face shot into shocking review beside hers in the reflection. "I'm interested in someone who wants this as much as I do, and you don't. Not yet. I'm not quite sure why, but you don't." The towel in his hands tumbled over her head, blinding her for a second.

Mina jerked and shoved at it, then his hands curled into the towel, using it to dry her hair. She froze, recognizing his intent as harmless.

"Not ever," she replied, shoving the towel up out of her eyes. "I won't be any man's whore."

"I see the mistake I made in making this a transaction." Hard lips thinned and he wrung the water from her hair with the towel. "You are free of your debt, and if you must know, I would have done as commanded if you'd but asked nicely. You are far too fascinating for me to see you die."

Her eyes narrowed. She'd stood before him practically naked and he'd not batted an eye, and now he was saying she was free of her debt, free of…everything. Mina stiffened. "What the hell kind of game are you playing?"

"Something rather akin to chess, I imagine. Sacrifice a pawn or two, and win the endgame. Oh, and Mina." He tipped her chin up, lowering his face. "I'm so many moves ahead of you that you'll never figure it out."

This time the kiss took her entirely by surprise. A

hard, demanding kiss that claimed her as if he owned her. The vanity bit into her back as she stumbled backward, capturing her towel, one hand clenching his collar for balance. *As if she'd ever find her balance again.*

It ended as suddenly as it had begun, leaving her confused and trembling slightly in her puddle of towels.

"What are you doing? I paid you your kiss!" Mina shoved at his chest, her eyes blazing with heat as she ducked under his arm, away from him. Heart hammering, she clutched the towel close to her, meek defense against the turbulence he wrought. If he touched her again…

Barrons reached out and slid one finger in the crevice between her breasts, tucking her sagging towel back into place. "That one," he said, with a dangerous smile, "that one I stole."

Damn him. Lust surged through her veins—pure, unadulterated lust—and with it came the heat of the craving, the world falling into shadows as her vision became nothing more than every shade of black and white. Her eyes had darkened with the hunger, she knew, and so would he. "Shall I name the punishment for theft, my lord?"

"Do you want to take it back? I'll let you, you know."

Of all the things he could have said to her… Mina's lips parted in surprise, her eyes slowly narrowing at his teasing tone.

All too late she realized the danger. For he knew now that he affected her. She would never again be able to dismiss him with hostility or coldness, for he'd seen inside her soul, seen that little spark inside her that yearned for heat, for touch, for passion. Every ounce of control she'd ever wielded in their encounters slipped away like grains of sand through her fingers, leaving her utterly helpless.

Do you want it back?

Yes.

"Keep it," she said instead. "And know that the debt between us is doubly paid."

"Very well."

Mina frowned. She'd expected an argument—or another attempt at seduction. "I don't understand."

"But then you never have understood my motives." With one last oblique smile, he tilted his head toward her, then stepped away and left her to dress in peace.

Four

STEAM LEAKED THROUGH A GRATE IN THE ROAD, EERIE in the early hours of the morning. In the east, faint hints of silver brightened the sky, but here on the very edges of Whitechapel, shadows seemed to stretch out and linger, each alley lost to pervading darkness.

The message had arrived but an hour earlier, long after Leo had seen the duchess into the hackney she'd insisted upon. A dozen theories sprang to mind about its meaning. He was playing deep and dangerous games these days, and a message from Blade, the infamous Devil of Whitechapel, could only mean one thing.

Revolution. The downfall of the prince consort.

Leo tucked the collar of his coat up around his jaw and started across Butcher Square, ignoring the vagrants flipping jacks in a nearby gutter. Their eyes lit on him, then moved back to the jacks, but he knew he'd been cataloged as surely as he knew his own name. One of the whores there eased back into the shadows and vanished, no doubt to bring word of his passing, or at least the passing of a seemingly rich young lord in this section of the city.

The cut of his coat was stark and unembellished, but the quality of it named him one of the Echelon or a minor blue-blood lord, no doubt. He didn't bother to disguise himself. There were enough blue bloods who would seek distraction in this part of the city, drawn by the no-rules excitement of the Pits, where men bled on the pale sand as they fought each other for coin, or the easy virtue of toffers, those whores seeking a way out of the East End and into warmer, more sumptuous beds.

Ratcatcher Gate loomed ahead of him. A man met him there, his flat green eyes narrowed and a sleeveless leather jerkin revealing the heavy metal spars of his mechanical arm. Leo was taller than most men, but this one had several inches on him and outweighed him immeasurably. Thank the devil he had permission to be here. In a duel or knife fight he had no match, but here in the rookeries, they didn't like to fight by what they termed "gentlemen's rules." Blade had set Leo on his backside often enough over the years for him to learn a healthy respect for the way they fought here.

Of course, he'd returned the favor.

"Rip." He nodded. "Got Blade's message. What's the matter?"

His brother-in-law wouldn't have sent for him unless it was urgent. The Devil of Whitechapel preferred to deal with his own problems rather than involve anyone else, and usually he dealt with them with swift, bloodied justice.

Blade was the only rogue blue blood who'd ever stood against the Echelon and survived. Fifty years ago, he'd escaped his execution in the Ivory Tower and made his way to Whitechapel where he'd roused the mob against the metaljackets the Echelon sent after him. It had been a massacre, but it had proven one thing to this part of London and to the Echelon—they were not invincible.

The king at the time had ceded Blade the rookeries and the Echelon pretended the matter was inconsequential, but everybody knew the truth. The human classes had adopted Blade as some kind of hero, and aristocratic children went to bed with their nannies whispering horrific stories about him in their ears. The myth was almost larger than the man himself these days.

"Think you oughta see it yourself," Rip replied, his deep voice pitched barely loud enough to hear. He uncrossed his massive arms from over his chest and jerked his head. "Charlie, you watch the gate. You make sure nothin' gets in, you understand?"

A cocky young lad shot them both a smile and a wink, leaning surreptitiously against a barrel under the shadow of the gate's overhang. Leo stiffened momentarily.

"Charlie." The boy nodded.

For a moment they stared at each other. The boy's eyes were blue, but the shock of familiarity he felt when he saw that face... Like looking in the damned mirror.

"Are you certain he's capable enough?" Leo asked, stalking after Rip.

"Lad's almost a man now," Rip replied. "And this ain't the sort o' place to pander to the weak. A boy tends to grow up fast."

Leo bit off his reply, guilt souring his mouth. Who was he to demand what Charlie did or didn't do? He'd given up his rights to that years ago when his own actions had infected the boy with the craving virus. Charlie might be his younger brother by blood, but Honoria—Blade's wife and Leo's half sister—had made it more than clear that he had no say in the boy's future.

"Startin' to look more 'n more like you as he ages." Rip glanced at Leo. "That could be dangerous."

Only Blade's most trusted knew the truth: that Leo's father had *not* been the Duke of Caine, but a gentleman scientist to whom Caine had given patronage years ago. Sir Artemus Todd was dead now, but he'd left his mark on the world in the form of three legitimate children—and Leo.

Not that Leo thought of that bastard as his father. If anyone ever discovered his secret, the prince consort would use it to see him hang.

"That could be dangerous," Leo replied quietly. "For both me and the boy."

"Blade's tryin' to convince 'im to try a beard and let his hair grow long."

"And what does Honoria think of this?" he asked dryly.

"It were 'er idea."

Leo didn't quite know what to think of that. She'd never truly forgiven him for what had happened to Charlie, though she welcomed him in her home and had even shared the cure for the craving virus with him when his own CV levels had grown high. She called him brother, but Leo had never truly understood why she'd helped him in the past.

It was easier with Lena, his younger sister. Despite the careful distance he tried to maintain, Lena insisted on dashing a kiss against his cheek as a greeting and sent him playful gifts each year for Christmas, despite the fact he didn't celebrate such a thing. Christmas meant little to any of the Echelon, those who'd been excommunicated from the church as soulless devils, but he had to admit that a part of him looked forward to her gifts each year. Using her skill with clockwork, she'd created a marching toy soldier for him last year. He didn't have a clue what he was supposed to do with it, but he'd set it out on display in his study—a little proudly.

"'Ere we are," Rip murmured, shouldering beneath an archway into an alley.

Tight grounds for an ambush. Leo's gaze flickered over the rooftops and spotted two of Blade's newly sworn men there in the shadows. The scent of blood washed over him, and he found the cause of it in the middle of a small group of men gathered in the alley.

Blade knelt over a body, torchlight gilding the stark bones of his face. His hair was darker now than it had been when they first met three years ago—thanks to Honoria's cure for the Fade—but other than that, he'd barely aged.

A trace of scarlet gleamed at his throat: a cravat in bold, embossed silk. His coat was black leather, its split tails separating as he knelt. No doubt beneath it would be a waistcoat in crushed velvet of some lurid color. Leo knew his brother-in-law too well.

"You sent for me?" Leo tugged at each finger of his gloves and slowly removed them.

Blade straightened, his shadow stretching out behind him. "Got meself a little problem," he said and stepped aside. The body at his feet was dressed in fine silk slacks, a crisp black coat, and—

Hell. Leo froze as he realized who it was. A pair of bloodied ribs gleamed in the lamplight, the heart missing. "Goethe," he said, meeting Blade's green eyes.

"Aye." Not a hint of warmth gleamed there. "Ain't nobody know 'ow 'e just up and appeared, 'ere in the 'Chapel. Or who killed 'im."

Leo took a measured step closer. "I can answer that, at least."

Blade gestured his lads to step back out of the way. Rip stayed, but then over the years he had earned the right to be here.

"Falcons," Leo murmured quietly. "At the Venetian Gardens last night. I saw it happen."

"*Falcons?*" Blade rubbed at his mouth, looking tired. "Christ Jaysus, do you know what you're suggestin'?"

"Aye. I know exactly what I'm saying."

"And the body turns up 'ere. 'Ow convenient."

"He's setting you up as a scapegoat." The prince consort had wanted Blade dead for years.

Blade snapped his fingers, gesturing to Rip and one of the new lads. "Get rid o' the body. Make sure it can't never be found."

"We'll 'ide it in Undertown." Rip wrapped a cloak around Goethe's body, hiding the garish signs of murder from view. Henley, Blade's newest gang member, grabbed the duke's boots and they hauled him up and vanished with him.

Not even a proper burial. Leo's gaze lingered on

them long after they'd vanished. He'd liked Goethe. The man played his own games on the Council— they all did—but at least he was honorable. For years Goethe had been sunk in grief over the loss of his consort. Only recently had he begun to eschew the dark clothes he preferred and actually attend societal events.

The night before Leo departed for Moscow, Goethe had even gotten top-hammered with him at the opera. All Leo could remember from that night was some ribald jest about the soprano, a rousing game of backgammon that he'd won, and the headache he'd traveled all the way to bloody Russia with.

"The dead don't care, you know?" Blade clapped a hand on his shoulder.

"I know." He looked down at the blood splashed on the cobbles. "For all he did, it seems a shame for him to just…disappear like that."

"Come and break your fast with your sister. We'll share a few glasses o' blud-wein to Goethe's memory. Like as not, we're the only ones who'd give a proper damn. The bastard and I 'ad our differences when we were younger, but 'e'd earned me respect."

"I don't know if that's wise. I've things to do—"

"They'll wait," Blade said. "And I've the feelin' there's more to this than's been said."

Leo could have denied it. Devil knew, Blade was aware that he couldn't force Leo to his will. Not the way he did with the rest of his men. An uneasy truce existed between them, two men both too well aware of their own positions of power.

Keeping that truce, that balance maintained, was an art form, and so Leo nodded. Besides, Blade was an

ally that he never underestimated, and in the past few
months they'd both signed on to an undertaking they
strongly believed in.

Removing the prince consort from power.

Treachery of the worst sort —or heroics, depend-
ing upon whether one was a member of the Echelon
or not.

Or simply a man who feared the depths the prince
consort could sink to, if left unopposed.

∽

Mina shipped herself into Casavian House inside a
trunk full of fine gowns from Madame Chevalier's,
along with a note for her maid. When the maid opened
the trunk inside the duchess's rooms, Mina straightened
out of the mess of froth and lace, causing a scream.

"Good…ness gracious, Your Grace. You gave me a
fright." Hannah clapped a hand to her chest.

Mina ushered the maid to an embroidered armchair
before she could wilt, then crossed to the window
and twitched the curtains aside. Her home was in the
middle of Mayfair, and there was not enough traffic
this time of the morning to hide the presence of a man
reading the broadsheets as he leaned against a wrought
iron fence opposite the house.

"It couldn't be helped."

"Of course, Your Grace." The maid wouldn't
mention a hint of this to anyone else. Hannah's
mechanical hand was hidden inside her glove but it
more than ensured her loyalty to Mina. No other
mech served within the Echelon, but Mina chose to
overlook the flaw and Hannah was eternally grateful.

Servants could always be bought, but it was easier to keep their loyalty if they were paid in currencies beyond gold.

A fluffy white cat lifted her head from the bed, her tail lashing. She examined Mina with golden eyes.

"I want you to send for Mr. Gow," Mina said. Her nerves were entirely stretched. Last night... She couldn't seem to forget a single thing. What had Barrons meant by any of it? To ask such a price of her and then not take the prize when it was offered.

You never did understand my motives...

Devil take him. It was hard to think of him as the son of her enemy when he was so charming. Far too easy to see him as just a man, and that could be dangerous for her.

There was an odd little silence as she picked up the cat, pressing her face into Boadicea's warm fur, and she realized Hannah was waiting, hands folded. "Mum?"

"Yes?"

"Do you wish to entertain him here or downstairs?" Hannah asked, and it sounded as if she were repeating herself.

"My study." She never liked having anyone else in her rooms. They were hers. Mina pressed a kiss to Boadicea's head. The feel of that warm body was comforting. "Then return here to see me dressed."

Hannah bobbed a curtsy and left. She'd not said a word about the ensemble Mina wore. The dress that Barrons had found for her to wear before he'd handed her up into a hackney was utterly ludicrous, a low-cut yellow walking gown devoid of anything resembling style. Everybody knew the Duchess of Casavian wouldn't be caught dead in such a thing, which was precisely the point. The image she'd perfected over the years as the very fashionable, untouchable duchess was foolproof. Nobody had even glanced twice at her as she entered the back of Madame Chevalier's shop.

Only one man had ever seen something else beneath the polished veneer. Mina turned and started tugging at her gloves. Last night had been disastrous in more ways than one. The bath and blud-wein, and the swift sleep she'd managed to snatch in his bed, had provided some distance, allowing her to clear her mind and focus on what *must* be considered more important.

The queen's note.

This was where her focus must lie, though she had no intention of allowing Barrons to slip her mind. His motives were just opaque enough for her to question them.

Fact: The prince consort had ordered Goethe murdered.

Supposition: He knew something about the notes she'd been delivering for the queen.

Mina frowned. No, he would have confronted her if he had. There'd not been a single hint that he suspected her of delivering such notes. Indeed, he'd tasked her only last week with increasing supervision over the queen's movements, which meant that he'd somehow discovered the affection his wife held for Goethe through other means.

Or was this a move against Goethe for some other reason? She couldn't discount that possibility.

Fact: She and Barrons were both witnesses, but how would they ever prove that the men had been Falcons?

Oh, she knew it, but she had not seen their faces. All she'd caught a glimpse of were shadowy figures in the night, cutting out the duke's heart. If she dared speak up, would that be *her* next time? Cold spiraled through her. She could almost feel the knife edge beneath her feet.

"At least I have you," she whispered. Boadicea chose that moment to sink in her claws and try to escape. Mina let the feline drop to the bed with an exasperated sigh. "Cats have no respect for a duchess." But the thought made her smile sadly as Boadicea started licking her paws.

Hannah returned promptly and helped her to remove the heavy gown. As she dressed, Mina was unable to stop her thoughts from drifting somewhere far away from fact.

Goethe was dead. That alone dealt her a pang of guilt and regret somewhere in her chest. She'd warned him, after all. What else could she have done?

Not given in to the queen and delivered the messages in the first place.

Queen Alexandra had caught her at a weak moment. "*Please, Your Grace… I should be forever grateful…*"

And Mina had given in, for in truth she knew there was very little pleasure in the queen's life. The prince consort saw to it that his pretty little human wife was well supplied with the laudanum she desired and otherwise kept her in her chambers, locked away from the world. As the queen's Mistress of Robes, Mina alone saw his petty cruelties. Pity was not an emotion she should let herself suffer, and yet she had allowed it to dictate actions she knew were dangerous.

Fact: Mina was going to have to tell the queen that the man she had come to care for was murdered.

Mina's shoulders slumped.

At least she had destroyed the note. Goethe was dead and the prince consort would eye his wife with suspicion, but he wouldn't know what the letter had contained. Or that Mina had delivered it herself.

"There we are, mum," Hannah murmured respectfully.

Mina came out of her thoughts and found herself dressed in a tight velvet day dress. It was so dark a blue as to be almost black, and gold epaulets gleamed on her shoulders. A spill of white lace framed the neckline of her jacket, with golden fringe outlining each layer of her bias-cut skirts. Eminently fashionable, but nobody else saw it as armor the way she did.

"Will you be turning in for the day after your meeting, mum?" Hannah asked, fetching Mina's hat and pinning her hair into a chignon.

"No." There was too much to do to sleep. The prince consort would know by now that Goethe was dead and that a woman had witnessed it. The theft of the airship would only draw further attention to the entire affair. She had to act quickly to allay the prince consort's suspicions while most of the Echelon slept the day away.

But first, Gow.

The man was waiting for her in her study, wearing a pair of slim-fitting trousers and a tweed coat. He was such a quiet, unassuming man that the eye practically begged to skip over him. His was a face that would blend into any crowd.

"Your Grace." He bowed as she locked the door behind her. "To what extent may I be of service?"

The House of Casavian's man-of-affairs, he'd served her father before he died and now herself. It wasn't until after her father's death, however, that she had become fully aware of the extent of Gow's resources.

First things first.

"I have a task for you," she said, wasting no time on polite necessities.

"Of course."

"I want you to find out everything you can about Leo Barrons."

A slim eyebrow rose. "The Duke of Caine's heir?"

"Yes."

"Personal, professional, financial?" he mused.

"Everything," she replied, her eyes narrowing slightly and the ghostly impression of a pair of lips haunting her own for a moment. Distracting her from the question that had begun to circulate in her mind while she traveled home—the question of why he'd been at the Venetian Gardens so soon after disembarking from the dirigible from Saint Petersburg. Certainly not for her.

"Most importantly…" she continued, "I want to know what his weaknesses are."

༺ ❧ ༻

The Warren lay directly in the heart of Whitechapel, a large house with heavy brick walls lining the accompanying yard and lights gleaming in the top layer of windows. The lower floor of the house was full of cobwebs and dust, the timber floorboards so creaky they threatened to break beneath each step, but upstairs was a gleaming haven of light and warmth, the scent of beeswax, elegant furnishings, and modern conveniences like hot water.

The only people who saw the upstairs were those Blade allowed within his refuge. He didn't think it wise to advertise precisely how well he lived to those that were potential enemies.

Dawn spilled through the polished windows of the small parlor as Blade ushered Leo inside. A young woman sprawled asleep on the daybed in front of the fireplace. Blade crossed to her side. Her eyelashes fluttered as Honoria slowly woke.

She was heavy with child now, her cheeks and upper arms fuller than Leo had ever seen them. The last few times he'd visited, she'd been in confinement. Leo crossed his arms and leaned against the doorway, nodding at her when she noticed him. "You look well."

Honoria struggled to sit upright. "It's ghastly," she said. "I cannot believe I fell asleep again." Her face softened as she smiled at Blade. "I was waiting for you to return."

Blade curled onto the daybed at her side, sliding a protective hand around her shoulders. He was often given to improper displays within the sanctity of the house, regardless of whether it was just Leo in attendance or all of his men. "I tol' you not to wait up."

"I told you I would," Honoria replied, a hint of stubbornness entering her voice.

An old argument, no doubt. Leo crossed slowly to the fireplace, holding his hands out to the warmth and

ignoring the pair of them as much as he could. He
never felt so much an outsider as he did when he was
at the Warren.

"What was the problem?" Honoria asked.

Blade swiftly told her the details and Honoria made
a small, distressed sound. "Not Goethe. He was such
a gentleman."

There was a sharp rap at the door. Rip's wife, Esme,
the housekeeper, popped her head inside. "Excuse
me." Her gaze slid over Leo and she nodded a greeting. "But there are a pair of Nighthawks at the door."

"Which ones?" The Nighthawks served the
Echelon as thief-takers. The group was comprised of
rogue blue bloods, those whose infection with the
craving hadn't been sanctioned by law. A rogue was
offered only two choices: join the Nighthawks or the
Coldrush Guards and serve, or be executed.

"Guild Master Garrett Reed and his wife, Lady
Peregrine," Esme replied.

"Rather quick on yer 'eels, ain't they, Barrons?"
Blade nodded to Esme. "See 'em in."

She disappeared and Honoria shared a concerned
glance with Blade. "At least Garrett's our ally."

"Aye." Blade's eyes met Leo's. "Could become
awkward for 'im, were this to be an official visit."

"Let's not make it official, then," Leo replied,
leaning against the mantel. "There's nothing for him
to see."

Blade usually liked playing games, but not at the
moment. His hand curled over Honoria's knee, a
frown darkening his brow. Anything that brought
Nighthawks—or bodies—into his territory when

his wife was in such a sensitive condition roused the darker side of his nature.

Garrett strode inside, handing his hat and coat to Esme. She took them, though a dry glance at Blade showed what she thought of this duty. Esme's role of housekeeper seemed to be more of an honorific than the actual role of a servant. It had taken Leo months to understand her precise position here.

On Garrett's heels came Lady Peregrine. Her hair was clipped at her chin, but it was a soft pale blond now, where once she'd dyed it a harsh black. Not the only change about her. She wore knee-high boots and tight black breeches. A lush lace bustle with a hint of skirt covered the indecent curves of her bottom, and her buttoned-up coat no doubt hid her armored corset. It was a feminine version of the harsh Nighthawk armor she'd once worn.

Leo glanced toward the window, schooling his features. Perry was hardly the sort to draw praise in a world where the Echelon was populated with diamond-bright beauties, but what he found attractive was that sense of strength. It was something all the fluff-buttoned debutantes in the world couldn't own.

Something that the Duchess of Casavian did, however. He was wise enough to realize that he appreciated a woman with a headstrong nature and a high intellect.

He frowned, tapping his fingers on the mantel. Last night came to mind again. He'd thought he'd finally slipped through Mina's barriers to the woman within, but in the end she had been able to resurrect those barriers with ease, leaving him to catch a bare glimpse of the heat within her. The kiss…the kiss had almost driven him out of his mind, and some part of her had liked submitting to him, but not altogether. The moment she'd stood up in the bath, with bubbles dripping down that glorious body, she'd disappeared again, like a valve closing.

He'd left her to sleep in his bloody bed alone, taking himself off to pace the rooftops as he waited for the sun to rise. He'd thought perhaps the cold air would do him some good. Not so. The fire was in his blood now.

A good thing he was a persistent bastard.

"Reed," Blade called, clasping hands with the guild master and tipping a nod toward Lady Peregrine. "An unexpected surprise."

Holding out a chair for his wife, Garrett then claimed the basket seat directly opposite Blade, his fingers curling over the cane arms. He'd grown into the position of guild master that he'd undertaken six months ago. Not many men would stare so directly at the Devil of Whitechapel like that.

"An unfortunate one," Perry replied.

"I have a witness claiming she saw the Duke of Goethe murdered on the edges of Whitechapel earlier this morning," Garrett said, adding, "By you, no less."

"I see." Blade leaned back into the seat, his eyes growing steely. "I trust you've got 'em in protective custody?"

"Of course," Garrett replied. "Somewhere nobody will be able to get to her, including you."

"Have you checked her for a Falcon's tattoo?" Leo asked.

A breath. Then Garrett asked softly, "Should I?"

"Most likely in her hair," Leo suggested. "Or if she doesn't have one, then I'm certain she's recently come into contact with someone who does."

Rubbing at the bridge of his nose, Garrett sighed. After years of being used, the Nighthawks had no love for the prince consort. "Bloody hell. So this is a plot. Do I even wish to know?"

"The prince consort sees Blade as a threat, so this is obviously a ploy against him," Leo murmured, circling the room to the decanter by the window. It was definitely time for some blood. For all of them. "You knew what we were setting out to do six months ago."

Nine men and women had made a decision one foggy morning to bring down the prince consort and restore peace to the city. Leo and Blade had been the instigators of that meeting, but Garrett and his wife had their own reasons for wanting to remove the madman from power.

Since that day, repeating rifles and supplies had been smuggled into the rookery, even cannons mounted on the walls, though those remained out of sight. Whitechapel was the base of operations, the heart of the effort to bring down the prince consort. Both Blade's ranks and the Nighthawks' rosters had swelled, men coming in by the dozens.

"Knowing isn't quite the same as being trapped between a rock and a hard place," Garrett replied, accepting the glass of blood that Leo offered him. "I've been summoned to the Tower to make a report to the prince consort as soon as I'm done here."

"Then go to the Tower," Leo said, crossing back

toward Blade. "Make your report. There's nothing to find."

"*Was* there something to find?" At his short nod, Garrett swore under his breath again. "So Goethe's dead?"

"Missin'," Blade corrected.

"The prince consort will insist there's a case to build." Garrett downed his blood in one swallow.

"Without a body you have nothing but a witness. Start searching for Goethe, but stay close to Goethe's house and his relations. The prince consort can't press you too closely on Whitechapel without going out of his way, and that's suspicious. You're simply following leads, questioning everyone—trying to find a link between Blade and Goethe when there really isn't one," Leo said.

"Keep us up-to-date," Blade insisted.

"We will," Garrett said, standing and offering Perry a hand. He locked eyes with Leo. "How goes that other matter you were dealing with?"

Leo grimaced. "I managed to meet with some of Wetherby's mechs last night at the Venetian Gardens. Wetherby wanted something public. I'm going to send him that three-pounder Hotchkiss cannon I got my hands on. Wetherby's certain he can create something similar for us to mount on the walls of the rookery, just in case." When revolution started fires in the city, they needed a stronghold where they could fall back if matters went badly.

A grim silence settled over the room. "So this is it," Perry said, letting go of a breath.

"This is it," Blade murmured, staring at nothing.

"Or the start of it, anyway. Once we got the guns, we can start movin' them to other parts of the city through Undertown."

"We'll try to make this as bloodless as possible," Leo said grimly. "A quiet coup, if I can get us into the Ivory Tower where we can take the prince consort prisoner and see him executed…but I'm not about to do this unprepared. If we don't need to use any of the weapons we're stockpiling, then I shall consider us lucky as all hell. He won't go quietly."

"But 'e'll go," Blade murmured, a dark light gleaming in his eyes.

"He'll go," Garrett agreed. "We cannot afford for him not to."

Five

"Extra, Extra, read all about it! Airship stolen from the Venetian Gardens last night by a gang of vigilantes! The pilot admits he was overpowered, and Lord M— demands more Nighthawks on the streets to protect good, loyal citizens!"

—Paperboy overheard by Leo Barrons

LEO HAD BARELY RETURNED FROM THE ROOKERY, easing his shoulders out of his coat, when his butler appeared with a carefully folded piece of parchment resting on a silver salver. The red wax seal bore the stamp of the Duke of Morioch, the current Chair for the Council of Dukes.

Leo slid the coat back over his shoulders and took the missive with a sigh. "No other messages?" he asked, feeling weary to the bone. No sleep in over twenty-four hours would do that to a body, and the previous month in Russia had been taxing. The Russian Court made the Echelon look like a bunch of lambs.

"Your father's footman arrived to schedule your chess game," Montgomery replied with a sonorous air. "Today at five, if it please my lord."

Not so much a request as a summons. Though he was the duke's heir, they'd barely spoken in more than three years, not since Leo had cost Caine much in the political arena by helping Blade duel Vickers, the Duke of Lannister.

The chess games, however, were regular occurrences that Leo indulged his father with, though he didn't know why he bothered or why the duke even requested them. They barely spoke and Caine trumped him almost every time, berating him for his lack of forethought.

No doubt the duke wanted to know about the Russian situation. Though his illness kept him indoors and out of polite society, Caine still hungered for control over the Council meetings Leo was forced to attend in his place.

Flipping his thumbnail beneath the wax, Leo broke the seal and jerked his gaze over the elegant gold writing. A meeting. At twelve. "*Ballocks*," he muttered.

"My lord?"

The enormous longcase clock in the hallway ticked with impertinence, a pointed reminder that Leo had barely half an hour to make the meeting. "Send for the steam coach. Where's Morrissey?" His valet would have to cut short his efforts today and be satisfied with simply laying out something for Leo to wear.

"I'll ring for him, my lord."

"Excellent." Sailing up the stairs, Leo examined the letter again. *A formal request for your presence in the face of a most unfortunate event…* He could well imagine what that would be.

Fifteen minutes later, he left poor Morrissey trailing behind him with a bottle of cologne as he descended the stairs. The man had had to make do with a mandarin-collared black coat that negated the need for anything fancy, like a cravat, and a pair of tight black trousers. Leo swung out the door with his top hat and an ebony-handled cane that concealed a diamond-edged sword.

He'd barely had time for a shave, though he had managed to tie his hair back in a neat queue. His hair was longer than he usually wore it and he'd considered cutting it, but something stopped him. The duchess's fingers making a fist in it as she tilted her mouth up to his, perhaps. Hardly the sort of thing a man was likely to forget.

She'd be there today. The thought fired his blood and left him tapping the top of the coach as he settled inside it and rested his elbow on the open window. At least there was one damned thing to look forward to.

❧

"You're late," Morioch said, tapping his fingers on the polished mahogany table.

It stretched across the Council chambers, surrounded by nine seats. The prince consort sat at the far end, with the queen's empty chair beside him and slightly behind. The queen herself was standing and staring through the windows out over the city. Maybe wishing for escape—or dreaming of it. The scent of laudanum often clung to her breath, and her eyes frequently held the distant gaze of someone in another world.

"I only received your missive a half hour ago," Leo replied, handing his top hat and cane to the nearest footman.

Morioch's lips thinned. "Can we call this session to order then?"

Leo smiled with a flash of bared teeth and took his time taking his seat. Only then did he let his gaze rest on the empty chair across from him. Goethe's chair.

"We're not all here yet," Lynch murmured. The former Nighthawk master's hair was dark and neatly combed. Wearing an unembellished gray suit with a black waistcoat, he fiddled with a gold pocket watch. His hawkish gray eyes pinned Morioch down as if he were a bug tacked to a lepidopterist's board.

Seven months ago, Lynch had dueled his uncle for the seat of the House of Bleight and was proving both a formidable adversary for the prince consort and a loyal ally for Leo and his quiet revolution. With the recent fracture of the Council—the loss of three dukes within the last three years—Leo was grateful to have someone he could count on for sense. Granted, Lynch didn't always side with him; the man was no puppet, after all, and they both had strong opinions, but it was still a relief to have someone else stand up against the prince consort's sporadic cruelties and small bouts of what Leo politely termed madness.

A tall man stepped out of the corner, his blond hair gleaming with faint reddish highlights. He withdrew a large piece of black silk from his waistcoat pocket. Leo stiffened, though he forced his fingers to keep

drumming on the table. Balfour was the prince
consort's spymaster—and the hand on the leash of
the Falcons.

Shaking out the silk, Balfour draped it over Goethe's
chair and stepped back against the wall, hands clasped
behind him.

Silence ruled the room, broken only by the
queen's startled gasp. A horrified expression crossed
her face, her gloved fingers touching her lips. She
hadn't known.

Despite himself, Leo glanced at the Duchess of
Casavian, who was sitting directly across from him.
He hadn't dared look at her when he entered; nobody
could know about last night. The small mechanical
jeweled spider she often wore tethered to her breast by
a pin crawled across her shoulder. Mina sat perfectly
still, her face so pale she might have been wearing rice
powder. As if sensing his gaze, she looked up, her eyes
meeting his. An expression of grief flickered through
them as she glanced sideways—at the queen, perhaps—
before she brought her expression under control.

Lynch was the first to break the silence. "When did
this happen?"

"This morning, my reports tell me." The prince
consort leaned back in his throne-like chair. "Your
young protégé Garrett Reed is working the case. A
young woman reports seeing Goethe on the edge of
Whitechapel before he was murdered by the Devil's
own hand—"

"Blade did this?" Lynch asked. "It seems highly out
of character. Also, what in blazes was Goethe doing
in Whitechapel?"

The prince consort's satisfaction dimmed slightly. "So the young lady reports."

"Mmm." Lynch scratched his jaw. "Perhaps I'd best discuss it with Garrett."

"I'm certain your man has it well in hand—"

"Of course, but we're speaking about the murder of a duke and the possibility of war with Whitechapel." Lynch's voice became flat with authority. "We would want to be absolutely certain that the Devil of Whitechapel is guilty before we commit to this. I needn't remind you what happened fifty years ago when King George attempted to extract Blade from the rookeries."

"The mobs rose," Leo murmured, "and the city burned, and despite all of our technology, we were forced back within the city limits."

The prince consort's lips thinned. "Time changes a great deal. Technology has improved. The presence of the Trojan cavalry sees to that."

The enormous steel horses were sent out in force, their iron-plated hooves crushing through a mob like a threshing machine. They were the first thing the prince consort had insisted on creating nearly thirteen years ago after he overthrew the human king and became regent.

Leo's fingers stilled. Thirteen years ago the prince consort had charged the royal blacksmiths with creating a weapon that could be used against the only thing that had ever challenged the Echelon: a mob. Could it have been serendipity, or something far more sinister? The first steps in some long-reaching plan to rid himself of those whose very presence challenged his rule?

Blade's legend gave the humans of the city hope. If Leo were in the prince consort's shoes, the first thing he would do would be to destroy that legend and prove that not even the Devil himself was untouchable.

And then? Leo's gaze shifted to that scrap of black silk. While the people in the streets might whisper that life would change, should their queen hold power, the truth remained—the ruling Council of Dukes were the only other gainsay to the prince consort, able to overrule him if they chose. And for years, the prince consort had held most of the vote, with four of the seven dukes in his pocket. The deceased Dukes of Lannister had both voted his way, and Morioch was fanatically loyal, as were the former Duke of Bleight and, of course, Caine. In the past three years, however, the Dukes of Lannister had both died; Lynch had overthrown Bleight; and Caine's illness had thrust Leo onto the Council as his proxy.

The only trump card the prince consort owned was the queen. She could, if pressed, overrule the Council's decision by right of regency.

Now two chairs stood empty: Goethe's chair and the one that the Dukes of Lannister had used.

What if Goethe's murder was simply the prince consort's way to even the score? If a new, amenable Council was instated, the prince consort would hold complete power again.

Dashed clever, if Leo was correct. Not just a move on Blade then, but on all of the dukes who opposed him.

Prepared to speak, Leo paused as movement caught

his eye. The queen was slowly coming toward the table. "You didn't tell me," she said, staring at that damning scrap of black silk. "You knew all morning, didn't you? That he was dead. That Manderlay was dead."

All eyes shot to her, including her husband's. He reached for her hand but she jerked it to her chest, staring down at him with wide, devastated eyes.

Manderlay. A rather more intimate title than Goethe. Leo was drawing conclusions, as he suspected several others were too.

"Your Highness," the duchess murmured. She slid out of her chair with extraordinary grace as she crossed to the queen's side. "I think it best if we retire to your chambers. You're looking peaked—"

"*Peaked?*"

"Alexandra," the prince consort said, the word heavily laced with reprimand. "Hardly the time to create a scene."

Instead of putting her in her place, as his words so often did, they seemed to ignite her. The queen's eyes blazed to life, her laudanum-soaked haze sliding off her as fury raised something Leo had never seen in her before.

"How *dare* you speak to me like that?" she demanded. "How dare you—"

The sound of the duchess's slap ricocheted around the chambers. Everybody froze as the queen drew in a harsh breath, her hand going to her reddened cheek.

The Duchess of Casavian seemed to collect herself, as if she too had been shocked by her own actions. "My prince, it seems Her Highness is overwrought by the excitement of the day. With your permission, I believe it time for her to retire."

"An excellent suggestion," the prince consort murmured. "Perhaps you should teach her some restraint, while you're at it. Or I will."

That was the first time he'd ever explicitly spoken of what went on behind closed doors. It wasn't the first time the queen had worn a bruise. It wouldn't be the last. The air in the chamber seemed to grow thinner, and Leo's fingers clenched on the table. "Your Highness—"

"Your opinion is not necessary—or desired—at this moment. My wife is overwhelmed. I think it time for her to rest." He gave the duchess a clipped nod.

The duchess replied with a more formal bow of the head. A little tremble started in the queen's hands but she hid it well, curling her pale silk gloves in her skirts.

There was nothing he could do, was there? To speak out would earn him little more than a spoken reprimand, but it might cost the queen far more than that. The prince consort could do as he liked with her. She was his wife, after all, no matter how poorly it sat. Still, the only thing keeping Leo's mouth shut at this moment was the knowledge that he could only cause the queen more pain.

Soon we'll be in a position to overthrow him. The thought eased some of the guilt. *Then nobody will ever lift a hand to her again.*

Slowly his gaze lifted to Lynch's, both of them sharing the same grim expression. Lynch gave a little shake of his head.

"Now, where were we?" Morioch drawled as the

duchess took the queen in hand, her fingers locking around one of those slender gloved wrists.

Leo couldn't help watching them leave the room while slowly sinking back into his seat. He also couldn't help frowning as the queen scurried to keep pace with the taller duchess.

It was the first time he'd ever been disappointed in the duchess.

Six

Rumors Unfounded, States the Prince Consort

Recent whisperings in the general populace and certain publications have put a strain on the government, with the news that the humanist revolutionary leader Mordecai Hughes, who was executed seven months ago, was not, in fact, truly the mastermind behind the humanist movement. Though the humanists have seemingly vanished back into the populace since Hughes was unmasked as Mercury and executed on crimes of treason, propaganda pamphlets perpetuating this rumor are now being widely circulated among the human classes.

The prince consort and the Council of Dukes have recently released a statement confirming that Hughes was indeed the mastermind behind the bombing of the Ivory Tower and the attempted terrorist attack at the opera last autumn. Persistent rumor among the lower classes, however, suggests that Mercury was never one person, but merely a persona worn by several humanists to protect the true mastermind.

Cause to wonder, perhaps, who truly is in charge

of the humanists? For if "Mercury" has many faces, someone must be in control. Despite the prince consort's assurances, argument suggests that we haven't seen the last of the humanists—or of the presumably faceless instigator behind this movement.

—London Standard

THE QUEEN'S BEDCHAMBERS WERE LIGHT AND AIRY as Mina marched her through the double doors. Gesturing for the maids to shut the doors and leave, she tipped her chin toward her one potential adversary in the room, the Countess of Baltimere.

Lady Baltimere's eyes locked on the reddening handprint on the queen's cheek. "Your Highness, would you care for some tea? Something—"

"That will be all." Mina used her iciest voice. Baltimere would only liberally lace the tea with laudanum. "The queen and I have matters to discuss."

Lady B. tipped her chin up. "Your Highness—"

"You heard her," the queen whispered, the afternoon light highlighting the dark shadows beneath her eyes.

A tilt of the head, one adversary to another, then Lady B. was gone, shutting the doors behind her.

And suddenly Mina didn't know what to say. Her shoulders slumped, her breath catching in her chest. "Your Highness—"

"Please. Don't." The queen crossed wearily to her dresser, sitting down and staring at her cheek in the mirror. Gently she lifted her hand toward the damning mark, touching it with the tip of her silk-clad fingers.

Mina's hand tingled, as if remembering the blow. Her skirts swished as she crossed the luxurious carpets. If only she'd said no to the exchange of letters. This would never have happened and the queen—

The sight of the queen crushed her. She looked utterly hollow, as if she were only an automaton— moving, breathing, speaking, but not there. Manipulated by someone else.

"I had to do it," Mina whispered, catching sight of herself in the mirror behind the queen. Her hands slid over those pale shoulders, squeezing gently. "You know I had to do it. We couldn't afford to let him know—"

"Is it true?" Those lifeless eyes caught hers in the reflection. "What he said about Manderlay? About the Devil of Whitechapel murdering him?"

Manderlay. A name only the queen used. Something caught in Mina's chest and lodged there. Of all the blows the queen had taken over the years, this was the worst. "Part of it. He's dead. I saw it happen." And hadn't stopped it. "But not by Blade's hand. It was at the Venetian Gardens last night when I went to pass along your note to him."

A single tear trailed down the queen's left cheek. "Who?"

"Falcons." Mina's head bowed, her thumbs stroking the queen's shoulders. "I couldn't stop it. I barely made it out of there myself, though I did manage to retrieve your note—"

"*My* note. That's why he died. This is because of me, isn't it?"

There was no answer to that, though Mina tried,

her mouth opening. *Of course not.* But she didn't truly believe it. Her own fault was in allowing this flirtation to escalate. Nothing came out of her mouth, and the queen's face screwed up in an expression Mina had never seen before: a mix of rage and grief and absolute devastation.

One of those gloved hands lashed out, smashing bottles of perfume off the dresser. Mina tried to catch them, exclaiming, "Alexa!" Another lash sent more bottles and the silver-backed brush tumbling in the other direction. A mess of cloying floral scent rose up as glass smashed on the floor, like a funeral gone badly wrong.

The queen fisted the enormous flacon of French perfume that her husband had given her for her birthday—and that she'd never worn. Mina held her hand out. "Please, don't—"

It hit the mirror, cracks spearing out in the polished surface, obliterating their reflections. Mina caught the queen's hands, trying to stop her. It would be far too easy to overpower her, human strength being nothing to her own, but she couldn't quite bring herself to do it. Instead she clung to Alexandra's arms, drawing the queen's smaller frame back against her chest. The queen jerked, rapidly losing strength. Each yank became more and more feeble until she finally halted, Mina holding her much like a marionette.

Alexandra let out a sob that sounded as if she had been broken inside somewhere.

"Please, don't," Mina whispered, turning the queen in her arms. Pressing Alexandra's face against her shoulder, she slid her hand through the other woman's hair.

"I'm so sorry. I should have saved him for you. I should have done something. I'm so, so sorry…" All of the so-called power she had accumulated over the years, and she couldn't do a damned thing to fix this situation.

Except to kill the prince consort. A task that she'd often considered while she watched as he turned a vibrant, powerful young woman into someone barely managing to hold herself together. He was too closely protected by his honor guard or by Falcons. And what would happen if she failed? Then Alexa would have nobody.

"No," the queen whispered, her tears leaching through Mina's dress. "No, I know you couldn't. I know you would have tried."

It was dangerous to do this, even here. Mina kept an eye on the door. If anyone opened it and saw them like this, there would be no hiding the truth anymore, but she couldn't let Alexandra go. The two women clung together, Mina making hushing noises as she stroked the queen's hair.

Far better to be patient. To bring him down through carefully planned means. Frustration burned in her breast—the same frustration she knew the queen felt. "We're so close to overthrowing him," Mina whispered. "Mercury's 'death' was a brief setback, but plans are continuing apace. Mercury's work creating an automaton army is being continued in the other segments of the humanists under my control. The Ironmonger enclaves have already produced their quota of the automatons."

That was their secret. They were building an army of automatons designed to encase a human within them, unlike the frequency-controlled metaljackets and the Trojan cavalry the Echelon commanded. Technology would provide what she herself could not—a way to destroy the man she hated above all others. A way to set her dearest friend free.

"I don't know if I can do this…anymore."

Squeezing her eyes shut, Mina pressed her lips against Alexandra's forehead. "Don't give up," she whispered fiercely. "Do you remember the day we first met?" *Strolling through the gardens behind the Ivory Tower on the day the human princess was to marry, and finding her sobbing behind the rosebushes.* "I told you then to be brave. That you could be the most powerful woman in the Empire, if you dared. You could be a queen and save your people from the Echelon's blood taxes and harsh laws."

Of course, neither of them had known then how difficult such a road would be. Mina had been all of sixteen and the queen but two years older. The then-princess had no allies. The entire Echelon backed the prince consort's regency, once he'd overthrown Alexa's father. For Mina, finding the princess sobbing in the garden on her wedding day, the future had not seemed so dire. Marriage was expected for both of them. They were both highborn, their roles in life mapped out long ago—until the death of her own father and her subsequent infection with the craving had changed Mina's life forever.

If she'd known…

Would you say the same thing to her again? Would you have set her on this path? Pushed her to marry a man who would slowly crush the life out of her?

She knew the answer to that, and it hurt terribly.

If she'd known the depths of the prince consort's evil, Mina would have taken Alexa by the hand and never looked back. Instead, she'd helped trap her friend in a cruel marriage.

She squeezed Alexa tight, hating herself just a little. *I'm so sorry. I didn't know. I didn't understand how bad it could be.* They were words that she could never utter. The only thing she could do was work to right this wrong.

"I want him dead," the queen whispered. "I cannot—I do not know how much longer I can last." Her voice broke just a little. "Every night I lie there, thinking about what would happen if I kept a knife under my pillow. If one night, once he was through with me, he would fall asleep and—"

"You would not succeed." Mina closed her eyes, squeezing them tight. "Even if you did, you're guarded only by Coldrush Guards and Falcons. *His* men. I couldn't get to you before they did as they wished, and I cannot say how far their loyalty to the Crown stretches." That was a thought that kept her awake most days. That Alexandra would do something rash and be cut down for it before Mina even knew.

"You're correct." But the words were lifeless, and suddenly Mina wondered if her queen truly cared whether she survived this or not.

Panic was a cold, spiraling coil deep inside her. "One day you're going to be free of him. I promise you. Then you can be the ruler you want to be, beloved by the people. The type of ruler your grandfather was. You can cast down the Echelon if you desire, and return the humans and mechs to their rightful places. Imagine all of those lives you're going to change—" Dreams that the queen had held for years, but Mina couldn't quite hide the desperate note in her voice. *Fight, damn you. Just a little longer.* "All of the plans we've dreamed over the years…come to fruition."

The queen stared hollowly at herself in the mirror. "Just once, I should like to be a woman first and not a queen."

"You are a woman." Mina kissed her cheek. "You're the strongest, bravest woman I know."

"You're my strength," Alexandra admitted, her gloved hand sliding over Mina's. "I would have given up long before this without you."

Would have… Mina let out a little breath of relief. "Give me time. Once we have enough of the Cyclops to defeat the prince consort's metaljackets, we can take action. I shall begin selling off some of our business ventures to raise capital and push it into the humanist quadrants. They can work faster with more men, more money… Give me until the end of the year at least… I will win you your freedom if I have to kill him myself."

Finally a spark of life came to light in the queen's eyes. "I know you would but we cannot rush. Not without risking his attention. If this fails, it will kill me."

"Then perhaps we can focus his attention elsewhere," Mina suggested, letting go of Alexandra. "Send him on a wild-goose chase hunting humanists where there are none? I've begun seeding rumors through the newspapers, suggesting that Mercury was simply a cover and that the prince consort executed the wrong man."

"A dangerous move."

"No more than most of them. The Nighthawks are showing increasing ambivalence toward his rule. I cannot see them tripping all over themselves to hunt down an imaginary revolutionary."

The queen looked around at the mess at her feet. "Thank you."

"For?"

"For being the one person I can rely on. For being my hope when I have none."

Something thickened in Mina's throat. "Always."

"That being said, I think…I think I would like to be alone for a little while. Would you send Lady Baltimere in?"

With her special *tea*. "Alexandra, I cannot see the good in it for you—"

"I'm not asking you to." This time a hint of steel edged the queen's tone. Their eyes met in the mirror, the queen's reddened and puffy.

Mina bowed. "As you wish."

"Just this once," Alexandra murmured, her gaze losing focus. "I just want to…not feel anything today."

Mina pressed a kiss to the queen's hair, her hopes dying a little. The doctors assured her the laudanum wouldn't hurt the queen—indeed, quite the opposite—but she had seen the way it changed her friend, leaving her but an empty, dreaming shell.

How much of her would be left once the prince

consort had callously carved away all of the pieces of her soul?

We could run away. Remember when we used to dream of that? But she said nothing, for the truth was that they were only pretty lies. The prince consort would never let the queen out of his grasp. They'd be lucky if they made it to Calais.

Unless I steal an airship. The bittersweet jest that made her think, of all things, of Barrons.

"Sleep well," she whispered, stepping away and gathering her skirts. "And remember that our day is coming. Sooner than you think."

"Mina." A slightly tremulous voice, followed by a deep breath. "You cannot leave yet."

She turned, trying not to look at that damning mark on the queen's cheek. "I should return to the Council."

"You know what he meant when he told you to take me in hand." Strength was returning to the queen's voice. She sat above the perfume battlefield, her skirts sweeping through the shards of glass.

"Please." Mina's throat constricted. "I don't want to—"

"Not my face," the queen instructed. "He won't want it to be visible. But make certain it bruises." Her chin lifted. "It wouldn't do for my husband to think he needs to add his own, and if I can bear it…by God, you can do it to me."

Sometimes being her queen's strength was Mina's own vile challenge.

Seven

"You're late."

Leo paused in the door of his father's study. "Father," he said, stripping off his coat and handing it to one of the hovering maids. "I've missed you too. The trip was successful"—only one assassination attempt by a Russian duke—"and the weather remained uneventful for our voyage, thanks for asking."

The Duke of Caine turned away from the fireplace, light flickering over his pale skin before he dragged the hood of his cape up, hiding his face. "Do you think yourself amusing?"

"Frequently."

The drapes were drawn, the room a smoky, heated den that Leo suspected the duke rarely ventured away from. A woman sat in the corner of the room, her fingers stilling on her needlework.

"Madeline," Leo murmured, crossing to press his lips against her cheek.

She was his father's oldest thrall, faint lines now forming around her dark eyes. A beautiful woman still, and one of the few who suffered Caine's temper with any sense of aplomb. "Leo," she replied, patting his cheek. "Look at you. You look like some dashing corsair."

He raked a hand over his hair, where it touched his collar. "So I've been told."

"Can you not do that elsewhere?" Caine snapped, gesturing to her.

Madeline's smile faded, her dark gaze locking on the duke. "Perhaps I should leave you both to your chess game," she demurred, though the faint lift of her brow indicated what she thought of Caine's rudeness. Gathering her things, she smiled at Leo. "You know where you may find me."

He'd much rather she'd stay. Her company was preferable to Caine's. "Later," he agreed.

His father owned six thralls, a sign of prosperity and influence, though, perhaps due to his illness, he'd begun to retire three of them. They were rarely kept in the manor house anymore, Caine having set them up in style in various houses around the city.

Leo himself supported two of his father's thralls. They'd been a generous gift for his eighteenth birthday, though now he wondered if that hadn't been his father's attempt to hide the onset of his mysterious illness. Caine had become more reclusive not long after.

The only thrall that remained in the house was Madeline, though Leo wasn't certain whose idea that had been.

He knew for a fact that Madeline refused Caine her flesh rights. She might have signed a thrall contract giving him unlimited access to her blood, but tradition dictated that a woman's body was hers to give as she desired. A gift that was seldom spoken of in society.

That left him somewhat uncertain why she tolerated the old bastard.

"Send for me when you're done," she told Caine, drawing his chair back for him in front of their chess game. "You've not fed today."

"I'll drink my blood from a bottle," the duke snapped.

"As you wish," she replied, making her way toward the door and closing it behind her with the faintest slam.

Leo stared at Caine for a long time. His father was many things, but seldom rude. "If I were Madeline, I would have slapped you for that. You owe her an apology."

"She's not my wife." The duke was peevish, settling in his chair and drawing his cloak around him as if he still felt the cold, despite the raging inferno that was the fire. "She needs to remember that."

"Perhaps you need to remember your manners." Leo crossed toward the chessboard. He took little pleasure in these visits; they were simply a duty to be performed. "Or are you forgetting them in your dotage?"

Caine's jaw tightened.

"Your illness?" Leo inquired. "Does it make you peevish?"

"I am *not* ill."

Leo sank down opposite him. A few years ago he might have still cared. Caine had burned away most of the empathy Leo had felt for him as a boy. Trying to please the old bastard had been an impossible task but one which Leo had set his mind to in every instance. But setting up Blade's duel with Vickers had caused a rift between them that seemed impossibly wide. Leo had…stopped caring. Or no, not completely, though he often wished he had. Perhaps he'd finally come to the realization that he would never truly please the man he called a father.

They had nothing in common in face or appearance. Leo took after his mother—and the man who'd sired him. The dark eyes he'd been gifted with were remarkably similar to Honoria's. Sometimes he wondered if Caine thought of that every time he looked at his wife's bastard son. The thought sent a vicious wave of emotion through Leo. Another way to twist the knife in Caine's chest.

They stared at each other across the chessboard.

"Don't the Russians have valets? Or scissors?"

"I've grown fond of my hair longer." At least he had now.

"Mmm." Caine leaned forward over the board, studying the pieces that were already in play. "Talk to me about the Russians."

So Leo did, falling back into the game they'd left off a month ago. He cut out all of the details Madeline might have enjoyed—the icy slash of wind against his cheeks as he peered over the prow of the dirigible, watching the Baltic pass by far below; the wonder of a foreign court; and the fiery burn of blood-laced vodka down his throat. He'd grown far too fond of that, sharing bottles of it with Captain Alexi as they laughed about the dangers of hunting boar in the Russian autumn and the far more dangerous pursuit of hunting Russian women.

Instead he named alliances, power plays, the puppet masters of the Russian Court, and discussed the treaty that the prince consort was intent on forging with the blood-thirsty Russians.

Caine was silent for a long time after he finished, staring at the chessboard Leo was halfheartedly negotiating. "You're not trying."

I haven't been trying for years. Still, his jaw twitched at the rebuke. Too many years of trying to please the man were ingrained in him.

Caine slammed his rook into place and glared at Leo over the board. "Check."

"So it is."

His bland acceptance seemed to enrage the duke. "Perhaps your attention's elsewhere, hmm? On something it shouldn't be."

He knew exactly what his father was suggesting. "Do tell."

"Who is she? I know you haven't availed yourself of Chloe or Cecilia since your return."

His thralls. Their eyes met and Leo saw the triumph in his father's. "You're having me watched?"

"They are my thralls, after all." The duke shrugged.

"Nice to know." Leo stood, giving the chessboard a barely concealed look of disgust. Chloe was not the sort to break his faith; the duke terrified her. Cecilia, however, would know where her dues were owed.

"Who is she?" Caine demanded again, moving with the kind of viperish grace that made Leo's breath catch just a little.

Caine blocked the path to the door. Leo met the duke's gaze. "You wouldn't approve."

"You might be surprised. She's clearly not thrall material or you'd not be restraining yourself. You always had a soft heart. I might be able to help with the marriage negotiations—"

"It's called respect, not weakness. And the negotiations are entirely between myself and the lady in question," Leo shot back, though it burned on the tip of his tongue that he was leading his father to believe him engaged in pursuit of a consort.

A laughable matter. Mina would never agree to such an alliance, and he was hardly certain where his own intentions lay.

He wanted her. Caine would never understand that. A political alliance was all that mattered to the duke, not a personal one. How many times had the duke told him that giving a woman his heart would only weaken him?

"I'll find out," the duke warned.

"No, you won't." Only Mina knew of his desires. "Not until the matter is decided."

He pushed past, surprised when Caine let him.

This was the only tool in his arsenal. He didn't have to stay. Didn't have to crawl after Caine's scraps of praise the way he once had, and Caine knew it too.

The duke followed him to the door, hovering on the threshold, as though he were afraid to cross it and enter the world of the living. "Are you going to see Madeline before you leave?"

"Of course I am," Leo replied, glancing back over his shoulder. "She's the main reason I still visit."

It could have been his imagination, but the duke seemed to flinch.

"Tell her I'm sorry," the duke called.

"Tell her yourself," Leo threw over his shoulder, taking the stairs two at a time. "I'm not your errand boy."

Not anymore, anyway.

&

Sunlight dappled the sitting room when Leo returned to Waverly Place, the home he shared with Cecilia and Chloe, his two thralls.

Only one of them would be home at this time of day. Cecilia would be out shopping, spending her allowance on small gems and silk gowns, or perhaps taking tea with her friends. Chloe preferred to read and also preferred her own company.

Her face lit up in a smile when he entered the room. However, her blond curls gleamed so brightly in the dying sunlight that he almost winced. He did not share Caine's aversion to sunlight, but he still preferred the dark of night.

"What are you doing out of bed at this time of the evening?" Chloe demanded, placing her book aside with a playful smile. "Have you even *been* to bed today?"

He shook his head. "Duty calls."

Chloe grimaced. "The duke."

Chloe's thrall contract had been signed between her father and the duke, leaving her with few other options in life. She'd been all of seventeen when Caine had passed over her leash to Leo—seventeen, somewhat frightened, and entirely unsuited for service as a thrall.

Leo shared his bed with Cecilia on occasion, though not his confidences. Chloe, however, had become a friend over the years, once it became clear that he would demand nothing of her that she did not wish to give. Her throat was unmarred by the fine silvery scars Cecilia flaunted, because she preferred to offer him the veins in her wrist for her fortnightly blood-lettings.

Leo took a breath, mulling over the thoughts that had been plaguing him since he'd left Caine House. "Chloe, I'm going to let you go."

There was no surprise in her green eyes, only a flare of nervousness. "To Caine?"

A relief to get the words out—and for her to take them so calmly. Cecilia would not accept his decision so easily. "No. If you wish, I shall arrange several meetings for you with prospective protectors." Passing a thrall contract on to another was not unheard of in the Echelon, though rare. Few wanted what had been marked by another man. "Or I would be willing to settle you with an annual stipend. You could live independently if you chose."

"An annual stipend," she said breathlessly, and he knew there would be no meetings to arrange on her behalf.

"A generous one. It is my hope that our friendship shall continue."

A sideways glance. "I should like that. However, that is entirely dependent on your wife's say in this."

He arched a brow. "I didn't say I was contemplating—"

"You didn't have to," Chloe said. "I would not be surprised to guess the name of the fortunate young woman you're interested in, either." A faint smile touched her lips. "The duchess does not seem the type to share."

Duchess…? He stared at her. "How did you—?"

"It's written all over your face when you see her, though I doubt that anyone else has noticed. I know you too well, my lord. You get this look in your eye, like Cecilia when she sees a plate of Cook's lemon tarts."

Clever, observant Chloe. She was the one Caine should have cultivated if he wanted a spy, though her loyalty would have made such a task difficult. "I'm not entirely certain what my interest holds in regard to the duchess, or whether any more shall come of this."

"I think you know. You would not do this if you weren't certain in some part of you."

Truth. He wanted Mina. Wanted to pursue her, to mark her as his, to claim her. Anything else would be a hard-won battle, but he didn't instantly deny the words. If she was his wife, then she would never belong to anyone else. That pleased the darker, hungrier side of his craving and stroked the darkness within that he'd fought so hard to contain over the years.

He'd been born a gentleman, but the hunger inside him was most definitely not.

"Besides, I think your doubt is misplaced."

"Is it?" he asked. "She's not the sort of woman to meekly submit to a consort contract." Besides that, the number of obstacles in his way—Caine included—was hardly insignificant.

"You're going to pursue her and you're going to win her."

"You should write propaganda pamphlets for the humanists," he said dryly. "Or enlistment posters." He stood, grateful that she had not railed against his barely formed decision. "Thank you," he said as he made his way toward the door.

"You should know," Chloe called, drawing his attention, "you're not the only one looking, my lord. Especially when you're not aware of her gaze. Though I should warn you... She doesn't look at you like Cecilia looks at her lemon tarts."

"Oh?" The words pleased him a little.

"She looks at you like a puzzle to be solved. Like a lion that has been staked near her and is threatening to tear its tether free. You are as much a threat to her as you are a fascination."

"Why do I think you're enjoying this?"

"I am. You've always been too certain of yourself." Her eyes twinkled. "And it wouldn't be worthwhile if it wasn't a difficult pursuit, now would it?"

❧

Gow was waiting for her as she descended the stairs that night. Mina peered at him from beneath the depths of the frothy black feathers that cascaded over her hair in a flirtatious little confection. She felt sick to her stomach, having spent most of the afternoon resting for the night ahead. She didn't look it, though. The finest applications of tinted powders made her radiant, hiding the dark circles beneath her eyes.

No sleep for her this afternoon, though she'd tried,

lying there with Boadicea snuggled to her chest, a warm contented purr rumbling through her. All she could see were the strategic marks she'd left on the queen's arms, bruises in the shape of her hands. The thought almost brought up her gorge again.

"Something that might interest you, Your Grace," Gow murmured, patting the file beneath his arm as she stepped onto the portico.

"One hopes." Gravel sprayed as her steam coach was brought around, one of the liveried footmen leaping down from his perch and setting out the small footstool for her to climb. The other footman opened the door and stepped aside. "I daresay you wouldn't have brought this to my attention at this precise moment unless it was important."

Gow simply handed over the file.

Nobody could get close enough in the luxuriant blackness of the evening to overhear them, yet Mina turned, using her body to shield the file as she flicked it open.

And caught her breath.

Grainy photographs filled it. She couldn't stop her heart from racing, a small, devilish smile curling over her painted lips as she flicked through image after image, one after the other.

Good Lord…

This was a blow that the Duke of Caine would never recover from. A way to finally earn justice for her father's death—and the part that Caine must have played in it.

She snapped the file closed. "The photos are only a suggestion of kinship. I want proof."

"As Your Grace wishes." Gow took the file back and retreated into the shadows.

Clicking together the gold-filigreed jeweled claws that sat on the fingertips of her right hand, she gathered herself and swept toward the carriage.

No sign of weakness could be allowed tonight.

⁓

Midnight chimed on the clock in the entrance hall to Lord Abney's London manor. Unfashionably early for her to arrive, as no decent ball truly started before midnight, but Mina was too full of nerves to care.

Taking a glass of champagne from the passing tray of a drone, she gestured for one of the loitering footmen to lace it with blood.

"Celebrating something?" a cool voice murmured.

Mina tipped her chin at the newcomers in welcome. "Indeed. Minor victories, Your Grace. Simply… placing a pawn where nobody shall see it coming for several moves yet." *Thought he was several moves ahead of her, did he?* She drained the entire glass, smiling at the Duke of Bleight and his wife.

The woman at Lynch's side was gowned in a spill of glorious green silk that set off the russet color of her hair. While not as dark red as Mina's own hair, neither was that color the end of the similarities between them. Rosalind Lynch, however, would never truly know how much Mina knew of her past—and the secrets Rosalind was keeping. After all, Mordecai, the man the prince consort had executed, had never been Mercury, but Rosalind had been. Once. Mina tipped her chin in a slower salute toward the Duchess of Bleight, a mark of respect to a fellow humanist.

"That sounds ominous," the woman replied, arching a brow.

"Let us hope your claws find other marks." Lynch's gaze dropped to the deadly filigreed jewelry Mina wore on her fingers.

"Trust me, Your Grace. You've no need to be concerned."

Those cold gray eyes settled on her with an intensity that made her slightly uneasy, but then he smiled. "Oh, I'm not concerned. I never did take you for a fool."

And no fool would attack a duke with ties to over four hundred Nighthawks. At least, not blatantly.

Something caught her eye over the Duchess of Bleight's shoulder. Barrons. He moved through the crowd, standing head and shoulders above a pack of debutantes in simpering white. They fluttered their fans as he passed, heated gazes following his black-clad frame. The disparity should have made her laugh. He looked like a wolf stalking through flocks of helpless little swans. Instead her smile grew sharper and she barely glanced at the duke and his wife as she murmured, "If you'll excuse me?"

This time she stalked him. Their eyes met and Barrons's left eyebrow twitched slightly in question before he crossed to the stairs, leaving her to follow if she wished.

Mina made her way through the growing crowd, following the trail of steam that heralded one of the servant drones. The room was full of them. She claimed another glass of champagne from the flat tray on the automaton's head, laced it heavily, and then followed Barrons to the gallery overlooking the main ballroom.

Her gown glimmered in the light as she climbed the stairs, each gold sequin rasping as it trailed over the marble steps. The full skirt cascaded like individual petals from her waist, golden at the interior and darkening to black at the tips of each petal. The bodice itself was sheer gold, the weight tugging at the delicate champagne-colored straps that clung to the very edges of her shoulders.

Shadows darkened the gallery, where the gaslights were turned low. Red damask wallpaper only gave it a more intimate feel. Mina was practically vibrating with nervousness as she saw the tall, elegant form leaning against the railing, watching the crowd below.

Barrons didn't bother to look at her, but she knew he was aware of her arrival. How could he not be? Tension vibrated in the air between them, an electric glide across her skin.

"You have a certain look in your eye tonight, Mina," he murmured, his eyes half-shuttered as he surveyed the ballroom. "I feel like prey."

He didn't look it. Tall, hard, and lean, with his rapier sheathed at his side, he looked like the king of his own jungle. Slowly his head turned, those dark eyes locking on her. Some trick of light gave hint to the striations of his irises—not black, not truly. Hints of warmth gleamed there, the color of molten chocolate. She was left at once overwhelmed and somewhat uncertain. Mina fought to regain her sense of equilibrium. She needed a damned victory tonight. Anything to take her mind off the queen's absence.

"A ridiculous assumption." Mina circled behind him. Barrons's head turned, tracking her movements as she trailed her filigreed claws over the back of his coat. "How could I ever harm you?"

"You seem to be lumping me with the rest of those addlepated fools who think you're a pretty little symbol." Turning, he caught her wrist, slowly lifting her clawed fingers to his lips. He never took his eyes off her as he pressed a kiss to the inside of her wrist, just over the pulse. The gentlest of touches, a ghostly caress. For a debutante, this would be considered a sign that he intended to pursue her for a thrall contract. "I know just how dangerous you can be, and just how clever your little ruse in the Council chambers is."

Shock froze her. "Ruse?"

"You vote like a pendulum, swinging one way and then the other, placating the prince consort just enough to appease him on items that matter little to you. But when it comes to something that appeals to your heart—or whatever game you're running—you don't back down. No one else has quite figured it out yet. They all think you're some puppet, dancing to his tune."

He'd guessed half of it. It was extraordinary—and proved just how closely he'd been watching her.

Dangerous. If anyone realized the game she and the queen were playing, they'd both be destroyed.

"Though I can hardly countenance what occurred in chambers today." Barrons lowered her hand from his lips, his thumb stroking where his mouth had left its burning mark. His lashes lowered and he dropped her hand.

Of course not. For you don't understand it. Still, her cheeks burned. She had no need to explain herself and yet… "If she'd said any more, he would have hurt her. The embarrassment of being chastised so publicly will perhaps suffice."

Sharp eyes bored into hers. "Then it was done out of mercy?"

"What does it matter?"

"It matters," he replied, turning and leaning on the rail, surveying the room once more. "It means that perhaps I was not mistaken about you."

A thousand thoughts coalesced. First and foremost, a warming buzz at his words that she shouldn't be feeling. There was no reason to desire his praise. "You do not like the way he treats her," she said instead, for she was a little curious herself. The very idea that Barrons had tried to speak today on behalf of the queen… Foolish and only bound to make Alexa's punishment more exacting if he hadn't stopped when he had, but… A ridiculous warmth spread in Mina's chest. There had been no strategy behind the move, simply a man voicing disapproval of the treatment of a woman, and how rare was that?

"I should have stopped it. I should have done more."

"She's not your wife. He would only have taken his anger over such a confrontation out on her."

"I know. It's why I didn't give voice to more." He glanced down. "And in not lifting voice, do we not condone it?"

A knife to her chest. Mina ran her polished claws over the rail, finding the prince consort in the room below. He laughed at something his pet spymaster, Balfour, had said. Hatred twisted the knife, her vision dipping to black and white shades for a moment as her hunger fought its way free. She closed her eyes and took a deep breath, letting it wash out of her, leaving only sadness and guilt in its wake. Perhaps she wasn't only furious at the prince consort. Perhaps some of that hatred was for herself.

"What can we do?" Somehow her thoughts found voice, dripping with bitterness. "As her husband, he *owns* her. He can beat her as often as he likes and *what can we do?*" Never, she'd promised herself, watching the queen slowly succumb to despair over the years. Never would she find herself in the same trap.

A slight warming prickle over her skin revealed how closely Barrons was watching her. Mina flushed, knowing she'd given something away.

"I thought you complicit in the queen's treatment, but you don't like it any more than I do." Slowly he reached out and brushed a strand of hair off her face, fingertips grazing her cheek. She backed away and his fingers dropped, but his focus didn't. "You don't like it because you see yourself in such a situation." Slow, questioning words, as if he were working through the thoughts himself. "Is that why you never married?"

"What could any man ever give me?" she asked instead. "I'm the head of my house, a woman on the Council. What man wouldn't try to take that from me?"

Instead of answering, Barrons actually smiled a

little. "Not all men are created equally. Perhaps you should find one who isn't threatened by your achievements. Someone who finds such accomplishments to be part of the fascination."

"I won't hold my breath."

"Perhaps you should open your eyes then. You might just realize he's closer than you think."

Every muscle in her body locked up tight. "What a fascinating little theory," she replied hollowly, while inside…shock rampaged through her system, followed closely by mistrust. This was part of a game, though she couldn't see what he thought he'd win from it. Fool her into thinking his pursuit was genuine and then… Then what? Did he think she would spill all of her secrets across the pillow one night? Or perhaps let her emotions hold sway until she was voting as he desired just to please him?

No. Barrons wasn't stupid, after all. What in blazes was his angle here?

But then you never have understood my motives…

She went pale. She *felt* it, all of the blood running from her extremities and washing out of her face, for if he wasn't playing games with her, that meant his words were real. For a moment she felt as if she'd caught a glimpse of his true intentions. *Her.* All along, he'd played for her.

No.

Breath coming just a little faster, she forced herself to school her features, hiding the maelstrom inside her, for this was exactly what she feared the most. To lose herself to a man.

In the silence, she realized he was watching her,

no doubt drawing his own damned conclusions, and Mina suddenly wanted to lash out, to force him off balance too so that she wasn't alone in this.

"Our secret is safe, if that is what puts that look in your eye," he murmured. "I've told no one what occurred."

"A strange thing that you should mention secrets…" She pressed closer, her skirts rasping against his pants as she placed her glass of champagne on the rail. "One wonders at yours."

"What makes you think I have any?"

"Everybody has secrets. It's just a matter of searching for them."

His gaze sharpened. This time he looked right through her, as if hunting for her own.

You'll never find them. Her lashes lowered and she lifted up onto her toes, one hand hesitantly pressed against his chest—the one with her claws. For a second she wondered if she were doing the right thing. Hesitation let her feel the warmth from his body, the enticing scent of bay rum curling through her nostrils, making her body tingle. Determination returned. She owed her father this. Turning her lips to his ear, she whispered, "I always wondered at your friendship with that rogue from the rookeries."

His head half turned. "The Devil of Whitechapel?"

"Did you know you look remarkably like one of the lads in his gang? One could say…the spitting image…"

Everything between them changed. Stillness radiated through his hard body, a silent menace. His hand came up, curling around her throat with soft, delicate fingers, the faint hint of a threat. "I wouldn't have expected to see you near the rookeries."

"Oh, I'm not that foolish. I sent someone else, a man of mine who's very good at tracking down things people don't want others to know. He followed you there this morning and now I have photographs, you see—"

Those fingers tightened. Not enough to restrict her breathing, but enough to set her heart to pounding. "Photographs of what?"

"The boy. Who is he, Barrons? Too old to be your get. A brother then... Caine's, perhaps?" She threw the lure into the wind, but he didn't bite as expected. "Not Caine's," she said slowly, her mind racing. Another thought sprang to mind. The icy-eyed Duke of Caine's image and a barely remembered memory of what his wife's portrait had looked like. Her father had had a copy of it. *Good God...*

"You're not his, are you?" Oh, he had the look of the duchess about him—her full mouth, mostly—but not the duke. There was nothing of the duke in his features. Excitement fired in her blood. "You're a bastard."

Those fingers tightened.

Mina sucked in a breath, her gaze lifting to his. Barrons's expression was emotionless, but his eyes... Goodness, she was right!

"An interesting theory. Do you know"—his eyes glittered—"I think I frightened you last night and again just now. Here you are, trying to find something—anything—to put me off balance."

"That's not a yes. Or a no."

He stepped closer, the sounds of the orchestra swirling around them. The hard press of his body was hypnotizing, and he lowered his head to hers, his breath whispering over her lips. "Are you frightened of your attraction to me?"

"I'll find the truth. You know I will. No matter how hard I have to dig."

"I am my father's son. I am *everything* he has made me. And if you dare threaten me"—his voice dropped to a whisper—"you had best be prepared to back up your claims. I know your weaknesses now, Mina." One hand slid around her waist, dragging her hips tight against his. "I know you want me. The question is, do you truly wish to destroy me, or are you simply trying to find a way to protect yourself from me? From this?" He ground his hips harshly against her.

She sucked in a sharp breath, but there was no escape. No answer. His mouth came down upon hers, hard and brutal, arms crushing her hard against his chest. The world staggered around her, or perhaps that was just them, with Barrons muscling her backward until her back struck the wall. His teeth hit hers, tongue forcing its way into her mouth. Mina's fingers curled in his coat collar, unable to do anything more against this onslaught than to yield.

Let us be honest. You want to yield, a secret little part of her whispered.

Music echoed through the ballroom, punctuated with laughter. *Oh God*. Somehow she managed to turn her head, just enough to whisper, "Not here."

Stillness leached through him. He bit at her ear, drawing back just enough to look at her, a scorching look that Mina returned. Then she boldly slid her hand into his hair and dragged him back against her, her mouth capturing his soft laugh.

Somewhere a door latch clicked open and he spilled her into the warm darkness of a room—a study perhaps, she couldn't tell—as he spun her around, her back hitting the door and slamming it shut. And then she was no longer simply *yielding* to him but kissing him back just as hard and fierce as he was, her filigreed claws raking down inside his coat, over his chest, tearing a stolen hiss from him.

"Yes," he whispered, a fist sinking into her skirts, cupping her bottom. Drawing her leg up until he pressed hard against the aching chasm of her thighs.

Mouth rasping over hers, he bit at her lip, thrusting just a little against her. Capturing her hands, he turned her and forced her up against the door, her breasts crushed against the timber. One knee wedged between her thighs, his teeth scraping against her neck. His tongue darted out to trace the leaping thump of her carotid as his fist curled in the back of her skirts. He forced them higher, cool air whispering over her stockinged calves.

Mina moaned, her nipples hard and aching against her corset. The doorknob pressed into her hip and she had the sudden shocking thought that if anyone turned it, they'd find her here, gasping and writhing as Barrons buried himself beneath her skirts. The rest of the ball was so close, yet nobody would ever suspect what was going on behind the door.

Somehow he had her skirts bunched between them, a hand sliding around her waist to boldly cup her between the thighs. Her eyes shot wide, her breath exhaling on a sharp gasp. The hard press of his body against her back and buttocks gave no yield, driving her directly against that hand. The other held her throat, tilting her head back so that his lips met no resistance when they traced the smooth line of her shoulder.

"Are you frightened of this?" he whispered, teeth sinking into the curve where her neck met her shoulder, sending a devastating ache all the way through her. Hard fingers cupped her, right where she wanted them. "Are you frightened of losing control?"

She couldn't speak. Could only give a muffled sob as her head fell forward, her forehead resting against the door. "Oh God."

This weakness in her…this longing… Only he knew of it. Only he could destroy her with a few simple touches.

Barrons's hips ground against her, forcing hers against the mocking cup of his hand. Exquisite sensation streaked through her. She knew what he wanted, and she couldn't stop herself from giving it to him. She could feel the tension in him relax a little as he felt her capitulation.

"Yes?" he whispered.

She rubbed against him again, aching where he touched her.

"Yes?" he demanded.

And curse her weakening body but she whispered, "Yes."

Silence filled the room. Only the vague sounds of the ball filtered through the door, mingling with their harsh breathing. Barrons's hand stilled, then slowly, slowly began gathering up fistfuls of her petticoats. He dragged them up out of his way with a whisper of noise. Mina ached badly at the sudden cease of sensation. She quivered at the thought of what was to come.

Then his lips caressed the sharp mark his teeth had left against her neck and his hand finally fell from her throat, curling possessively down over her breast. "I've never been your enemy, Mina," he whispered.

And then those clever fingers slid through the slit in her drawers until they found hot, wet flesh. Sinfully wet. Betraying her last secret to him.

Mina's lips parted on a silent gasp as he traced slow, steady circles around where she wanted him most. She couldn't help herself. Her hand slid between her body and the door, finding his through the acres of petticoats and guiding him exactly where she wanted him. *There.* This time her breath was almost a sob.

"There's no rush, my love." His lips nuzzled her ear, but his fingers pressed hard against her and she almost screamed.

She hadn't been touched in so long, and never like this. Always, always, she'd controlled her liaisons. It went against everything in her to let him do this to her.

Or no, she had no aspirations.

She had no control when it came to him. He was her master, taking the breath from her lungs and the words from her lips. Taking everything he damned well wanted from her and leaving her moaning helplessly like this as he fucked her with his fingers. Sliding just his fingertips inside her until she shamelessly arched her hips to give him better access, silently begging him to fill her.

Thighs falling apart, she couldn't stop the cascade of sensation. Of his breath, wet against her ear, or his teeth, sinking into the soft flesh of her lobe. Her body was bucking against his hand, pressing harder, wanting the release that he promised. The hand between her legs stroked, delicious tension unfurling, and she bit back a sob. Barrons pressed against her, crushing her body against the door so that she couldn't move, not even a twitch, forcing her to let his fingers do the work so that she was completely under his control.

"Let it out, Mina." A hot whisper against her skin. "Let me hear you come."

A swift shake of the head. *Oh God.* Her claws raked the door, sinking into the timber. Biting her lip, she relished the small pain as her hips jerked against his touch.

And then it was sweeping over her like a fever. Somewhere a soft moan sounded. Herself. She collapsed against the door, firm hands capturing her and holding her there, quivering, as a strangled sort of noise came from her throat. Fingers brushed against her mouth and she sank her teeth into them, moaning softly as his other hand whispered over her wet skin, making slow, devastating circles with his fingertips that knotted her tight again and pushed her over that exquisite edge. This time she came with a gasp, almost a scream, buried against his fingers.

Mina shook her head, silky hair tumbling down

around her shoulders. "Stop," she begged. "No more." *I can't take any more.*

The world dropped away, leaving her a quivering mess. Somehow she found herself in his arms, her face pressed against the smooth, clean linen of his shirt as he held her against the door, making quiet *shushing* noises. A hand, so gentle, stroked over her hair, as if to soothe her in the aftermath of something that had been so shockingly potent, her bones still felt burned to ashes.

Mina clung to him. Time seemed to stop and she could hardly breathe, some part of her not daring to break the spell. She was no stranger to sex, but this... this tenderness... She didn't understand it. Nor could she pull away from it. This, more than anything, drew her like a moth to a flame. Had any man ever held her in his arms like this, quietly waiting for her to come back to herself?

She knew the answer to that. *No.* She'd never allowed any man to touch her like this, even if he'd had the inclination. Only Barrons didn't bother to ask.

And she wanted it. She wanted to be weak enough to lean on him, to let him hold her. Someone she could lean against to catch her breath, just for a moment, even though she knew she could never rely on him. Just a fancy, a dream, a foolish little wish. Her fingers flexed in his coat and then she gathered herself and withdrew from his arms, her skirts tumbling down her stockinged legs.

Mina pressed her hands against her cheeks. So hot. And she was throbbing too, her body crying out for more, telling her that this was not done yet.

"Mina," Barrons murmured, lifting a hand to her hot cheek. "Are you all right?"

At that she breathed a laugh. All right? Shocked, broken, shattered. Shaken to the core. But not all right. She didn't think she'd ever feel like herself again. "I'm fine."

Leo cupped her face in both hands and forced her gaze to his, trying to see the truth of that. In the darkness, he could barely make out her features, but even here he could see the bottomless black of her eyes. Her hunger.

His heart was pounding, his own need a flush of heat through his veins. That she had let him do that to her… That she had wanted it. Blood and glory, he wanted more—had to hold himself back—for what he saw in her eyes was hunger, but wariness too. She wasn't ready, and he'd long known this to be a game of patience between them. A game of seduction. He had to take this step by step or he would risk frightening her away.

Letting out a shaky breath, he pressed his lips to her forehead gently, feeling the tremble within her. Eight long years he'd wanted her, and now she was in his arms…but he still didn't have her. And it was clear from her threat that she was trying to find some way to restore her control of this situation.

Did he dare trust her? She had to be wondering the same thing. So how could he demand she give her body over to him if he did not share some of his intent with her?

His gut clenched, but he forced the words out. "If you want the truth, Mina, you have in your hands information that could ruin me. You could cut at the Duke of Caine while you're at it, but you'll never bring your father back. You'll never slake that empty hole inside yourself that you think vengeance will fill." His thumb stroked her jaw. "All you'll do is destroy me. Not him. Me."

Those dark eyes lifted to his, widening in shock—and then uncertainty.

"Your choice," he whispered. "I know you're frightened of what's happening between us, but in this…you have all the power."

"You're a fool," she blurted out. "To tell me of this."

"Maybe." He *was* a fool. When it came to her, he was the worst kind, and damn him for it, but he couldn't help himself. "Or maybe I think I know you, just a little. Maybe I'm the only one who'll ever risk getting close enough to know all of you. You can either run from that or ruin me so that you feel safe, but I don't think you want to." He brushed that same thumb against her lip, his voice dropping. "But the choice is yours, in this and everything between us. I won't deny that I want you, Mina, but you're the one who's going to have to take that step, and so I choose to trust you with this."

With that, he took a step back, his hands dropping from her face. Mina stared after him, her fingers brushing against her lips as though she still felt his touch.

Slipping the door open, he paused on the threshold. "You have nothing to fear from me. You never did."

Then he closed the door behind him, leaving

her to gather herself and hoping that he'd made the right decision.

❧

Mina stared into the fireplace in her study, rolling the cut crystal glass against her lips and seeing nothing. She'd left the ball early, too shattered to stay and make pleasantries when inside she was boiling like a storm.

Choices.

Barrons had all but admitted he was a bastard, and she could pursue this if she wished. She had the ability to finally ruin the Duke of Caine—to bring down the man who'd had a hand in her father's death.

And in doing so she'd destroy the only man who'd somehow managed to touch beneath her smooth, glossy surface. The only man with the strength of will to match hers. She wouldn't deny that was part of the attraction. Standing in her gilded ivory tower, she was untouchable—except by Barrons. Nobody else dared try to scale her walls, and she'd thought once that she wished it that way.

I won't deny that I want you, Mina... But the question was, what did he want from her? And could she afford to pay that price?

Damn him, why had he told her the truth? Why had he put this power into her hands, then walked away? She could destroy him; he had to know that.

She owed her father that much.

Didn't she?

The fire slowly swam back into focus, hot flame licking brutally at wood. Mina stared at it for a moment longer, then turned to the desk with Gow's incriminating file upon it. Her hands quivered a little as she flipped it open and stared at the photographs.

"Damn you," she whispered, her decision made.

She didn't look as she cast the entire file into the flames. She couldn't. There went her vengeance, the final door closing on her past and leaving her with an uncertain future.

Instead she grabbed her cloak and made her way upstairs to change into something a little more comfortable for the night, something that nobody would ever recognize her in.

There was work to be done.

Eight

SIR GIDEON SCOTT KNEW THAT SOMETHING WAS BOTH-
ering her. Head of the Humans First political party, he
held a great deal of respect among his peers, though
many of the Echelon's blue bloods sneered at his
politics. Once the son of a minor house, he'd carved
out a name for himself with those same politics. The
prince consort tolerated him because Scott worked as
a pacifist between the strident human classes and the
Echelon. Not for him the cry of war on the lips of
nearly every humanist.

Not in public, at least.

Sir Gideon poured a generous finger of whiskey
into a glass and waved a dash of blood over the top
of it for her. His study was wallpapered in burgundy
and cream, the scent of cheroots lingering with beeswax and rich leather. A man's room, and one that
frequently saw use as a base for the aspiring politicians
who made up the party.

Taking the glass, Mina paced to the window and
glanced out. "The prince consort's going to raise the
blood taxes," she said finally. The draining factories

which were used to collect and store the blood gathered in the taxes had all been struck hard by the humanists more than six months ago. Not those humanists under her orders, but others within the group who'd taken matters into their own hands. One of her direst frustrations was her lack of control. She could direct matters, pull strings, provide financial backing, but at heart, each man and woman associated with the cause had their own free will.

But was that not the very heart of the cause? To gain the human classes their freedom and revolutionize the Echelon?

Yes, but burning the draining factories had created a cycle of events she had been hoping to avoid. The loss of the facilities and blood storage created a vacuum that needed to be filled. The blood taxes would rise, and ultimately, the humans would suffer. If they dared raise their voices now, the prince consort would simply unleash the Trojan cavalry.

As a girl, she'd struggled with the weight of her humanity and the future mapped out for her: either a thrall or consort contract to a powerful lord, then a life of luxury under his protection. Hardly devastating, but for her it might as well have been a prison. She knew she'd have slowly wilted over the years in such a role, her eager mind shuttered and stunted by the lack of something more. Without a doubt, she knew she'd have ended up bitter. Most likely sinking her frustrations into the pursuit of fashion, spending countless pounds her patron provided for her and truly desiring none of it.

When her father infected her with his blood on his

deathbed, she'd been willing, even eager, to accept. One of the lucky humans; so many others didn't have that choice, and she understood why it rankled.

Alexa had been a kindred soul, dreaming of something else in life, begging for her moment to appear—that moment when fate separated her from destiny. Her enthusiasm had been contagious, and Mina threw herself headlong into the cause. Why should she be the only young girl able to sidestep her fate? Why could a human not choose her destiny?

And it wasn't as if she owed the Echelon anything. Indeed, she often thought of them as a faceless kind of enemy, mocking and ridiculing her when she'd first made her appearance as a blue blood.

Sir Gideon sighed. "How much?"

"They're talking double—"

"*Double?* The taxes are already high, damn it! Half the people in the poorer sections of the city can't afford to offer more blood. They're malnourished and impoverished, living in conditions I wouldn't even condemn a rat to. This is the type of tax hike that could kill."

"There's a rumor that he's considering dropping the minimum mandatory age," she added, sipping her smoky liquor. It burned, giving her at least the sensation of warmth. "Perhaps to children as young as twelve."

Sir Gideon paled. "No. The Echelon's blood supplies cannot be so dire as that. I won't believe it."

"Of course they're not that dire, but the humanists who burned the factories were never caught—only Mercury, their leader." Or the man who had sacrificed himself as Mercury. "This is retribution. A means to punish the populace for hiding their humanist brethren among them. A sign that such an outrage will not be tolerated again."

"I'll take it to Humans First," he declared. "With this warning, we can be prepared to argue against it, perhaps rally some—"

"No!" Rallying a gathering to protest had never worked in the past, and she didn't want those crushed and lifeless bodies on her own conscience. That had been one of her many mistakes in the past, and she'd never forgive herself for it. Stealth and secrecy were the best means to bring the prince consort down. Everything depended on the secret army of automatons the humanists were building beneath London. "I'm only warning you so that you may know what to expect. I intend to vote against it in Council, but it will depend on the others."

"Is there anything that I *can* do?" he asked bitterly.

"Yes, there is. I need you to begin selling off some of our investments—" She began outlining the ones she intended to see auctioned for the cause. The sooner they could flood the mechs and humanists with money, the sooner the Cyclops could be built.

Sir Gideon sighed as she took her leave. "Thank you for the warning, then. I'll do my best to prepare the poorer classes of the city."

Mina kissed him on the cheek. Scott was one of the few she trusted, and he'd earned her friendship over the years. "Send word when you've restructured my assets."

Sunlight streamed through the carriage window as Mina made her way to her nine o'clock appointment. Leading this double life often left her tired, and she napped as the carriage swayed.

Galloway's Aeronautics had purchased an old abandoned factory at Southwark. A series of enormous sheds that faced the Thames, with roofs that could be opened by an elaborate system of pulleys, they housed dozens of dirigibles in various stages of completion.

This was the way of the future. She could see it so clearly in her mind's eye. An investment in Galloway's ventures was high-risk, but Mina was certain it would pay a rich reward for her ventures.

Plus, the part of her that was always her queen's coldly noted that an attack from the air would be the last thing the prince consort expected. He'd had artillery towers mounted throughout London, thanks to his ever-increasing fear of France's air fleet, but Mina knew their locations. There was a clear path to the Ivory Tower, if she sought to use it. All she needed was for Galloway to build enough dirigibles to use when her humanists decided to strike.

Not that Galloway was aware of that.

Joining the group of investors for Galloway's latest demonstration, she listened with half an ear as Galloway proceeded to explain his latest innovation—a pleasure cruiser like that he'd designed for Lord Matheson. Mina glanced sideways, stillness slinking through her muscles. A glimpse of darkness caught her eye, a man slipping through the crowd at her back, weaving his way among the men as he moved toward her. Her gut knotted up tight and

Mina resolutely turned her attention to Galloway, though she heard not a word of what he was saying. She was too busy straining to listen to what Barrons was doing.

There was a wall of heat and steel at her back, creating the faintest of predatory stirrings that made her breath catch and her nipples harden. Her grip shifted on her parasol. "What are you doing here?"

"Hoping that you'd be here," Barrons murmured, and one hand splayed over the small of her back. "You spoke of Galloway the other night and I'd heard of this demonstration. It seemed a good chance to see you again."

"Enjoy the view then," she snapped, feeling somewhat breathless.

"I am." Those fingers rippled over her spine in the faintest of caresses. "But I'm more interested in what you think about the future of aeronautics."

Mina twirled her parasol, the point grinding into the stone floor. She should never have given him an inch the other night, should have kept herself cold and walled off.

As if you had a choice.

Her cheeks heated as she thought about the taste of his mouth, nipples tightening at the flush of remembrance. *His fingers becoming a fist in her hair...*

Barrons's hand curled over her hip, his breath whispering along the back of her neck as if he could sense her sudden flare of desire.

"Gentlemen...and lady." Mr. Galloway tilted his head toward her. "If you would step this way, please. I wish to show you my latest design...the *Gilded Falcon*."

A hand curled around her arm. "Stay. I want to see more of the *Lionheart*."

The others set off after Galloway, a flock of black-coated businessmen. Some were of the Echelon and some were human investors, economics creating equality for the first time in years. Mina stared longingly after them. "What do you want?"

"You're in danger," he murmured. "We all are."

That piqued her interest. Her gaze traveled toward the *Lionheart*. The enormous gray envelope floated aloft, steel cables encircling it and holding the enclosed gondola beneath it. It was one of the dirigibles created for passenger use, rather than the closely guarded plans for a warship that she'd seen in the back offices of Galloway's, where he was building an air fleet to keep the ravaging humanists of France at bay, should they attack. It was one of the prince consort's ever growing irrationalities and private commissions, and strangely enough, one of the few things she agreed upon with him. France was potentially dangerous.

"I wish to see inside," she said. At least the cabin of the *Lionheart* would protect them from curious ears.

Barrons helped her climb the roll-away ladder to the cabin, his hands steadying her. Not that she needed the help, but she said nothing. Most of the Echelon didn't know the limits of her endurance and strength, and she intended to keep it that way. Prancing across the rooftops of London, and slipping in and out of places where she didn't want to be followed, gave a girl remarkable dexterity.

The door closed behind them and Mina ran her fingers along the flight console, resting her parasol in the corner. "I'm always in danger. More specifics, if you will."

"It's a theory," Barrons said. "Why did Goethe die?"

She knew the answer to that, but she shrugged. "Who would know?"

"He opposed the suggested increase in the blood taxes as soon as the prince consort gave us the briefing note, and with the death of several of the prince consort's pocket dukes, it's clear that he's losing power. Malloryn, Goethe, Lynch, and I were dismissive of the blood-tax bill. The prince consort knows he can't push it past our blockade in Council, and if he wants to get his bills through, he's going to have to remove some of the obstacles in his path."

An intriguing thought. "You think he's going after the Council?"

"All of us," Barrons concurred with a tip of the head to her. "You don't always vote as he wills."

Only often enough to make the prince consort think her allegiances were sympathetic.

"I'm protected." She had to be. Too many of her male relatives had tried to remove her over the years, threatened by the thought of a woman in power. "But thank you for the warning. I hadn't thought of Goethe's death in those terms." Barrons's body blocked her path, though she didn't think it deliberate. "Was that everything?"

Barrons glanced through the glass, surveying the factory. Galloway's group was farther away now, examining the semi-rigid construction of the pleasure cruiser. Tension etched itself across his broad shoulders. "Perhaps I simply wished to get you alone."

"To warn me about dangerous plots?" Her voice held a teasing lightness to it.

Faint humor stirred in his expression, his right brow twitching. "No, Duchess. I was thinking of something far more interesting than that. Perhaps it's the presence of the dirigible. Reminds me of the other night. Of... debts owed. And paid."

"So you lured me here under false pretenses?" she replied, taking a step to the side when he took one toward her.

Barrons smiled, a lazy stretch of the mouth. "Would you have come if I'd told you I planned on kissing you?"

Yes. No. Her smile froze. "I've decided your kisses are bad for my health."

"Precisely." Another step had her pressing back against the far wall.

"Besides, the other night was different. I owed you a kiss, and a Duvall always pays their debts."

"And last night?" The overwhelming presence of his body was palpable now. A whiff of bay rum came off him, lingering in her nostrils and making her mouth water, just a little.

"Barrons," she warned.

"Last night," he murmured. "You didn't owe me anything."

Mina ducked beneath his arm, bumping into the console. "Last night, I learned some rather interesting facts."

"Have you decided what you're going to do with that information?"

"Not yet," she declared. *Make of that what you will.*

Barrons crossed his arms over his broad chest, those implacable black eyes boring a hole through her. He grunted and looked away. "Well, you're predictable at least. A mere mention of a kiss and you're suddenly throwing blackmail in my face." His eyelids grew heavy, then a sidelong glance made her breath catch. "No talk of kissing then. No games, no duchess. Just you and me. Tell me what you think of Galloway's plans to standardize air travel for the common people of England."

"Why are you interested in my views?" she asked suspiciously.

"Because you interest me." He shrugged out of his coat and hung it on a brass hook on the wall. His crisp waistcoat was dark gray with thin cream pinstripes, cut to fit his broad shoulders and narrowing to define the leanness of his hips. An eyebrow arched. "We could always discuss the weather, if you prefer. Something mundane?"

Despite herself she was drawn. "I think Galloway is a solid investment, though I understand the risks involved. The rest of Europe is beginning to race headlong into the skies, following France and the colonies' examples. Travel will be expensive at first, mostly first-class passengers, though I see a need—and a desire—for the common classes to seek passage in the future—and of course it would help significantly with long-haul freighting. One day, we'll be able to board a dirigible in the morning and be in Manhattan City within a day. You mark my words."

The console spread out before her, providing an incomprehensible display for the unlearned, but

Mina had been reading Galloway's design manuals for months. *Here's the switch for the boilers for the engines for extra speed... The deflation device for the envelope...* She traced another switch. *The ballonet air valve...*

"You like the idea of flying." His hands settled on either side of her hips as he leaned forward, examining the console over her shoulder. That large body surrounded her, leaving her desperately aware of how close he stood.

Flying. The sort of thing she'd dreamed of as a girl, when she first heard of France's airships, until the death of her parents had cost her all of her naive fantasies. Still... Her fingers traced the sleek mahogany steering wheel for the horizontal and vertical stabilizers. "Do you know who I admired most as a girl?"

"Who?"

"Grace O'Malley," she admitted, letting her lace-clad fingers drop from the wheel. "The Pirate Queen."

At that Barrons stepped to the side, twisting to rest his hips against the console so he could see her properly. A sudden smile lit his entire face. "You wanted to be Grace, didn't you?"

"My brother Stephen and I played pirates." Even she couldn't stop herself from smiling at such remembrance—and the very incongruity of the thought. Who would ever suspect it of the very proper Duchess of Casavian?

"What did you like about her?"

"She was brave. Fearless. Willing to defy Queen Elizabeth herself. And, of course, she had red hair like me. Stephen was always Edward Teach. He preferred the villain. We would run about the hills at Eton

Grange during the summer, with real swords. Father allowed it as it helped teach us both swordplay." She opened herself up just a little to him. "What did you play at?"

His dark eyes sobered, his arms crossing over his chest. "I had no brothers or sisters. My only companion was my weapons master." A slight pause. "Master Baldock was a former Falcon who did not consider play a very useful means of development."

Mina's smile faded as she examined him. "There were no other children your age?"

"Only one. The daughter of an inventor the Duke of Caine gave patronage to. I used to put mechanical spiders in her bed. Honoria despised me."

"You sound like my cousin Peter."

"Careful," he warned. "I knew Peter. We were of an age at Eton. That's hardly a compliment."

"Was I seeking to turn you up fancy?" she replied, shrugging her shoulder a little flirtatiously.

The light in his eyes flared with interest and Mina stilled. *What are you doing?* She turned away, focusing on the console again. It was too easy to forget herself around him.

"Do you know what I like about flying?" he asked.

"What?"

"There are no boundaries. No England, no France, no Russia… Simply wondrous places, the likes of which you've never seen before. I never realized how much I was missing out on, until the mission to Saint Petersburg."

Mina's breath caught. "What was it like?"

"Cold." He gave a swift laugh. "Very cold at first.

We were still bundled in furs into March, and the dirigible struggled with the temperature. Ice kept forming on the propellers, but it was wonderful. A modern-day Venice, they call Saint Petersburg. Full of palaces the likes of which you can barely imagine, akin to the magnificence of Versailles. And gold-domed monasteries. Their Orthodox Church has not rescinded their blue bloods. Perhaps it dares not. The blue bloods rule completely. It's the most dangerous place I've ever been."

Her mind took her to the places he spoke of. Ancient monasteries…palaces…a city of canals. Something stirred in her breast, an unmerciful itch.

"Have you ever traveled abroad?" he asked.

"There was no time for my Grand Tour. My father died when I was seventeen, and that put an end to that." It put an end to a lot of things, actually.

He eyed her, that mischievous gleam making her heart tick faster. "I should take you to Paris. We'll fly there on one of Galloway's dirigibles and tour Versailles, or what's left of it, or sip champagne from your shoe."

She'd never imagined this playful side to him. "You're forgetting that France is full of humanists. And why would I go to Paris with *you*?"

Barrons's eyes practically smoldered. He stepped closer, the backs of his fingers brushing against her hip. "To make love on a bed smothered in rose petals while we drink champagne and argue immeasurably, and I strip all of these skirts and petticoats off you."

"You're a romantic," she accused, unable to believe it herself.

"I could fuck you here and now," he whispered, stepping closer again until she was looking up at him, all of the words fleeing her startled mind. His hand grew bolder, sliding up her corseted hip, his thumb brushing against the fullness of her breast. "But I think you need a little romance in your life, Mina. A little adventure. And God knows, I do."

Leaning closer, his mouth brushed against her forehead, his lips smooth and cool against her skin. Mina shut her eyes, her hand curling around the wheel as if to hold herself upright against the sway of his magnetism. His mouth traced her cheek, breath whispering into her ear: "I want to make love to you on silk sheets. To melt all that ice and find out if underneath all of this silky-smooth skin beats a heart of pure fire, like I suspect it does."

His thumb brushed back and forth, teasing at her nipple. Mina whimpered, backed against the console. His hand slid lower, a knowing caress against the silk covering her abdomen. "You liked what I did to you last night."

Fingers cupped her between the thighs, rubbing gently, her skirts tangled between them. "I've made no secret of the fact that I want to be your lover. All you have to do is say yes. I'm certain if I write a reasonable check, Master Galloway can outfit the *Lionheart* by the end of the day. I'll even let you fly it, if you want…"

The words were temptation indeed. Mina stared at him helplessly. "I can't," she whispered, the debt of her responsibilities sinking like lead through her chest.

He mistook her denial for a challenge, and a kiss

scalded the smooth skin below her ear. He painted delicate butterfly caresses on her cheeks as he bunched the material between her legs, his fingers working a delicious friction as he sought to seduce her to his cause.

Clinging to his waistcoat, she shot a glance around the workshop. Galloway's group was still exploring the *Gilded Falcon*, like a flock of well-dressed penguins. "Barrons!"

"Part your legs."

She shook her head, then gasped as his fingers increased their mastery. Her hand gripped his wrist.

"Nobody can see. It's just you and me here." The devilish light in his eyes dared her. "Come to Paris," he whispered and she bit her lip as her entire body trembled. "Come and make love with me in a bourgeois hotel tucked in some hidden alley. Come, Mina."

If anyone glanced up and saw them... Everything inside her tightened at the thought. A new flush of urgency lit through her veins like white fire. She lost her mind. All she wanted was to tear at the intervening layers of fabric between them, to rake her nails down his bare flesh. To fill that beckoning ache deep within her.

To say yes.

"Come."

The word stole her wits, sending her over the edge. Mina grabbed at the console, pressing her other hand to her lips and sinking her teeth into it as a breathy noise tore from her throat. Barrons's thigh pressed between hers as his hand withdrew, and she gasped out her pleasure.

The world reeled around her, leaving her with only Barrons for balance. The dark heat of him evaporated off his coat, until all she wanted to do was bury herself in his arms and fight to still the raging heat in her blood.

Instead she pushed at him, forcing him to back away a step, leaving her hot, flushed, and aching. At the sight of the satisfied smile curling over his mouth, she slapped his arm. A husky laugh hummed through his body. She wanted to kiss him so much that she ached. She'd never felt like this before. "You're a madman."

"And you, my duchess, are exquisite." His expression sobered. "Come with me."

"I can't," she told him, stepping out of the way of the press of his body. She needed some space to clear her mind. Her blood might be cooling, but the merest breath of his cologne did damaging things to her insides, setting her nerves alight again. "Some of us have responsibilities. And can you imagine the scandal?"

"I've never given any particular care to what others think of me."

That made her furious. "Of course you haven't! For it wouldn't truly matter to your reputation if I said yes. I can't be your lover. I can't afford to be. And"—her brow darkened, though she wasn't certain if she was angry at him or herself—"I'm not quite certain it would be worth my downfall."

Snatching at her hat, Mina started for the door in a swish of skirts, her blood boiling. All she knew was that she had to get away from him.

Barrons strode after her, heels echoing on the metal walkway as she hurried down the stairs. "Mina, wait."

"No!"

One of Galloway's men saw them coming and started, unclasping his hands from behind his back. "May I help you, sir?"

"He was just leaving," Mina told the fellow coolly.

"Actually," Barrons replied, "I want to place an order for something like this." His soft laugh followed her, meant for her ears alone. "I'm told the cost is substantial…but I live in hope of a trip to Paris in the near future."

Nine

THE MOMENT SHE STEPPED INSIDE HER HOME, MINA LET out a sigh of relief. Here she could rub at her temples to try and still the pounding headache Barrons's words had caused.

Slipping through the hallways, she avoided most of the staff by dint of her supernatural hearing. The sun had nearly reached its zenith, leaving her desperate to reach her bed. Two days without sleep left her feeling slow-witted and dull, as evidenced by what had occurred at Galloway's. If she'd been in her right frame of mind, she'd have laughed in his face.

Instead she'd melted like flavored ices in the sun.

What was she doing? She might have destroyed the evidence against him, but she still despised his father. Her feelings for Barrons were far more uncertain.

If she stripped away the history between them and looked at him as just a man, she had to admit that she found him quite charming and humorous at times.

Come to Paris… Make love to me… Mina swallowed. A foolish part of her was almost tempted.

If she were honest with herself, she almost... liked him.

A scream cut through the stillness of the early morning silence. Mina froze, her heart jacking into her throat and her foolish daydreams vanishing. That had come from her bedroom. Another one followed it, dying to a helpless sob.

Yanking the door open, she stepped inside, the hilt of a knife warming her palm. Her maid, Hannah, sobbed in the middle of the room, her hand pressed to her mouth and the curtains stirring over the open sash of the windowpane.

"What in blazes is—" Mina's gaze fell on the bloodied mess in the middle of her bed. Her gloves made a slapping sound as they hit the floor.

"Oh, Your Grace...Your Grace..."

She ignored the maid's helpless sobs and took a step closer, her face draining of heat. Bloodied fur. That was all she could see. Someone had been in her house. In her room. Someone had... Her mind shied away from the thought.

"I swear I didn't hear anyone come in! I don't know how...how it came to pass."

Mina crossed to the window, moving as if through a nightmare. Twitching aside the curtains, she stared down at the street with its early-morning passersby, gentlemen in tweed coats and top hats making their way to their place of employment. Across the road, the same man who'd been watching the house the day before looked up from his newspaper, meeting her eyes.

The slightest hint of a smile tugged his moustache

upward and he tipped his hat to her, tucked his folded newspaper under his arm, and sauntered away with a whistle.

Mina's fingers curled into the window frame. A message from Balfour—or the prince consort, no less. Why? They couldn't know about her humanist plans or else there would have been no message, merely an escort of Coldrush Guards.

What if that had been Hannah or one of her other servants? If a Falcon could get at her here, then what did that mean for those that surrounded her?

"You're dismissed," she said hoarsely.

"Of course, Your Grace. Let me ring for Grimsby…" The maid caught her teary breath. "And then I'll see that poor…poor Boa—"

"Dismissed," Mina repeated sharply, turning on the girl. "I'll provide you a reference and a generous stipend, but I want you gone by luncheon."

Hannah's jaw dropped, her eyes welling up again. Mina forced herself not to weaken. *Oh, you dear girl, I'm trying to save your life. Far better to be well away from here.*

"Yes, Your Grace," Hannah whispered, proffering a curtsy. "I shall send Grimsby up."

From the footsteps on the stairs, he was already on his way. Her father's faithful butler had been with the household since the day she was born.

The door clicked behind Hannah, giving her a moment of peace. Mina shut her hot eyes, wilting a little. *This is war*, her mind kept saying, *but it doesn't feel like it*. No, it felt like the only place she'd ever been safe was gone now. They'd been in her

bedchambers. And her cat—fat, pampered Boadicea…
Mina couldn't even look at her.

Taking a deep shuddering breath, she gathered
herself. Not the time for weakness. She had to…
to collect herself. Protect her household, her loyal
staff members…

Only then could she turn to the bed. A shaking
hand reached out, flipping the bed pane over the cat's
body. Still warm.

That was the thought that undid her.

A sob caught her by surprise. Mina bit into her
knuckles, her knees going out from under her.
Pressing her face against the counterpane and moaning
into it as her hands curled into claws in the carpet.
She wanted to scream her pain and rage out into the
world. All of her losses compounded upon her—her
brother, Stephen; her grief-stricken mother; and her
father, slowly fading before her eyes. All she'd ever
wanted was to create a safe place for herself and
those she loved, and Balfour had sent his Falcons to
destroy it.

Mina grabbed the edge of the counterpane as she
dragged herself onto her knees. Barrons's warning rang
in her ears. If they meant to cow her…

I will kill the prince consort. I'll kill them all.

"Your Grace!" Grimsby's voice intruded, his hands
clutching at her shoulders. "Your Grace, you must
get up."

She turned and somehow his arms slid around her,
rocking her against his shoulder.

"Phillips, please remove the bedspread and see Her
Grace's cat buried outside in the garden. Beneath the

roses, if you would. Miss Boadicea always liked to play there. Would you like that, Your Grace?"

She nodded, her face buried in the stiff starchiness of his collar, clinging to him.

"Then see that you shut the door. Her Grace is not to be disturbed, and this is not to be mentioned," Grimsby warned.

Movement shifted around her. She wanted none of it. Then the door clicked shut, leaving her in a wretched state on the floor in her butler's arms.

"There, there," he murmured. "I've set the footmen to searching every inch of the house and checking the windows and doors. I assume they came through the bedroom window."

"They're gone," she whispered, pulling back and pressing at her dry face. Nausea swirled through her.

Grimsby saw the look on her face and pressed her head down hurriedly. "Take deep breaths, Your Grace. Nice and slow."

She did, surrendering herself into his care. When was the last time anyone had looked after her?

Barrons flashed into her mind again. The bath. The way he'd toweled her off so tenderly. A mirage in her mind, for it wasn't real—but for the first time, she wished she'd been weak enough to turn away when her father demanded that he infect her with the craving so that she could rule the House of Casavian in his absence. Weak enough to sign a thrall contract with some blue-blood lord to be pampered and protected for the rest of her life, or until the contract expired.

Cold enough to turn away the day she'd found the

crown princess crying in the garden the morning of her wedding.

Regret left a bitter aftertaste in her mouth. *But you didn't make those choices. You chose* this *path. Now don't drop your head because it's turning into a horrible slog.*

"You won't protect poor Hannah by sending her away," Grimsby murmured. "You know she's safer here beneath this roof."

Mina shook her head, trying to hold her breath to calm herself.

"If you see her on her way, she'll be alone in the world," he continued. "Here, she can be guarded, now that we know what to expect."

Grinding her hands into her eyes, she wiped away her grief. "Tell her...tell her that I didn't mean it."

"There's also a message from the Duke of Morioch downstairs, calling a session of Council to order. It just arrived," he said gently.

"Council?" For Morioch to be calling a Council session in the middle of the day... Something was afoot, or else they'd have waited until night. The darkness twisting inside her grew until the room sprang into black-and-white clarity. The scent of blood filled her nostrils, bringing with it a wave of red-hot fury the likes of which she'd never felt before.

"Yes, Your Grace."

Anger burned hot and furious, but she caught herself on the verge of it. Giving in to what she wanted to do would only bring further grief on her household and destroy her carefully nurtured plans.

Be patient. A mockery of the very words she'd whispered to her queen. Only now could she fully understand how it felt to receive them in the face of such pain. That, and that alone, stopped the wash of red heat through her veins, letting her think again. Her queen had borne far worse than this, a thousand times over, and only recently had she let it begin to wear on her nerves.

Mina would go to Council, sit at the prince consort's table, and smile as she sipped her blud-wein. She owed it to Alexandra.

And in her head she would assuage her grief and anger by plotting the prince consort's downfall in excruciating, explicit detail.

PART TWO
THE BETRAYAL

"If an injury has to be done to a man it should be so severe that his vengeance need not be feared."

—Niccolò Machiavelli

Ten

MINA UNPINNED HER MECHANICAL SPIDER BROOCH, letting her fingers brush against the wall where she deposited it as she walked past. The device could record sound from up to thirty feet away, with almost an hour's worth of tape spooled in its tiny body. All she had to do was activate the tracking beacon in her pocket, and she would be able to find it again.

Barrons stood at the top of the stairs that led to the Council chambers, speaking to the Duke of Malloryn. The two had formerly been close friends, though the relationship had become strained over the years, she'd noticed.

As Malloryn caught sight of her, Barrons turned, his dark gaze pinning her with an intensity she couldn't miss. Malloryn gave her figure a lazy perusal but Barrons cut straight to her face, his eyebrow arching as if in question.

There was no way Barrons could see any sign of what had happened in her expression. She was flawless, her hair curled back artfully and her lips painted the vibrant red that only she dared wear. Still, the sensation left her slightly restless. Did he see some sign of what had occurred?

"Malloryn." She tipped her head to the other duke.

"My dear Lady Aramina," Malloryn murmured in that mocking drawl he always affected. He was rarely serious, at least in public, though the sharp cut of his eyes showed his true nature. In the privacy of his bedroom, he'd been an entirely different man, but that had been many years ago. He continued, "Two Council sessions called in two days. Something's afoot."

"Perhaps the Nighthawks have word of Goethe's final hours," she replied.

"Perhaps." Barrons looked unconvinced, however.

"Someone tried to kill me this morning," Malloryn continued. "I was just discussing the matter with Barrons."

Both of them looked at Malloryn sharply. He shrugged. "They already know they tried to kill me. Why keep it secret?" He glanced at the Council chambers. "They're right in there, after all. We all just pretend we don't know."

"You were not assaulted?" she murmured to Barrons.

"No." His eyes asked the question his mouth didn't.

She nodded, almost imperceptibly, feeling that sharp, stabbing ache in her chest again. Even Malloryn saw it, but then he saw a great deal. Too many underestimated the dashing young duke. Of all the members of the Council, she thought perhaps he was the most dangerous. Knowledge was power, after all, and Malloryn had a network in place to rival Balfour's.

Malloryn leaned closer to Barrons and whispered, "Rather interesting that you weren't targeted. Looks like someone is trying to remove half the Council."

The doors chose that moment to open, two unflappable footmen holding them wide.

Malloryn flashed her a cool smile. "I think I'll go see what Balfour's up to."

His departure left her alone in the hallway. The last time she'd been alone with him, he'd pinned her to the console of an airship and done wicked things to her. It seemed a lifetime ago. At the moment, she couldn't even summon a smile.

"Are you all right?"

She wanted to confide in him, the thought bringing a rush of pain to her chest. *My cat, he killed my cat... His men were in my house, in my room...* None of it would make sense to him though, and there were too many ears nearby.

Her hesitation spoke volumes. Somehow she managed a weak smile. "I survive. As always." *That's the one thing I am very good at doing.*

"You took a blow, though," he said quietly. "I can see it in your eyes."

"I'm tired," she said. "I didn't sleep this morning."

"Mina?" Just that.

Suddenly the urge was too great to deny. "They killed my cat. They left her in the middle of my bed."

Not a word, nor a single change in his expression, but she felt as though the world faded around them, as if his gaze sharpened until he could see all the way through her. As if he reached out to touch her somehow, but his body never moved. "I'm sorry." A quick glance into the room. "They're trying to frighten you, Mina. A warning, that's all this is."

"I know." Somehow she could breathe a little easier. "I've said too much."

"Perhaps that's the problem. We councilors never say enough to each other. Together—"

The sound of someone coughing cut off his words. This was not the place to be having this discussion. Barrons tipped his head to her in a nod and entered the chambers.

Yet she understood what he meant. *Together we could be a threat to him.* The idea had never occurred to her before, and it slowed her strides as she followed him inside. The Council of Dukes rising up to overthrow the prince consort?

Half the time they were at each other's throats. Ridiculous even to assume that they could wield their power to remove this cancerous boil on the nation's backside. Or that they would.

Never discount any possibility. And if it meant that the prince consort was overthrown sooner, freeing the queen…

A dangerous supposition. All it would take to destroy everything she'd worked for would be one set of loose lips seeking to gain favor.

Wait, she told herself. *And see.*

❧

Council was called to order, Morioch taking the Chair's seat. He flashed a smirk at Leo, who stilled. The cadaverous old bastard had always despised him, and the smile made Leo uneasy.

Beware a blue blood's smile, for it is full of teeth. An old human saying he'd heard in the streets.

The doors swung wide, hitting the walls with a crash. Every head in the room turned at the entrance, and shocked gasps spilled through the room. The pair of Coldrush Guards at the door both jerked at their blades until the prince consort called for them to be sheathed.

"A guest," the prince consort said as the man entered, the hood of his cloak fluttering back from his brow.

"What the hell is all this about?" the Duke of Caine snarled, waving a gold embossed letter in his hand.

That wasn't what had drawn the gasps, however. The duke wore white, from head to toe, his silvery fine hair carefully pomaded back from his pale brow. There was no color in his face, his skin, his hair... Even his irises were no longer cerulean but an almost colorless, milky blue, like a calcium pool.

The Fade, in all its spectacular glory. The final, end stages of the craving virus, a sign that a man was turning irrevocably into a vampire.

Leo's gut knotted tight.

A hundred years ago, a rash of vampires had torn apart half the city, slaughtering thousands. For that was another effect of the disease, the descent into irrational blood-lust.

By law, anyone approaching the Fade was to be executed once the percentage of craving virus in their blood reached the seventies.

"Blood and glory." Morioch gasped. He staggered back. "Guards! Guards!"

"I wouldn't." Caine cast the guards a filthy look

as he strode toward the table. He stared them all down, one eyebrow arched. "My craving virus levels are in the nineties, after all. I'm stronger and faster than any man in this room. None of you could stop me if I chose to tear out your throats." The Duke of Lannister's former chair squealed as Caine dragged it across the floor. He flicked the black shroud onto the floor and took his place.

Circumstance put him directly at the end of the table, facing the prince consort. Not a hint of expression explained what this was about.

"Father?" Leo murmured.

"Not now."

The prince consort looked nonplussed for once. "How…how is this even possible?"

For Caine had not evolved as a vampire normally did, hunched and bent over, his eyes filming with blindness and his voice losing itself to a pitch few humans could even hear. Nor was he ruled by the insane blood-lusts from which they suffered, though his hungers were deep.

"It appears I have evolved," Caine said. "I am reaching the end stages of my metamorphosis."

"You're a vampire!" Morioch couldn't seem to control his revulsion.

"Indeed." The faintest of smiles played over Caine's hard mouth. "In the truest sense of the word. I am what blue bloods were always meant to become."

Why the hell was he here? Most of the time Caine locked himself away in the depths of his house, trying to avoid the sunlight, as it hurt his eyes dreadfully and burned his pale, sensitive skin.

To have come out into the light… Leo's gaze fell uneasily on the letter that Caine had flicked onto the table, then toward the three guards in the room, noticing their pistols and swords, while Leo had nothing more than his blood-letting pouch on him.

"Explain yourself," Lynch demanded, his voice cold and hard. "And why we should not consider you a threat."

Caine held out his hands, his fingernails translucent— and sharp. "I am a vampire," he explained, "who has managed to retain all his senses. What else do you need to know?"

"He is fully in control," Leo admitted. After all, he'd known for years, horrified at first, keeping an eye out for the moment when by law he should have been forced to call for an executioner. Caine had vanished for a period of three months, touring the Orient, or so he had said. When he returned, his state had evolved to the point it was clear any chance Leo had of executing him was minute.

Something had stopped him from trying. Caine was lucid in a way most blue bloods weren't at that stage. His blood-lust was entirely manageable, his needs seen to by Madeline and bottles of blood bought from the draining factories. He slept a great deal of the time, and when he was awake, he seemed sometimes catatonic. Rather catlike in a way. Content to sit by the fire to warm his cold blood, with his lap rug over his knees. Oh, he still liked to play the game and listen to word of court, but his existence had become almost…meditative.

"How did this occur?" the prince consort asked flatly.

Caine flashed his sharpened teeth, revealing canines that had elongated into sharpened points. "The answers are in the Orient. That is all I will say of the matter."

The Orient. Where the craving virus had originated, kept under the strict control of the White Court that ruled the Forbidden City until an intrepid explorer named Sir Nicodemus Banks had become infected with their precious virus and fled back to Europe, infecting half of the continent's aristocrats along the way.

Every court, from Spain to England, had paid gold to receive what seemed like a boon—strength, faster reflexes, prime healing rates, a certain sense of indestructibility…even a taste of immortality, if you wished.

Only Italy had held firm, naming the creatures that evolved from the virus demons and monsters.

That position spread throughout the Church, the Spanish Inquisition burning the country's blue bloods at the stake. The French had been equally as efficient, executing most of their aristocracy. Only the Russians and the English Echelon had held firm, crushing the human classes beneath their heel and creating an automaton army to protect themselves from the mob.

As for the Russians, who yoked their humans as serfs and paid little heed to the care the Echelon took not to kill when they drank their blood…life was cheap on the Russian steppes.

Silence reigned in the room. The prince consort let out his breath, his fingers splayed on the table. "This is…unanticipated." His eyes cut to Leo. "And should have been reported."

"I had no intention of making myself the target of some botched execution attempt." Caine laced his hands over his middle.

The prince consort nodded and Leo tensed. Not the prince consort's plan today, then. He had something else on his mind. Something important enough to dismiss what should have drawn more scrutiny.

"You seem hale and of sound mind," the prince consort said. "In this respect, I see no choice but to absolve you of the crime of concealing such a state. All in favor?"

Neither the Duchess of Casavian nor Lynch raised their hands. The rest gave their hesitant approval. After all, if they said nay, then who intended to imprison Caine?

"I would, of course, like to know more about this." The prince consort's smile was tight.

Caine bowed his head in deference. It was not entirely without wariness. "We shall speak privately. Now what did you mean by sending me this letter?"

Leo couldn't take his eyes off it.

"A grave tale, Your Grace." The prince consort paced, his hands behind him. "One of lies, of treachery…of betrayal."

"What the hell are you referring to?" Caine snapped.

"The cuckoo in your nest, Your Grace."

The world went still. Leo froze, every muscle in his body locking tight, not quite daring to look at the prince consort. This couldn't be happening. Instinct

screamed at him to run but he couldn't move. In all
of his nightmares of this moment—and there had been
many—he'd shouted down the accusation, fought it,
anything other than simply sit here, but it felt as if
this were another dream, slightly watered down at
the edges.

All he could see was the duchess's pale face as she
stared at him with wide eyes.

You. You were the only one with that information… The
betrayal was another knife edge, though he'd handed it
to her. He'd dared her to stab him in the back with it
the second he turned…and she had. Of all the blows,
that was one of the greatest. For he'd thought, for a
moment, that something fragile and tentative existed
between them.

Caine's laughter broke the silence, a sharp, rusty
sound. Then it cut off as if with a razor. "You *dare* try
and call my son a bastard? Be very careful about what
you're claiming, my prince. I will not be mocked. Not
even by you."

A meaty slap sounded and something slid across the
enormous table toward the duke. Finally Leo could
move again, his head spinning as he looked at the file
and the photographs that spewed out of it as it came
to a halt on the polished mahogany. Photographs
of Charlie.

Caine looked up. Their eyes met for just the briefest of moments. And Leo knew that Caine was going
to cut him loose.

All these fucking years, protecting the bastard from
the world, protecting Caine's own bloody secrets.
Don't you dare do this to me. I supported you. I stood by

you for years, no matter what you did to me. You…you were the only father I knew.

The duke's gaze dropped. And there was Leo's answer. Incredulousness filled him, the final blow to send him reeling.

Slowly, Caine reached out and flipped open the file. "What are these?"

Over. It was all over. Leo couldn't breathe.

The prince consort leaned on the back of his chair, his fingers digging into it as he gave Leo a vicious smile. "Photographs, Your Grace, of your wife's bastard's half brother in the rookeries. Indeed, it explains a great deal about Barrons's dabbling in matters that didn't concern him." Blade's duel with Vickers flashed to mind. "My man has been digging. Turns out the boy's name is Charlie Todd, son of the late Sir Artemus Todd, over whom you once held patronage." The prince consort's voice turned soft, as if in sympathy.

"Barrons had to know the truth. There's no other reason for him to visit the rookeries so often, and he did take in the boy's older sister, Miss Lena Todd, last year. Gave her a debut, in fact. Why else, if not to give his sister a chance? I'm so terribly, terribly sorry to reveal the truth of your wife's betrayal in such a manner, but I cannot allow her bastard to interrupt my court anymore."

Everyone's eyes were on Leo. The aging Duke of Morioch actually laughed under his breath, the sound cutting through Leo like a knife.

Caine slowly closed the file. "I see. And what do you intend to do with the boy?"

"I would see him named rogue—"

Destroyed. His entire reputation and all he'd worked for shattered. But worse than that, worse than everything…his father wouldn't even look at him.

"—except he has not only taken the benefits of the craving virus illegally, but he has lied to the court. To you and me, to all of us. And his allegiance has been made clear over the years in the way he's perverted justice by seeing the Devil of Whitechapel freed after his duel and—"

"During the incident with me and Mercury?" A new voice spoke up. Lynch. "I do recall Barrons standing in support of myself when you would have left me on the executioner's block." A brief smile. "Erroneously, of course." Slowly he let his gaze run across all of the Council members, including the very silent Lady Aramina. "In fact I rather recall Barrons standing in defense of several that sit here today."

"Perhaps I should revisit the judgment of that action too," the prince consort spat.

"In the wake of Goethe's sudden disappearance, that would leave us down…three councilors, would it not? How…inconvenient." Lynch barely blinked.

Movement shifted at the table as each duke tried not to look at any of the others. Lynch's words were a reminder that those who had stood against the prince consort in the past were slowly being whittled away.

"Only two," the prince consort replied after a long, drawn-out moment. "Caine holds his seat—Barrons only held his vote during his…incapacitation."

Leo finally managed to look along the table to the person sitting at the very end in her creamy skirts and pearl-net bodice. His mind went white-hot with betrayal.

The photographs loomed in front of her. Aramina stared at them, her face dead-pale. As if feeling the weight of his gaze, she slowly looked up and flinched.

Barrons let out a soft exhale of a laugh. The one time he'd misjudged someone so completely... "You treacherous bitch," he whispered under his breath, knowing that she heard him.

"Judgment, my prince?" Morioch called.

"Let us not be hasty," Caine retorted, drumming his fingers in a slow, controlled pattern on the table.

"You would have to put it to a vote," Lynch pointed out. "And you know what mine will be."

"As mine," Malloryn added.

Auvry, damn him. Leo let out a harsh breath. Their differences over the past year had torn them apart, but they'd once been friends. He wasn't alone here. Their votes wouldn't be enough to save him—Lynch and Auvry couldn't turn the tide of the Council—but it was a welcome balm for the ache in his chest that cleaved him in two.

The prince consort leaned back in his chair, his hands clasped over his middle. "No, no, I don't think we'll put it to a vote. I think we'll let the queen decide."

Only she could overrule the entire Council, though she did so rarely.

Lynch let out a breath. "Very well. Exile? Banishment? What shall we—"

"Execution," the prince consort breathed into the room.

Leo's head jerked up. *What?*

"What do you say, my love?" The prince consort slid his hand over his wife's, where it rested on the table. "For the sin of lying about his birth, he could be absolved, but I fear his intentions go far deeper than that. He has moved against us, plotted for years to commit treason—"

"Treason?" Lynch demanded in shock.

"And your proof?" For the first time Barrons found his voice—and his feet. There was no way he was going to let the bastard pin this on him.

"The Devil of Whitechapel—"

"Sir Henry?" he countered. "Whom the queen knighted herself? How was aiding him during that duel treason?"

"For the simple reason that he's plotting to overthrow me. He's been stockpiling weapons in the rookery for months. Far more than are needed to defend that hellhole, and you've been meeting with him regularly. Or do you deny it?"

Deny something that was, in essence, the truth? For in a way, they *had* been preparing to commit treason.

"Your very silence condemns you." The prince consort gestured to the pair of Coldrush Guards. "Arrest him." He looked down at his wife. "On my lady's command."

The queen stared blankly at the table in front of her. Everyone's breath caught. She wasn't always obedient, but something about the vacant way she stared raised the hackles down Leo's spine. The prince consort had done something to her. Hurt her or threatened her after the incident the other day.

The queen jerked her head in a nod. "Y-yes."

No.

"Send him to the Tower to be executed." The prince consort's smile spread, and he caressed his wife's face, ignoring her flinch. "I want his head mounted on the walls."

Executed.

Hands caught him roughly by the arms and forced him to his knees. The room was in an uproar, dukes calling out across the table, but he could only see two faces. His father, his mouth slightly open as if in shock, the only one still seated; and the duchess, curse her blood, as she circled the table, going to the queen's side.

The room went dark as his hunger rose. He could feel his rage building. Not like this. The prince consort had outplayed him—and well. Must have been eyes on the rookery. Eyes on him. Of course. He should have guessed it. The prince consort wanted to regain control of the Council, and now he was making his move against all those that threatened it.

"You said in your message that he would be spared," the Duke of Caine called, looking up at his prince, his ally. "If I didn't deny it."

The prince consort didn't even bother to look at him, too busy gloating as he smiled at Leo. "I changed my mind."

The world went black for just a second. For the first time in his life, Leo let his demons rule him, and it was as if the world suddenly shot into vital blood-soaked clarity.

Both guards went down beneath his hand and

then he snatched at acres of silk, drawing Mina back against his chest and bringing his blood-letting knife up against her throat.

The room froze. Mina sucked in a breath, her heart thumping in her chest. He could feel it all the way through her slim back.

"Kill him," the prince consort snarled.

"No!" the queen screamed, on her feet at last, the dead look fading from her expression. "He'll hurt her."

"She'll heal."

"Not from this," Leo promised, taking a step back to keep them all in view, but the instant he said it, the red haze washed from his vision. *No. Not her*, the darkness in him whispered.

He let out a breath. Couldn't let them see it.

"Don't follow us," he snapped, stepping back against the heavy brass doors, dragging the duchess with him. "Or I swear to the blood that I'll kill her."

Eleven

"WHAT ARE YOU DOING?" MINA STAGGERED DOWN the stairs, ruthlessly hauled by Barrons. "Where are you taking me?"

She couldn't catch her breath. All she could see were those damning photographs—the same ones Gow had given her the other night. But she'd burned them. How the devil had the prince consort gotten his hands on them and worked out what she had?

Gow. He'd been in her household for years as one of the few she could rely on to get the information she needed. So bland and unassuming, never asking for anything more than he was owed.

The Falcons were not only assassins but also spies. It wasn't beyond belief to imagine that the prince consort would try to infiltrate all of their houses. Indeed, she often vetted prospective employees *very* carefully. But what if the spy had already been there, trusted under her father, inherited by her? She hadn't queried the employees she already had.

But Gow as the spy made too much sense not to be true.

She'd done this. Cast Barrons to the lions as carelessly as if she'd done it deliberately, and from the harsh look in his eyes, he'd never forgive her.

Barrons hauled her to the side of the spiral staircase that circled the center of the Ivory Tower and peered over the rail. "Damn it," he muttered under his breath, shooting a look above them. From the sound of voices and tramping feet, at least a dozen Coldrush Guards were swarming down on them from above, and more were heading up from below. A bell rang somewhere, pealing out its warning.

He was trapped here.

Or was he? There was a rushing sound in her ears as she stared at the hard line of his jaw and that jaunty ruby that hung from his ear. She could get him out. If she dared.

Sacrifices must be made, the queen's voice whispered in her head. *For the greater good.*

Not this. Not him. Biting her lip, Mina refused to examine the unsettling sensation burning in her chest. She owed Barrons a debt for his actions the other night with the Falcons—and so did the queen. It was as simple as that.

Grabbing his sleeve, she gestured downward. It was like trying to haul a statue with her bare hands. "I know another way out…one that very few people know about."

"Why the hell wouldn't I think it a trap?"

"Because if you're cornered, I can't predict what you'll do to me," she shot back, staring into those dark eyes and willing him to see that she spoke the truth. "And I never wanted…this."

For a moment his expression tightened, not anger or fury but grief. And she felt again how she had in that moment the prince consort had dropped his devastating words into the room—when Barrons had looked up, just once, and known that everything he'd fought for was lost.

Heart twisting, her grip softened on his sleeve.

"I made a mistake," she whispered. "This is my fault. Please, let me undo some of the damage."

And he wanted to believe her. She could see the yearning in his expression, that of a man with no other allies in this moment and who desperately wanted one. Then his face hardened. "If you betray me again, I promise I will destroy you before they kill me. Do you understand?"

Somehow she nodded, swallowing hard against the lump in her throat.

"Then show me how to get out of here."

※

There was nowhere to go. All of his properties would be compromised, including those that belonged to the families of his friends and thralls.

Nowhere to go… Or perhaps only one place the prince consort wouldn't dare follow him.

Whitechapel.

The secret tunnel spilled them out at the base of Crowe Tower. One of the four smaller towers that circled the Ivory Tower, Crowe Tower was so named for the flock of ravens that circled its peak.

Peering around the edge of a stone gateway, Leo saw dozens of Coldrush Guards streaming into the Ivory

Tower. Nobody had seen him and the duchess vanish into one of the smaller sitting rooms with a mirror hiding a secret passage he'd never known existed.

"Let me go," the duchess whispered. "I swear I won't sound the alarm."

He dragged her forward into the shadows of the royal stables. "Your word lost its value for me half an hour ago. Besides, I might still need a hostage."

Brandy-brown eyes raked the walls and the main gates that led to the tower. "If you were by yourself, you could scale the walls. I can't. Not in this." A gesture to her full, creamy skirts. Finally she gave him a look filled with defiance. "And I wouldn't, either."

Scaling the walls would leave him with his hands too full to carry her. "It's a good thing we're not going over the walls then."

Capturing her wrist, he dragged her inside the stables. A long, low hall, it was filled with the gleam of copper and the muted silence of a place that held nothing living.

"You're mad," the duchess said, guessing what he planned to do.

"Not yet."

Nobody had bothered to shut the main gates, no doubt presuming he wouldn't make it out of the Tower. Half a dozen Coldrush Guards were guarding the gates, armed with pikes and the electric stunners used to bring a blue blood down.

They weren't, however, watching the stables.

Dragging the duchess up in front of him, Barrons set the boilers on the massive Trojan horse he'd chosen to a low hum. Hundreds of the horses stood in silent rows within the stables, their copper-plated hides gleaming. They stood eight foot tall at the withers, their enormous soup-plate hooves shod with hard steel.

"Have you ever ridden one of these things?" the duchess hissed, clinging to the arm he'd wrapped tightly around her waist.

"Once," he replied, sliding his legs into the pressure grooves on the plated saddle. The steam horse stepped forward a step in response to the pressure from his thighs.

Most commonly controlled by the small radio frequency their handlers used, they could also be ridden. Each squeeze of his thighs compressed the pressure plates until the copper destrier danced sideways out of its row. Steam snorted from its nostrils as Barrons gathered up the reins. The boiler was almost at full capacity, heat burning between his legs.

"*Once?*"

"I was curious. Are you ready?"

"No! Barrons, don't do this. I need to be *here*. You don't understand what you're doing. I've helped you so far—"

Another squeeze with his thighs and the horse reared up on its powerful hind legs, dancing forward a step. *Hmm. Not so hard then.* The duchess shrieked, her hand clutching at his sleeve. Then he leaned forward, releasing the reins, and the creature leaped into a thunderous, lurching gallop.

The Coldrush Guards barely had time to turn before he was upon them, the Trojan horse smashing through their ranks and leaving screams behind. A horn sounded the alarm but they were through the gates, galloping out onto the thoroughfare beside the Thames. People saw the beast and screamed, darting out of the way.

"The cavalry!" someone bellowed. "They're unleashing the cavalry!"

Then it was mayhem as everyone sought to get out of the way.

He'd not planned for this. Even here, in the heart of the city, the crowd was terrified of the enormous metal beast—and what it usually signified. When the cavalry were unleashed, the prince consort didn't care if not everyone they crushed were rioting against him. Coaches jerked into side streets and a cart crashed into the back of an omnibus as the driver swore, the whites of his eyes gleaming as he tried to drag his vehicle out of the way of what he presumed would be death.

The rope on the man's cart snapped and half a dozen wine barrels crashed onto the cobbles, two of them smashing in a spill of claret and the other four rolling directly in front of the mechanical horse.

The duchess screamed, bringing her arm up in front of her eyes.

"Hold on." Leo leaned forward, trying to work out what move would send the creature into a jump.

"*Barrons!*"

One enormous hoof shattered a cask. The mechanical horse simply plowed through the mess, sending barrel staves and wooden slats tumbling. Leo looked behind him at the remains, then urged the destrier onward.

❧

Lynch leaned out the window and watched as the streets erupted into mayhem. Dozens of Coldrush Guards poured out of the base of the tower, the streets full of screaming people and mayhem. He didn't smile. He wanted to, though.

"Do you mean to tell me he's escaped?" the prince consort screamed behind him at the guard who'd brought the news. "How the hell could he manage to get out of the Tower unseen? And then through the gates before anyone knew of it?"

"I'm n-not entirely certain, your—"

"Lynch!" the prince consort snapped. "I want him found! I want—"

Lynch crossed his arms over his chest as he turned. "You forget, my prince. You yourself said I might no longer be a Nighthawk when I joined the Echelon. This is no task for a duke."

Their gazes clashed. The prince consort actually bared his teeth, then searched the room, flashing over Malloryn and Caine... Lingering there. "Caine?"

The pale head lifted, those eerie bluish eyes locking on the prince. "This is no task for a duke," Caine whispered and stared his prince in the eye.

It was the first time he'd ever outright defied his ally. Lynch caught his breath. A broken alliance?

"There's no need to find him," Morioch called.

His words stilled the room.

"There's only one place he can go." Morioch gave a sinister little smile. "The rookeries, my prince."

The prince consort traced his fingers over the back of his chair, his face still pale. He wouldn't look at Caine. "You ask for proof of treason? Let us give

Blade a chance to prove his loyalty, then. Morioch, take control of the Coldrush Guards and the metal-jacket legions. Tell Blade that he has twelve hours to deliver up Barrons."

"And if he doesn't?" Morioch asked, a vicious anticipatory gleam in his eye.

"Then burn him out," the prince consort snapped, striding for the door. "Burn the rookeries to the ground."

Twelve

"WHO'S THERE?"

Leo hauled the Trojan horse to a sliding halt, its hooves dancing on the cobbles. A figure stood on the top of Ratcatcher Gate, leaning on a fairly intimidating cannon.

"Ease off, Dandy," a lad called, sliding down the sides of the gate and landing in the streets. "He's one o' ours."

Charlie dusted himself off as he landed, straightening until he was almost as tall as Leo himself, though far leaner. "Barrons." He grinned. "You appear to 'ave stolen a Trojan horse."

The shock of seeing Charlie was another blow. The lad's smile faded a fraction as Leo said nothing.

For years he'd avoided Charlie as much as he could, knowing that the lad knew the truth about who'd infected him with the craving virus. Not one of Leo's finest moments. He'd deliberately sabotaged the vaccine that the boy's father—his father—intended to inject himself with, not realizing that Sir Artemus Todd intended to inject his younger son as well.

The duchess twisted to look at him when he didn't answer, her slender body lithe in his arms. Leo cleared his throat. "Charlie." There was nothing more to say. The reality of the situation was beginning to weigh him down again.

"'Ere, lads." Blade's voice carried out of the shadows, the man himself followed closely by Rip's hulking form. "Leave off and get back to duty."

Three young boys appeared out of nowhere on the rooftops and scampered away. All of them wore the same jerkin with a pair of crossed daggers branded into the leather over their chests, the sign of the Reapers, Blade's gang.

"Why, look at you." Blade strode forward, his hands shoved into the pockets of his long leather coat and a curious expression on his face. Catching the reins of the horse, he eyed the duchess. "Gretna's that way," he said, tipping his head toward the north.

Amazing how Leo had managed to hold himself together through that thrilling ride, but the familiar sight of Whitechapel—of Blade and Charlie and the rest of the men—was a punch to the chest, reminding him of the nightmare, and of everything that he'd lost. "They know," he said, his voice roughening. All of a sudden the rookeries didn't look as inviting as they once had. Damn it, what had he been thinking? There was nowhere safe from the prince consort, nowhere.

Blade's eyes narrowed, sorting through the implications of those two words.

"I shouldn't have come here." Leo started backing the horse up. "I'm sorry. I don't know what I was thinking."

"You ain't got nowhere else to go." Blade snatched at the reins, holding Leo in place, then eyed the duchess. "Dangerous 'ostage."

"Circumstances and all. Blade, you don't understand." Although Leo was starting to. "I just gave him a bloody invitation to start a war. You know what he wants. He'll use this to—"

"Not 'ere," Blade snapped. "Back at the Warren. Now."

"I should never—"

Blade snatched the duchess out of Leo's arms in a froth of white skirts. "'Ello again, princess." He tossed her toward Rip, who caught her in his arms. "Make sure she don't go nowhere. Might be some value in 'er yet."

"Barrons!" the duchess snapped, one hand curling in the giant's collar, her eyes flaring wide.

Leo's eyes narrowed.

Blade slapped a hand on his knee. "Don't make me throw you over me shoulder too. It ain't seemly."

A half dozen of Blade's men were watching, having followed him out of the alley. Charlie shot Leo a grin, leaning against the gate with his arms crossed in amusement, as if silently daring him to throw down with Blade.

Leo didn't have the strength of will right now to argue. Rubbing at the bridge of his nose he sighed, then slid his leg over the horse's rump and landed with a stagger at Blade's side. "You're a fool."

"We always knew it would come to this," Blade replied in a low voice. "You ain't the cause. You're just the catalyst. Besides, 'Onoria would wring me bloody neck if I let you leave and do somethin' noble and stupid, like sacrifice yourself."

Tossing the reins to Charlie, Blade lifted his voice. "Spread the word, boys. It's martial law in the rookeries. Women and children inside at all times, and I want the menfolk out 'ere on the walls." Blade slung an arm over Leo's shoulder and started leading him toward the Warren. "And look sharp! As soon as you spot a pasty face, I want to 'ear of it."

∽

Blade's insouciance wore off the closer they got to the Warren. Snapping orders at those they met, he forced Leo through the door and shut it behind them. Rip was inside, the struggling duchess in his arms and his metal hand clapped over her mouth.

"'Ow'd they find out?" Blade asked.

"I trusted someone I shouldn't have." A dark look at the duchess.

Blade laughed under his breath. "Always the pretty ones you gotta watch your back wit'. Wouldn'ta thought you'd lose your 'ead over the Ice Queen, though."

"What the devil is going on?" a voice called from the top of the stairs, and Honoria appeared with a shawl draped over her shoulders. "Is that the Duchess of Casavian?" Her eyes widened. "Did you kidnap the duchess, Blade? Are you insane?"

"Not me, luv." Blade started up the stairs, jerking a thumb over his shoulder. "Your brother decided life were gettin' borin'. Thought 'e'd turn pirate or somethin'."

Brother, she mouthed. "Blade—"

"It's all right," Leo called, following him. "No point hiding the truth anymore. The prince consort called me out on it an hour ago." He paused at her side. "They know I'm a bastard."

Her dark eyes softened. "And?"

"The prince consort wants my head on a spike."

Honoria's breath rushed out of her and she looked at Blade, half shaking her head. "No. No, I won't let them—"

"It's all right, luv." Blade squeezed her hand. "'E ain't goin' nowhere. The prince consort wants 'is 'ead? Then 'e's goin' to 'ave to go through me."

Warm arms curled around Leo as Honoria hugged him. He staggered back a step, taken by surprise. Her heavily rounded stomach was a barrier between them, making him slightly uncomfortable, but that didn't stop her. And then her shoulders shook and he realized she was crying.

He couldn't ever recall Honoria crying. Honoria, who was made of firmer pluck than most men.

Blade shrugged and made a circular motion in front of his stomach, mouthing, "*The baby.*"

"We won't let anything happen to you," Honoria said, lifting her head and drying her eyes with the back of her hand. "I promise."

The very idea that she intended to protect him struck him by surprise. "Honor…" He had no idea what to say to her. And then it hit him. The duke hadn't stood by him. Only Lynch and Malloryn had offered a word of defiance. But this…

His sister. His arms curled around her and he

lowered his chin onto the top of her head, soaking up the sensation of her warm body. Closing his eyes and resting, just for a moment. He was so fucking exhausted, and somehow insulated, as if the true effects of the day hadn't yet penetrated.

He'd needed this so badly. For someone to give a damn, to stand by him, even if that would start an all-out war.

The press of her pregnancy was a brutal reminder, though. Everything had a consequence. He'd learned that with Charlie. He opened his eyes and found Blade watching. "I can't stay."

"*What?*" Honoria lifted her head.

"The rookery defenses haven't been completed." He couldn't look at her. To do that would somehow break him. "And the weapons you've stockpiled aren't enough. Not yet. He'll throw everything he has at you. Fifty years ago, when you forced the Echelon out of the rookeries, they learned from that mistake. They won't misjudge you—or the people here—again. I can't stay. I can't give him an excuse to push this to war." Not a single expression flickered over Blade's face. "Damn you, look at her. She could give birth at any moment."

"You don't think I know that?" For the first time, Blade's composure wavered.

"So it's true," the Duchess of Casavian whispered. "You're planning to overthrow the prince consort."

Blade shot her a look that had Leo stepping between them. He'd acted before he thought about it, poised on the balls of his feet.

They all noticed. Blade shared a glance with Honoria that Leo couldn't read.

"Perhaps we should all take the night to think about it," Honoria suggested. "No matter what the decision, one thing is eminently clear. The duchess cannot be released, not yet."

"Don't 'ave to keep 'er 'ere, either."

The words were deadly soft. A threat. Leo stiffened. "I brought her into this, and I will see her out of it. Safely."

Blade gave him a long, slow look. "She stabbed you inna back once. Don't you forget that."

"I won't." *Never again.* "But she's *my* hostage. Not yours."

"Fine. 'Onor, see 'em to some rooms to freshen up. You oughta get some rest whilst I go rouse the lads. We'll see what the prince consort's first move is, and work out 'ow this gets played."

❧

The small room they took her to was surprisingly clean and smelled like beeswax. Mina stumbled over the stoop and jerked to a halt. Barrons murmured something under his breath at the tall giant who'd bundled her here—Rip, she thought he'd called him—then stepped inside and shut the door behind them.

Alone together.

Mina wrapped her arms around herself. So much was going through her mind, but in a day of revelations, the one that was most startling was the fact that both Barrons and Blade did indeed seem to be working to overthrow the prince consort.

All these years, she and the queen had thought themselves alone, maneuvering pieces into play until they finally had enough money and resources to begin actively working against the prince consort. The humanist movement had already been in place, so Mina had simply started pushing some much-needed funds their way and helping with recruitment, until she'd slowly become the heart of the movement.

Did she dare trust Barrons with the truth? That they were working on the same side? Mina opened her mouth, then shut it again. Too many years and too many secrets made her cautious. She needed to know more before she committed herself to this.

And for the first time, she felt desperately alone. She and Alexandra had always worked together on this. Any step she made was a threat against the queen herself, if handled incorrectly.

After all, neither Barrons nor Blade had made mention of who they intended to see in power once the prince consort was overthrown. And Barrons... He was not himself, that much was clear. There was no sign of the man who'd managed to sneak beneath her defenses. The man who'd dried her off so tenderly and whispered in her ear of Paris. She wanted that man back. He was just a shell now. Weary. Exhausted. Lashing out at her. Potentially dangerous.

"I know what it must seem like," she said quietly. "But I want you to know that I never betrayed you."

"No?"

Just that. Mina took a deep breath. "It's my fault indirectly. I set my man-of-affairs, Gow, to...to finding something I could use against you. Gow must have gone to the prince consort with the information I'd requested."

"Did you wish to ruin me so badly?"

"I-I—" She didn't know what to say. There was a bitter taste in her mouth, and how could she explain her actions when she didn't truly understand them herself? *You frighten me* didn't seem to be answer enough.

Those dark eyes watched her, drawing their own conclusions, no doubt. Mouth thinning, he turned away, examining the barred windows. "The problem with trust is that once it's broken, it's very difficult to restore again. Do you know, you almost look guilty. And I almost believe you." Barrons looked up, his voice turning to smoked honey. "But I don't."

"What do you intend to do to me?"

"Blade's correct. You know too much now."

"I can't stay here. I have to go back."

"Why? Lord Branson's ball tomorrow night? Or an appointment with your milliner in the morning?"

She backed away, keeping a chair between them. "You wouldn't understand." Without her, Alexa had no one to truly protect her. And she'd been in such a rare mood this morning—to actually condemn Barrons to death when the prince consort requested it, without even challenging him. That wasn't the woman that Mina knew. He'd done something to her. Hurt her. The bruises she'd left on her queen hadn't been enough.

"Please," she said, seeing no other way out of this. "I'll do anything you want. Just let me go."

Barrons's eyes became half-lidded at her words. "*Anything?*" he murmured, tipping the chair out of his way and stepping toward her.

Mina's back hit the wall as his hand slid around her

throat, fingers stroking the pulse of her carotid. Those black eyes were bottomless, empty chasms where she stared directly into the face of his hunger as he gave himself over to his darker side. Her throat went dry, heat blazing behind her eyes as her own hunger ascended. The room went dark as her vision changed, becoming sharper.

Too long since she'd last sipped some blood, combined with a horrendous day. There'd been no time to grieve for Boadicea, not truly, and the rush and excitement of their escape from the Ivory Tower had stirred her blood. Saliva wet her mouth. She wanted blood. Wanted it with a fierce ache.

Mina turned her face to the side, closing her eyes until she thought she had herself under control. The nearness of his body didn't help, that thumb stroking her throat. Back and forth. Mina bared her teeth and snatched at his wrist. "Don't."

Thick lashes shuttered his eyes as his gaze dropped, fingers tracing her collarbone and lower, hand turning, the back of his knuckles leaving a tickling sensation against the smooth slope of her inner breast. He looked back up, a challenge there. "I thought you said 'anything.'"

An odd mix of desire and revulsion filled her, washing her hunger back down into the depths within her. She wanted him, but not like this. It was an ugliness that he asked of her to clearly mark the change in their relationship.

"I won't let you make me your whore." Not even for Alexa? After everything the queen had endured over the past decade while married to the prince consort?

His hand froze against her skin, a horrified look flashing across his face before he smothered it. "Perhaps I wasn't asking you to be my *whore*."

He pushed away from her and Mina slumped against the wall, feeling the loss of his heat. What the hell had he been asking for, then? Her eyes narrowed to slits.

Barrons paced to the door.

"Wait."

He lingered, half glancing over his shoulder.

"What do you intend to do with me?"

"Christ, Mina. Quite frankly, you're the least of my concerns." He yanked at the doorknob and she couldn't help noting the stiff line of his shoulders and the weary, almost beaten way he carried himself.

A part of her felt an odd kinship with him. Her tongue pressed against the roof of her mouth, words hesitating there. How much had she longed for a kind word when she'd been in his position? When the entire world—her family and status—had almost been stripped from her?

"Barrons."

"Yes?"

Clearly he had no intention of making this easy for her, and she could let it continue, truly she could. Let him build this wall of distance between them until she was safely walled back in.

Ice princess. In her gleaming ivory tower… A part of her had never liked those words, though they'd protected her. A part of her didn't like *herself* very much when she looked at it that way. Because walling her heart off was safe and she'd needed that so badly once, but she was stronger now. She'd caught a glimpse of what it could be like for someone to tear down those walls.

And this wasn't about her. She wasn't the one hurting so badly now, though there was almost no sign of hurt in Barrons's composure.

"I've never seen you so uncertain," she said. "You're always so confident at court. It's…part of the reason you intrigue me so much."

He didn't say anything, but she could feel him listening.

Silence stretched out. She tried another tack. "I know what you're feeling. As if the whole world has turned upside down, including your place in it." As though there was nothing left in the world beyond the dogged determination to fight for survival. Duel after duel, familiar faces falling beneath her blade… How they'd turned on her then, when suddenly she was no longer a niece or a cousin, but the path to power.

"Do you?" The words were almost broken.

"You forget who I am."

"No, I don't." And his eyes told her in that moment, that he saw only what she wanted him to see—what the world saw. He no longer saw her.

It had threatened her, the uncanny way he seemed to know her, but now its loss was almost unbearable.

Something of it must have shown on her face. His harsh expression softened, just a hint. "I can cope with the loss of power, of position. What man can't forge himself anew? Do you know what the worst thing is, though?" He waited for her to answer, then never gave her the chance. "It's Caine. I knew he wasn't my father, and he was never the type to act the role, but things changed in recent years, once it became obvious that he was facing the Fade. For the first time in my life, he needed me. And damn me for a fool, but I gave him everything he needed. I protected him, no matter what the cost, and today he couldn't even look at me. Not one word of protest. He wouldn't even take that much bloody risk."

"Maybe he couldn't." A generous assessment, but she didn't share that thought with him. Barrons was too lost in his own grief and anger, and she…she knew exactly how that felt. "It will fade," she said quietly. "The feeling of betrayal, of loss."

"How do you know?"

Mina ignored the sharpness of his words. "I have lost a father too, and more than that, far more." Her fingers twitched, aching to toy with her skirts. "When my brother, Stephen, died, I was fourteen. It was a duel, something reckless that my cousin Peter had led him into. Of course, my family was devastated, my mother more so than most. He was…" A deep breath. "He was the kind of brother who always made me feel like I was welcome at his side. He was the one who taught me blade work, when I was five. Hardly the pursuit of a young lady, as my mother frequently stated, but Stephen insisted on it. Won her over with charm, like most people. He had the entire household wrapped around his little finger."

She didn't want to look up at him, but something drew her gaze. A peculiar prickling, as if he were focusing all of his attention on her. Mina reached out and gestured to the wall beside her. Slowly he sat.

Folding her legs under her, she sat beside him. Their shoulders brushed against each other.

"When he died, it was like a little piece of me died too. There went my laughter, my sense of order, for such a long time. My mother vanished into her grief, and my father turned his entire focus onto his experiments and the pursuit of a way to heal even death. I was left to my own devices. Peter became heir presumptive, and my father could barely stir himself to protest.

"It's the worst kind of feeling—to be useless, ignored, left to your own devices. I felt invisible, and then my debut came, and of course, every blue-blood lord wanted to have me for his thrall. No longer invisible." She gave a bitter laugh. "But still not seen. And Father began to fall further and further into his work. Someone had to manage the duchy's finances and deal with creditors.

"For over a year I managed the duchy, and then Father started growing ill. We thought it the Fade at first. Paling, losing time, losing his strength…taking to bed for long periods of time." This time she couldn't hide the grief underlying her words. "He kept saying it was Caine, that your father had done it to him. My mother and I feared poison, but what kind of poison could afflict a blue blood? We're invulnerable to illness. I'd never been so frightened in my life."

Thought flickered behind his eyes. "I know you don't want to hear this, but…if it were poison, I doubt Caine had anything to do with it."

"Of course you'd say that—"

"I believe it," he countered, then studied her.

"Caine's not the sort to hide behind poison. It's the sort of thing he'd think a weak person would rely on to defeat his enemies." As if some thought drove it, all of the expression vanished from his face. "For years he beat me for every minor infraction, but he always insisted upon holding the rod himself. 'A weaker man makes others do what he must,' he used to say. 'I take no pleasure from this, but by grace and glory, I shall make you a man.'" Barrons scraped a trembling hand over his exhausted face. "If he'd intended to see your father dead, he'd have held the pistol or the sword himself."

Troubling. "It's what my father said," she insisted. A surge of hate welled up inside her, but she didn't know what to think. A little part of her—the part that had spent years watching her enemy—knew that his words were true.

"But did he speak of what he believed Caine to have done?"

No. Mina frowned, picturing her father lying in his bed, so pale that she'd almost feared he was exhibiting signs of the Fade. Racked with pain that tore screams from his lips. They'd had to tie him to the bed in the end. "It wasn't a natural death."

"Peter?" he suggested.

"If Peter had been responsible, he'd have been unable to keep it a secret."

"I remember him. A bloody popinjay, if I recall. You're probably right. He'd have been crowing about it from here to Greenwich if he'd been behind it." His voice lowered. "I remember the day you dueled him for the position of heir."

Not her kindest moment. "I had to. He was threatening to marry me off to that cockroach Martin Astbury and to see my mother placed in an asylum once he became duke." This time she let the bitterness surface. "She didn't take my father's death well."

Vastly an understatement. Her mother had essentially died the day Stephen had. Her father's death had merely been the opening act in a grave-digging service. Her mother had lasted all of three months after Mina's father passed, and a part of Mina would never forgive her.

Stephen hadn't been the only one who'd needed her. Mina pushed to her feet, pacing to the window. She felt as though her skin was on inside out. Revealing so much had never been her intention. Indeed, it made her feel terribly uncomfortable. But at least Barrons's anger had subsided.

"So you see, I understand very well what it's like to lose everything. It will pass, this feeling, though it never entirely vanishes." She traced her fingertips along the window ledge, disturbing particles of dust. "It's always there, like a ghost in the room."

Movement shifted behind her. Light footsteps tracing hers. A shadow fell across her shoulders. Though he wasn't touching her, she could feel him at her back like a brightly burning coil. "You're right." His voice dropped to a harsh whisper. "I'm acting like a child."

"No. It's not… It hurts." She turned. "Right now it hurts, because those who should have cared for you weren't there to protect you. Or if they were, they didn't raise their voices when they should have."

The look he gave her— "Why are you telling me this?"

Something unfurled deep in her chest. "Because nobody was there to tell me."

Just because she had never shown it didn't mean that the hurt hadn't been there, deep inside. In a way, it was easier to pretend that she didn't feel anything. Easier to concentrate on her plans, one foot in front of the other. Cement her status as duchess. Earn her place on the Council. Then later, to gather the humanist movement together and give its believers some sense of purpose. Or had that been another part of giving herself a way to forget her pain?

She stared at him somewhat defiantly. "We're not enemies, not anymore. I don't know what the truth is about my father's death but…perhaps you're right. I've cataloged Caine's faults and weaknesses. Poison… it's not like him." Mina licked dry lips. "I won't betray you. I won't breathe a word of what you're doing here. I'll say I was blindfolded the entire time—"

And just like that, she lost him. Fury glittered in his eyes and he turned on his heel. "Christ." A bitter laugh, thrown over his shoulder. "You know, you almost had me there. You almost made me believe you gave a damn—"

"Barrons! Wait!" She went after him.

The door slammed in her face. Mina held her fists up in frustration, then rested them helplessly on the door. From the sound of his harsh breathing, he was still on the other side.

"I meant it," she said, pressing her fingertips against the polished wood grain and resting her forehead

there. "I meant every word. It's just—I can't stay—"
You don't understand.

And I can't tell you...

The only answer was the sound of angry footsteps echoing down the hall.

❦

"She says she didn't do it," Leo said, staring into the fireplace.

"Do you believe her?" Honoria asked.

He clenched and unclenched his fist, watching the play of tendons across his knuckles. "I want to. Perhaps that's part of the problem. I don't know if I can see the truth." Something he'd never admitted to anyone else before. "Not when it comes to her."

"You look tired," Honoria said.

Drained was a more accurate assessment. He stared into the flickering flames in the grate. "I spent years dreaming of this moment. I used to lie in bed and plan how I would react; whether I'd stare the prince consort in the eye and deny it, or rage against it, or call him an imbecile." *God.* He looked up at the ceiling. What a fool he'd been. "I did nothing. I just sat there. I *couldn't* say anything."

And he didn't feel anything either, not really. A little numb, now that the initial shock had worn off. Worn thin, as if he'd lost a piece of himself, but the greatest loss was the most unexpected one.

There was nothing left of the tentative bond he'd thought existed between himself and the duchess. She'd finally let him see a piece of her beneath that guarded veneer. He'd felt as though he'd reached for her and she'd begun to reach back. She existed in his thoughts; she always had. Hell, he'd even come to hope that she could be his, that he could have something akin to what his sisters had. He wasn't fool enough to dream of love, for he didn't understand it. Didn't have a bloody clue what it meant, truly, but he'd hoped for…something.

Obviously he had overestimated the situation.

The duchess's one desire was to return to her gilded life. And why not? What would she want with a bastard? With a man who was nothing? He had nothing to give her now but himself, and he knew how cheap a gift that was.

If only he could *make* her want him, prove he had some worth left.

"Well," Honoria said, her hand sliding over the small of his back, "the truth is out. There's nothing to be gained by sitting here and dwelling on it. Now we must plan what we will do for the future."

Despite himself, he smiled a little at her, though the effort soon slipped. Honoria would never change. Practical almost to a fault, but he liked the way she said "we." They'd made their peace over the years about his involvement in Charlie's illness, but he'd never truly felt as if she'd forgiven him.

His smile faded. "How ironic… Here I am standing on your doorstep, begging for help."

Four years ago, she'd been a stranger to him, the daughter that Todd had loved more than him. The little girl who'd grown up in Caine House while Todd still had the duke's patronage. How he'd hated her as a child.

When Todd had been murdered by Vickers, the Duke of Lannister, she'd fled into Whitechapel with Charlie and Lena, with barely a handful of coins and the clothes on their back. Leo had turned her away from his door when she came begging for money after she lost her position of employment. Though he'd tried to hide her traces and steer Vickers's manhunt in the opposite direction, he hadn't done *enough*. He'd never forgive himself for it. "Honor, I——"

"A wise man once reminded me that I would never have married him if you'd given me money back then."

Leo let out a slow breath and said gruffly, "Now I know the baby's stolen your wits. You're referring to Blade as wise."

"He has his moments." Honoria reached up on her toes and kissed his cheek. "I never thanked you for that."

"For not helping you when I should have?" It had plagued him for years.

"For driving me straight into his arms when I was too proud to go there of my own volition."

"I've done horrible things to you over the years."

"The mechanical spiders in my bed when I was a little girl living at Caine House?" An arch of the brow. "All I can say is that I wouldn't sleep too deeply, if I were you."

However, the laugh that she gave him belied the words. Leo sighed, his head lowering in thought.

"Do you know what the problem is, Leo?"

He glanced at her. "What?"

"I forgave you," she said solemnly. "Years ago."

The words floored him. "But—"

"You never forgave yourself. I feel it in you every time you're with me. There's a door between us that I can't breach. I see how close you and Lena have become, and I wish… I wish we all shared that. Charlie thinks you're smashing. You can do no wrong in his eyes."

Christ. "But I was the one who infected him." His own infection with the craving had come from an untested vaccine Todd had used on him as a lad, when he'd been so desperate for a father's approval that he'd even sought Todd out, mouthing his humanist platitudes. Todd had despised blue bloods, and as soon as signs of infection sprang up, he'd turned his back on Leo—despite the fact Leo's turning had been Todd's fault.

Leo had never been a vengeance-minded man, but when he'd learned years later that Todd had perfected the vaccine and planned to use it on himself… Leo's fist clenched. "I swapped the vial for the one Todd used on me. I didn't once consider that he might use it on someone else. I-I thought it justice."

"I know that now." Her fingers laced through his. "Father has his share of the blame for that. He treated you abominably." It had to be a bitter confession, considering how much she'd adored her father.

There were no words. Leo stared down at their linked hands. "Thank you," he said in a hoarse voice.

Honoria gave him a weary smile. "You should go to bed. Tomorrow won't seem half as grim."

No, it would be much, much worse, but he didn't give voice to his thoughts. Kissing the back of her hand, he said his good nights and turned toward the door.

"Need I ask which bed you will be staying in?" There was a deceptive lightness to her tone.

Leo paused by the door. That was finished between him and Mina. "My own," he said roughly.

∽✑∾

There was no point banging on the door or screaming for help. There were bars over the window; not the first time this room had been used for this purpose. Mina tried to pick the lock on the door, but it turned out to be bolted on the outside too.

"Rot." Scraping a hand over her mouth, she turned again to survey the room.

She was at the very back of the house on the top floor. Peering through the window, she could see a brick yard below, with strands of ivy choking the walls. If she could get outside, perhaps on the roof, then she had some chance of getting away.

After all, nobody ever expected a duchess to be able to climb, and they would be watching for people entering the rookeries, not exiting it.

Standing on the bed, Mina reached up and tested the ceiling. Plaster. A smile curved over her lips, and then she ripped a large swathe off her skirts and wrapped it around her fist. Built to hold men, she suspected, but not blue bloods.

Plaster dust rained down upon her as she punched a hole through the ceiling. Every couple of seconds she'd pause and listen, but nobody seemed close enough to hear her. By the time she'd cleared a hole large enough to slip through, a fine layer of white dust powdered her shoulders.

Dashing off a note to Barrons, she left the piece of paper in the middle of the bed, then hauled herself up through the hole. The roof above was good solid tile, so easier to go back down rather than through it. Smashing her way through the ceiling, she found herself in the bedroom next to hers. A man's room, by the look of it. Mina swiftly raided his wardrobe for trousers, a large white shirt made of rough material, and a belt to hold it all together. Knotting her hair into a tight chignon, she quickly searched the room, finding a dagger beneath the mattress.

Never let it be said that the Duchess of Casavian needed a man to do her dirty work.

It was quick work to unlatch the window and slip out onto the ledge. Catching hold of the gutter, she hauled herself onto the tiled roof and lay flat for a moment, scanning the horizon. Houses pressed close on either side of the Warren, built crooked or on a slant, so that it almost seemed as though they leaned upon each other. A thick velvety darkness softened the sky in the west. Night then. She could feel her blood thundering through her veins. Night was a blue blood's natural habitat. Nothing to fear. Not for her.

Mina peered toward the city and the enormous Ivory Tower that kept guard over all of London, clearly visible even from here.

Time to keep her promise to her queen.

Thirteen

"What do you think?" The prince consort sipped his blud-wein, staring out over the entire city of London beneath him. His city. "Do you think it collaboration?"

"I doubt it, Your Highness." A voice from the shadows as Balfour stepped forward. "My man in her employ specifically stated that she asked for information on how to destroy Barrons."

The curtains flipped closed. "Unfortunately, then, the duchess seems due for a disappointment. The Crown does not deal with ransoms or threats. He can have her. Saves me the need to bury her when the time comes."

A bow. "As you wish."

—A conversation between co-conspirators

HE TRIED TO STAY AWAY. TRULY HE DID.

Leo unlatched the heavy bolt guarding the duchess's door and rapped on it with his knuckles. "Your Grace?"

Leaning closer, he listened to the echoing silence. Suspicion bloomed.

Leo shoved the door open. There was a duchess-sized hole in the ceiling, and the bedding was littered with straw, plaster, and the ragged remains of her skirts. A note was tucked neatly on the top of the pile, mocking him. He swore under his breath and flicked it open.

> *I did ask you nicely to let me go. Give my regards to the Devil of Whitechapel, and tell him to send my man-of-affairs the bill for any damage.*
>
> *Regards,*
> *Lady Aramina Duvall*

Leo shoved his head through the hole in the roof. Barely three feet in front of him was another hole.

"Honoria!" he called, striding out into the hallway and into the next bedroom.

It had clearly been ransacked. While he'd been sipping blood with his sister and trying to gather his thoughts, the duchess had been plotting her escape like a seasoned criminal.

The swish of skirts caught his ear and Honoria paused in the doorway, trying to catch her breath. "Good heavens, what are you—" She looked up at the gaping hole in the ceiling and then the not-quite-closed window. "What in blazes…?"

Leo jerked the window open and peered out. Twilight limned the rookery, washing away the harsh stains of the day. Warm flickering candlelight sputtered in several nearby windows; no cool gaslight here. "She's gone."

It was almost a twenty-foot drop. Entirely possible

for a blue blood, and he had to start thinking of her as such now, not merely a woman. Baring his teeth, he looked up at the roof. A single strand of cotton was caught on the edge of the slate tiles. *There*. She'd gone over the rooftops.

A distant shout caught his ear, followed by several more. What the hell was she thinking? Of all nights, this would be the worst to be out on the streets. She'd be lucky if she were only accosted by Coldrush Guards.

"Where are you going?" Honoria asked.

"After her," he replied, slinging a leg over the windowsill.

"Perhaps you should leave her be. There's more than enough excitement for everybody to handle at the moment, and she's…she's a duchess, Leo."

Leave her be? *No*. She was the only damned variable he could control at the moment. He could no sooner let her go than he could change the weather.

"A duchess who knows entirely too much about our plans." He crouched on the windowsill. "Stay here with Esme. I'll bring her back."

"Leo?"

He paused.

"Are you certain that's the true reason?"

"Of course I'm certain," he lied.

❦

Fires burned in barrels past the wall that circled Whitechapel. In the distance Mina could hear the roar of a gathering mob and see the gleam of steel as several makeshift weapons were thrust in the air.

Crouching low on the roof, she surveyed the wall. It was more heavily patrolled than she'd expected. The mob might be unruly, their armor and weapons crafted out of whatever they could lay to hand, but Blade's men moved ruthlessly through the night, alert to the faintest hint of noise.

If the Devil of Whitechapel got his hands on her, she was quite certain he'd act swiftly to remove any perceived threat.

The ring of iron-shod feet echoed on distant cobbles. Metaljacket legions by the sound of it, the ground forces of the Echelon's automaton army. No doubt some of the models would be spitfires, capable of burning half the rookery to the ground with the flamethrower cannons strapped to their arms. She had to get out of here before this entire mess degenerated into a massacre.

Timing the guards along the walls, she leaned forward on her hands and the balls of her feet. A shadow slipped past in the night and Mina wasted no time, running up the tiled slope of a roof and leaping up to catch hold of the edge of the wall. She hung there for a moment, her shoulders straining, listening as the guards kept walking.

Not quite as easy as she'd imagined it would be. Gritting her teeth, she dug her toes into the wall and hauled herself up, inch by inch. Determination was her ally; there were so many times people—men—had told her she wouldn't be able to do something in her life. She'd proved them all wrong.

A horn screamed through the night and Mina crouched low. She wasn't the cause. The stamping metal feet had fallen silent, evidently reaching their destination, leaving the racket of a dozen dogs howling as the noise echoed through the cold night.

No houses leaned up against the wall on the outside. Mina eyed the distance to the ground, then slung her legs over the edge of the wall. Twisting, she let her body lower until she hung, prepared to drop into the alley below.

Free.

A hand snagged her wrist. Mina gasped and looked up into eyes black as Hades. The flickering firelight was unforgiving, casting a pall over his lean features and highlighting the stark cut of his jaw.

"Going somewhere?" Barrons gave her a tight, frigid smile.

The fierce intensity of his regard burned through her as she dangled against the wall. "Just out for a stroll," she replied.

Mina leaned into his grip, forcing him closer to the edge, then ran her legs up the wall, smashing her heel into his chest. It jerked her wrist from his grasp and she flipped backward, tumbling through the air. The ground flashed into view and she twisted her hips, landing lightly on her feet like a cat, her hands slapping the ground.

Looking up, she met those startled eyes and a certain reckless urge overtook her. *Stir the devil*. Pressing her stinging fingertips to her lips, she blew him a kiss, then darted back down a shadowy street.

The second she was out of sight, Mina grimaced and let herself favor her right ankle. Blue blood she might be, but invincible she was not.

There was no doubt he'd follow. Mina hauled herself over a wall and up onto the rooftops. A swift glance behind showed a shadow rippling after her and she ran faster, sprinting up the gable on a roof.

Leaping across onto the next rooftop, she caught a glimpse of light flickering nearby. The legion. And the only place Barrons wouldn't dare follow her.

Sliding down a roof on her bottom and feet, she could hear her pursuer hot on her heels. Faster than she was and far more sure-footed on the rooftops. Mina accelerated, scrambling for the edge of the roof. Barrons slipped and slid after her, nearly on her heels.

"Damn you." A hand snatched at her shirt.

Mina judged the edge of the gutter and, catching a foot in it, slowed her descent just enough to twist as she dropped. Instead of landing in the street below, she caught the gutter and hung for a moment before hauling herself back up. Barrons landed below with a muffled curse, thinking that her destination.

The devilish part of her couldn't resist shooting him a smile, and then she was gone again. Four streets and she'd make the legion. She could hear them now, the roar of the mob in Whitechapel swelling. The streets and houses nearby were almost deserted.

Mina darted across a rooftop—

And a blur of shadow came out of nowhere, smashing into her and sending them both tumbling down the sharp incline of the roof.

Barrons flung a hand out, shoving it into the gutter. Mina smashed into him, but his other arm curled around her, tucking her in tight against his heavier body as she lay half on top of him. The world didn't stop spinning. Slowly she looked up, breathing hard, the air driven out of her in the fall.

"Not a good night for a stroll," he growled, glancing below. A torch gleamed as a gilded carriage rolled around the corner of the street below, dozens of metaljackets trotting along beside it. Two handlers sat on the top of the carriage, wielding the small spike-topped control boxes that signaled the automatons to move.

Barrons drove her face into his chest. "If you make a sound, Duchess…"

No threat. There was none needed. Strong fingers cupped the back of her head, while his other arm curled around her. Beneath her his body was hard steel, each muscle molding the softness of her curves. His heartbeat thundered beneath her ear, reminding her that he was alive. That she held the resolution of that in her hands.

Looking up, she saw the gleaming blackness of his eyes. "If I wanted you dead," she whispered, "all I'd have to do is scream."

He could have slammed a hand over her mouth. Instead the silence stretched out between them and she knew he was giving her the chance, testing her for the truth of what had happened in the Ivory Tower.

Mina let her shoulders slump. The chance of escape vanished like a fluttering moth. For the only way to do so now was to betray him to the very men who wanted his head.

And Barrons knew it.

❧

Leo's head dropped back onto the tiles and he let out a shaky breath. Somehow his hand had entwined in the knot of her chignon and he kept her pinned atop him, her head resting on his chest.

The duchess had been only seconds away from escaping. A part of him knew she wouldn't scream for help, but another smaller part was filled with doubt. He'd never felt so bloody uncertain in his life. About everything.

So he gave her the chance. He could get back behind the safety of the walls of Whitechapel before any of those nodcocks below caught him, though he'd have to sacrifice the duchess to do it.

And damn her, but she didn't say a word.

What the hell did that mean?

The press of her soft body caught his attention. Leo's mouth firmed, but he kept his head cocked, listening to the sounds coming from below.

They were close enough to Ratcatcher Gate to hear what was being said. If he tilted his head to the right, he could actually see Blade standing on top of the wall. Blade held one arm up and the mob's restless cries stilled to a murmur, then nothing at all. Silence ruled the rookeries, proving beyond a doubt who owned it.

"Looks like some fancy coach got turned 'bout and made its way to the 'Chapel," Blade called, to the laughter of his men. Then his voice grew flat and hard. "State your name and your business 'ere."

The tramp of metal feet slammed to a halt, then a ringing voice cried out, "Morioch."

Leo tensed. No friend of his. The cadaverous old duke was firmly in the prince consort's pocket.

The duchess gave a little wiggle as she shifted to

look, her hip pressing hard against his cock. The treacherous thing hardened.

Any other woman would have taken instant advantage. Not the duchess. Her head was tilted to the side, listening too. Then her eyes widened and her head jerked up as she realized his predicament.

Their faces were a bare inch from each other. The startled look in her eyes was almost comical until she began to relax, one inch at a time, her body softening over his. "Men," she murmured, "are entirely predictable."

"Not all men, Your Grace," he shot back. "That thing, however, has a mind of its own."

"Morioch." Blade laughed in the distance, but it sounded more like a threat. "Me old friend Morioch."

The carriage door opened and footmen darted forward with a stool. One held Morioch's hand as he alighted from the carriage, wearing burnished gold armor and a white, Georgian-style wig. He'd been born in that era, after all.

"You have something the prince consort wants."

Blade rested one foot on the wall, leaning on his thigh. "Do I? And you thought you'd bring a legion o' metaljackets 'ere to politely ask for it back?"

"To take custody of the criminal."

"Criminal, eh? 'Fraid Your Grace'll 'ave to be more specific than that."

Another round of laughter behind the wall. Half the men here had earned that title.

Leo could almost picture the tight smile Morioch would be wearing right now. The duke despised rogue blue bloods.

"I'm well aware—as are you—that Leo Barrons entered Whitechapel earlier today. He is to be tried for treason and executed. I would encourage you to hand over the criminal with as little ceremony as necessary."

Leo held his breath. He knew what Blade had said to him earlier, but a small part of him—still raw from Caine's defection—wondered if the same would apply now.

"What'd 'e do?"

"That's strictly Council business."

"And now we got ourselves a little problem." Blade's voice carried in the night. He had the skills of a showman at times, modulating both voice and appearance to suit the moment. "You ain't 'avin' 'im."

The breath went out of Leo.

"You weren't certain, were you?" the duchess whispered in his arms.

"Shut the hell up."

And she did. But he could feel her watching him, the trace of her gaze lighting up every nerve in his body until he felt raw.

"Don't be a fool," Morioch called.

"Oh, I ain't," Blade replied. "Gave me word o' safe passage to Barrons earlier. You don't want me to break me word."

"What you need to remember, you little cur, is that you have a wife now. Don't make me cut her throat in front of you, for I shall make that my priority if I'm forced to take the rookery."

"Hell." Morioch was insane to make a statement like that. Firelight danced over Blade's grim

expression. If one didn't know him, one would think
him entirely capable of anything in that moment.

"Did you just threaten my wife?" A knife couldn't
have been sharper than Blade's voice. The murmur
of the rookery lads behind him lifted to a dull roar,
sensing the sudden predatory intensity of their leader.

Morioch shifted. "Look around you," he snapped,
trying to save face. "I've got a legion of spitfires."

"You think that makes you safe? You just threatened my *wife*," Blade repeated softly, his words
distinctly clear of cockney now.

Dangerous. Leo had seen Blade like this before: eyes
blackened with the craving, his hunger stirring to the
surface. Utterly ruthless in that moment.

"Shut your saucebox and get out of my sight,"
Blade said. "Go home to that fancy manor you got on
Blakeley Square and pray that you got enough guards
to keep me and my lads out. And if you ever"—he
punctuated his words with a pointed finger—"threaten
my wife again, I'll make sure that the last things you
ever see are these." Holding up the pair of razors
he wore at his belt, he flicked them open. Firelight
flashed on the steel.

Morioch didn't flinch, but his face tightened as he
realized his error. He was, after all, standing in the
aptly named Butcher Square. This was where Blade
had carved out his legend in blood. "You have until
morning," the duke said, turning toward the carriage.
"If your answer hasn't changed by then, I shall be
forced to dig Barrons out myself."

The footman slammed the door behind the duke
after he entered the carriage, the troop of metaljackets

taking a uniform step to the side. Blade watched with glittering eyes as the carriage wheeled around, returning to the Ivory Tower. The metaljackets remained behind, falling into rank with a single, echoing step, then becoming silent as they faced the rookery.

"Come," Leo demanded, his fingers digging into the duchess's upper arms.

A flash of fire lit her eyes, like flame set to brandy. "Let me go. You and I both know this is foolishness. You'll never keep me."

A sudden surge of hot frustration licked at him. He rolled her onto her back on the roof, coming over her. The duchess sucked in a little gasp as all of his weight pressed her down.

"No." He bit the word off, challenging her. Devil take him, but this was a madness he couldn't deny. His hands softened on her arms and he rested on his elbows, staring down at her, at her beautiful treacherous face. "You had your chance. All you had to do was call for help."

"I know you find this difficult to believe, but I don't actually wish your death on my hands." The snap of temper in her voice was like a lash. Was that a hint of guilt?

"No?"

"*No.*"

Truth? Or carefully planned lies? Leo rolled off her. "Why are you so bloody desperate to get back to the Ivory Tower?"

"Wasn't it that milliner's appointment I simply couldn't miss in the morning?"

The duchess was back in her place. Lady Aramina

at her coolest, arching a disdainful brow as if to deter some young buck.

The ache in his chest grew. Leo pushed to his feet and held out his hand to her. Whatever had begun between them that night at the Venetian Gardens was simply a mirage. She was his reluctant captive, and he had no intention of letting her go. One more staggering loss on top of the rest of them. He could almost feel his face shutting down, emotion blunting within him. Even the ever-present burn of the craving's hunger was a distant thing tonight.

He didn't think she'd take his hand, but something softened in her eyes as she absorbed the change in him.

"The gentleman returns," she murmured.

"Hardly."

But she caught his fingers, her slight weight barely dragging at him as he hauled her upright. She staggered a step or two, her palms splaying against his chest. That faint hint of seduction sucked at him again, especially as her lashes fluttered over her eyes and she slowly looked up at him. The pale gleam of her face was particularly taunting, for it wasn't the Duchess of Casavian he stared at. Not in this moment. Just as he was comprised of two halves, split in two at this moment, so was she.

Mina.

He steeled himself.

"Come." He pushed away from her. "I'd like to oblige your milliner, but I'm afraid you'll have to reschedule."

Fourteen

"The best-laid plans…and all that rot…"

—Blade, the Devil of Whitechapel

AFTER SNATCHING A COUPLE OF HOURS OF GRAINY-EYED sleep, Leo swung his legs off the edge of the narrow cot and sank his head into his hands. He felt worse than he had when he'd lain down, which felt like mere minutes ago and was probably hours.

Sleep was a luxury few of them could afford, but he'd had to snatch some of it to clear his head. Rubbing at his eyes, he found some sense of alertness. Caine had often deprived him of sleep during his almost-militant training as a youth.

"Your enemies won't wait for you to be well-rested, my lad."

They certainly wouldn't. And they'd proven to be much closer to home than he'd imagined. *Didn't they, Father?*

At least the bastard had given him a good grounding

for this war. He was already dressed, lacking only the protective leather body armor Blade had given him. Dragging it on, he exited the room, his wits sharpening with every second.

The room across the hallway was silent.

Pausing at her door, Leo listened. The sound of the duchess's soft breathing assured him she was still there. The tension in his gut unwound just a little. Not that she could go anywhere, since he'd used a pair of manacles to bind her to the bed.

Just let her go. Stop this madness. There was no point to it, nothing beyond the halfhearted reasons he'd given to Honoria. The duchess knew only what the prince consort already suspected. Hardly cause to keep her here against her will like this...

But he turned away grimly, letting his hand fall as he made his way through the house. Letting her go would be the final sign of defeat. He would have nothing then, only memories of the man he'd once been.

War had been on their minds ever since he, Blade, Lynch, Will Carver, and Garrett Reed had first discussed overthrowing the prince consort. Months' worth of preparations greeted him as he stalked through the dark streets toward the wall. Some of them he recognized as his own suggestions, and a small hint of pride burned in him. There was his mark upon the world, something that he could still call his own.

The wall was lightly manned, though he saw dozens of boots sprawled under blankets in nearby houses, men snatching sleep where they could. Along the top of the wall, Blade had fitted heavy cannons into the slots his men had created in months past. Each cannon was highly modified, prepared to fire scattered shot, which was one of the best ways to take down a metaljacket.

The automatons could splash liquid fire against the walls if they got close enough, and the heavy metal plates protected most of their clockwork inner organs from outside machinations, but their limbs were their weakness. Most of the metaljacket handlers wielded a stable of ten automatons with their high-frequency controllers. Trying to get one of the drones back on its feet once it was down, while wielding nine other automatons… That was a skill in itself.

Of course, all they had to do was get close enough to burn the rookeries. The Echelon's blacksmiths had long since rediscovered the secrets of Greek fire, and the spitfire models were difficult to stop. If Morioch launched them at Blade, he and his people would be in serious trouble.

Leo nodded at passing men, his hands shoved in his pockets as he waited his turn for the iron ladder that was bolted to the wall. Some men nearby were using grappling guns to lift themselves swiftly to the top, something that would be necessary if the cry sounded and Morioch attacked.

Finally he reached the top. Silvery light glistened in the east, knotting up his stomach. He knew what Blade had said last night, but Morioch would soon be back to hear a final answer. All these men could die because of him.

"You look like 'ell." Rip's deep voice jolted Leo out of his distraction. The giant watched the gleaming

horde below. He had a flask of blood in his hand and
was nonchalantly sipping from it.

Leo leaned on the ramparts beside him. Two hundred metaljackets, if he wasn't mistaken, with more of
them coming in overnight. Gold plate gleamed at the
back, identifying the spitfires. The rest were common
automatons, the least valuable of the prince consort's
steel army.

"I've been better." The tightly packed alleyways
surrounding the rookery gave them a slight advantage.
Morioch had flooded the streets he could see with
metaljackets, but they'd be forced to attack the walls
in narrow units.

"Blade's ordered 'ouses pulled down in the streets
out there to block the way," Rip replied, offering him
the flask. "That's where 'e is now. They got to come
at us from only one o' three places now."

Leo took a pull from the flask. Spiced blud-wein
with something far more potent added. *Christ*. His dry
throat rebelled, and he coughed and handed it back.
"A clear sign he's not going to surrender me."

"That leech knows 'e ain't." Rip shrugged, his steel
shoulder joint rippling with the movement. A cutaway
leather jerkin hid his massive chest but revealed the
biomechanical arm he'd refused to hide since his marriage to Esme. Fingerless leather gloves concealed his
hands, gloves with razors cut into the back of them.
A single punch could kill a man. "We ain't 'idin'
our intentions none, and 'e'll be mad as 'ops after
last night."

"He'll come and put on a show." Morioch
always liked to perform. Leo pointed to a place in

the square where the sun would hit, come dawn. "Probably there."

Rip eyed the expanse. "Could 'it 'im from 'ere."

"Won't kill him. He's a blue blood, and if I know him, he'll be wearing heavily reinforced armor the likes of what he wore last night."

Rip spat over the wall. "Ain't no bricky lad. Got a streak o' yellow wide as London Bridge."

"He's not here to fight. He's here to crush you. There's no honor gained in engaging an enemy that's beneath you, and that's how he sees this." That's how most of the Echelon saw the human classes, the mechs, and especially Blade. A mistake on their part, Leo had long thought, but then he'd always been considered a progressive. No matter how many times Caine had tried to force his views on him, Leo had never been able to conceal his curiosity.

Why crush the human classes beneath their heel? As far as he could see, it only stirred resentment. The colonies seemed to have some sort of system in place where their blue bloods worked side by side with the human classes. Why couldn't England do that?

Why does a mechanical hand make a man less than human? Why should only the legitimate sons of highly ranked lords be gifted with the blood rites? Why them? Why not others?

A thousand whys over the years.

All those questions he'd asked himself. Plans he'd dreamed of. Changes to the way the Echelon controlled the country. Swept away in the ashes of a single day.

He stared dully over the scene. The rows of automatons were almost eerie in the predawn stillness. Men would shift and shuffle in place, but not these.

Leo frowned. A single frequency to control them... Each handler's control device was specifically coded to their stable of ten, but the frequency remained the same. "Unless..."

"What?" Rip asked.

Leo shook his head, scraping at the stubble on his jaw. "Nobody's managed to bring back one of the handlers' control devices?"

"No. Why?"

"I'm just...thinking." He paced along the wall, staring at the Echelon's army. "Several of my business enterprises are in communications, and the recent invention of radio frequency and telegraphs. It's the way of the future, but progress is slow. Interruptions affect the efficiency of radio frequency all of the time. The frequency must be pitched precisely..." He trailed off, catching a glimpse of Rip's expression.

"I'm listenin'," Rip assured him. "You're sayin' change the frequency and it'll drive the automatons barmy?"

"Mmm." Possibly. He understood the basics of how the metaljackets worked, though warfare had never been his priority. "The frequency resonates with a chip in the metaljackets' heads."

"Off with their 'eads, then?"

"Maybe." Both of them eyed the heavily plated steel helms staring back at them. "Take out the handlers and you crush the army. The Echelon's been aware of that for a long time, so the handlers

will be heavily guarded. Or could we create something? Something to interfere with the radio waves?
Perhaps to change them?" He'd need one of the
Echelon's carefully guarded blacksmiths to do it—or
perhaps one of the mechs who worked steel in
the enclaves.

No. This kind of thing was most likely beyond
them. Leo slammed his fist down on the wall. It
could work if he had the right tools, the right people.
"Anyone know how to work steel here? Any escaped
mechs? Or a...a scientist..."

Honoria. The closest thing he had to a scientist.
Sir Artemus Todd had been a lauded member of the
Royal Society. Most who spoke of him called him a
genius, and although his main field of work had been
trying to discover a cure for the craving, there were
rumors he'd dabbled in mechanics, creating plans for
several highly advanced automatons and a pistol he'd
modified with firebolt bullets that could take even a
blue blood down. Honoria had apprenticed with him
as a young woman.

Leo had seen her in action. Hell, she'd engineered
the vaccine her father had discovered, using it on
Leo's thralls and offering him all of her notes to
present to the Royal Society so that the vaccine
could be delivered to the masses. It was the first step
in loosening the prince consort's stranglehold on
the Echelon after he'd discovered a device that had
been thought, at the time, to be the only cure for
the craving.

For the first time, Leo's head felt clear. "I need one
of the frequency control devices."

"Dawn ain't far. They'll 'ave 'em locked up tighter than a nun's drawers."

"I'll need a few men then. Who?" Rip knew Blade's lads better than he would.

Rip turned and put his fingers into his mouth to whistle sharply. Heads jerked up all along the wall, but he waved them down. "Send for Charlie, Lark, and Tin Man," he bellowed.

Charlie. A cold ring circled the back of Leo's neck. "I'm not taking the boy into that."

"Lad's a craver and 'e's a right prig. Got fingers on 'im like one o' them concert pianists. Can fan you up before you e'en know 'e's there."

"And if I get him killed, Honoria will strip the hide off me." Not to mention that he already owed the lad an unrepayable debt.

"Don't let 'im spill any claret, then." Rip's gaze was merciless. "I can't leave these walls, not 'til Blade gets back. And you want the best." A faint tip of the head. "'E's the best. Devilish cocky 'bout it, but 'e's damned good."

Leo ground his teeth together.

"You think I'd send 'im if I thought 'e wouldn't come back? Blood don't mean much to most o' us 'ere, but you see this?" Rip flexed the inside of his wrist, revealing the tattoo there. "Lad's as much a part o' me family as 'e is yours."

More so. "Fine, I'll take him."

Wasn't as if they all wouldn't be among it when the war began anyway, but somehow, commanding troops on a battlefield was far easier when they weren't your flesh and blood.

"Need help, kitten?" Charlie called, leaning over the edge of the rooftop.

"'Ow 'bout you sod off?" Lark snarled, ignoring the hand the boy extended and scaling the wall as if she were part monkey. The girl had been Charlie's almost constant companion ever since he arrived at the rookery.

"Tsk, tsk. Such language." Charlie sounded almost precisely like he was mimicking Honoria. "From a lady too." He grinned and danced out of the way.

Lark flicked something from her wrist—the small steel whip she carried at her hip—its end lashing around Charlie's boot and sending him sprawling on the roof. He hit it with an *oof*.

"Where the hell did you get that?" Charlie asked.

"Needed somethin' to deal with impertinent gits who think they're a great deal cleverer 'n they are."

Charlie found his feet and winced. "It shocked me."

"Wouldn't know much about that," she replied. "I'm just a slum brat with—"

"If you two don't shut up," Leo ground out, dragging himself onto the roof, "I'm going to wring both your necks."

The pair fell silent. They'd been bickering since they left the wall, treating the whole thing like a romp in the park. If they hadn't been so bloody good at what they did, he'd have sent them back to Rip an hour ago.

He'd started this venture with the idea of protecting them, keeping them safely out of the way while he and Tin Man did the heavy work. Charlie had considered his plan carefully, waited all of two seconds, then sketched out an alternative idea that sounded utterly ruthless, insanely dangerous, and like something nobody in their right mind would come up with.

Before he knew it, Leo was swearing under his breath as he tried to keep up with the two of them. Charlie had snatched two of the handlers' control devices before anyone even knew they were there, and Lark led the diversion while Leo and Tin Man got Charlie the hell out of there.

Leo had to remind himself that they'd both lived, though he wasn't certain how long it was going to be before he changed that state of affairs. Pausing at the base of the wall, he picked up the grappling guns they'd hidden before they ventured out. Charlie aimed his grappling gun and triggered the hook, watching it soar into the sky. Lark barely had a chance to grab hers before Charlie slung an arm around her hips and triggered the recoil. "Allow me, milady."

With a feminine curse and a masculine laugh, the pair of them sailed up over the wall that circled Whitechapel.

"When did I get so bloody old?" Leo growled as Tin Man handled his grappling device.

The man was mute—someone had cut out his tongue years ago—but his eyes were eloquent enough. He clapped a hand on Leo's shoulder twice, a faint smile on his scarred lips as he vanished after them. As far as Leo was aware, the man was some kind of father or uncle to Lark.

Leo followed suit. The rush of air past his body as he jerked to the top of the wall was exhilarating.

"'Ave fun?" Rip unscrewed his flask and handed it to him.

Leo drained it. Served the bastard right. "They're completely insane. Think they're invulnerable, both of them trying to outdo each other like it was a *fucking* game. Snatch the handler. All the rage in the streets of the rookery."

Rip snorted. "Blade tells 'em they're gonna give 'im gray 'airs."

At least Leo wasn't alone in this. "We got two of them," he said gruffly, removing the control devices from the leather bag that was slung across his chest. "Where'd they go?"

"Out of reach, I'd imagine." Rip eyed the control device Leo handed him, turning it this way and that. "Think you know what to do with this?"

"Not a clue," Leo replied, examining the device in his own hands. "That's why I brought back two of them. Now, if you'd excuse me, I'd best go see if Honoria wants to tinker with me."

❧

Honoria bit her lip, staring at the mess of springs and cogs in the back of the opened device. "I'm not entirely certain I know what to do, Leo. This is more akin to Lena's work than mine."

He knew his younger sister had great skill with clockwork toys and transformationals—which were all the rage after she'd created one for the Scandinavian verwulfen ambassadors—but it was difficult to imagine

his pretty, fashion-plate sister manipulating the work-
ings of the control device. Besides… "She's not here.
All we have are you and me."

A shiver went through Honoria's body and she
paced, wincing a little as she chewed on her knuckle.
A little out of character, he thought, though perhaps
the state of the rookery's affairs concerned her more
than she'd let on.

"I understand how the device works and what
each piece is," he said, picking up a pair of thin
pliers. He poked at some wires, trying to make sense
of them. "They used Leyden jars to store the charge
before they managed to fine-tune it, but now… The
capacitor must be here somewhere. Here's the spark-
gap…high-voltage induction coil… All of it based
on Hertz's work, of course. This piece sends out the
signal, I believe, though I'm not quite certain how to
change it—or if it will even correlate with the matching chip in the metaljacket's head once I do." He
looked up. "Honoria?"

She blinked.

"Have you heard a word I've said?"

The restless shift of her knuckles in the small of
her back caught his attention. Leo frowned. "Are you
all right?"

"I'm…frightened." Honoria rubbed the small of
her back, her face paling. For the first time he looked
at her, truly looked. Saw the fine white lines around
her eyes and the darker shadows beneath them. Saw
too the way she kept knuckling her back.

"Blazes," he whispered. "You're having pains,
aren't you?"

Her throat worked as she swallowed. "It's been happening on and off for a few weeks. The midwife said it's quite normal, and that if I were to lie down, it would most likely subside. But…they've been growing stronger all night. I've been trying to hold it in, but what am I going to do?"

"I'll get Blade. I'll tell him—"

"No!" Honoria caught his wrist, bending forward and gasping a little, as though to ease some sort of internal pain. Her face screwed up in a grimace, and Leo winced under the sudden assault on his wrist.

It seemed to go on forever, and then she let out an expulsion of breath and started panting. "Don't…tell him. Not now. He cannot afford to be distracted. I *won't* distract him right now." Her expression firmed. "I can hold it. I can. I know I can."

"Blood and blazes." Leo scraped a hand over his mouth, nearly stabbing himself in the eye with the pliers. What the devil was he supposed to do? His mouth went dry. This was entirely outside his realm of understanding, but he could understand her desperation. Honoria would never admit it, but there was fear in her eyes—for her husband, for her baby, and for herself. "Esme," he said. "I'll fetch Esme."

"Don't leave me alone." Her fingers tightened pitifully.

Leo rubbed a hand over the small of her back and gently directed her to an armchair in the corner of her laboratory. "I'll only be gone a minute. I need to fetch Esme." Coherent thought began to form in his head. A plan. *God.* "Esme will know how to fetch the midwife. I don't see any reason why we need to tell

Blade right at this moment. It's entirely possible this is being brought about by the emotion of the moment and that the pains will subside as they usually do. Is this correct?"

That look of trust on her face… It killed him.

"I want you to stay here, and I'll return as soon as I've found her."

❦

It wasn't as simple as that, it seemed.

"They're firing the rookeries!" Lark called, darting into the room.

Leo helped lower his sister onto the edge of the bed. Honoria was biting her lip, though she'd not uttered a single sound since he returned.

"Where's the midwife?" he demanded. *Christ*, Honoria didn't need to hear that.

"I can't find 'er," Lark replied. "'Ouses are all abandoned. Everyone who can 'old a pitchfork's up on the walls. There's burnin' in other parts of the city too."

"Blade—" Honoria cried weakly as Esme rubbed her back. "Oh God—what if they burn the walls? What if—"

"They're not going to get through the walls," Leo replied, taking her hand in his and squeezing it. "Look at me. Blade knows what he's doing and what he'd be up against. They've been stockpiling weapons and supplies for months now—"

"What about Lena? And Will?" Honoria's eyes filled with tears. "Lena was supposed to be here for this. She said she'd *be here*."

He didn't dare give his little sister and her husband

too much thought. They'd be safe. They *had* to be. "No doubt Will is aware of what's occurring. He'll make his way here with Lena, or he'll take her somewhere safe." For such a small woman, Honoria had one hell of a grip. Leo ground his teeth, ignoring the pressure.

"If there are fires burning elsewhere in the city, then the mobs are rising. The Echelon won't be able to focus all of their attention here. It's all right, Honor. Blade's not going to get hurt." A ball of emotion tightened in his throat. "I *won't* let him get hurt. I promise I'll watch his back for you."

"You're going to join the fighting?" Esme asked.

"I'm not much use here." This was women's business, and Honoria needed to know her little family would be safe. He'd brought this all down upon them. This was his sister and his niece or nephew. The least he could do was make certain they and her husband survived the war.

No matter what he had to do. He turned to Lark. "Keep looking for the midwife. I'll ask the duchess if she's had any experience in this."

Blinking through tear-glazed eyes, Honoria whispered, "Don't let him get hurt."

"I won't." Leo kissed her cheek. "Now you make sure you look after yourself and this baby."

◦◦◦

The door banged open.

Mina stepped away from the window and the sight of the ruddy glow on the horizon as Barrons strode inside. A manacle dangled from her wrist, and part of the headboard was broken. His mouth tightened when he saw her standing free.

"Still here," she said, lifting her wrist and displaying her iron trappings. He'd chained her to the bed, of all things.

"I see I keep underestimating you," he replied, shooting a quick glance through the window.

Mina smoothed her skirts. She could feel the tension in him; he didn't give a damn about her freeing herself. Something had happened.

"What do you know of childbirth?" he asked.

"A little. I attended the queen two years ago when her son was born not breathing." Possibly the most horrific experience in her life. That poor baby that Alexa had wanted so very much, that *Mina* had wanted… "Why? Is it—" An image flashed to mind of the heavily pregnant young woman she'd caught a glimpse of when she first arrived. "Blade's wife's been put to bed, hasn't she?"

"My sister." Hesitation caught his next words, then he met her eyes. "They're searching for the midwife, but there's been no sign of her. Esme's asking some of the…women of ill repute outside if they've dealt with a birth, but it concerns me. I've seen the reports on hygiene and birth fatalities in the East End—"

"Barrons, are you asking me if I can attend your sister?"

There was something she thought she'd never see in his eyes. "Do you know what to do? Can you help her? If anything happened to her—" He swore then, raking a hand through his gilded hair as he glanced once more at the edges of Whitechapel. "I should never have come here. Honoria should have been resting these last few weeks, not dealing with this. If I hadn't—"

"From my very brief experience, birth is unpredictable at best. It might have happened regardless." At least all of the books and treatises she'd read in preparation for Alexa's birthing had claimed such. Still, she was a little shocked. After last night and everything that had happened the day before, she thought she'd be the last person he'd come to for help.

Did he trust her? The thought stilled her breath. She hadn't realized how much she'd wanted such a thing until it was lost.

They both stared at each other.

I'm sorry. Mina's chin tipped up. "Take me to her," she said softly. "I'll do my best to help, though that may be little enough indeed."

Some of the tension in the firm line of his shoulders softened. "Thank you."

Mina held up her wrist. "The key?"

Barrons dug it out of his pocket. His hands were gentle on her wrist as he unlocked it. The scent of smoke clung to his coat and Mina leaned into him a little, balancing on her toes as she breathed it in.

"If you run"—the words were silk over steel—"I will catch you. No matter how far or fast you run, I will always catch you."

"What if I don't want you to catch me?" she dared ask, rocking back on her heels.

Their eyes met. His were implacable. He tugged the manacles loose, a muscle working in his jaw as if he fought some strong emotion. "If you didn't want me to catch you…then you should have taken your chances with Morioch. It's far too late for that now, Duchess."

⤳

The moment she stepped inside the birthing chamber, the smell of it brought back all of the helplessness she'd felt when she'd held Alexa's hand through her traumatic delivery. It didn't matter what she'd said to Barrons. She couldn't do this.

"Your Grace." A dark-haired woman turned from the birthing stool, relief melting the tension from her face. "Have you any experience with difficult births?"

"Difficult?"

"The baby's turned," the woman replied. "It's not coming as it should. Or so Dolly says." She turned back to the blond whore kneeling between Honoria's thighs and feeling her distended stomach.

"What…what do you mean?" Honoria panted, struggling to sit up. "Esme, what's wrong? What's wrong with my baby?"

"I don't… It's the…" Esme lost her words.

A sharp rap at the door preceded its opening. A middle-aged woman wearing a scarf and a faded purple hat stepped inside briskly, a small medical bag at her side.

"Mrs. Parsons." Esme hurried to the newcomer and clasped her hand. "Oh, thank goodness they've managed to find you. We're having a devil of a time."

The midwife, Mina presumed. She edged toward the door. "It seems you've matters well in hand—"

Mrs. Parsons surveyed the room with a cool-eyed

glance. "Hot water," she demanded. "And I'll need some clean cloths and laudanum. Here, let me have a look at the situation."

With that, Mina found herself in charge of fetching the required items with Esme. Anything to leave the room.

When she returned, Mrs. Parsons had just finished her exam and was washing her hands. "The baby is in the breech position," she said quietly to the pair of them. "I've tried to turn it, but quite honestly, I've always felt Mrs. Rachinger is proportionately inadequate, which is why I originally sent her to the obstetrician. We had hoped that the child would not be overlarge but... I could be wrong, we shall see as the labor progresses—if it progresses—but..."

"Cephalopelvic disproportion?" Mina asked. It was quite common, especially among malnourished women or simply those of narrow proportion.

"So the obstetrician believes." There was no doubt on Mrs. Parsons's face, however.

"I have seen this once before," Mina said. "The queen's son was born not breathing because it was decided that she was more important than the child." That moment, when the baby had been delivered, Alexa had seen him and given a groggy cry. "*My little boy...*" she'd whispered in a voice that broke Mina's heart before they took him away. She'd screamed then and struggled. Mina had forced herself to pin the queen down so that the doctors could stop her bleeding.

"If the child were in the correct position I might attempt a forceps delivery. However, there's little option at this stage. The obstetrician must be sent for. The only way to save either child or mother is to deliver by cesarean," Mrs. Parsons said. "A choice must be made."

Esme's lips parted on a soft cry. "No," she whispered. "No. It will devastate her. Can we not save both?"

"It's a risky procedure, Mrs. Doolan," Mrs. Parsons replied bluntly.

"And there's no way to fetch the obstetrician now," Esme whispered. "He's located in Clerkenwell."

Mina gestured Mrs. Parsons to the side. "Have you attended any cesareans with an obstetrician?"

"Several. I help Dr. Phillips on occasion. He suffers from shaking palsy and sometimes his hands aren't as steady as he'd like."

"So you've performed a cesarean?"

"Twice. But you cannot possibly think I could perform such an operation! I know what I'm doing, but the risks are too high. She could suffer from internal bleeding or even hemorrhage to death, and I'm not a surgeon."

Time to take a gamble. "What if you could perform the operation? You would know where to make the incisions, if nothing else. And what if I could guarantee that I could stop any bleeding?"

"How?"

"My craving virus levels are moderate," Mina continued. "But a blue blood's blood can heal almost any wound."

"Infecting her with the craving in the process."

"Yes, but Honoria will live and so will the baby. Blade's a blue blood—I have little doubt he'd rather see his wife live, no matter the change—"

"She won't catch the virus." Esme suddenly spoke up, interrupting them. Honoria was gasping through another contraction and Dolly knelt at her feet by the birthing stool, rubbing her hand. "She's been vaccinated against the craving."

Of course. One of those vaccinations Barrons had been particularly keen on championing. There was little doubt he'd have seen his family inoculated.

Honoria broke off, panting. "Might not...stop the bleeding," she whispered. "I'm not entirely... certain what the vaccination would do...if your blood mingled with mine. If it affects the healing..."

Though they'd been speaking quietly, evidently the room had heard the plan. Four sets of eyes stared at her.

"Then we test it," Mina said grimly. "Does anyone have a scalpel or a blade?"

&

"They're fallin' back!" Blade bellowed.

Dozens of men lifted their arms and roared, the sound spreading along the entire wall. Leo scraped a hand over his face, trying to remove some of the soot and grime.

So far Morioch's attempts to breach the rookery had been driven back. "He's not throwing everything he's got at you yet," Leo murmured, examining the orderly ranks of automatons.

Blade's smile never slipped as he waved his fist along with the men. "I know." Their eyes met and Blade lowered his arm. "Testin' us for weaknesses."

"He'll find them." He himself had, upon inspection

of the wall. Built from whatever people could get their hands on over fifty years ago, the wall had certain places he'd hit if he were trying to destroy it.

"As to that, I've got plans." Blade pointed at the fires burning in other parts of the city. "They can't afford to send all their forces at us. That'll 'old 'em a bit, enough mebbe to finish Morioch off."

Leo considered the golden blazes highlighting the night. Three of them, by the look of it. "Or they'll send the Trojan cavalry out in force and crush the mobs there, then hit you with the spitfires. They don't need me alive, just dead. All they've got to do is burn us to the ground."

"Aye." Blade's gaze darkened. "But they need *me* alive, to execute me in public so they can prove I'm dead, once and for all."

Killing a legend. "Perhaps." Leo eyed the fires again, noting where they were. "No sign of Will yet?"

Blade sobered. He looked at the fires too, particularly the one to the west, near the verwulfen ambassador's house. "'E'll get 'ere when 'e can, and all them verwulfen 'e's got."

Neither of them voiced the other option—that the prince consort's forces would have hit there hard, knowing that Will was likely to come to Blade's aid with dozens of the newly freed verwulfen. A single verwulfen in a berserker rage could cut through half an army by itself.

The image of Lena's face flashed into Leo's mind. His laughing sister; that was the way he'd always thought of her: the girl who smiled, even when she had nothing to smile about, because she lived to see others happy. She kept her pain private so as not to alarm anyone. Something he understood all too clearly, despite different methods. His own pain was hidden through indifference.

It ached inside him now. This was why they'd been so long in planning their offensive. People would die and neither he, Blade, Lynch, nor Garrett wanted to see familiar faces among the dead. If Lena was out there, she'd be by Will's side, both the safest and most dangerous place to be at the moment.

She'd be safe. Will would die before he let anything happen to her. But the words didn't sound as confident in Leo's own head. War was brutal and violent and unforgiving. People died. People who shouldn't have or people who should—there was little distinction.

"Blade!" A voice cut through the laughter and bellowing of the men on the wall.

Lark scrambled up beside them like a cat, her face pale. Blade's spine straightened, his body locking tight. "'Onoria?"

"She's lyin' in." Lark sounded nervous. "The duchess said you ought to come."

"But it ain't 'er time yet," Blade blurted, panic tightening his features. He turned to Leo. "She were right, weren't she? When you saw 'er last?"

Leo tried to think of something to say and Blade saw it. "Honor didn't want to distract you," he said.

"Bloody 'ell."

Lark looked very small all of a sudden. "They won't let me in, but I don't... I don't think it's goin' real well. I could 'ear 'er screamin'."

If Blade had been pale before, it was as nothing

compared to now. Leo caught his arm, holding him up. "Steady."

"I *can't* go," Blade whispered, looking around. "I've got to 'old the wall. If they overrun us, they'll burn us and she won't 'ave a chance to escape."

Leo tipped his chin up, catching Rip's attention. Firelight leered over the man's brutal face as he clapped someone on the back, then strolled closer with a nonchalant step. Despite that, tension tightened the fine lines around his eyes.

"Go and see to her," Leo said. "Rip and I will hold the wall. Nothing's going to happen anytime soon. Not yet. Morioch's still playing cat-and-mouse."

Blade clasped his arm, giving it a squeeze, the relief on his face palpable. "Thank you."

Fifteen

PACING OUTSIDE THE DOOR, MINA FELT EVERY HAIR ON her body lift. She was no longer alone.

The Devil of Whitechapel appeared at the top of the staircase, his face pale and his eyes as black as Hades. There was no sign of the man she'd seen earlier; this was a predator, tight with tension and the need to kill. Prepared to defend every inch of the place he called his own.

A muffled sound of pain echoed from inside the bedroom. Blade's attention shifted, and for a moment, his face contorted. Not a blue blood, not a predator now, just a man listening to his wife cry out and completely helpless because of it.

"Lark said the baby's coming," he said, his words strangely lacking any hint of his usual accent.

Mina took a deep breath as he strode closer. "It's not going well. The child's in a breech position, and the midwife seems to feel that Honoria is too narrow through the hips to give birth successfully. However, if we don't get the baby out soon…"

Those black eyes stared at her, then he scraped a

trembling hand over his mouth. "No. No, this can't be happening."

Mina reached out and touched his arm. He tensed. "There is a chance we could perform a cesarean on her. Mrs. Parsons has performed such operations before and—"

"Cut it out of her? What about Honoria? What about—"

"We'll use my blood to heal her wound. It will significantly lower the risk of scarring and infection, and I've already tested her to see if her vaccination will interfere with the craving virus's ability to heal. It doesn't."

He looked lost. "Is there no other way?"

"None of us are obstetricians and we cannot wait to find one. I feel we must take this chance or lose it forever."

Blade rubbed his mouth again, his gaze staring at something she couldn't see. "And you want my approval?"

"Your approval," Mina said, "and your help. Your wife is very frightened right now. With her scientific background, she knows too well the risk of this pregnancy. I know it's hardly the done thing for a man to attend his wife, but if you could be there…to hold her hand, to talk to her and calm her fears—"

"I'll do it."

Thank goodness. She didn't fully understand the relationship between Honoria and her husband, but he seemed to care very strongly for her, enough to overcome a man's instinctive fear of the birthing room.

"Let's do this then," Blade said. "Before I lose me nerve."

"Wait." She caught his arm. "How is the battle faring?"

A dangerous look from those green eyes. "You ain't about to be rescued, princess. Barrons and Rip are 'oldin' the wall. Morioch's only playin' with us for now."

The familiar sound of his accent let her breathe a little easier. There was something entirely too intense about him when his inner demon held sway. A sense of...danger.

"Barrons," she murmured, her mind flashing to the hints of fire she'd seen in the distance and the sounds of shouting. He'd be right at the forefront of the fighting, no doubt. For a moment, she felt ill.

"Well, I'll be damned..." he murmured. "Barrons?"

A hint of heat surfaced in her cheeks. Mina straightened. "I don't know what you're speaking about. Come. And make sure you wash your hands. You practically reek of blood and smoke."

❧

"'Ere they come again," Rip murmured.

"How many waves of this can the walls take?" Leo asked. Morioch hadn't sent the spitfires in yet; no doubt the fear of uncontained fires stayed his hand. He'd see if he could bring them down with just the metaljackets.

Rip shrugged. "This wall were only ever a symbol. Not built as a means to stop an army."

Not many then, by the sound of it. "We need to bring

the battle down into the streets. Stop them before they hit us too hard."

"They'll grind us up against our own wall," Rip pointed out.

"Not if we're coming at them from both sides."

The pair of them shared a look. Firelight flickered off the giant's green eyes, a considering expression on his face. "We go through Undertown. Come at 'em from behind before they even know we're there."

"You need to stay here, to be a figurehead for the men and lead this force." A deep breath. "Who do you suggest should lead the other force?"

Rip stared at him. "You know who I'm goin' to suggest."

Christ. "They won't follow me. They're Blade's men. Not mine."

"None o' the lads know warfare," Rip countered. "They know these streets, 'ow to ambush a gent, 'ow to fight, 'ow to kill... But you know tactics. You know 'ow Morioch thinks, 'ow the metaljackets work... All you need's a few o' the lads to direct the men and make it clear we're workin' for you."

A certain kind of bleakness settled over him. He was used to command, to control. Why then did he feel so bloody uncertain?

You wouldn't have hesitated three days ago.

Leo crushed his eyes shut. Where was the "old Leo" with his confidence and his air of command? Would he ever be that man again?

"I'll do it." He'd made his sister and Blade too many promises—and this was what he was trained for. With a breathless laugh, he offered a silent prayer of thanks to Caine for teaching him the art of war.

"Good. You'll need men. Tin Man, Dalloway, Higgins, and Charlie to help direct you." Rip held up a hand. "No arguin'. This is my command, my choices. I'll select the rest to go with you." A slow, fierce smile slid over the man's hard mouth. "Time to make metal bleed."

❧

The room stank of chloroform.

Honoria's head sagged back and forth, vaguely aware, as Esme held the cloth over her mouth and nose. Blade sat at her side, his fingers clenched in hers and that dark-eyed stare locked on her abdomen.

When Mina had suggested such an operation—knowing the procedure theoretically but not practically—she'd never imagined there would be so many layers of flesh to cut through. Mrs. Parsons worked with swift efficiency, using both scalpel and scissors from her kit and a pair of clamps. Using Lister's suggestions for antiseptic on the area and then on her hands, Mrs. Parsons had set to work.

Mina only managed to watch for a minute or two, then looked away, swallowing hard. Honoria made a small moan in her throat, her eyelashes fluttering against her cheeks.

"It's all right, luv," Blade murmured in her ear. "I'm 'ere. I've got you."

"Baby?" she murmured vaguely.

"The baby's fine." Blade looked away from her

imploring gaze, patting her hand. "Nothin's gonna 'appen to either of you."

Honoria's head lolled, her consciousness dipping again.

"What are your CV levels coming in at?" Mina asked Blade, to distract them all.

"'Bout forty-eight percent."

Higher than her own. The higher the virus percentage in the blood, the stronger its healing capabilities would be. "Perhaps we should use your blood to heal her. Mine are thirty-six percent."

"If this works," Esme said, "imagine the possibilities. The area of obstetrics would significantly improve if we could guarantee swift healing rates and lack of infection."

Infection was often the cause of maternal mortality, and judging from her softened frame, Esme had her own stake in this.

"They would need to be vaccinated first."

"Ladies, please attend, if you would," Mrs. Parsons said. "Your Grace, would you hand me the clamps?"

It helped if she tried not to think of what she was seeing as a human body. Walling herself off from the procedure, Mina simply moved as Mrs. Parsons directed, holding various metal instruments and squishy body parts out of the way as Parsons continued her swift incisions. Finally a pair of feet appeared, straining inside a thin gelatinous sack. It was the most amazing and disgusting thing Mina had ever seen.

"Oh," she said.

The wet sucking sound as the baby emerged was not at all what she'd expected. Mina held up the soft linens as a small, weakly struggling, slimy baby was deposited into her arms. Mrs. Parsons cleared the sack off its face and shoved a finger inside its throat to clear the airway. Its mouth opened in a silent squawk, and then suddenly, as if something had been cut, sound erupted. A hearty cry that made Mina jump.

"It's a girl!" Mrs. Parsons cried, relief leaving her red and perspiring.

"A girl?" Blade said in a shaky voice. "I've a daughter?"

Mina swiftly wrapped the child up, holding her awkwardly. "Here. Look at her."

Another feeble squall split the air. The baby had a wealth of dark hair plastered to her scalp, and her reddened face was all wrinkled up. Blade stared at her as if Mina had just offered to show him the moon.

"Just look at 'er," he whispered, reaching out to touch the tiny shaking fist that was poking out of the blankets. "'Onor, look, luv. She's so beautiful. Just like you."

"I think perhaps we'd best wait to show her until after we've stitched her back together," Mina suggested. "Esme?"

Esme surrendered the chloroform-soaked cloth to Dolly and gently took the baby from Mina's arms. "Hello there, beautiful. Let me take her and clean her up."

"Give me your wrist," Mina said, taking Blade's hand.

Making a neat little slash in Blade's wrist, Mina used one of Honoria's syringes to pour his blood into the wound that Mrs. Parsons was hastily clamping together. It was a matter of minutes before the first thin layer of membrane began to almost visibly heal itself and Mina let out her breath.

"It's working," she said excitedly.

Blade looked up sharply. "You weren't certain?"

"There's always an element of risk." Blade was a hard man to look in the eyes at such a moment.

Within half an hour Mrs. Parsons was placing silk sutures into the outer abdominal cut. The area around the incision was red and swollen, but so far the hastily mended edges of the wound seemed to be knitting together. Taking the cloth away from Honoria's face, Mina prepared a mixture of laudanum, should Honoria need it when she came to.

Before long, her eyelashes started groggily fluttering against her cheeks. Sweat plastered her hair to her scalp and Blade gently brushed it off her forehead. As she and Mrs. Parsons cleaned up, Mina couldn't help stealing glances at them.

The Devil of Whitechapel in his fiercest moment. She smothered a smile and went to answer the rap at the door. Esme beamed at her as she returned with the baby, newly cleaned and somewhat prettier to look at for it.

"How is she?" Esme asked.

"She's taken some laudanum, but the wound appears to be healing well." Amazingly well. There was almost no sign of an incision.

"What are we going to call her?" Esme said, crossing the room to the bedside.

"Emmaline," Honoria whispered, reaching out to touch the baby's head with a shaking hand. "Oh, she's so tiny."

"Emmaline Grace," Blade repeated as Esme settled the baby in his arms and he held her down for Honoria to peek at.

Both Mina and Esme shared a glance as Blade swallowed the lump in his throat. Mina had never felt a stronger sense of satisfaction, though a little part of her remained aware that of this group, she was the one standing on the outside, looking in.

Sixteen

"PULL BACK!" LEO BELLOWED, WAVING HIS ARM AT THE line of men behind him. A bull of a man that Rip had introduced as Dalloway cupped his hands around his mouth and trumpeted the same words, making nearby men wince.

Leo looked up at the roofline and flicked two signals that Rip had taught him. Dozens of lads appeared in the smoky shadows, brandishing nets. Made of tightly woven metal strands, they were heavy, requiring two men to drag them, but as they arced up into the air and dropped over the horde of metaljackets pressing him and his sortie of men, their use became swiftly apparent.

Metaljackets went down, entangled in the mesh.

The rest of the rookery gang moved in with brutal efficiency, wielding the short, heavy metal clubs the rookery lads seemed to favor. Leo instructed them to aim for the back of the metaljackets' helms, where the control chip was located, and the knees, to shatter the joints. Anything to keep them out of action.

"Spitfire!" Higgins roared, darting out of a nearby

alley. Fire bloomed, spewing forth from the alley and catching his sleeve. Higgins screamed, dropping to the ground as the greenish flames licked up over his skin and clothes, igniting like a match set to dry tinder.

Nothing to do for him, not now, but Leo clenched his teeth and beckoned his men out of the way. A glance at Charlie confirmed the boy was ready. Leo scrambled up onto the roof behind him, trying to keep up. As blue bloods, the pair of them could move faster than any human—and could heal from things no man here could.

No point going after the spitfire. The rookery men scattered, using diversionary tactics as the huge automaton clanked out of the alley, its flamethrower cannon lifted in front of it. Instead, Leo spied the trio of metaljackets carefully guarding a handler. The man worked his control device, twisting dials and flipping a couple of switches to make the metal automaton turn and clank after Leo's lads.

Charlie sailed across the gap of the alley, landing on the rooftop opposite them and crouching low. The handler never looked up.

It was done swiftly. Charlie sent a metaljacket staggering into the others, and Leo used the opportunity to grab the handler and slide his knife up between the man's ribs. The handler gurgled and quivered in Leo's arms, his weight slumping. Leo held him for a second longer, then let him drop, slipping the device from his lax fingers.

Charlie kicked the back of one of the metaljackets' knees out from under it.

"Don't destroy them," Leo snapped. He twisted a dial and looked at the metaljackets expectantly.

One of them swung an arm directly at his head and he ducked to the side.

"Give me that," Charlie said, tugging the device from Leo's hands. He darted back out of the way and started fiddling with the controls. After several seconds—and helpless jerking moves—one of the metaljackets strode toward the wall and punched it, brick dust coughing into the alley. It drew back, repeating the gesture again and again.

"This row controls this drone," Charlie said, turning his attention to the second row. The metaljacket behind Leo lurched forward, and he had to step aside. "Sorry," Charlie muttered. He corrected a dial. The metaljacket straightened up and turned to attention, both of them falling in together.

"Now for the main one." Charlie's eyes gleamed as he turned his attention to the spitfire.

He only burned one building before he managed to figure out which button *not* to press.

Charlie swung up onto the spitfire's shoulders, his legs dangling down over its chest and his elbows resting on its helm as he wielded the control device. "Lark is not going to believe this." He grinned. "Tally-ho!" One flick of his fingers and the spitfire lurched forward, Charlie riding him into battle with the pair of metaljackets clanking along behind him.

"Don't let him get hurt," Leo snapped at a pair of men, who turned and trotted after the boy.

Seventeen

NOBODY WAS WATCHING HER THIS TIME.

Mina asked for a change of clothing to clean up, and Esme found an older shirt, short coat, and trousers that belonged to Charlie.

"I'm so terribly sorry," Esme said. "You're much taller than Honoria or me. I'm afraid there's little else to be had at the moment. However, I could send—"

"They're perfect," Mina interrupted, barely able to contain her glee. Washing up by herself, she swiftly dressed and cracked open the door. Nobody lurked nearby.

Moving quickly, she saw Blade's coat and holster slung carelessly over the back of a chair in the washroom from when he'd cleaned up, and stole them and his knife. The pair of pistols were larger than she was used to, the rounds built to contain a mix of chemical that would explode on impact. Not the sort of weapon used indiscriminately, these were designed to kill. A firebolt could take half a man's torso apart.

Perfect.

It was a tense minute as she made her way back

down to the kitchens and checked for Esme. No sign of her, but voices broke out upstairs and she recognized Blade's distinctive cockney. If he found his coat and pistols missing…

Time to move.

Slipping through the door, she nodded to a pair of prostitutes who were organizing bandages. Esme's voice rang out across the courtyard as she directed a lad to help split firewood. Tugging her cap down over her eyes—and distinctive hair—Mina turned the other way.

Fighting could be heard in the east, where Morioch directed his forces. Mina turned deeper into the rookery instead. She'd have to take the long way and then circle back around toward the Ivory Tower once she was free of Whitechapel.

Her nerves were buzzing. Being so far from the City left her feeling slightly powerless. Anything could have happened to Alexa in the meantime. That moment when the queen had blankly agreed to Barrons's execution—that wasn't the Alexandra she knew.

Mina needed to get back, to find out what was wrong with her friend and protect her if need be. If the queen gave up when they were so close…

She couldn't allow that to happen.

Even if she left Barrons behind to face the consequences himself?

"Focus," she whispered to herself, ducking between barrels and into the shadows. Barrons had no meaning in this. The queen was her concern. Not a man she was only just coming to understand, to know.

And what if Blade and Barrons were the allies she

and the queen had been so desperately searching for? What if this was the moment in which fate shifted, if she dared throw her cause in with them?

Blood and damnation. She couldn't afford to falter. They'd made no mention of who they wanted to see in power once this attempt was made—and if it succeeded. And every moment she hesitated was one in which the queen might succumb to her ever-growing despair.

Her decision was made. Alexandra needed her.

Pausing in an alley, Mina peered around the corner. Laundry lines were strung between houses but bare of washing. An almost eerie silence echoed in this section of the rookery, darkness sitting heavily in the streets. Empty of life and laughter and the whisper of human heartbeats. Blade had no doubt commanded every able body for the wall.

She could see it in the distance. This section was only lightly manned, with most of Blade's forces directed toward the threat of Morioch. Hardly difficult to slip up and over without being seen, if one was a blue blood.

A little prickle of unease swept over her skin and she paused.

Nothing moved. No harsh breath or whispered words, but she couldn't fight the sensation that somebody was nearby.

Metal rasped on the cobbled streets. A steady *click-click-click* noise. What the devil was that?

Sneaking a glance, she saw a tiny shadow bobbing its way out into the streets. It marched with deliberate movements, its metal arms swinging at its sides and its feet making the tinny noise she could hear. A clock-work soldier? A toy?

The wind blew her way, carrying with it the scent of smoke...and something else. Something she was quite familiar with, thanks to her work with the humanists.

TNT.

Highly explosive.

Her gaze narrowed on that marching clockwork. Its body was full and round, large enough to carry a charge sufficient to destroy a house.

Bloody hell. Morioch was in charge of provisional warfare; he always had been. While she and the rest of the councilors had directed their attentions elsewhere—to building the city and trade contacts—Morioch had been directly involved in working with the spitfires and metaljacket legions.

And why else would he be sitting outside the rookery, throwing a few metaljackets at the walls here and there, almost as if testing its defenses? Morioch wasn't a cautious man by nature—a planner, certainly—but when it came to an attack, he was deliberate and effective. A shark with a contingency for everything.

He wasn't wary of Blade. He was simply waiting for another type of assault to succeed, one that would destroy the very heart of the rookery.

The little clockwork soldier ticked on, heading straight for the Warren. The metaljackets were directed by radio frequency, their handlers forced to remain within two hundred feet of their assigned automatons at all times. If the clockwork soldier worked on the same principles, then the handler had to be somewhere near.

She couldn't risk touching the clockwork in case it exploded, but the handler… Oh yes. The handler was a different matter entirely.

❧

"That was easier than expected," Leo said, staring at the shattered formation below as he wiped blood from his forehead. A stray bullet had clipped him as he climbed the wall.

Rip clapped hands with him, jerking him into a rough embrace. "Good work. Like puttin' 'em in a mincer." His hard green gaze raked the streets. "Though I wonder why he'd keep most of 'is forces back."

"Because 'e's plannin' summat." Blade's voice came directly out of the darkness behind them.

Both men turned. Blade pushed away from the top of the ladder, wearing lightly plated body armor and an expression that warned others to tread lightly.

"How is she?" Leo demanded, his heart in his throat. "And the baby?"

Blade gave him a tight little smile. "I've a daughter. Emmaline Grace Rachinger."

Rip laughed and clasped Blade's hand, drawing him in for a meaty slap against the back. "Bloody 'ell. Wait 'til the lads get word o' that. They'll be linin' up from 'ere to the city when she's sixteen…"

"Anyone touches 'er and he's a dead man." Blade saw the expression on Leo's face and the smile slipped off his own. "She's fine. They 'ad to cut the baby out o' 'er." A faint expression of respect crossed his face. "Your duchess's idea, actually. Then 'ealed 'er up with me blood. Mrs. Parsons thinks she'll be right as rain. She ain't never seen a wound 'eal like that before."

Your duchess… Leo ignored it but the thought sent a shiver beneath his skin. Some part of him liked those words. The darker, predatory part of him. It didn't make sense, but for a moment he felt somewhat less adrift. "Congratulations. You're a father."

"Aye, and no time to enjoy it. Now"—his expression hardened—"the stakes just got 'igher. Morioch's grandfather were the Butcher o' Culloden, weren't 'e?"

Leo nodded. Culloden was something he preferred not to think of, a time when the English blue bloods had risen against the Scottish verwulfen clans and crushed them, turning those verwulfen left alive over to slavery or throwing them into the Manchester Pits to fight to the death for the crowds. Though he personally considered it a dark time in blue-blood history, others still whispered that perhaps they shouldn't have left *any* verwulfen alive. Not everyone was pleased with the new laws regarding the verwulfens' newly legal status, Morioch chief among them.

"And the duke were never shy about cuttin' a throat." Blade leaned on the wall. "Rip, I want you to lead a team down into the tunnels of Undertown. It's the only other way into the rookery, barrin' the wall."

"And me?" Leo asked.

"I want you back at the Warren to relieve Tin Man. Keep an eye on things there for me."

Guard duty. A part of him bristled—as a blue blood he was worth more here, and at least the fighting took his mind off matters—but Blade rarely did anything without a reason. "You think he'll attack the Warren?"

"It's what I'd do." Their eyes met and Blade's went black with hunger for a moment, a reminder that the man before him could be utterly ruthless when he wanted to be.

"You wouldn't kill women and children."

"No, but ain't nobody else knows that. I'd capture 'em and 'old 'em for ransom. I don't think Morioch's got it in 'im to be quite as benevolent."

The words were stark. Blade stared down at the amassed forces below with a cold, almost calculating gleam in his eyes. For years he'd been the Devil of Whitechapel, a man whose name was whispered into small ears by nannies all through the city's mansions, warning aristocratic children to behave or else the Devil would come and steal them away.

Honoria's presence in his life had softened some of those edges, humanized him in a way Leo would never have expected; yet the merest hint of a threat to his wife and daughter brought out everything in Blade that was dangerous. He would kill to defend his own, and he would be utterly ruthless in doing it if need be. Morioch might eventually be able to take the rookery, but he would do it through a hail of raining fire.

"I want you to get 'em out," Blade said quietly. "If things go wrong 'ere for me. Get 'em out through Undertown and try to find Will."

"It won't come to that—"

Blade cut him off with a harsh glare. "You ever get

one o' those feelin's? Where you don't think it's gonna
end well for you? I got it now. The prince consort
can't afford to let me live. It's either 'im or me this
time. 'E won't stop 'til it's done, no matter 'ow many
lives 'e needs to throw away, and I need to know that
my wife and my daughter are in safe 'ands. You're the
only man I'd trust with this, because they belong to
you too. Do this for me. Promise me."

They belong to you too... "You're not going to die,
you stubborn bastard. You are *not* going to leave me
to tell my sister that she's a widow."

"Aye." Blade looked out over the wall once more.
"Just keep an eye on 'em at the Warren. You see red
smoke, and you get 'em out and don't come back." A
long hesitation. "No matter what she begs you to do."

"She'll hate me for leaving you behind."

"She'll live." Blade looked at him. "That's all I
need to know."

⤬

The artillery started up almost five minutes after he'd
left the wall. Leo gritted his teeth together, striding
away from the white flashes illuminating the night
behind him. A stronger offensive this time.

Blade didn't think he could hold the wall. What
the hell was Leo going to do? This lay on his shoulders. *Think, damn it.* The control devices. If he could
manipulate the frequency somehow... That had to be
the way out of this.

Sound exploded as Blade and his men fired back.
Someone in Morioch's forces had a revolving gun,
based on the design of the Hotchkiss revolving

cannon—able to fire almost sixty-eight rounds per minute. The sharp hammer-strike *rat-a-tat* of the gun cut through the stillness of the rookery. Then Blade was shouting and Leo could almost hear the return fire focus on that area. It fell silent a minute later.

A stronger strike, but not as hard as Morioch should have sent in. If that were him... His strides slowed as the Warren came into sight. If that were him he'd have leveled the walls already, what with the artillery and legions Morioch had under his command, or he'd be damned close to it.

Blade was correct. Morioch was waiting for something.

But what?

It lifted the hairs along his spine. With Rip leading men down into Undertown, Morioch couldn't come at them from that direction.

Esme had marshaled the women at the Warren with military efficiency. Leo nodded to Tin Man, the guard, as he passed him and prowled through the yard. A dozen strategies worked through his head. Obviously the prince consort's intelligence on the rookery was better than they'd been led to believe.

How would *he* do it?

Take Honoria and you had the key to destroying the Devil of Whitechapel. If the prince consort knew about Leo's relationship with her, then he certainly knew how much Blade doted on her. Anyone in the rookery could tell you that.

Leo's blood ran cold, a wash of unfamiliar feeling.

Taking the steps two at a time, he ghosted through the almost-silent Warren to his sister's room. Voices murmured within and Leo didn't bother knocking. He jerked the door open, startling both a bed-bound Honoria and a slim woman he presumed was Mrs. Parsons. The sensation died a little, though his gaze raked the room, taking in the shuttered windows and the small fire warming the hearth. Nobody here. Perhaps he was mistaken. Perhaps Morioch would be too arrogant to risk such a move.

"Sir!" the midwife protested. "What are you doing in here?"

"It's all right, Ann," Honoria murmured, looking up from the small weight cradled on the pillows beside her. Dark shadows circled her eyes and she looked pale with exhaustion, her voice whisper-soft, but the smile that softened her face was radiant. "Look, Leo. You're an uncle."

An uncle.

Until that moment, the baby had been an abstract thing, an idea that he couldn't quite seem to comprehend.

Ignoring Mrs. Parsons's clear disapproval, Leo crossed toward the bed. Honoria twitched aside the blanket with a wince, revealing a tiny little button nose that was set over rosebud-shaped lips. Emmaline had hair as dark as a raven. Leo's breath caught, despite the sense of urgency he felt, and he leaned on the bed and held out a trembling finger to stroke the baby's cheek. So soft. "Oh, Honor, she's beautiful. She looks just like you, thank goodness."

Honoria's smile lost none of its warmth. "She's so little. I'm afraid to pick her up."

"You shouldn't anyway, not in your condition,"

Mrs. Parsons admonished. "You're not to move for weeks yet."

Weeks… That buzzing sensation lit beneath his skin, demanding that he scratch it.

"Emma," he murmured. With her tiny eyelashes shut tight over her eyes, the baby yawned.

"Would you care to hold her?" Honoria asked.

"Mrs. Rachinger," Mrs. Parsons murmured in disapproval. "It's hardly the done thing… He shouldn't even be in here. The birthing chambers are no place for a man."

"He's my brother," Honoria shot back. She tried to shift and then gasped.

"Easy," he warned, "don't tax yourself." As she settled, he couldn't help noticing the ring of perspiration at her temples. She wasn't going to be able to move anytime soon, no matter what Blade had said. He'd never been so fucking uncertain in his life. This was not the way he'd been raised. The Duke of Caine had seen fit to carve him into a weapon, to be ruthless if need be, but none of his childhood lessons had ever covered what to do when other people were involved. People that he cared about.

How the hell was he going to get her out of here if something went wrong? And the baby? His gaze drifted to that downy head again.

"Here," Mrs. Parsons said with a huff of indignation. "I told you not to move."

The midwife eased the bundle into his hands, and Leo felt a ring of cold around the back of his neck as he found himself completely in charge of his niece. More blankets than baby at this stage.

"How do I hold her?" He gingerly tried to cup his hand beneath her head. Emmaline's little lip trembled, and her entire face screwed up as if she were going to cry. His stomach dropped. "I don't think I'm—"

"Like this," Mrs. Parsons said and repositioned the baby in his arms.

Beneath the blankets he could just make out the shape and weight of her, all tiny broomstick arms and legs, and a wobbling head. She smelled like Esme's lavender soap.

Emma yawned again, a task that looked like it exhausted her. Blinking sleepily she rested against his chest, her dark eyelashes lowering against her pink cheeks. Her tiny fingers curled around one of his, and in that moment, he fell completely and irrevocably in love with her.

A breathless, painful moment.

If something went wrong, he would get her out. Both her and Honoria, no matter what he had to do. *I promise*, he thought, feeling those fingers circle his. Pride and arrogance gave way to crystal clarity. He was useless here, waiting for word from the wall, but Blade was correct. He would kill half the Echelon to keep his niece and sister safe, even if he died himself in the process.

"She has her father's sense of timing," he murmured, forcing the thoughts aside.

"As long as she doesn't inherit his taste in fashion, we should be all right," his sister replied.

They shared a smile, and he wondered, for the first time, what it would be like to hold his own daughter in his arms. To guess at her future, what she would be like...

He'd never been so enamored of a woman that he'd ever considered marrying one or fathering children with her. Only...the duchess, and he wasn't quite certain what his interest in her signified, or if he could trust her. The thought washed the smile from his lips. Speaking of... She was rather significantly absent at the moment.

"The duchess?" he asked.

"One moment we're speaking of babies, and the next you're asking about the duchess. My, my," Honoria teased wearily. "I wonder what I should read into that?"

"We're in the middle of a war, Honor. And I'm not entirely certain I trust her—"

Emmaline made a sound in her sleep and he froze, looking helplessly at Mrs. Parsons. She slid her arms beneath his niece and returned her to Honoria's side on the bed.

"The duchess went with Mrs. Doolan," Mrs. Parsons announced. "And I think it quite enough time to have had your visit, sir. Your sister needs her rest."

"With Esme?" There'd been no sign of the duchess in the courtyard.

"Have you heard from Lena?" Honoria asked sleepily.

A quick glance at Mrs. Parsons. Even he knew better than to upset Honoria in this condition. "No. Not yet." He didn't mention the fires burning in that section of the city, nor his certainty that Will wouldn't rest at home if he knew his former master was being attacked by the prince consort. "I'm certain they'll be along as soon as they can."

"Perhaps they shouldn't come."

"Will won't let anything happen to her." Mrs. Parsons had presented Leo with the perfect opportunity to take his leave—and he was growing increasingly curious about the duchess's whereabouts. *If I were her and the opportunity presented itself, I'd run.*

"Time for you to rest, Honor. I'll check in on you from time to time."

She caught his fingers. "Let me know if anything happens, or if Lena arrives. I feel so helpless lying here."

That, he certainly understood. Leo squeezed her fingers. Honoria had never been the type of woman to wring her hands and wait at home for the menfolk to arrive. She was the first to push up her sleeves and take control of a situation. "I'll send word immediately. You should take some inspiration from your daughter and get some sleep."

Instantly her attention turned to the new object of her fascination. Leo excused himself and eased the door shut on the room.

One glimpse out the window at the end of the hallway showed the bustle of women in the courtyard below. There was, however, no sign of a certain devious duchess.

His heart skipped a beat. The yard was a sort of organized chaos. The perfect opportunity to escape, if one had a mind to. He jerked open the door to her room and found only a weighted silence. For a second, he gave in to the fierce urge inside him, tossing the bedding aside and raking it over. She'd taken nothing from here. Devil take her. The thought didn't still the fierce anger pumping hard through the veins in his temples. Where the hell was she? Leo took a shuddering breath to cool his temper.

In the distance, the sharp crack of rifle fire kept Blade and the rest of his men pinned down at the wall. If she were out in that, she'd be a fool.

The duchess was no fool. He closed the last door quietly, thinking hard. He could search the Warren from top to bottom, but it was pointless. He knew, in the cold burning pit in his chest, that she was gone. Knew too that she was far too rational to try and escape via Morioch. They'd never been allies. No, she'd go elsewhere. Find a quiet, out-of-the-way place to slip back into the safety of the city.

And for a moment he thought about letting her go. This irrational fascination of his was beginning to be noticed, if Honoria's words were any measure. He should let Mina go and deal with his own problems, his own family. What might have become a cat-and-mouse game between them over the years was no longer a game he could play. Not with the rookery under siege and his family under threat. He had other concerns…

No. The world instantly turned to shadows as the hunger within him surged to the fore with brutal force. Leo swallowed hard, grinding his teeth until color flooded back into the world. *Stop telling yourself lies…*

There was no way he could let her go.

Eighteen

BELLS TOLLED IN THE DISTANCE, RINGING OUT THE midnight peal. As if on cue, a sudden belching cough of flame roared in the distance, followed by screams and brutish yelling.

Morioch was making a full-scale attack on the wall.

Just in time to divert attention away from the interior of the Warren. Mina crouched low in an alley. The farther one went from the heart of the rookeries, the dirtier and more cramped and crowded the streets grew. Fish bones littered the dirt underfoot, along with a healthy stew of scent, ripe and unidentifiable.

"Time to move," someone whispered in the stillness of the night.

"Meet you in the middle," another man agreed and laughed.

Mina looked directly across the street at the grimy window there, catching a hint of reflection. Two men, dressed in dark clothes. One of them peeled away, and as he went, a pair of tinny steps echoed him. Two clockwork soldiers then.

Tracing the first man's steps in the window, she

waited, her heart hammering through her veins. This sort of work was unknown to her. For years she'd flitted across rooftops and into the depths of the enclaves and Undertown, forming her alliances, pushing the humanist movement into action, and meeting with the men and women who ran her and the queen's secret business empire. Danger wasn't unexpected but not like this…stalking a man with lethal intent. If a blue blood could sweat, she had a feeling her palms would be wet around the hilt of the knife by now.

It was the perfect time to make her escape, but leaving wasn't an option. She hadn't brought that baby into the world only to see its life threatened now, and there were helpless women and children everywhere.

Besides, if Morioch crushed Whitechapel, the prince consort would be one step closer to winning the war.

She hadn't thought about it in terms like that before. What if she was making a mistake in running back to the queen? Here were allies, strong allies, if she could find a way to control them and harness them to the queen's cause.

No time to think of that now. *Later.* She was very good at compartmentalizing her problems, and right now, the bomber who'd stepped in front of her was the more immediate concern.

Wielding one of the radio-control frequency boxes, he stuck to the shadows as much as he could. Mina slipped along behind him.

Somewhere near the wall a screaming whistle sounded and an explosion lit the night. One of Blade's modified cannons, no doubt. A perfect time to make her move, while the bomber was distracted.

Grabbing him from behind, she jerked her knee into the back of his and brought the knife to his throat. "Don't move."

The man stiffened. He was her height, but leaner and smelling faintly of chemicals. Leather padding filled out his jerkin, along with what felt like metal inserts.

"Aiming for the Warren, are we?"

"Bugger you."

Not the confirmation she'd hoped for, but where else would they be attacking? "How big a blast radius are the clockworks designed to achieve?" she demanded, pressing the knife hard against his skin to make her point.

"Want to find out?" he snapped, holding up the control box.

"Last year, when the humanists set off a bomb in the Ivory Tower, the damage was approximately forty feet wide, and that clockwork bomb was ten times the size of yours. Right now, we're standing far enough away that even if you do detonate it, the impact might knock us off our feet but we're not in immediate danger." And she'd heal, not that he needed to know that. "Besides, the detonation would alert men. How long do you think it would take for them to realize you and your friend are here?" A nasty little smile. "So go ahead. Detonate it."

"I don't think 'e needs to," someone said from behind. The sound of a trigger being thumbed back echoed loudly in the night. "Don't move, princess. I've got a bead right between your shoulder blades."

Mina froze. She hadn't heard a sound. The breeze cut around her body, bringing with it the scent of leather, herring pie, and explosives.

She tilted her head to the side, catching sight of the man standing several feet behind her. His voice sounded somewhat familiar. Mina's mind raced.

"You're one of Blade's men," she said, recognizing him from when Blade had dragged her down off the Trojan horse. He'd been at Blade's side. She rarely forgot faces.

"Damn it, Henley," the man in her arms gurgled. "Kill her."

All along there *had* been a spy in the rookery. One of Balfour's Falcons, she had to presume, which meant he was far more dangerous than he seemed.

"Step away from Dougal and put the knife on the ground. I know what you are. Any sudden moves and I'll pull this trigger, then all the king's 'orses won't be able to put you back together again."

"Firebolt bullets, I presume?"

"Oh, no. Somethin' of our own. Trust me when I says you won't like it."

The moment she stepped away from his companion, she was dead. The same way Goethe had been. Mina's eyes narrowed on the marching clockwork soldier ambling toward the Warren. She had to stop it before it murdered dozens of women and children.

"Change of plans," she said and whipped Dougal around, between her and Henley.

Too late. The Falcon had pulled the trigger as she began to move. Dougal jerked and screamed, and Mina... Something sparked through Dougal's body and lifted her off her feet. She hit the cobbles, her head smacking down hard, unable to breathe for a second, her lungs catching and clenching on nothing. Mina blinked, her heart thundering in her chest. What the hell—?

It felt like she'd been hit at the elbow with a metal pipe. When her lungs finally opened up, the stink of burning hair and flesh nearly made her gag.

She heard the Falcon curse under his breath as the little clockwork soldier ground to a ticking halt.

Move, she screamed at herself. Her body didn't want to. Her heart felt like it was trying to punch its way out of her chest, and *dear God*, what was wrong with her hand? Where was the knife? She lifted her head just enough to blink away the blinding flash in her eyes. Her right hand—the one that had held the knife—was blistered and burned.

She finally found the source of the stink. Dougal's body jerked on the ground, a small tripod-shaped anchor attached to his chest. A thin metal line ran back toward the strangely shaped pistol Henley had in his hand. He stared down at where Dougal's heels drummed on the cobbles, and when he looked up…

Somehow Mina forced her body to roll, clutching her aching hand to her chest as she found her feet. The world swayed as she staggered upright, stumbling against a building. Henley tossed aside the smoldering pistol in his hand and drew a knife.

"So the duchess is not entirely defenseless." A nasty little smile twisted his mouth. "You'll pay for that. I'll cut it out of your 'ide."

Where was her own knife? Where—

There. Moonlight gleamed off the blade. Mina scrambled for her knife and Henley lashed out at her with his, a diamond-sharp flash of pain raking across her ribs. Her fingers didn't want to work properly, but somehow she closed them around the hilt and spun.

A little tickling burn danced in her fingers and the slash at her side as the craving virus started to heal her. Not soon enough, though. Henley danced forward and grabbed her wrist as she slashed at him. All she could see was his own knife driving toward her face. She gave a twist, but it would be too late and—

Something slammed into the pair of them, driving her into the nearest house.

Back hitting the wall, she landed on her backside, agony jerking through her burned palm. Grunts filled the air—the sound of flesh hitting flesh. A shape materialized, hard and lean, moving like liquid shadow as he slammed Henley back against the wall, one hand tightening around the man's neck and the other forcing the man's own knife into his throat.

Henley jerked, but Barrons held him pinned, waiting as he kicked his heels against the wall, blood dripping from his shoes onto the dirty street. Finally the kicking stopped. Barrons snarled and discarded Henley's body like an old rag, turning on her. Fury made him look even larger.

He was breathing hard, eyes blazing with black fire. Mina made herself very small. Barrons was always cool and in control, but at the moment his craving was in full ascendancy. Blue bloods all had their own inner darkness, but she'd never seen his hold sway like this.

Dangerous, her instincts whispered.

And so she didn't move.

"Are you injured?" His voice sounded cold and distant.

Mina shook her head. "Not really. Barrons, I—"

"I know what you were doing. We're not going to speak of it right at this moment. Right now, I have to get you back to the Warren." He caught her upper arm and jerked her to her feet.

Mina staggered against him, wincing as her raw palm grazed his coat. A little animallike sound of pain came from her throat and Barrons froze.

"I thought you said you weren't hurt." If anything, he sounded even more furious, but his hands were gentle when he caught her chin and tilted it to the side, examining her face. All of that strength…so finely controlled. "Where?"

"He shot the other man with some sort of current-stimulating device." Mina offered her hands for inspection. "I was holding on to the knife at the time."

Cool fingers curled her palm up so that he could inspect the damage. "I can smell blood." Tight, perfectly pronounced words, but they made her shiver. She could smell blood too.

Barrons had always seemed so charming, so urbane, so completely in control of himself and the darkness that stirred beneath the surface. It excited her a little to know that he owned such a dark edge. The part of her that she hid deep inside herself—her own brutal hungers—shifted and stirred through her middle, a rush of blood tingling through her veins. A heavy stillness settled between them, as if he felt it stirring too, both of them far too aware of the consequences of the hunger.

She found herself leaning closer, her eyelids growing heavy with a smoky hypnotism. Her teeth ached,
throat suddenly dry with need. Barrons was so still
it was almost a warning, but she could sense every
muscle locking hard in his body, his focus on her
narrowing until the world seemed to disappear around
them. All she knew was the hunger. All she could see
was the corded muscle in his throat working as he
swallowed, the vein there punching against the skin.
He wanted it. She wanted it.

A cool breeze cut across her bared skin, sweeping
away some of the red that had brightened her vision.
Good God, what was she doing?

"A mere cut," Mina murmured, dragging her hands
out of his. She felt breathless again, like she had when
she first hit the ground, her gut muscles locked tight.
She'd almost taken his blood. Heat flooded her cheeks.
"We don't have time for this. They've got some
sort of clockwork device filled with explosives." She
pointed to the clockwork standing frozen in the street
and the dropped control frequency box. "There was
another man with another device. They're marching
on the Warren."

Again Barrons seemed to search her eyes. "So you
decided to stop them?"

For the first time in years, Mina couldn't hold
a man's gaze. She looked away. "Consider it my
charitable act for the day, but if we don't hurry up and
catch him, it will all have been for naught."

That stirred him to action. "Which way did the
other bomber go?"

"That way." She pointed.

"Follow me."

Grabbing the frequency controller, she took it with her, in case someone else happened to activate the device. Barrons moved mercilessly, barely giving her time to keep up with him, ducking and weaving through streets and alleys, hunting through the night. From the black gleam of his eyes, his hunger was still in ascendancy. Her own vision was still darkened. Neither of them had the street-smart instincts of one of the rookery-born, but she could scent a man now, and the sharp tang of chemical. The predator inside her would be able to track him no matter how far he ran.

"There," she whispered, pausing beside Barrons as he peered around the corner.

The Warren loomed ahead of them, several of the whores visible through the archway that led into the yard behind it. The little mechanical man marched steadily toward it, tracing the shadows that ran along the walls here.

"Where's the controller?" There was no sign of him in the streets.

Leo had a pistol in his hand, his gaze searching the rooftops. "Damn it. Can't see him."

"How well can you shoot? Could you hit the clockwork?"

Their eyes met, a sense of that long-ago camaraderie from the Venetian Gardens springing to life. "Yes."

"We don't have time to find the controller," she said, eyeing the Warren. "The blast radius has to be smaller than forty feet. I can smell the nitroglycerin inside it, and from the size of the clockwork soldier's body, it cannot hold enough of Nobel's blasting powder to harm the Warren from here. Shoot it."

"Are you insane?"

"We don't have a choice," she snapped.

Another second to hesitate, then he nodded, stepping out into the street and into a marksman's stance.

The sound was almost instantaneous, the pistol retort echoing a second before a wall of noise exploded down the street. Light bloomed, the wall beside her shaking and leaving the soles of her boots vibrating.

Barrons was on his knees, one arm thrown over his face to shield it as a flare of orange light washed over him. He fell back onto his other hand as the force of it hit him, his hair dancing in the windblast. Bits of glass and debris tore his sleeve, filling the air with the scent of blood, and then suddenly the wind vanished, leaving the hot flicker of orange flame playing over his chiseled face as he lowered his arm.

Her ears were ringing. Mina staggered to his side, catching his arm. "Are you all right?" she yelled.

Nodding grimly, he stared at the wreckage in front of them. Blood dripped down the side of his face from a gash near his eyebrow. Mina touched it gently until he looked up, pushing her hand away.

The bomb had obliterated half the street and several houses. If she concentrated, she could just make out the sound of frightened screams cutting through the ringing in her ears. Dozens of women and children tumbled out of the Warren, staring at the gaping hole in the street.

"That was larger than expected," Barrons mouthed at her.

"I'm not a scientist," she snapped back. Movement shifted; a man fleeing across the roof opposite them. Mina pointed, and Barrons snatched up his pistol again, aimed, and then fired.

The fellow catapulted off the roof, the body hitting the ground so hard she could almost imagine the sound of it.

⤜❦⤏

Shadows materialized out of the looming darkness of the streets. Blade thundered into view, his face drawn tight with terror and his fists pumping at his sides. He saw the Warren, standing safe and whole, and staggered to a halt, black eyes raking over the bomb's devastation. Mina hovered behind Barrons, her shoulder pressing against his.

"They're safe. The duchess and I were patrolling the vicinity when we came across the bombs." The two men clasped hands and Blade's shoulders slumped in relief. Mina couldn't take her eyes off Barrons. Why lie like that? Their eyes met. Barrons glanced away with a carefully neutral expression as he explained the situation, leaving out certain details, such as why precisely she'd been helping him.

"Thought she was—" Blade couldn't say any more.

"This was what Morioch was waiting for." The sound of artillery faded and Barrons's gaze cut toward the wall. "Sounds like they're retreating for the moment."

"That bastard." Fear gave way to an almost feral fury on Blade's face. "That bleeding coward." His hands dipped to his belt and returned with one of those barbaric unsheathed razors he favored. "I swore if he touched my wife I'd return the favor—"

"That's not your greatest concern," Mina broke in. All eyes were suddenly upon her, including Barrons's. "I recognized one of your enforcers. He was helping the two men who tried to bomb the Warren."

Recognition lit Barrons's dark eyes and he swore. "Henley. I didn't note it 'til now, but she's correct. He was trying to kill her."

If anything, Blade's expression darkened further. "Where is he?"

"No longer breathing," Barrons replied. "I took care of it."

"That means Morioch knows your defenses, your weaknesses, your strengths," Mina said.

"He was obviously counting on Henley and his men to destroy the Warren and break the heart of the rookery. If that had happened, we'd have come running back," Barrons said grimly, "and he would have hit the wall with everything he had."

"You cannot assume Henley was the lone Falcon slipped into your ranks," Mina finished. "Why else would the duke call off the attack? He must know it failed."

Blade's nostrils flared with fury. "Barrons, I want you on guard here, just in case there is someone else. I'll leave Tin Man at the gate, but I want you inside where nobody can see you. Get yourself cleaned up. I'll check on Honor and then…" His voice turned silky soft. "Then I'm gonna make sure that bastard don't ever forget the first mistake he made in this war."

Mina couldn't help a shiver.

∽

Her room looked like it had been ransacked when Leo
returned her to it. "Did you do that?" Mina asked,
trying to shrug out of her borrowed coat. Her arm
caught in the sleeve, and her right fingers were too
badly burned still to be of much use. Skin, new and
pink, stretched over them and she tried not to think
too much about what they looked like as she tried to
wriggle out of the coat. Tingling pinpricks made three
of her fingers numb as the craving virus healed her.

"I was trying to find out what you'd taken with
you." Hands curled around her upper arms, the press
of his fingers firm enough for her to feel his innate
strength. "Hold still."

Liar. The room was almost destroyed. It spoke of
a recklessness and anger that she'd rarely seen Barrons
display. A hint of chaos beneath that cool, calm mien
he always wore.

But what had stirred it to the surface? Her disappearance? Or something else?

Barrons stripped the coat off her carefully, then
turned her to face him. No sign on his face of the
chaos around them. Only dark smudges of ash and
dirt, his hair roughened, and a faint burn mark along
his stubbled jaw. Smoke clung to his hardened body
armor, burning her sensitive nostrils, but underneath
that was the heated scent of bay rum and starched
linen, scents that she always unconsciously associated
with Barrons.

The shock of the explosion had left her almost
numb, but now her ears were ringing and her heart
raced as the reality of the situation penetrated. She was

in the middle of a war, with no allies and no way of getting back to her queen.

Doubt and confusion were two emotions she rarely encountered. Her plans saw to that. If something went wrong, she always had another option to fall back on. But she'd failed. She'd made choices—the safety of the women and children here over the safety of her queen. Nothing in the past two days had gone according to plan, and she was well out of her depth.

With a man who didn't trust her, yet had still lied to protect her. A man who…might be an ally? If she could trust him…

I don't know what I'm doing.

So tempting to reach out and wipe some of that dirt and ash from his skin, to press her lips lightly against his. Not to take him to bed or to push at the blazing, dangerous connection between them, but something else that made her skin feel hot and tight and her chest clench up, like a vise winched tighter around her lungs.

If he reached out and took her in his arms, she wouldn't push him away at the moment, but she wasn't quite certain how to ask for it.

"Why did you lie to Blade?" she whispered instead.

Dark lashes blanketed his eyes. His fingers found the buttons on her shirt and he started undoing them. Mina slapped at his hand with her good one, but he simply pushed her back against the door and pinned her there.

"Behave," he warned, "or I'll take my belt to you."

That made her jaw drop open, a little curl of heat flickering low in her abdomen. Not entirely an unwelcome thought, as troubling as that seemed.

"If you think I will drop such questioning simply because you've turned into a brutish thug," she warned, "then you are very much mistaken. You lied to him about my aborted escape. Why?"

Those eyes looked up, filled with a troubling darkness. "Blade is not someone I would push at the best of times, most especially when his voice changes and his grammar corrects itself. That's when he's at his most dangerous, when the hunger is completely in control of him."

Blood-lust. She shivered. "You're protecting me."

No answer passed his lips, but she saw the truth in his eyes, and it floored her. He didn't trust her; that much was clear. But though he doubted her and had to be wondering why she was so adamant to return to court, his fingers gently peeled her shirt open, his eyes probing for the cause of her pain. "Where are you hurt?"

The moment was lost. Mina dragged her shirt from his fingers, closing it over her corset. The fine French lace was the worse for wear now, a little like herself. "I'm fine."

"Mina, I can smell it."

Smell it—? Then she realized what he meant. The little slash under her ribs wept blood against her skin, soaking into her corset. "It's nothing," she murmured, pushing away from him. Not enough blood in the last couple of days conspired to weaken her. If she'd been stronger, this should have healed by now.

"Duchess, let me see what—"

"It will heal." *Duchess.* That hated word. Trust was an ambiguous thing in the air between them. No reason not to show him but…it felt uncomfortably

like she was opening herself up to him. "I shouldn't
see why you give a damn."

His eyes narrowed. "So be it."

The world upended as he caught her around the
waist and gently lifted her up against his shoulder.
Mina snatched at his shirt with her good hand,
tempted to kick him. "Put me down."

"As my lady wishes." She didn't like the tone he
was using, like all that anger was leashed, just beneath
the surface. Then she didn't have time to think about
it. Her backside hit the seat of a chair and Barrons
jerked the shirt down over her shoulders, trapping her
arms. "It seems I won't have to use my belt, after all."

"What are you doing?"

He tugged the sleeve carefully over her burned
hand, then slipped the other off her left wrist with considerably less aplomb. "Getting some bloody answers."

Her wrists were dragged behind her and something looped around them. Her shirt. Mina's mouth
dropped open, then she kicked out. "Don't you dare
tie me up." She might as well not have bothered. The
shirtsleeve pulled tight around her wrists, and he tied
her to the lower rung of the chair.

Mina brought her boot heel down on the rung at
the front. The vibration ricocheted up her leg, but the
rung didn't break on the first strike. Barrons caught
her knees before she could do it again, trapping her.

Breathing hard, she glared at him.

"You're bleeding again." That black gaze dropped
to her side and the corset she wore. His cheekbones
tightened with a fierceness she recognized, his lips
parting as his gaze locked on her breasts.

"Of course I am, you manhandling oaf!" She strained to move her knee under his heated palm. Couldn't shift him. "Get off me!"

Something heated his expression. Something that made her body still. "Or?" he murmured, fingers wrapping around the inside of her knees as he forced her legs to part.

Mina forgot how to breathe.

"You need blood," he said. "And with your wounds, mine will give you more of what you need than anything human."

Her gaze shot to his, her heart stumbling a little. *His blood.* She'd never once taken from the vein. It was socially unacceptable for a woman, and more than that, she liked being in control of her own blood-lust.

"No, no, it's fine. If you just fetch me…" Her voice trailed off as he withdrew the small, leather-bound fléchette case from inside his shirt. Mina swallowed. She could still feel the imprint of his hands on the inside of her knees. "What are you doing?"

He opened the case and selected a sharp blood-letting razor. Setting it aside, he began to roll up his sleeve, the veins on the inside of his wrists pulsing. *Oh God.* Mina's tongue darted over her lips, her gaze focusing on the pale skin of his forearm.

"Do I have any choice in this?" she demanded.

"Of course." Barrons set the razor to his skin, slicing sharply across the vein. Blood welled, the almost bluish color that gave blue bloods their name. Putting the razor down, he caught her gaze. "You can choose not to drink it."

Hardly a choice at all. She could scent it now, her mouth watering as she twisted in her bonds. The wound at her side pulled, reminding her of her weakness. Cursing him, Mina stilled, looking up once more. A hot, wicked flush started burning deep within, the scent of her arousal flavoring the air.

Barrons's expression tightened, as if he too were aware of it. Stepping between her spread legs, he looked down at her for a long moment, then held his wrist out, blood spilling into the hollow of his palm. Barrons's nostrils flared, but he held himself still, waiting for her to take what he offered.

"Damn you." The world was nothing but shadows. Something swelled up within her: a need so fierce she'd never felt it before.

Blood-lust.

It wasn't the same as sipping her blood from a champagne flute or lacing her brandy with it. Mina bit her lip, focusing on that dark splash. He rested a boot between her parted thighs and leaned on it, holding the bloodied slash closer to her, tendons clenching in his forearm as if she wasn't the only one fighting personal demons.

"Your choice." A mocking whisper.

Mina looked up, seeing the dare in those devil-black eyes, the intensity in his expression. He wanted this as much as she did.

So be it. Mina leaned forward, her tongue darting out to trace the small, already-healing slash. She never took her eyes off him.

The taste of it exploded through her body. A breathy gasp and then she bent her head and pressed her lips against the cut, her dry throat working. Moaning a little. Pulling that sweetness inside her body. Drowning in its volcanic heat.

Sensation cascaded through her and her thighs clenched, locking around his boot. Rubbing against it until he drew back, straightening and circling behind her, leaving her with only his wrist pressed against her lips. It wasn't enough. She pressed her knees together tightly, fighting the building ache between her thighs, an ache that wouldn't go away, building like the pressure of a storm front. It left her restless, her teeth sinking into the tender flesh of his forearm as she sucked hard, hoping that he burned just as much as she did.

Barrons's fist clenched. A swift jerk on the back of the chair and she tilted backward, her lips breaking from his skin in a shocked gasp.

He leaned down, claiming her mouth with his own, tasting the blood there. One fist in her hair. A strange upside-down kiss that made her restless again, her hips shifting on the seat and her nipples hardening. *More.* Oh God, she wanted more.

Then his hand was moving down her body, sliding over her breast and lower. Teasing across her stomach, between her thighs, pressing hard there. Mina cried out and his tongue plunged into her mouth. He was merciless. Absolutely, single-mindedly merciless. Two fingers rode over her sensitive flesh until she was rubbing against him herself, determined to bring that storm cresting over her.

Mina's thighs clenched around his hand. Suddenly there was a hand over her mouth and she came with a scream, her hands jerking against her bonds, her entire body rigid.

Then his hand was gone and the world came into focus again, slightly blurred around the edges. He was saying something. Harsh words delivered right next to her ear. Mina sucked in a sharp breath, her body still molten. Still twitching in places.

"…Do you want to know the damnable truth, Duchess? No matter how much I want to walk away, to let you leave, I can't do it." His hand caught her throat, tilting her head back and pinning her there, balanced on the edge of the precipice. Black eyes blazed in the center of her vision. "You enthrall me. I feel my heart beating and it's all you, you, *you.*"

You. Mina's eyes shot wide as his face lowered. That dangerous mouth closed over hers again, tongue thrusting past her lips and teeth, forcing the kiss upon her.

The thin veneer of civility washed away, drowning her in a man that was more primal than rational. This…this was what the craving meant, what lust meant. This was the choice he'd offered, one that she hadn't anticipated.

And one that undid her.

Yes. She made that choice again, with her whole body screaming the word. Past time for games, for fear. Tiptoeing around each other for years, because maybe a part of her had always known it would be like this. Consumed. Stripped bare. All that she was, offered up to him on a platter.

Then he was coming up for air, breathing hard. "I hate the hold you have on me."

More shocking words, an honesty of sorts. It seemed sacrilegious not to reply in kind. "No, you don't," she whispered. "You would love it, if only you too had such a hold on me."

All four feet of the chair hit the floor, jerking her forward. Breathing hard, half-dazed, she collapsed against her bonds, shuddering in every nerve of her body.

Boot heels echoed on the timber floor. Barrons circled her slowly in a dangerous prowl. Blackened eyes locked on hers. Leaning down, he caught the edge of the chair seat and dragged her forward until her knees hit his. Control was a knife edge within him.

Slowly he reached out, hands tugging the pins from her hair and scattering them disdainfully until it tumbled loosely down her back. Barrons twisted her hair into a rope, then wrapped it around her throat, the ends of it tickling her jaw.

"And do I not have such a hold?" Soft, dangerous words.

She *couldn't* answer that.

Instead she bit his thumb. Heat flared in his eyes at the feel of her teeth, his breath catching. "I will never let any man own me," she said, kissing the bite mark to soothe it. "But you can try."

At the sound of her sultry whisper, he let her go. Her hair unraveled, tumbling down around her shoulders. Neither of them looked away.

"Then I will."

Hands slid over her hips, then under her thighs. Somehow he lifted her into his lap as he settled on the chair beneath her. Barrons dragged her forward with one hard thrust, seating himself fully beneath her, his muscled thighs clenching beneath hers.

He brushed her hair back over her shoulders, baring her corset to his gaze. Thumbnails scraped over her skin, bringing the barest shiver to the fore. His eyes were shadowed now, unreadable. Palms cupped her breasts through the stiff boning of her stays. Mina twisted uneasily, pulling at her wrists.

"Let me go."

"No." He leaned forward and bit her throat, one thumb sweeping beneath her corset and rasping over her nipple.

The sensation shot all the way through her. "*Please*." She twisted again, feeling the hard steel of his erection rock between her thighs. "If we do this, I want to touch you."

"*No*." His voice came a little harder, fingers dipping and rolling her nipple between them, breath warm against her throat as his lips grazed her skin. "We don't always get what we want, Duchess."

Duchess. The correct way to address her, and yet it only emphasized the distance between them. A hand slid down her calf, tugging her boot off, making quick work of the other one before he settled her more firmly in his lap.

"Now," he murmured, a strange light in his eyes, "let us see who's telling the truth."

Obviously he was still smarting over that "*never let any man own her*" comment. "About what? About how desperately you want me, Barrons?"

He stilled, the backs of his fingers brushing over her corset, then looked up slowly with dark, dangerous eyes. "I already admitted that. That makes you the liar. Are you lying, Duchess?" His thumb swirled dangerous circles around her hardened nipple, sending a hint of seduction through her corset. "Do you want me too?"

"Do you need me to want you?" she countered and his face darkened as if she'd struck a direct blow.

"No, you're right." Something cleared in his expression. He caught her hips between his hands and ground her against him, earning a hiss. "I just need you to want *this*."

This was safe. She bit her lip, letting her hips ride over his again. Silent confirmation.

"I'm not going to be gentle, Mina—"

Mina. It threw her out of the moment, forming a connection between them that she shouldn't want, and yet her heart clenched in her chest.

"Not tonight. I want you to remember this." He lowered his head, tugging at the top of her corset. Her nipple tumbled free, drawing his heated gaze. "I want to mark you so that you can't deny this tomorrow."

"Then mark me," she whispered. "Make me feel it."

Teeth bit her nipple, drawing a cry from her lips. The pain was sharp, swallowed in warmth as his mouth softened over her, sucking at her. Exquisite. She felt it between her legs, as though his mouth were there instead.

His hands jerked at her trousers, tugging at her buttons, then ripping the fabric down her legs until his hands hit her thighs. Bending her knees up between them, he stripped the trousers off. Her drawers went with them, his mouth finding hers as she gasped at the shock of her sudden nakedness, his teeth sinking into her bottom lip.

No time to think about it. He spread her thighs wide in his lap, tearing at the buttons holding his own trousers closed until his cock jutted free. Lifting her hips, he hissed as the blunt head of his cock wedged between her slick thighs. Her entire focus narrowed to the sensation of their joining, as if nothing else mattered. Barrons looked at her and she saw the silent question in his eyes.

She had no answer. None but this… Inch by inch, she impaled herself upon him.

The shock of it stole her breath. *Oh God*. Then she was moving, the muscles in her thighs straining as she rolled her hips. Or tried to. The ties at her wrist dug in, giving her no leverage.

Large hands slid under her bottom, holding her there. The feel of him stretched her inside like a molten brand. "You're at my mercy, Duchess." His cool whisper shivered over her skin, a taunting smile darkening his lips. Muscles bunching in his arms, he lifted her hips until the blunt head of his crown threatened to leave her, then slowly let her sink back down.

"Do you want this?" A hiss escaped him as his cock glided all the way back in again. Mina buried her face against his shoulder, shuddering. She nodded.

Again those hands lifted her, holding her at the very edge. "Then beg me," he demanded. "Tell me how much you want it. How much you want *me*."

Years' worth of secret desire burned between them. Mina shook her head, and he rubbed the blunt head of his cock against her sensitive flesh. The ache of withdrawal was bittersweet, and she realized that he was telling her the truth.

He would take no more unless she surrendered to him.

"Why is it so bloody important?"

His eyes darkened as he held her there, face-to-face, his body threatening—promising—to breach hers again, if only she whispered those few little words. And she could tell from the stiffening line of his jaw that he wasn't going to answer her.

"I want you." *There, damn you.* "I've always wanted you." She nipped at his lip. "And I want this—" Her words ended on a hiss as he thrust back inside her. "All of this. All of you."

"I'm not letting you go." A part of her didn't care. Teeth sank into her arm as he turned his head to the side and bit her. "*Never*, Mina. This is the only thing that makes sense anymore."

Somehow she dragged a hand free of the shirt and cupped his face, tilting his mouth to hers in a whisper of a kiss. Those damning words burrowed deep inside her soul. She couldn't let him say any more.

She wanted to hear them too badly.

Tongue thrusting into her mouth, he slid her up and down in carefully controlled glides, his cock gliding wetly between them. Mina moaned, clenching her inner muscles. She didn't want slow. She didn't want controlled. She wanted to drive him crazy, to finally see the darkness that lurked under his skin.

He broke the kiss, lip curling in a silent snarl as he lowered her back down and she squeezed *harder*.

"Damn you." The breath exploded out of him, the whites of his eyes gleaming as he nipped at her chin. Muscle bulged in his forearms as he urged her up, thrusting his cock into her harder, faster, until she could feel the burn between them.

Nibbling along his jawline, she bit his earlobe gently. "Fuck me, Barrons." A dirty little whisper that earned her a hard thrust. *Yes.* Mina reveled in it. "Untie me. Let me touch you," she murmured, gasping for each breath as he pounded into her. He liked her to beg, did he? "Please. *Please.*"

Barrons tore at the shirt holding her other hand and she sank both of her hands into his hair, curling her palms against his scalp as she tried to press closer. Barrons caught her under the bottom, thighs straining as he lifted her out of the chair.

One step. Two. Her back hit the bed as he followed her down, Barrons's entire weight crushing her down into the mattress as he slid back inside her. She couldn't stop herself from writhing beneath him. He was plunging into her now, years of pent-up tension between them coming to the fore. The tendons in his throat tightened, his teeth bared as he clenched his eyes shut. So close. Her heart reveled in it. She couldn't take her eyes off his face.

Barrons ground to a halt, his breath harsh and muted against her shoulder as he shuddered. "You are the devil, you know that?"

"Don't stop," she whispered.

"I don't intend to." The next thrust was slow and deep. He laughed under his breath. "But you make me forget myself. A gentleman always takes care of his lady…" The smokiness of his voice spilled heat all the way through her.

"You are taking care of me."

Easing up onto his elbows, he shifted the angle of her hips, the next thrust taking her by surprise. She felt it deep within her, her entire body tightening and her nails digging into his upper arms. Not quite certain if she liked the raw intensity of this feeling.

"Mmm." He closed his eyes, lips parted. "That feels good. So fucking good."

Mina writhed, trying to tempt him. "I like it when you lose control."

His eyes opened. A dangerous challenge filled them. "You first, Your Grace." Rolling onto one elbow, he slid his hand between them, fingers gliding down through the thatch of red hair between her thighs and over slick, sensitive skin. Mina grabbed his shoulders, holding on for dear life. With his hips pinning hers, she had no escape. It was shockingly intense. She couldn't hide from him here—couldn't control *any* of this…

"No. No," she moaned, shaking her head, crying out as he stroked the small, hard bud just above where they joined. Her entire body shook.

"Yes." Barrons slid her knee up, her heel resting on the indentation of his buttock as he rocked his cock into her. Filling her so deeply that she ached.

Pleasure was a hot, wicked flush in her abdomen. She couldn't stop her body from clenching around his as he slowly fucked his way into her. A strangled sound tore from her throat, one hand fisting in the sheets as she shook her head, trying to deny it.

"Do you ever touch yourself?" he whispered.

Their eyes met. A finger stroked over her lazily and Mina bit her lip as her body arched helplessly.

"You do," he whispered. "Don't you?" Another lazy stroke, his fingertip circling that swollen bud.

Mina held her breath, her hips arching up, up…

He bit her ear, the words a hot temptation. "Do you think of me when you do it?"

The words followed her over the edge. She couldn't control herself, thrashing beneath him, her nails scoring desperate marks in his flesh. Her entire body shook, locked around his.

The second she felt herself coming down from the edge he thrust hard, riding over something deep inside her. Mina came again with a shocked cry, clutching at the hard sinew of his shoulders.

Again. Her eyes shot wide and she threw her head back as he surged inside her. Hard, wet slaps. Flesh against flesh as he finally let her hips tilt back down until she could manage the explosive sensations inside her. She was shaking all over.

With a rough growl, Barrons quivered, spilling his hot seed inside her. "Mina," he breathed, collapsing atop her. "*God.*"

A little blaze of warmth lit inside her at the sound of her name and she reached out, hesitated, then rested her hand on his back, feeling the breath shudder through him. A tenuous touch, a silent question. Wanting to ask him to say her name again. *Mina,* he'd whispered, and it shivered inside her, all hot and molten.

Damn him, what was he doing to her?

It was all she could do to hold him. She had no energy left. Just enough to lie there, completely shattered, as his weight settled firmly on her, sinking them both into the mattress. Her ribs compressed and she couldn't quite get enough breath, but when he moved to shift off her, she dragged him back down.

For the longest time, she clung to him and he held her, his face nuzzled against her throat. His breathing softened, his heart pounding against her breasts where they were crushed to his chest. She could feel him inside her still, wet and thick and softening…

Barrons finally lifted his head. "Hell," he whispered gruffly. "I didn't hurt you?"

Mina shook her head. "I'm not breakable, Barrons."

He rolled off her, and she caught a flash of dark, dark eyes as the sudden rush of air left her feeling startlingly naked. The ache of his body echoed within her, and she could still feel the ghostly press of his weight upon her. Her hand lifted as he turned. Then hesitated.

Barrons scraped a hand over his face as he sat on the edge of the bed. "I never meant for that to happen," he said, his hands clasped, elbows resting on his knees.

In that moment she felt a distance between them that seemed like one she would never—could never—breach. Biting her lip, Mina sat up, drawing the sheet to her breasts. The sashaying tickle of her unbound hair curled against her lower back. And her hand hovered there, not quite daring to touch him.

"Not like that. I just thought I should give you blood to help heal you. *Christ*—" He cupped his hands over his face and dragged them down until they formed clasped palms in front of his mouth.

Was that regret she heard in his voice? Mina's heart dipped and she forced herself to reach out. Her hand slid down the long, smooth muscle on the right side of his spine, tracing the dips of each vertebra. Barrons tilted his head toward her, the smooth profile of his face catching her gaze. Mina opened her mouth, but the words couldn't come out.

"And I don't regret it," he told her somewhat fiercely. "I should. For treating you like that, for taking what I've wanted for so many years… But I wouldn't take it back, Your Grace. I wouldn't change a thing."

"I don't regret it either," she whispered.

Doubt darkened his expression. "I don't even know if you mean those words." His voice grew tight. "But I want you to. Perhaps I want it too much." His head bowed, the words roughening even further. "You're free to go. I have no right to keep you here. I have no claim upon you."

What? Mina froze.

As he stood, her fingers fell from his back, dragging over the taut muscle of his buttocks. Barrons hauled his trousers on and snatched his shirt from the ground. Two steps took him to the door, and there he hesitated.

There was no expression on his face as he turned, his hand hovering on the doorknob. "You're the only thing tying me to the past, and perhaps it's time to let you go. Perhaps it's time to let it all go." A world of regret echoed in his eyes. "I'm sorry that I kept you long after I should have. If you get dressed, I shall escort you to the wall. It's as far as I can go, unfortunately, but I have no doubt you'll make it home safely."

And then he was gone, his footsteps echoing briskly down the hallway while her heart slowly started beating again in her chest.

I thought you said that you couldn't let me go.

Nineteen

PRIDE KEPT HER IMMOBILE FOR LONG SECONDS. PRIDE, that strange burning feeling somewhere in her chest and, more practically, a lack of clothes.

The room was a mess. So was she. Dragging herself to her feet, Mina tucked the sheet in between her breasts to anchor it around her.

His final words echoed in her ears: *Perhaps it's time to let you go.* She was going home, back to her queen… and all she could feel was a lump of solid iron weighing her chest down.

This was what she'd wanted, wasn't it? Mina pressed her knuckles to her lips. She didn't know what to do.

For years she'd had a plan and moved toward it. Barrons had never been supposed to happen. And good God, what if he could help her?

What if she was making the biggest mistake of her life?

She didn't have time to think her way through this mess. She had to make this choice, and she had to make it *now*. War was coming and the rookeries would burn beneath it, destroying people she'd come to know—and even admire a little. And Barrons would stay here until the end, trying to protect the people he cared for.

They'd make sure he died, Morioch and the prince consort and all his Falcons… But she could stop that from happening.

Oh God… Mina sailed out of the room after him, clad in nothing but the bedsheet and filled with an absolute terror of the unknown. Her choice, such as it was, had been made.

❧

"Don't you dare walk away from me."

He was halfway down the stairs when the duchess's voice rang through the hallway. Leo spun on his heel. Sailing down the hallway with what looked like the bedsheet wrapped around her, the duchess looked as though she were going to faint. Her cheeks were dangerously pale, red marks marring her throat from the scrape of his stubble and her mouth kiss-swollen.

His heart jacked into his throat. Walking away from her had been the hardest thing he'd ever done. The right thing to do, though it had nearly killed him. He didn't think he could do it again. "What are you doing?"

"There are certain matters we need to discuss."

He couldn't do this. "Not now. There's very little time for you to escape. If you get dressed—"

"I'm not going anywhere."

Leo couldn't say a damned thing. A surge of fierce want nearly brought him to his knees. *Don't do this. Please don't do this…* "If this is a game—" His throat thickened.

The door at the top of the stairs opened and Blade stepped out, the sound of soft murmurs behind him. He half closed the door, green eyes raking the duchess from head to toe. "That the latest fashion in the city?"

Her cheeks bloomed with spots of red. "I need to speak to you as well as Barrons. Give me a moment to get dressed and meet me in the parlor."

Blade arched a brow. "Did you just forget where you are, luv?"

She turned on him, furious and glorious. "Do you want me to help you defeat Morioch or not?"

Leo's gaze locked on her. Hard.

"As me ladyship commands," Blade said after a faint hesitation. "But I ain't got a lot o' time right now for games."

"No, right now you need a way to save the rookery and your wife. And I need clothing," she told Blade.

Blade considered her for a long moment. "I'll fetch you summat, but Leo's playin' lady's maid."

"Considering he's directly responsible for the demise of my last set of clothes, I'll accept that condition."

Blade laughed under his breath. "Didn't you tell me one time that she ain't so bad once you clip 'er claws?" he murmured to Leo as he shut his door behind him, presumably to fetch the duchess something to wear.

Finding himself the recipient of that hot amber stare, Leo cut her off with an abrupt slice of the hand.

"Not here," he said, climbing the stairs. "If you have something to say to me, then we'll do it in private." The last thing he wanted was his brother-in-law chortling under his breath about the situation.

"I have something to say, all right." She turned, dragging her voluminous sheeted skirts behind her as she marched back to her designated rooms.

Oh, there was fire beneath the ice, of a certainty. Leo strode after her, shutting the door behind him with a sharp click. "My apologies. I thought you wanted to leave, and I have things to see to, if I'm to see my family safe. *Christ*, what did you expect? Did you want me to beg you to stay?"

He glanced at the bed and its mess of blankets, feeling a heated throb cut through him. Guilt. Anger. Hurt. Emotions he wasn't entirely certain he was in control of. It had taken *everything* in him to let her go. "We *fucked*, Mina," he said, enunciating the word clearly. "Nothing more. I must have missed the moment when you actually laid yourself on the line, gave me a damned inch in this or trusted me enough to—"

"That moment happened right here," she yelled, pointing at the chair. "Do you honestly think I would simply give myself to anyone? To a man I didn't... didn't want?"

That slowed him down. He glared at the chair, fragments of memory assaulting him and arousing him instantly. Hot little cries of pleasure in his ear, her nails raking down his back... Dangerous thoughts. They turned him from his purpose, made him forget everything he needed to remember about her. The duchess had been raised to play games. She excelled at them. And somehow, what he wanted from her was not just to win, not anymore. This had become more than a game. "It didn't mean anything. You said so yourself."

"I lied. It meant more to *me*!" she cried, her eyes glittering with fierceness and rage and...something that made his gut muscles clench as if for a blow. "Why are you angry with me? Do you want me to tell the truth? I wanted this to happen. I've wanted it for *years*!"

"Why are you angry with *me*?" he countered with arms flung wide, though his breath caught. He couldn't let himself believe it... Because if she was lying to him... "You were the one who said you didn't want me, that I had no hold over you. So why be angry now? Isn't this what you want?"

Mina cupped her palms around her upper arms as if to brace herself against the words echoing in the room. "I don't know what I want. I don't know how to do this. I don't know what you want from me."

Did he dare answer that? The words were a strangled admission of something he'd never let himself admit. "You know what I want."

Someone to give a damn about him. Someone to care. A warm bed to crawl into when he returned home from court in the early hours of the morning. Soft, welcoming arms and a sleepy, murmured greeting. A smile in the darkness as he tipped her face up to his to kiss it.

Everything that he saw in Blade's face when he looked at Honoria, or Lena's tender smile when she cupped her hand against Will's cheek when she thought they were alone. He wanted that. He wanted it so fiercely that sometimes he thought he'd choke on it, and yet he'd never dared put it into words.

Those bright eyes closed, her head lowering. "Then perhaps I don't know how to give it."

A pregnant pause thickened the air between them, full of want and need and everything unspoken. This was the precipice. The moment in which either of them could take a step forward to meet somewhere in the middle...or never meet at all. A moment full of risk, but he felt stronger now because of a hope there that hadn't existed before.

He hadn't understood the depths he'd sunk to until then. A bleak place full of shadows that threatened to envelop him. But there was a light now. A glint of a future. He just had to take it by both hands.

And so he did. He stepped forward, his hands cupping her cheeks and tipping her chin up. Mina looked at him, her eyes full of something he'd never seen there before. "Why?" Her voice was raw. "Why me?"

His thumbs stroked the silk of her cheeks. "Because it was always you."

Again more silence as she digested the words, her eyes so far away that he felt for a moment as if he'd lost her. The light from the window reflected in her irises.

"I like it when you call me 'Mina,'" she admitted. "It drove me insane at first that you would dare, but...I miss it. You're the only one who does, did you know that? The only one with the courage to do so. You always push me. *Always*. And sometimes I'm not ready to be pushed. Sometimes it scares me that you get under my skin the way you do." She took a shaky breath, hands curling in his shirt. "You frighten me, but I'm trying…I'm trying to stop pushing you away. It's not easy for me."

With her hair tumbled down around her shoulders and her hands clinging to his shirt, she looked far younger than she ever had.

He'd never, ever expected her to yield. But she had. And that was all he'd been asking for, really, for her to meet him halfway. Halfway to…whatever the hell this was.

Leo slid his arms around her, crushing her against his chest, his hand cradling her scalp. So small in his arms. As if that backbone of steel was finally threatening to crumble…and he didn't want it to. Curling his fingers in her hair, he tipped her face up to his and pressed a kiss to her lips, tasting the sweet heat of her mouth.

And that spark between them hissed to life again. A connection he'd never been able to fight, no matter how much he knew this was a fool's dream. Moaning deep in his throat, he pressed her back against the wall, following her with his hands and mouth. Mina was liquid fire in his arms. Everything changed. *Everything.* No more holding back. Her teeth bumped his in their desperate attempt to consume each other. Lashes fluttered against his cheeks as she sought to breathe, hand twining in his hair. *Oh God*, her breasts. His hands cupped them, mouth dropping to her throat, where he could taste the faint saltiness of her skin, lower, nipping at her collarbone…

A hand pushed against the middle of his chest and he drew back, gasping for breath, his blood a conflagration of need.

But the look on her face stopped him from taking more, the way she searched his eyes as if looking for the answer to some question he didn't know. Mina licked her lips, face paling. "There's something I need to tell you. And if I don't tell you now…"

The air between them charged with something potent, something dangerous. He studied her gaze. "What?"

"For the last ten years," she said, her voice dropping to a whisper, "I've been working to overthrow the prince consort. I have the means to do it too, if I can find the manpower."

The entire floor dropped out from beneath him.

Part Three
The Tower

Twenty

"So you been workin' to overthrow the prince consort for years." Blade leaned against the fireplace in the parlor.

"Yes," the duchess replied. Blade's enormous tomcat, Puss, jumped into her lap. Mina hesitantly scratched its scarred ears and it leered at her, if cats could be said to leer. There was something sad in her eyes as she dragged the cat into her arms, her chest vibrating with its purr. "It began the year I ascended to the duchy."

She'd lost her cat, Leo recalled. Found its body butchered in the center of her bed. He stretched his arm out along the back of the daybed, his fingers brushing against her shoulder. Just that, but she gave him a grateful look.

"I seem to recall you votin' 'is way several times," Blade replied.

"Of course. There could never be any doubts cast my way. So I voted for him when the outcome was unaffected by my choice or when it was a small concession or even on those rare occasions when we agreed." Stroking the cat, she glanced at Blade. "You doubt me and yet you never asked why I voted for you to live three years ago."

A Council vote in which Mina, as the seventh councilor, had held Blade's life entirely in her hands. Leo stirred. *He'd* wondered.

"Thought you wanted Vickers dead, which I did for you," Blade replied, his eyes narrowing.

"Partly, but you had already dueled with the duke—and won. The prince consort wished you dead for it. And we were never friends, Blade. But I let you live."

"Why?" Leo asked.

Taking a deep breath, Mina licked her lips. "Because I have never worked alone."

You could have heard a pin drop in that moment. Leo's fingers curled into her shoulder, mind racing. Who was she protecting? Not once had the duchess ever revealed an alliance. No friendships, no romantic entanglements, barely any strategic associations at court.

But her words came back to him, about voting for the prince consort on smaller matters, keeping her cards entirely close to her chest. If she'd had an alliance, then it was one that must never be guessed. Someone she could be seen with and never have doubt cast upon their precise relationship.

Someone no one would believe…

He sucked in a sharp breath, incredulous. Of course. The one person she could spend time with and never be suspected, because the prince consort had *asked* her to take his wife in hand. "The queen," he whispered,

knowing it for the truth and yet instantly rejecting it.
"The queen is doing this."

The human queen everyone saw as a puppet.
The same bloody woman who'd simply sat there
without a hint of protest when the prince consort
condemned him.

Mina nodded very minimally.

"Strike me blind," Blade breathed. "The bloody
queen."

"She knighted Blade so that he would be in a
position to fight Vickers," Leo said. "That's why you
voted for him to live."

"Usually we plan our moves, but Blade storming
into the Ivory Tower to rescue Honoria was too good
an opportunity to pass up," Mina admitted. "Alexandra
obviously saw some purpose to keeping you alive, so I
followed her lead, hoping it was for the best."

Bloody hell. Leo's mind was working, still throwing
up moments that seemed, in hindsight, something that
should have alerted him at the time. All these years the
two women had been playing the court in tandem. He
couldn't quite describe the way he felt.

"So 'ow'd you plan on overthrowin' 'im?"

"She's the leader of the humanist party," Leo said.

The duchess continued, repeating everything that
she'd told him earlier. About channeling funds through
Sir Gideon Scott, the head of the Humans First political party, of how she and the queen had sold most
of the jewelry the prince consort had given her and
mortgaged the House of Casavian's unentailed properties to create a business company. Small investments at
first. Shipping, insurance, bonds, the Exchange…even

a coffee plantation in the colonies that reaped reward. Building on that with every step over the years until the funds had begun flowing in.

The extent of it was stunning. Too impossible to believe. But he did. He had to. There was no other explanation for this, and Mina's knowledge of the humanists was too comprehensive for her to be making this up.

All these years, they'd been fighting on the same side. She wasn't the enemy; she never had been. And though he had admired her for her wits and courage, that was nothing compared to how he felt now. He felt as if the floor had dropped out from under him again.

The analytical part of his brain that never stopped working threw another thought into his sphere. Outing his parentage was a move that would have gained her plans nothing. Indeed, removing him as Caine's proxy would have been a setback for her plans. Leo had long voted for progress on the Council but Caine would not have.

She had never meant for his bastardry to become general knowledge. There had been no intent of betrayal.

For the first time in days, he felt like he could breathe again.

"Who else is involved?" Leo asked when she paused for breath.

"Only Sir Gideon, the queen, and me," she replied, but her gaze dipped.

His hand reached out and caught hers, giving it a warning squeeze. "The truth?"

She clearly didn't want to speak, but finally the strength seeped out of her shoulders. "And Malloryn."

"Malloryn?" Of all people, he'd never suspected his former friend.

"He has a network of informers to rival Balfour's Falcons. He was the first to discover something was going on, and when he confronted me with it, I managed to offer him something he wanted in return."

He could imagine only too well what that something was. Rage stormed inside him as he realized why his former friend had suddenly started turning away from him when Leo had made it clear he intended to pursue the duchess. "You."

"Malloryn's many things, but to be swayed by a woman? No. He wants power and revenge. Most of all, he wanted the main alliance out of the way—the prince consort and his puppets: Morioch, Caine, and the late Duke of Bleight. I offered him a chance to destroy those four and a place on the new Council, should we succeed." Mina looked him in the eye. "Though we were lovers for a time."

She'd not been innocent, but the idea of his own bloody friend in her bed—

Blade laughed, a disbelieving sound. "*Bloody 'ell*. 'Onor's not gonna believe this…"

There was a sudden commotion in the yard, and Blade's head jerked up as if scenting danger. Leo found his feet, one hand staying the duchess where she sat. His other hand strayed to the pistol at his belt.

Shouts caught his ear. Leo strode to the window. There were torches in the courtyard, shapes striding in under the gate…tall men. And there, glancing up at the Warren from beneath a ragged gray cloak, was a pale, heart-shaped face with bronze eyes. His heart squeezed in his chest. "*Lena.*"

He didn't realize how much he'd feared for her until that moment. Shooting the duchess one last glance, he hurried through the door to the landing. He hadn't seen Will, but that didn't mean he wasn't there. Where his wife went, Will followed. Unless—

Then his sister was standing in the doorway at the bottom of the stairs, a huge man draped over her shoulder as she tried to help him inside. Barely tall enough to reach Leo's shoulder, yet somehow she kept her husband on his feet.

Lena's weary eyes met his, relief widening them. "Oh thank goodness. Oh, Leo! I didn't know what had happened to you."

Blade thundered down the stairs past him and caught Will under the arm. Leo followed, squeezing Lena's shoulder and planting a kiss on her tearstained cheek before she urged him to help her husband. Will stank of blood and smoke, his teeth bared in pain as they shouldered him through the door.

"Upstairs," Blade commanded.

With a grunt, Leo bent to lift Will's legs. Will snarled and Lena grabbed his hand. "Easy. Easy, Will. It's Leo and Blade."

They staggered their way up the stairs with him, cursing and swearing. Will towered over both of them by a good few inches, his shoulders broad enough to make getting him through the door a hassle. Every step made blood weep at Will's side, and Leo's arm was warm with it.

Lena bit her lip. Her husband's enormous body shook violently as they eased him onto the daybed the duchess had vacated. "You're safe now. We're both safe. We're at the Warren."

Blade jerked Lena against him in a quick hug before snapping orders at the trio of men who'd followed him in, all exhausted verwulfen by the look of them.

"Christ, don't you look a right treat," Blade said when they cleared the room, then knelt over Will in a rough hug and thumped his back. Strain lines tightened around his mouth. "Thought you weren't comin' 'ome to me, you big brute."

Leo turned away to give the two men privacy. The relationship between them was complex. Blade had rescued the lad from a cage at the age of fifteen and taught him what the words "safety" and "home" meant. They weren't brothers, nor father and son, but family all the same.

Lena threw herself into Leo's arms the second he turned and he clung to her, resting his chin on her head. Crushing his eyes closed as he breathed in the smoky scent of her. *Thank God.*

"They attacked the house," Lena said as she drew back. "We didn't even know what was happening, but Max helped Will get me out. The whole city's afire with riots and metaljackets. Word on the streets claimed you'd been sentenced as a traitor and the prince consort had given Blade 'til morning to surrender you. That it was war between the Ivory Tower and the rookeries." She dashed at her welling eyes with her dirty sleeve. "Will was hurt badly trying to get us to safety, but we knew we had to be here." She looked at her husband. "He wouldn't let me tend it. Not until he knew I was safe."

Blade had taken over, ushering Will onto his back on the sofa and peeling him out of his bloodied shirt. He saw the stab wound and winced. "'E's 'ealin'. Need to get some food into 'im."

The loupe virus that verwulfen suffered from could heal almost anything, though it took its toll. The verwulfen were insanely strong and virtually unstoppable in battle, but once the fight was over, their entire systems shut down for them to recuperate. And now that he had gotten his wife to safety, Will slumped back on the sofa and passed out.

"I know how he feels," Lena said with a weary smile. She too was verwulfen now.

"Stay awake," Blade told her. "We need to know what's goin' on in the city."

"Insanity. Master Reed was arrested earlier this morning, as well as several high-ranking Nighthawks. Lynch was thrown in the dungeons last night for refusing to assist in Leo's capture."

"They're still alive?" Leo demanded.

A helpless shrug. "There are fires all over that section of town. The Coldrush Guards have surrounded the Nighthawks Guild and have warned them not to attempt anything."

"Shit, were 'opin' Reed might be able to get Morioch off me back." Blade and Leo shared a glance. "We won a brief reprieve, but Morioch'll be back, and this time he'll come in strength." One of the verwulfen returned with bread and a bowl of clean water, and Blade dismissed him to tend his own wounds. "Sorry, luv," Blade muttered. "Looks like you might've come to the wrong 'aven. Least you can 'elp me get 'Onor and the baby out—"

"Baby?" Lena demanded. "She's had the baby?"

"A little girl." Both pride and fear softened Blade's voice. "Emmaline Grace."

"I'm an aunt?"

Leo cut his hand through the air to still her. "You can see her later. I'm sorry, Lena, there's no time at the moment." He turned to Mina. "Morioch will return. The rookery will fall. These points are certain. We don't have the men or the manpower here to defeat a full legion of metaljackets."

The duchess circled the daybed, wearing Blade's shirt and a pair of leggings. Her feet were bare, her glorious red hair tumbling around her kiss-ravaged face.

Their eyes met and then her gaze turned to Lena.

"My sister," he told her. Lena gasped and looked up at him. "It's all right," he said. "The Council knows the truth. That's what set off this entire catastrophe."

"No, it ain't," Blade muttered from where he was cleaning Will's wound with the water. "Only, some of us is arrogant enough to think it."

Lena eyed the duchess warily. "Leo, what's going on?"

"Her Grace is helping us with our little problem." He helped Lena to sit in a padded armchair, handing her a piece of the bread. There was blood at her temples.

"You can trust her." He gestured for Mina to continue her story as he examined the lump hidden in Lena's dark hair. The skin was red, but whatever cut she'd suffered had closed already. "Lena's aware of the humanists—"

"I know."

And Mina would. Lena had once been a spy for the humanists until it grew too dangerous.

"Seems a day o' revelations," Blade muttered, tearing a strip off his own shirt to bandage Will's side. "Turns out we finally found that money trail for the 'umanist movement that we were lookin' for when we got you out. Meet the puppet master 'erself."

Lena shoved to her feet, fierce anger blazing in her eyes. Leo caught her before she leaped for the duchess, her fingers curled into fists. "Someone threatened me," Lena hissed. "Told me to destroy the prince consort's alliance with the Scandinavian verwulfen clans or they'd hurt my brother Charlie. Someone in the Ivory Tower, a humanist who was also a blue blood. It was you, wasn't it?"

"Yes." The duchess stilled. "Although I made a farce of supporting the Scandinavian alliance, it was deemed dangerous to the cause. We didn't wish the prince consort to have an alliance with anyone. We were trying to cut his political opportunities out from under him."

Tears gleamed in Lena's eyes. "You bitch."

"I never intended to hurt the boy," Mina said softly, looking up at Leo. "It was…a gambit. I needed her cooperation for just a little longer…"

"I believe you," he said, catching Lena against his chest. "Lena, we don't have time to hold grudges." He stroked her cheek. "I trust the duchess. I have to."

"Thank you," Mina murmured.

"Don't think you're forgiven." Lena glared.

"If she gets us out o' this mess," Blade said, "then she'll 'ave earned me forgiveness." He looked up. "But not before it."

Mina picked the cat up again and curled her face into the top of Puss's head, seeking refuge with her one ally in the room. Leo settled Lena back into her chair. She had been verwulfen for only a year. Trying to adjust to the changes in her body was difficult at times, particularly controlling the fierce emotions that a verwulfen was prone to suffer.

"Sun's goin' to come up soon and Morioch's gonna 'it us with everythin' 'e 'as," Blade continued. "I'm more interested in the part where you show us 'ow to defeat 'im."

"She means the Cyclops automatons," Lena said. "The ones Mercury wanted me to create last year."

"Thought you said there weren't enough of 'em," Blade said. "That Mercury ceased her activities with only a little over a 'undred or so."

"There aren't enough," Mina interrupted. "Not in Mercury's quadrant, but Mercury—or Rosalind Lynch, rather—was not the only one creating them for me. We needed a figurehead, someone to rouse the people, and so the legend of Mercury was created. In secret we had other humanist cells quietly at work in other quadrants of the city. Mercury was not aware of them."

"So why ain't you attacked yet?" Blade asked.

"We have the Cyclops, but we don't have the men to handle them," she replied. "Rosalind's decision to 'retire' from the position of Mercury, following her marriage to Lynch, has been a recent setback. Mercury drew men to the humanist banner and gave the masses something to cheer for." Mina took a deep breath, meeting Leo's eyes. "We were planning to be at full strength within the next two years, but I'm taking a risk here. You have men"—this at Blade—"and the Nighthawks if we can free them. You also have a figurehead. Every human man, woman, and child knows the name of the Devil of Whitechapel. All you'd need to do is rise up against the prince consort and they'd follow you. The mob has always been something the prince consort fears."

"And in return?" Blade asked. "What do you get?"

"Precisely what we want. The prince consort overthrown, preferably dead, and the queen on the throne, ruling as she was always meant to rule."

"The people like her, but support's been waning the last few years," Leo pointed out quietly. "Over some of the decisions she's made."

"They were never her decisions," Mina shot back fiercely. "If the Devil of Whitechapel storms into the Ivory Tower and then bends knee before her…they'll yield. And she can earn their trust the hard way."

"Is she strong enough to do it? All of us at court know she dabbles with laudanum."

Mina's cheeks flushed. "She *will* give it up. It simply…it eases her burden at times. You don't know what he's like behind closed doors." This time she included the whole room in her glance. "He takes out every slight and challenge he receives on her. When Blade defeated Vickers because she gave him the chance…there were so many bruises. I will never atone for that. For leaving her there to face that. For telling her not to defy him. For not killing him when I have had the chance." Head bowing, she whispered, "How could I ask her to give up the one thing that gives her relief when there is no end in sight?"

This was not simply an alliance between two powerless women, Leo realized. "You love her."

"More than anything. She is my dearest friend, my only friend. The sister that I never had."

Those shining eyes told him everything about her reasons.

"If I send you off with a bunch o' the lads, you think you can use the Cyclops to defeat Morioch?" Blade asked.

"Can you hold the rookery until we return?" she asked.

Blade narrowed his eyes. "I'll 'ave to, won't I?"

Tension thickened in the air. Leo turned to Lena. "In aid of that, I have a question for you."

"Yes?" his sister asked.

"What do you know about frequencies?"

Twenty-one

TWILIGHT SETTLED OVER THE CITY, SMOKY-EDGED AND restless. The sun was a molten ball in the sky as it sank, casting the west into a dirty orange smudge through the haze. If Mina looked hard enough, she could just make out the needlelike spire of the Ivory Tower. All of the fires in the city had been put out during the day, except for the one near the Nighthawks' guild head-quarters. The fires were signs of rebellions crushed and dampened in other parts of the city, no doubt.

Hold on, she whispered to herself. *Just hold on, Alexa. I'm coming to get you.*

"Your body armor's ready," a smooth voice murmured behind her.

Just the sound of it sent a shiver across her skin. Mina turned, seeking Barrons out in the shadows of the room. Once a prison, now it seemed a haven of sorts. It was easier to let down her guard here when there were just the two of them. Especially now that she'd revealed everything. It created an intimate little silence between them, the vague beginnings of trust she'd thought long gone.

Leo wore unrelieved black from head to toe. Sunlight winked through the ruby stud in his ear. The sight was so familiar that she felt a little clench in her chest, but when she stepped away from the window, crossing toward him, he gave no sign that he felt it too.

Blade had delegated the pair of them to prepare, while he sorted through his men for those dexterous enough to handle the Cyclops. A hard balance. Take too many and the wall would fall. Mina knew only too well what she was asking of him. Admiration bloomed like a reluctant flower. The Devil of Whitechapel was a dangerous man but, she was starting to realize, he was also incredibly loyal and protective of those he considered his own. A man who weighed the risks of halving his forces, knowing that if he erred on either side, their mission would fail.

And his people would die.

Morioch might have fallen back for most of the day, after his ruse with the clockwork bombs had failed, but she could hear the marching step of metal feet in the distance, even through the closed window. The rest of the Echelon's automatons, half of them ceremonial, no doubt. Morioch was so determined to win the rookery that he was stripping valuable defenses from the Ivory Tower.

There couldn't be a better opportunity, could there? Mina rubbed at her chest, trying to ease her doubt.

Barrons held up a brass-plated protective leather corset that would buckle over her shirt. Outwardly he seemed relaxed but she sensed the same inner tension within him. "It's one of Lark's, apparently."

It should fit. The young woman was of a height

with her, though Mina couldn't help wondering if she'd be able to breathe. She held out her hand and he responded with a rather bland look that said everything.

"It won't be the first time I've played lady's maid for you." Although there was a challenging glint in his eyes, his voice was rougher than it ought to be and a shadow of stubble decorated his cheeks. Mina recognized a bone-deep weariness that had nothing to do with lack of sleep. He'd had one shock after another in the last few days, and though she could see him slowly putting himself back together, the experiences still haunted his eyes at moments.

She didn't have the heart to insist he wait outside. "How does it work?"

"Hold your arms up." Barrons tugged the laces as loose as he could, then slipped it over her head, sliding it down over her shoulders and setting it into place over her hips and waist. His hands smoothed over her hips, pausing for just a moment. She could almost feel the tension building in his body. Mina dragged her hair over her shoulder, holding it there.

"You're nervous." His clever fingers pulled at her laces, his breath ghosting over the back of her neck.

No point in denying it. She felt ready to fly out of her skin. "I'm trying not to think about it."

"You can trust Blade—"

"I wouldn't have ever mentioned it if I didn't think I could trust him."

The press of his body was somehow comforting, even as his fingers slowed. "Then what's bothering you?"

"I'm well out of my depth here." It felt strange to admit to a weakness. "I have no information. I don't know what's going on at court, if the queen's still well, if all of the humanists I've set into place are still free—" *If Hannah and Grimsby and the rest of her people were safe…*

"Breathe," he suggested. Warm fingers curled over her shoulders, abandoning any pretense at lacing her up. He dragged her back against his body, pressing his lips lightly to the back of her neck. "And tell me what the real problem is."

Mina stood arrested. *The real problem…?* She opened her mouth, then paused, letting his thumbs dig into the tense muscles of her shoulders through her silk shirt. Working her way through the turmoil in her mind. "What if I have one chance and I destroy it by moving too quickly? Surprise is our only weapon."

"What if you have one chance…and you never take it?"

The words were a blistering realization. Mina glanced over her shoulder helplessly.

"You need to trust in yourself—in all of us. The Ivory Tower is going to fall, Mina, sooner or later. There are too many voices that refuse to be silenced, too many people the prince consort's crushed. He cannot kill them all. And I know, in here"—he thumped his fist against his heart—"that when we rise, the whole of London will rise with us. He can't defeat that, Mina. That's how I know we're going to win."

She could barely think, blinded by the surety in his voice—and the sudden realization that this was the only man who had ever understood her on any level.

The truce between them was a tenuous one, but she could feel him reaching out to her. Mina stayed very still, softening under the slow circles of his thumbs. *I'm tired of pulling away.*

What if you have one chance…and you never take it?

The words echoed in her ears and beat in her heart, like the opening strains of a waltz, growing stronger, steadier, as the players found their confidence. Wondering in that moment if this was all that the pair of them would ever have—stolen moments shrouded in secrecy.

"Lean forward," he suggested.

Without thinking, Mina turned, gripping his face and lifting up onto her toes. She only had a second to see the shocked look in his eyes, and then her lips met his. A strangled sound came from his throat, then his hands slid over her hips, jerking her roughly against him. He kissed her with everything he had.

This man would never be easy to manage. She could never hide herself from him. He'd demand everything of her and still ask for more, and she wasn't certain she could give it. But this…

Mina pressed him back against the wall, sliding her hungry hands down over his chest. His own caressed her arse, grinding her hips against him, letting her feel just how much he wanted her. She wanted more, wanted to feel the smooth glide of his skin beneath hers. Mina's hands yanked at his shirt, dragging it out of his pants, her palms seeking the coolness of his skin beneath. Roaming the tautness of his flat stomach, feeling the ripple of his abdominals quiver beneath her touch, and up over the hard planes of his chest.

More.

Mina bit his lip, jerking her hands out to tug at his buttons. One hit the floor. She didn't care. Barrons pushed her away just long enough to jerk the damned shirt over his head with a snarl, baring all of that skin to her gaze, to her touch. He caught her wrists and dragged her back against him, holding her there.

"Not that I'm complaining," he gasped, the words so rough and raw that it pulled at something deep inside her, "but what did I say to bring this about?"

Her heart twisted in her chest, all of the doubt washing down on her again. "Maybe I'm just thinking about the future. About tonight. We're going to war, Barrons. What if I never get this chance with you? What if I never get to make love to you?"

His expression sharpened, understanding what she was truly suggesting. *People died. Even blue bloods. Especially those she cared about.*

"I thought we'd covered that." He took the easy way out.

"You tied me to a chair. I would hardly call what happened here before 'making love.' Something more akin to war."

Fingertips skittered down her face. "We've got but an hour or two, love." Leaning closer, his voice dropped several octaves. "That's hardly time enough for what I have in mind to do to you."

A little thrill whispered over her skin. "You're a resourceful man. I'm certain you'll come up with something."

"Something? Hmm?" His expression darkened, teeth nipping at her jaw, her throat. "I think we can do better than that." The press of his body against her earned a gasp. Taking her wrists in one hand left the other free to explore, and he used it with devastating effect.

"Barrons?" She wriggled against his hold.

"Yes?" His fingers paused, trailing over her leather-clad thigh.

Her lashes lowered. "I liked the way you kissed me. That time at your secret house, in your bathroom."

Not so much the method of kissing—he excelled at that but the look in his eyes as he did it, the way he stared at her as if she were the most beautiful thing he'd ever seen. As if he saw every facet of her: strengths, her weaknesses, the way she girded her armor against the world... Saw it and understood all of it.

Long, slow moments trickled by. "Did you?" His eyes blackened, far more intense than they'd been. Burning right through her.

Barrons leaned down and caught her beneath her bottom, lifting her up into his strong arms. He kissed her, slow and deep, striding toward the bed with her legs wrapped around his hips. The armored corset came off, then her undershirt and chemise, leaving her pale flesh bared to his gaze as she tumbled onto her back on the bed. Leo's eyes drank her in, fingertips skating up over her ribs and brushing against the undersides of her full breasts. A square of dying sunlight from the window gilded the hard muscle in his shoulders, catching the faded tips of his eyelashes.

Mina's breath caught. He was an astoundingly handsome man, all hard planes and lean angles, with those dark, fathomless eyes. Only she knew what lurked there. A man of impressive strength of will. Being beaten down, facing the loss of all he knew had cut any softness from him, but instead of destroying him, she could see it making him anew. Like a blade, forged in hot coals and hammered out slowly to hone its edges.

There was a softening in her at the thought. She cupped his face and he leaned into it instinctively, seeking more from the touch. She didn't like to see him hurting, though it was necessary if he wanted to move through all of this.

Leo's pulse raged in his throat as he knelt over her, callused palms rasping up over her breasts. "I never thought you'd ever surrender to me," he admitted, kneeling over her.

"This is not a surrender." Her hands pressed flat against the heavy slab of his chest, her body tensing.

"No?" The muscle in his biceps flexed as he lowered himself over her, her hands giving way slowly, those dark eyes watching her as he brushed his lips against her breast. "Then what do you call it, Mina?"

Her hands tensed.

"Let me in," he whispered, his breath stirring over her sensitive flesh, his tongue darting over her nipple and sending shivers across her skin. "Stop fighting me. Let me make love to you. Let me show you all the ways I've been dreaming of to pleasure you over the years."

She couldn't stop a shaky breath. Surrender was a word she didn't like. It spoke too much of leaving herself unprotected, leaving her heart bared and wide open. But she had asked this of him. Her arms yielded, her eyes closing softly. Her fingertips grazed his lean flanks as she let her hands fall to the bed.

She was the picture of submission, but she couldn't help feeling as though a part of her steeled itself.

"What do you have to fear?" he asked gently, his body weight hovering over her as if her hands were still between them. "I won't hurt you." Lips brushed against her jaw, her throat... Silken caresses she felt to the bone, with her eyes clenched tightly shut.

His mouth trailed up her cheek. More devastatingly light caresses. Over her brow and eyes, her eyelashes rasping his soft lips. Taking her chin, he tipped her mouth up to his, the weight of his body softening upon hers as he rested on one arm. His tongue caressed hers in light, slow circles, his entire body seeming to wrap around her as if he were melting into her. The kind of kisses that stole her breath and made her dizzy.

Everything that she'd asked for. Mina blinked hotly as she drew back from the kiss, her bones feeling like weighted lead and her skin flushed and heated. It was a little disorienting. She wanted it so much and yet...

Leo rested his forehead against hers, breathing in the scent of her. "What's wrong?"

"Nothing's wrong." She wanted more of that kissing and reached for him, but he held her down, wrists pinned to the bed.

Meeting that gaze was hard. In it was a silent demand. "Talk to me," he said, then his expression softened. "Please."

"I just... This is..." Mina looked away. "I've always believed that loving someone is giving them the power to destroy you," she whispered. "It's... I feel like—I can't—"

"You already have the power to destroy me."

Her breath caught.

"And it's terrifying," he admitted. "I feel like I'm standing in an entirely new world, a world I don't know, but one full of so much possibility. But the thing that frightens me the most is that I fear I'm standing here alone. That loss would be greater than anything I've suffered this week."

She opened her mouth—then hesitated.

"And you won't say it. You won't tell me that I'm not alone in this, but then I think of what you just asked of me. 'Kiss me. The way you did once.'" A small furrow worked its way between his brows, his gaze absorbing the details of her face. "And I think I know what you're really asking."

"It's not just—" Did she have the nerve to say this? "I want you to be careful," she blurted. "Tonight."

Another slow look that seemed to see right through her. "You lost your entire family." This time his kiss was a feather stroke of lips against hers. His hands softened on her wrists and the sheets rustled beneath them as he moved slowly, deepening the caress. "It makes sense for you to be nervous to let yourself care for someone."

She'd never even admitted it to herself, but it was true. Though she'd taken lovers, she'd kept them at arm's length, and there'd only been one true friendship since her parents died... Mina felt the choking weight of something in her throat. She nodded.

"And a part of you is lonely," he murmured, kissing her jaw. "But you don't know if you can trust me—"

"Of course I trust you. I wouldn't—"

"Trust me not to leave you," he corrected. "Trust me not to die, if you let yourself care."

She fell silent again, so full of feeling that she was afraid if she opened her mouth to speak it would all come welling out.

"It's a risk," he admitted. "But if you don't take it, then you'll never truly live, Mina. And I admit I'm biased. I want you to take that risk." His voice grew husky. "I want you to be my Grace O'Malley— fearless and defiant, despite the odds."

"I want to be that girl too. I want her back... But I'm so frightened that she died with Stephen, with my mother and father—"

"Then forge her anew." A hot, molten whisper against her skin.

Silence. Nothing except the pounding of their hearts. Mina let out the breath she'd sucked in. "Yes," she said. "I could." Perhaps he wasn't the only one finding himself again.

This time when he kissed her, she could sense the change. No holding back. Not for either of them.

A kiss to change her world. Suddenly, surrendering didn't seem like it would be such a bad thing. He knew her fears, her hopes... He knew, without her even saying, what she really wanted.

Mina's tongue plunged into his mouth as she set herself free. Taking what she wanted from him and demanding the same. Barrons—God, she had to stop thinking of him like that. Not now, when his hands and mouth wrought such delicious damage on her body...

"Leo," she whispered in his ear as he caressed the

full curve of her breast. The word was a shocking
intimacy between them, and his eyes lit up with
something heated before he tugged her trousers down
her legs. His were gone too, the proud jut of his cock
angling against the flat plane of his stomach. She hadn't
had time to admire him before, but she did now—
from the tempting trail of dark hair leading south from
his navel to the chiseled vee of his hips... Mina held
out a hand to him and he lowered himself over her.

"Say it again," he demanded.

"Leo..."

The whisper of his skin against hers made her writhe.
A hot mouth closed over the rosy bud of her nipple and
she gasped, hands sinking into his hair and encouraging
him lower, her eyes clenched shut as she threw herself
into the sensations. His heated tongue dipped into her
navel, the gravel of his stubble rasping against sensitive
skin as he moved lower. Mina's fist curled in his hair
as he cupped her bottom in both hands and spread her
thighs, leaning down to devour her.

"Blood and glory!" Her eyes shot open, staring
at the ceiling as her hips worked beneath him. She
was shameless.

And so was he. The things he did to her with his
mouth... The heated coil tightened within her, leaving her wet and gasping, demanding more with harsh
whispers and her own hands clenching in his hair.
Her sex throbbed at the sight of those broad shoulders
spreading her thighs apart... Mina threw her head
back with a cry as his tongue circled her, thrusting
deep into her molten body.

The sounds she made... It wasn't her, and yet

somehow she felt like she'd never existed like this before, never given herself over to a man to be loved like this. Pleasure mounted within her until she felt as though she were on the verge of falling. Mina held her breath, her body arching—

Leo lifted his mouth, a devastating smile curling over his lips as he wiped them with the back of his hand.

"What are you doing?" she demanded, her hips collapsing back on the bed with an explosive exhale of air from her lungs. She lifted her head weakly from the pillow. So damned close...

Hunger filled his eyes, the blackened heat of the craving. Mina's heart thundered to a halt in her chest at the sight.

"I'm taking what is mine."

This time, when he pressed her into the bed, there was a sense of urgency to their actions. Hooking her knee up against his chest, he drove into her, his eyes lost to anything but lust and his lip curled in a silent snarl. The feel of his hard body inside her... She'd forgotten how large he was, how delicious it felt to be utterly, utterly claimed.

Mina clutched at him, unable to take her eyes off his face, until she could no longer hold herself together. She shattered with a cry, fingernails biting into the sleek muscles of his back, leaving little red marks on his shoulders. The angle was shockingly intimate, her knee trapped so that she couldn't escape the flood of sensation. She came again, her entire body shaking as he buried himself inside her with short, hard thrusts, knowing exactly what he was doing to her.

A quiver ran through his shoulders. "Mina," he said, burying his face in her throat as he thrust a little deeper. A gasp was torn from his lips. "Damn it…" He filled her again, long and hard. "Wanted to take this slower…"

She met his eyes and saw the feral need there—Leo Barrons stripped of all his cultured finesse, all of his smooth, seductive devices lost in a shattering haze of need. And suddenly she wanted to drive him beyond control, to prove that he was just as much hers as she was his.

A tight clenching of her body around his wrought another strangled groan. He knew what she was doing, thrusting harder, deeper…until her entire body ached with possession. And still it wasn't enough. She wanted to shatter him.

Nails digging into his back, she bit at his throat and jaw, sharp, stinging nips that made him groan. The *hunger* within her was violent, shocking, completely unrestrained. Yet there was something missing, and by the blood, she knew what it was… Sinking her teeth into the corded tendons in his neck, she bit just hard enough to make his hips jerk.

"Fuck." Hardly the tender love words she'd imagined, but somehow rawer, more primitive for it.

He came with a violent shudder, rocking hard into her, his entire body shaking as he gave himself over to her. The sight of his face, his eyes clenched shut and his mouth parted in ecstasy, did something to her deep inside.

Mine, the hunger inside her purred. But something within her wanted more.

Her mind raced. She'd never drunk fresh from the

vein before the other day. Control was vital, and yet a part of her felt sleekly fulfilled, as if some darker recess of her nature had unfurled itself, glutting itself on the lack of control, the fierce, primitive nature of what had just occurred between them. Reveling in a claiming that was possessive and fierce, owing nothing to the rational part of her mind. Perhaps she'd been suppressing her needs for so long that she hadn't truly understood the darkest part of herself.

Leo collapsed atop her. When he tried to move, Mina curled her arms around him and held him tight, feeling him still inside her. She needed to hold him right now, a little afraid of what had occurred between them. Her entire body was wrung out with the intensity, but she couldn't deny that her heart thundered in her chest, reminding her of the gloriousness of living. She felt dangerously alive, the predator inside her still alert.

Leo finally lifted his face from the pillow. "That wasn't entirely what I intended."

"No?" Mina nuzzled her face against his throat. "Perhaps it's what I planned instead."

His eyelids lowered, only the dark hint of his pupils watching her. Leo slowly withdrew from her body, leaving her wet and aching and loving every moment of it. He curled her into his strong arms, tucking her back into the hollow of his chest and hips. A position that could be either a prison—or total protection.

Mina relaxed her head back onto the pillow of his arm, kissing his biceps.

"You like it when I lose control," he murmured.

"Of course I do. Surrender goes both ways, my love."

"My love?" he repeated with a questioning lilt, tracing skittering circles over her hip.

Mina froze at the realization of what she'd said. Feeling it, Leo kissed the back of her neck and settled in against her, his breath shivering over her skin. "Do you need blood?"

The sharp ache of unfulfillment echoed sharply within her, yet she was nervous. Leo rolled over her and reached for his leather-bound kit, taking out a small razor and testing it against his thumb. He looked at her, accurately reading her expression.

"I know how much you want it, how much you fear it." He held the razor out to her. "And I know this means another surrender for you, but think of it this way: you've been holding your hunger in check for years. Tonight, what we do is dangerous. I want you sharp and alert, and this will grant you that."

At what point had control become fear? Mina eyed the razor. Her mouth watered, nostrils flaring. Everything in her went predatory still.

In the silence she could hear his heart beating. He lay down and stretched one arm above him, cupping his head in his palm, eyeing her with the type of smile she'd never seen on his face before. Completely relaxed and open, with a faint hint of boyishness. Dragging the tip of the razor over his own skin, he let the smile die as her interest flared.

Heart hammering, Mina reached out and took it from him, letting its sharp edge glide down his abdomen just enough to leave a white pressure line on his skin. With her vision enhanced, she could make out every tiny blond hair on his body, the faint lines at the corners of his eyes, even the grain of his dark stubble. She wanted to lick her way up his body, trailing the razor with her.

"You're making me want things I've never wanted before." She let a tiny bead of blood well near his nipple as she pressed the razor harder. Leo sucked in a taut hiss of breath, but his gaze never left hers.

"Perhaps I'm simply encouraging you to do what you've always secretly wanted to, even if that means merely admitting it to yourself." His other hand slid up her thigh, helping her straddle him. "I like it when *you* lose control. I like seeing this part of you, knowing that no one else ever has. Even Malloryn."

Tangled red hair tumbled over her shoulders as she looked up. "You're jealous."

"Of course I am." She saw the same hint of possession in his eyes that she knew dwelled in hers. Almost a challenge.

"You shouldn't be." Reaching out, she touched her fingertip to the droplet of blood on his chest and sucked it into her mouth. The taste of it exploded through her, igniting her senses. Beneath her his cock surged, pressing against wet, sensitive flesh.

"Where?" he asked, knowing the decision had been made.

Mina's heart raced. She knew, even before her vision shattered into shadows, where she wanted to take him. The perfect imprint of her teeth still marred the column of his throat.

Leo saw the direction of her gaze and tilted his head to the side. "Take me, then. Mark me."

And so she did.

Twenty-two

UNDERTOWN EXISTED DEEP BENEATH THE ROOKERIES and streets of the East End, a mishmash of tunnels and hidey-holes carved into the old, abandoned, and partially collapsed train tunnels of the Eastern Underground link. Three years ago a vampire haunting Whitechapel had culled most of the denizens that lived down there, until Blade and Honoria killed it. The slasher gangs that frequently haunted the rookeries had killed the remaining humans, selling their blood to the Echelon's draining factories or to those rogue blue bloods who could pay coin for it on the black market. Now only desperation drove people to seek refuge down here in the dank, whispering darkness.

Desperation *and* revolution.

Splashing along the tunnels, Mina counted quietly under her breath as they reached each intersection. Tiny marks were chiseled onto the tunnel walls, indicating which way to go. Not that any of the others understood them.

"Bold," Leo murmured. "To create an automaton army right in the midst of the enclaves."

"Who would know?" she asked, aware of how closely he followed. Ever since the blood-letting she'd been hyperaware of him, her senses transformed until she wondered how long she'd been only half-asleep and unaware of it. It excited her, even as caution reared. She could feel her blood rushing through her veins, the ache of his claiming deep within her body.

"Kincaid rules the enclaves and he's our man, through and through. Any Echelon inspections are always carried out with advance notice. They're not looking for revolutionaries. Not in the enclaves. They think the mechs nothing but brutes, too stupid to overthrow them and less even than human. Besides, Mercury kept the prince consort's spies busy."

"If Rosalind Lynch finds out she was only a decoy for you, she's going to be furious."

"The Duchess of Bleight is far more practical than that," she countered. "She'll see the purpose behind it."

"Are you so certain of that?"

No. Rosalind had been a practical, utterly ruthless woman. Until Lynch came along and somehow swayed her into giving up her work. Now, as the Duchess of Bleight, Rosalind was proving to be a political thorn in the prince consort's side with him none the wiser about her previous identity, but Mina hadn't forgotten the lesson. Even a ruthless woman could have her head turned by a man, with disastrous consequences.

A part of her could understand the temptation.

"The Duchess of Bleight would have to discover such a truth first, and I'm hardly about to reveal my hand to her," Mina replied. "Here. This tunnel. We're getting closer."

Wispy tendrils of steam filled the tunnel as they turned down it, Blade's men sloshing along behind. Another couple of hundred feet and the hellish red glow of the enclaves began seeping through the grates above them. Mina began to relax. Almost there. A ladder appeared and she reached on her tiptoes to grasp it.

"Do you know the one thing that still makes me curious?" Leo's hard body framed her own as he reached up and unlatched the ladder.

"What?"

"Why you give a damn about restoring human rights and setting the queen in power. Or even how you two came to be involved."

"It's complicated."

"It always is." He held out his cupped hands, gesturing for her to use them to climb up.

Not one token protest about how perhaps he should go first. As she stepped into his cupped palms and used them to haul herself up to the lower rungs of the iron ladder, she frowned. Perhaps she feared her intolerances, not his. She was always waiting for him to protest her abilities, when he'd shown not the slightest indication of doing so.

With a deep breath, she relented, telling him about her first meeting with the princess. Leo listened as he climbed, following at her heels so that his hard body almost caged her in.

Turning the sewer cover at the top, Mina gritted her teeth and gave it an almighty shove. The metal cover shifted sideways, a spill of orange light blinding her. Strategically placed behind a row of boilers, the cover hid anyone trying to sneak in, but she could see hazy figures shoveling coal into the boilers and men lurching past with wheelbarrows.

Easing herself through the hole brought her into a world of heat, the kind that shimmered in the air and rained sweat down every brow she could see. Staying low, she kept watch as she gestured for Leo and several of the others to follow.

"Stay here," she murmured to the scarred brute they'd called Tin Man. "I need to find Kincaid first. Make sure none of the men are seen."

The mute man nodded and Leo fell into step beside her as she scurried through the shadows behind the row of boilers, darting through hissing steam and along the wall to the end of the massive foundry.

"Devil take it, it's like hell in here," Leo murmured.

One of the many reasons the mechs were so bound to the humanist cause. If humans had few rights, mechs had even less. They were forced to work in the enclaves until their mech debt—the cost of their mechanical enhancements—was paid off, working steel to create the Echelon's dreadnought ships and automaton armies, or crafting even finer works in the smaller foundries closer to the edge of the enclave walls, where clock-work organs and mechanical hands fetched top dollar.

"Must be second shift," she said, catching a glimpse of a slim shape moving through the overseer's offices above them. "That looks like Maggie Doyle, Kincaid's assistant."

"Will she know you?"

"She'll know me," Mina replied grimly. Whether Maggie would send for Kincaid was another matter.

Time to find out. Mina rose out of the darkness and set off purposefully toward the metal stairs leading to the overseer's office. Nobody even glanced at them as they climbed, the workers too busy trying to make their quota.

The door opened and Maggie shut it behind her, glaring through narrowed eyes. "What do you want?"

"A word with Kincaid," Mina replied coolly.

"He's busy."

"He'll want to hear me out."

"Busy," Maggie repeated, but this time her sloe-shaped eyes slid over Leo, as if in curiosity. "He's got two girls in there with him. I ain't interruptin'."

Indeed, now that she concentrated, Mina could just make out a hint of giggling coming from the inner offices. "Allow me," she said, stepping past Maggie and reaching for the door.

"You can't just—" The words cut off as Leo no doubt dealt with her.

Striding across the office, Mina didn't bother to knock. "Kincaid?" Jerking the other door open, she found him immediately. Naked as the day he'd been born, with one girl splayed beneath him on an old sofa and the other wrapped over his broad back like a blanket.

A set of evil blue eyes locked on her, and he raked his thick black hair out of his face as he straightened to his knees, cock rampant in front of him and some strange steel contraption seemingly wrapped around his waist, prongs like little steel spider legs caressing his hips. "My mysterious Madame M.," he said. "Come to join the fun?"

"Come to extend an invitation to you," Mina replied. There was some kind of mechanical device running down the back of his thighs, bolts sticking out of the skin. As he shifted, she saw them embedded in his calves too, pistons hissing in the support frame as he moved. An exoskeleton? "I've got something much more enjoyable in mind."

Kincaid glanced at the girl beneath him. "Really? You wouldn't believe what Clara can do with—"

"It's time," Mina interrupted.

That caught his attention. A ripple of something hard and mercenary danced over his features. He snapped his fingers at the two girls. "Leave us."

"Oh, but—"

"Now," he told the pouting girl at his back.

"Excellent prosthesis," Mina murmured as the girl snatched up her shirt and stalked past, steel gleaming at her hip.

The second girl—Clara, she thought—stalked across the floorboards, draping a shirt over her shoulders without buttoning it. Her voluptuous curves taunted in the gaslight and even Mina arched a brow as she stopped in front of Leo, trailing her fingers over his shoulder.

"How 'bout you? Want to play with me?" There was no sign of a mechanical body part, which she'd have to have to live in the enclaves.

"Sorry, sweetheart," Leo replied, his gaze meeting Mina's with a challenge. "I've got everything I want right in front of me."

Mina felt heat rising in her cheeks.

A cynical snort came from behind. Kincaid had laced himself into his leather trousers, thank goodness, and was eyeing Leo with considerable mistrust. "Who's the leech?"

"A friend of mine," she replied.

That made his eyes narrow. "Out," Kincaid commanded Clara, circling Leo as if he were some muscled gladiator in the Pits in the East End, where men wagered on blood and death.

She didn't have time for this—and she also wasn't entirely certain how Kincaid would react. The mech was a dangerous man, used to ruling his enclaves with an iron fist—literally. She'd seen him kill men for the smallest of infractions, and he despised blue bloods.

"Leo Barrons," Leo said, holding out his hand.

Kincaid gripped it, squeezing hard. Mina took a step forward but Leo's swift glance spoke volumes and she froze. Muscle strained in his forearm as Kincaid tightened his iron grip with a nasty grin, and it was a surprise to see that Leo was taller than the burly mech.

"Got a good grip on you." Kincaid laughed. "Come on, why don't you show me how good?"

A mocking arch of the brow. "I don't need to. I already know my cock's bigger than yours."

That startled a laugh out of Kincaid, and Mina watched with bated breath as he released Leo's hand and stepped back with narrowed eyes. "Barrons, eh? You're the one with the price on your head."

"Don't go getting any ideas. In short order, nobody's going to have any coin to pay that reward."

Kincaid scratched his jaw. Almost as if someone

blew out the flame on a match, his entire demeanor changed, leaving her wondering just what kind of man Kincaid truly was. "We're not ready," he said bluntly. "The Echelon's been squeezing our resources, pushin' our quotas. Haven't had a bloody chance to sneak in any work on the Cyclops." All business.

"We'll take what you have," she replied.

"And ruin the bloody lot?" A scowl darkened his brow and he took a step toward her.

Leo somehow just happened to be standing in the way, looking down at the shorter man as he picked a fanciful clockwork paperweight off his desk and rolled it over the back of his deft fingers. Nothing in his expression changed but Mina had that breathless feeling that they were walking the edge of a knife again and that he was daring Kincaid to push him.

"You're not the only pocket of revolutionists producing the Cyclops," she admitted. "There are four hidden foundries in the city. This is merely the largest."

That made Kincaid's eyes narrow.

"Men can't speak of what they don't know," she reminded him.

"They're all risin' up?"

"As many of them as we can outfit with the Cyclops." All of the humanists she could summon, anyway. The message she'd sent to Sir Gideon Scott would hopefully have found him by now.

Their job wasn't to wait. Sir Gideon could rouse the humanists in their network and fit out the Cyclops in the other sectors. She needed this sector, however, to crush Morioch's forces and spare the rookery.

A devilish gleam burned in those blue eyes. "We're taking the Tower?"

"A slight detour first, then, yes, the Tower."

Kincaid snatched up a metal brace from the desk, drawing it over his head and fixing the leather straps in place to support his iron arm. He hooked a pair of small chains onto the steel hydraulics in his forearm. "Been waitin' on this moment for a long time, lass. My steel wants to taste blood. Blue blood." A pair of thin blades shot out through his steel knuckles.

"Just remember—some of the blue bloods are on our side," she warned. "If we do this, you follow my command."

There was a momentary pause. Then Kincaid graced her with a dangerous smile. "Of course. Wouldn't dream otherwise."

⤝⤞

"Bloody hell."

Leo rapped a knuckle against one of the steel breast-plates on the first Cyclops. They gleamed in the darkness as Kincaid lifted his phosphorescent smuggler's lantern, dozens of them...no, hundreds...stretching into the cavernous warehouse buried deep beneath the enclaves. All of them faceless, with thin, glass eye slits at the throat through which a man inside could peer as he operated the massive device. They stood a good three feet taller than the largest spitfire, wielding enormous flame-throwing cannons fitted to their arms.

"It reminds me of an old tale I once read about rumors of a hidden, long-lost army in the Orient," Leo murmured.

Mina came into view, her hand sliding over the elbow joint of the Cyclops in front of him. "You've read Sir Nicodemus Banks's *Travels to the Orient*?"

Few blue bloods gave a damn about their origins. Banks had written of his journeys through such foreign lands, including rumors of the Emperors of the White Court hunting for word of the craving virus when the whispers first came to their attention and then deliberately infecting themselves with it to become gods to their people.

"Curiosity is my greatest affliction," he admitted wryly. "I like to know how things work. Why they work. Where they come from."

The human classes in France had dealt with their blue-blood aristocracy during the Revolution, and the Spaniards had used the Inquisition with theirs. Leo paused for a moment, wondering if he was on the brink of the downfall of the remaining blue bloods in London. *Change*, he told himself, *is the way of the future*.

Perhaps England could forge a new way forward, involving mechs, humans, *and* blue bloods, the way the other countries hadn't.

"How does it work?" he asked.

"Like this." She couldn't hide the proud glint in her eyes as she reached up and pressed something high on the breastplate. With a faint hiss, it swung open, revealing a cavity inside where a man could stand, and levers and buttons with which to manipulate it.

"It's amazing." He circled the first iron soldier, peering at it from all angles. "A vast improvement on the metaljackets."

"Having a human to drive it makes it far more

efficient," she replied, hopping up inside the cavity and
sliding her feet into the hollow legs, hooking her boots
into the feet molds. She strapped the leather harnesses
to her thighs and tugged them tight. The boilers on the
thing hissed to life with a press of a button, the Cyclops
vibrating. Sliding the chest harness over her shoulders,
Mina manipulated a set of levers with brisk efficiency,
and one of the arms jerked to attention, pointing a
flamethrower-mounted arm directly at his face.

"Are they difficult to manage?" He peered inside,
his face inches from her thighs. She had legs like a
dancer or a duelist.

For the first time, she looked uncertain. "Not truly.
One wields it physically. If I take a step, it moves with
me, but they will require a certain amount of instruction before one launches them into battle."

Tension filled him. *How much time did they have?*
"We'd be better off using the mechs to drive them.
They, at least, know what everything does. Blade's
men can clear the way until we have some semblance
of control."

Her gaze slid to Kincaid.

"Don't doubt yourself," he murmured, sliding a
palm over her thigh and squeezing it. "He's not going
to make a move. If he'd wanted to, he'd have done
it by now, while you weren't here." Taking a deep
breath, he continued, "You cannot understand how
in awe I am of you, Mina. To create all of this, right
beneath the prince consort's nose… To start with
nothing and build an army large enough to shake the
foundations of the Ivory Tower… You are the most
fearless, amazing woman I know."

OF SILK AND STEAM

"I worked with the queen and others—"

"Yes, but you were the catalyst." He stepped up onto the Cyclops's bent knee, until his face was of a height with hers, leaving her trapped in her harness. Leo brushed his fingers against her cheek, using the other hand to support himself. "Don't you like compliments?"

"I'm used to flattery."

Comments on her beauty. He'd seen the way she shrugged such things off in the past. Leo traced the path of her jaw. "I remember the first time I ever saw you. It was the duel with Peter. You were breathtaking—fierce and aloof and so coldly focused on what you were doing. Determined beyond all means. I wondered then what you could make of yourself." He looked around. "This far surpasses even my expectations."

Something caught his eye. A leather cap drawn low over a young man's face as he darted behind a Cyclops. Leo swore under his breath as he stepped down for a closer look. *Charlie.* Who was supposed to be at the rookery.

A hand tightened around his arm as he took a step toward the lad. "Don't," she said, leaning precariously out of the Cyclops's shell.

"You knew he was here?"

"I saw him but a minute ago. There's nothing to be done now. We cannot send him back, and indeed, I don't believe he'd go. He might as well stay with us—it's the safest place for him."

"You don't understand."

That earned him an arched brow. "Enlighten me."

He didn't want to. What man wanted to speak of his greatest shame? But Mina was watching him with a steady gaze. It couldn't have been easy for her to offer him her trust with so much at stake. And if he wanted to prove himself worthy of it...

"I can't let him get hurt," Leo said, looking away and sliding his hands into his pockets. He presented the very picture of a man of repose, but inside... inside his heart was lead. He added softly, "I caused Charlie's infection with the craving virus. I hated his father—my father. So much so that I sabotaged the vaccine Todd was preparing to inject into himself. I didn't realize Todd intended to use the same vaccination on his son. Charlie...he nearly died, Mina, because of me."

Understanding softened her eyes, then they turned thoughtful. "Your guilt is blinding you. He's not a boy anymore, Leo, but a young man, restless with the cage you're trying to force him into. If you and Blade keep trying to smother him, sooner or later, he will do something foolish—something risky—just to escape it. And if I can see that, then you're closer to that point than you realize."

Leo opened his mouth. Then closed it. He scraped a hand over his stubbled jaw. *Bloody hell.* "So you think I should let him come along?"

"If he wants to come, then he can suit up in one of the Cyclops. It's the safest place for him. I'm quite happy to make it clear that he either follows our orders precisely, or I shall see him chained up in one of the cells for unruly mechs."

"No, I'll do it." He glanced across the room, jaw

tightening. "Just give me a minute, or I'm likely to say something else to him entirely."

"Very well. Here, help me finish strapping in. It will show you what to do."

The next minute was a quiet one, as Mina showed him each control and how it worked. Leo threw himself into the task, pushing Charlie to the back of his mind. Or trying to.

He felt eyes upon him. "Why did you hate your father so much?" she asked.

Leo reached out, helping to strap her buckles into place, taking his time with the answer. He locked the last one tight, testing it across her shoulders, before resting his hands on her hips and looking up. He felt like he was cutting open an old wound, long years of ugly emotions oozing up inside him like an infection that needed to be lanced.

"Perhaps the correct word is not 'hate.' Perhaps it's because I wanted him to be something he wasn't." There were razor blades in his throat. "Todd made it quite clear he never gave a damn about me."

"You hoped for such recognition once?"

"I knew from an early age that the duke was not my father. He told me on the morning of my sixth birthday." Not the best present he'd ever received. "Let us simply say that Caine was a rather cold, exacting 'father.' I remembered Todd from his time serving under Caine's patronage. He was polite, highly intelligent, and driven. Of course, I began to imagine him to be something else; more of a dream than a reality. When I was thirteen, Caine suggested I visit with him. He told me I should learn something of the scientific advances of the time, and it fit with my schooling."

Mina was no fool. "He wanted you to see your father for who he was."

No denying it. Leo's voice roughened. "It didn't matter how harshly Caine treated me, because he wasn't my father. My real father wouldn't have treated me like that, or so I thought. So I began to take instruction with Todd once a week.

"He was obsessed with a cure for the craving and so was his new patron, Vickers. And I wanted to please him. You may find this somewhat ironic, but Todd was one of the first humanists in London. A founding member."

"I know." She hesitated. "He was responsible for developing the plans for the Cyclops. I've always likened him to da Vinci."

"Truly?" That surprised him. Todd had always been mechanically minded but... Leo's hand roved over the Cyclops's steel flank. He could not conceive of a man who could create such a work of mechanical art and still be such a cold bastard.

"So what happened?"

"My fourteenth birthday came—and Caine officially applied to the Council of Dukes to recommend me for the blood rites." The crowning achievement of every aristocratic son's childhood. Only those deemed worthy were infected with the craving virus during their fifteenth birthday rites. "But of course, by that stage I had begun to parrot Todd's humanist sympathies in a bid to earn his respect."

"You didn't want to be a blue blood?"

"I didn't know what I wanted. I only knew that Todd would despise me if I were a blue blood." A remarkable piece of foresight. "Of course, my application was approved. For all intents and purposes, I was Caine's son. I couldn't avoid it except... Todd was working on a vaccine. He promised me it would stop me from becoming 'a monster.'"

The sympathy on her face was too much to handle. "It didn't," he said brusquely. "It was untested, and within weeks I began to show signs of the virus. My visits with Todd ended and Caine helped me hide the fact that I was already infected until after the blood rites."

"And Todd turned his back on you."

"In a way." That wasn't the worst of it. "Caine saw fit to provide me with copies of Todd's journals, where he detailed all of his experiments, including that of Subject 13, whom he tested with the fifth variant of the vaccine. I was clever enough to follow the trail of the dates mentioned. It had to be me. 'Subject 13—though a healthy young man—shows signs of the virus. Variant Five is defective. I will continue to find willing participants in these trials until I meet with success,'" Leo quoted. "Todd was using me for a trial because he did not dare complete these experiments under Vickers's notice. Vickers didn't want a vaccine. He wanted a cure."

"And when Todd finally found a vaccine that worked, you sabotaged it before he could use it."

"An eye for an eye," he murmured. "I kept abreast of his work after the blood rites. Todd despised what I'd become, but it didn't change the way he treated me.

That…it told me everything I needed to know about his feelings for me. I think my 'lessons' catered to his sense of importance—a captive audience, so to speak—and I never told him that I knew what he'd done. Just waited until he finally worked out the solution.

"By that time he'd tested it on Honoria and Lena. I'll never mention it to them, but if he'd truly given a damn about them, he'd never have used them like that. Honoria was always his favorite, but he still vaccinated her before he used it on himself. And when it came time for his attempt…I swapped the vaccines."

"I don't blame you. He sounds like a horrible man. Anyone who makes the Duke of Caine look like the hero—"

"He's not," Leo said quickly. "And neither am I. I didn't…I didn't like the man I became. It wasn't until Honoria turned up on my doorstep four years ago that I realized that there had been consequences to my actions. My selfishness nearly killed my half brother, and not once had I considered that Todd might have used it on someone else." He swallowed, feeling slightly ill. "It's a hard thing to look at yourself in the mirror and not like what you see. Or worse, to see your father looking back at you. Both of them."

"It's even harder to admit that," she told him. "Or to seek to change your ways." A slight bow of the head. "You would not be the man you are now if your actions had not caused Charlie's infection. You would still be angry and bitter toward a father you barely knew, careless of consequences. Perhaps… perhaps despite all of the pain you've been dealt, you have become a better man for it."

It almost undid him. Leo looked away, swallowing against the bitter shards in his throat. Yet, in a sense it rebuilt a part of him that he'd feared lost. She gave him an anchor against the tide of despair that had swept him away... God, how long had it been? Only a couple of days ago?

In the shadows, dozens of mechs swarmed over the Cyclops suits, fitting themselves into the interiors. Leo watched, but his mind wasn't on them.

What had he lost, truly? Caine's face sprang to mind. Nothing worth such grief. This...what he saw here. This was his legacy. His deeds, not the extent of property he'd owned or people who didn't give a damn about him. And Mina. Of everything, she had become the most important.

Reaching out, he brought her fingers to his lips. "Thank you."

He tried to let her hand go, but Mina turned it, cupping his cheek in her palm as she stroked his face with her thumb. Her eyes were soft and contemplative. "Sometimes I grow so angry when I think of all that has befallen me. But then...where would I be if it had not? The queen would be a stranger. I would most likely be trapped in a thrall contract, and"—her voice dropped to a whisper—"I would never have met you."

The words rocked him to the core. Was she saying what he thought she was? "I thought you wanted to be free of me." Deceptively casual words. His gut muscles locked tight in anticipation of her answer. Nothing of the future had been discussed between them.

"I did." Her eyes were shining bright.

"And now?"

"I'm not entirely certain." A pained whisper as she studied his face. Still wary, still cautious. "It was easier before I knew the type of man you were—before the prince consort tried to destroy you. I don't know if I would have let you seduce me then. Now?" Mina took a deep breath. "When this is all over, I want you to be my lover on a permanent basis."

Not enough. Never enough. He wanted her and he wanted her forever, and if she wouldn't dare take that step, then he would. "When this is all over," he whispered, stepping up onto the Cyclops's bent knee so that their faces were but an inch apart, "I'm going to ask you to be my wife."

Her shocked intake of breath stole his. "Leo—"

Sliding a hand around her nape, he drew her mouth to his, tasting the sweetness of it in soft, hungry kisses that gave way to something far more possessive. He wasn't lost anymore, unable to determine his future or second-guessing every decision he made… The words were a rash declaration, but they rang so true that a part of him ached.

He knew what he wanted now.

This. Her. The dark depths of his hunger rose, a brutal claiming that stirred his very soul. Drawing back, he cupped her face, forcing her to look at him. "I'm going to make you mine, Mina."

Her pulse flickered in her throat like a rabbit's. She wet her lips. "If this were a different world, I might say yes."

He'd pushed her far enough. Any more and she might run. Leo stepped back, letting go of the Cyclops's arm. "Then let's go forge another world together."

Twenty-three

LENA SLID HER PHOSPHORUS-LENS GOGGLES UP ONTO her head, chewing on her lip as she peered out into the darkness. Will was a warm, steady presence at her back, one of his hands splayed over her hip. He was a comfort in the dark night, his job only to protect her on this dangerous mission.

Perched on the rooftop with him, overlooking the crowd of metaljackets, she fiddled with the frequency on the control device Leo had given her. A few adjustments earlier had altered the control pad into something that amplified the waves that controlled the automatons. She'd tried to alter the frequency, but the metaljackets only seemed to respond to something of a similar wavelength. "Please let it work," she whispered, glancing at Blade perched high up on the rookery walls.

Wave after wave of automatons stared at the wall, a larger assault than had been launched so far. Blade's expression was grim, even from this distance. There was no way the walls could withstand this kind of assault, and from the look of the front row of metaljackets, Morioch was sending in his spitfires to burn the rookeries.

Images burned through her head, making her perspire. Honoria, in bed with her niece...helpless as fire leaped from house to house. The houses were so closely packed that the spitfires would barely need to use their flame-throwing cannons once the first house caught.

"It'll work," Will murmured, hunting the shadows for anyone who might have seen them.

His complete confidence in her abilities made her heart soar. Taking a steady breath, Lena watched as Morioch lifted his arm in the air.

"Burn them out!" he yelled, and his arm dropped, just as more than four hundred metaljackets took a step forward, iron boots ringing simultaneously on the cobbles.

Time to find out if her device worked.

∞

Blade tensed, one arm lifted in the air as he watched Morioch's arm drop and the metaljackets surge forward as one. Flanked by plain metaljackets, the spitfires came first, their flame-throwing cannons dropping into place as they aimed at the walls.

Seemed Morioch wasn't going to bother with destroying a legend and creating a martyr. He just wanted the rookeries destroyed. *Christ*, the walls were only lightly manned, barely enough to deflect heavy artillery. Where the hell were Leo and the duchess? *Honor...* Blade's breath caught in his chest, panic a cold spiral through him. An image of his daughter's sleeping face flashed to mind. Two people he'd die for, if that were necessary to keep them safe. "Sorry, luv," he whispered into the night, knowing Honoria would never forgive him if he didn't come home to her, if he didn't keep the promises he'd made when he left her trying grimly not to cry.

His gut twisted, his arm starting to drop to urge his own men on and—

One by one the metaljackets went mad.

Blade caught his arm in mid-descent. "Hold!" he roared. The demon of his hunger, his craving, wasn't on him now and he had to make do with only slightly enhanced vision. Never before had he been so frightened that he'd been unable to rouse it.

"Bloody 'ell," Rip said.

Flame spurted into the air as a spitfire spun in circles, unleashing jets of liquid Greek fire across its compatriots. Several of the metaljackets simply slumped to the ground, the ones behind them grinding straight over the top of them. Mayhem. Sheer, glorious mayhem.

"It worked," he said incredulously, eyeing the nearby rooftop where Lena worked her device.

"Only within a certain range." Rip pointed at the far side of the wall, where metaljackets advanced grimly on the rookery.

"I'll take advantage o' whatever Lady Luck can send me." A vicious note descended into his voice. This time the darkness of his craving swept up over him, the edges of his shadowy vision tinged with red. No fear now. Only the violent desire to do as much damage as possible before the metaljackets reached the walls.

This time when he lifted his arm, there was no doubt. "Into the streets, boys! And aim for the joints!"

A roar shook the wall as men slung grappling hooks into the wall, then leaped into the melee below.

Twenty-four

THE ENORMOUS CLANKING CREATURE THAT ENVELOPED Leo was less difficult to control than he'd expected, though he'd needed most of the half-hour walk through the streets to work out what everything did.

Charlie, of course, had taken to the Cyclops as if he'd built them himself. The lad was amusing himself by running at walls, then performing backflips.

Ahead of him, Mina's arm went up—or at least, the metal fist of the automaton. "They're fighting," she yelled. "Kincaid, take the east. We'll hit them from the south. Grind them up against the walls!"

Half of the mechs clanked after Kincaid, leaving Leo and Mina with the band of Blade's men and about a hundred mechs suited up. Leo strode forward, his own legs working within the Cyclops. Pneumatic pistons hissed beneath him as the creature clattered over the cobbles. His thighs strained with effort.

"Morioch's ahead," Mina said to him, her dark eyes visible behind the thin eye slit of the automaton.

"He's mine," Leo returned, grimly anticipating the

look on the duke's face when Leo came crashing out of an alleyway.

"Don't get yourself killed," Mina said.

Recognizing her nervousness for what it was, he forced a smile. "Isn't that my line?"

A roll of the eyes. "I was waiting for it."

The straps of the leather harness bit into his shoulders as he shrugged. It was so damned close in here, the weight of the metal seeming to loom against his skin. Heat bloomed along his spine where the boilers sat. "I make a habit of not irritating women who could set me on fire. Besides, logic dictates you're more competent in this thing than I am."

A long considering look. "Watch my back then." A concession he'd earned by not trying to keep her out of the fighting.

"Always," he replied and then worked the lever that set his Cyclops into motion.

Fire spewed over houses outside the walls as Leo strode forth with his contingent. Spitfires were going insane, marching on their own metaljackets as Blade's rookery lads protected the base of the wall. A golden carriage stood in the midst of a dozen metaljackets, with Morioch on top of it shouting for order. Several handlers furiously worked their controls.

Leo's eyes narrowed on the duke. Advancing through the tide of metaljackets, he smashed several of them out of his way with his enormous metal fists. The Cyclops was hard work; he jerked on the controls and gritted his teeth as metaljackets swarmed him. An enormous steel boot came up into his field of vision, kicking one of the clinging metaljackets in the head. A flash of Charlie's eyes caught his through the eye slit, and Leo could tell the lad was grinning.

The wave of Cyclops joining the fight crushed the Echelon's metaljackets. Flame spewed across the square, though both sides were careful not to overuse it. Greek fire burned like the fires of hell once it hit anything and was notoriously uncontrollable.

Morioch was screaming, his gaunt face wide with horror as he looked at the tide of Cyclops. Leo waved on the men behind him as he set his shoulder into the side of the carriage and tried to push it over.

It rocked from side to side as they joined him. Morioch danced on top of it, trying to keep his balance. The entire thing tipped on edge...and went down with a resounding crash. Morioch tumbled through the fallen carcasses of his metaljackets.

Stomping forward, Leo grabbed him by the throat. He hauled the duke up until his feet dangled, then pressed the button that kept his helmet sealed. It opened with a hiss, steam curling the hair at his temples. "Surprise," he told the duke.

"Barrons!" Morioch gritted his teeth and kicked at him. "You treacherous snake!" A knife appeared in his hand and Leo smashed it away with his metal fist. The duke screamed in pain. "What have you done?" he howled, wild eyes looking at the carnage surrounding them.

"Not me, Your Grace."

Mina clanked up beside him, releasing her own helm. Morioch's eyes widened when he saw her.

"Me," she said. "Are you going to kill him?"

"No." Blade strode out of the clinging pall of smoke, the pair of razors in his hands. "I am. Put 'im down. I'll give 'im a fightin' chance, at least."

"Is that wise?" Mina asked.

"I ain't a murderer," Blade shot back. His eyes focused on Morioch as Leo dropped him. "Now, what was that you were sayin' 'bout me wife?"

⤜⤛

Soot and ash stained the air, the houses lit by the glare of fire. Most of the handlers had been killed or captured. Metaljackets stood in silent rows or littered the square.

They'd won, though they couldn't have done it alone. One Cyclops was worth four of the metaljackets, it was true, but at this stage they'd been vastly outnumbered and untrained. Only Lena's frequency-altering device working in conjunction with the Cyclops had won them the day.

Leo kept his helm open, breathing in the hot, smoky air. Better than being trapped inside his helmet, his own breath blowing back into his face. "Roughly eight hundred metaljackets," he announced, returning from his count. "Which means a good number of the Echelon's forces."

The little group huddled on the top of Morioch's splayed carriage made up the war council; Blade, Rip, Will, Lena, Kincaid, and the duchess.

"They'll still have the ceremonial automatons," Mina replied, staring at the map someone had brought from the rookeries. She stabbed a finger into the heart of it. "And the walls guarding the Ivory Tower are immense. Nobody's ever brought them down. They're impenetrable, and no doubt any hidden access routes were blocked after our escape."

Blade scowled. "So we 'it the gates? Smash 'em to pieces?"

"Spoken like a true brute." Mina looked up at him, her eyes alight. "A good way to lose half your men. There are cannons mounted on the wall. You wouldn't make it within a hundred feet." She tipped her head toward the rookery walls. "And this time, we'll be in Morioch's position."

"Then what do you propose?" Lena asked.

"We need more men—more of the Cyclops in action," she replied. "We've called on the extent of Kincaid's enclaves, but there are three other secret factories storing Cyclops."

"Funny thing, luv," Blade replied. "All the men we got to pilot them is right 'ere."

Leo released the breastplate of the Cyclops and undid the harness. Hot air washed over his skin, but at least it was clean. A breeze of some description. "Mina's contacted Sir Gideon Scott. We can only assume he's spreading the word among the humanist forces in the city and outfitting humanists at the Ironmonger enclaves."

"A mob." Kincaid scratched at his roughened jaw. "Send them in first and let the Coldrush Guards on the walls focus on them."

"No," Mina snapped. "I won't countenance useless deaths. Here." She pointed to a spot on the map. "What we need is here."

"The Nighthawks Guild." Leo hauled himself on

top of the carriage and peered at the map. "A whole army of blue bloods."

She shot him a grateful look. "Our plan of attack is to march on the Ivory Tower—Blade can lead that force, keep their attention. Take Kincaid and his mechs with you. Then another group attacks the Coldrush Guards pinning the Nighthawks down, and then the Nighthawks go to the Moorgate and Cripplegate enclaves—they're the closest to the guild. They arm themselves with the Cyclops there and assault the Ivory Tower from the south."

"Will can lead that force," Leo murmured.

Will scowled. "If you think I'm—"

"We *need* you to do it," Blade repeated firmly. "I know you wanna stay at me side, but this is war, lad. We need someone we can trust and that the Nighthawks would recognize and obey. Get 'em to the enclaves where the second and third lot o' Cyclops are, and suit up. I'll meet you at the Tower."

Will wavered. He'd been Blade's second-in-command until he received his promotion to verwulfen ambassador. Leo could see the sense in Blade's words, but Will would be fighting the protective instincts of a verwulfen—everything that told him to protect his master.

"I'm going too," Lena said.

That refocused Will's attention. "Like hell you are. This is war, Lena. You need to be at your sister's side."

"How do you plan to work the Cyclops?" she asked with a sweet little smile. "Rosalind showed me how they work when she was trying to recruit me to create them. You don't have time to figure that out. Does he, Duchess?"

"Time is of the essence," Mina replied.

"*And* I know how to work this," Lena added, lifting her frequency-altering device. "There will be more metaljackets."

"Still no word on 'ow we're gettin' past the wall," Kincaid said.

Leo smiled. "Leave that to Mina and me."

Mina arched a brow at him.

"Care to take that trip to Paris?" he asked, reaching out a hand to help her to her feet.

She understood immediately. "I assume we'll be making a brief stopover."

"Courtesy of the good Mr. Galloway."

❧

"What about me?" Charlie demanded, when the leaders were giving out the orders.

"Us," Lark corrected, though she looked decidedly less enthusiastic than Charlie.

Leo paused at Blade's side, checking over his weapons. Blade stilled, shooting the lad a hard look. At his questioning glance, Leo shrugged. He didn't want the boy in the melee any more than Blade did, but Mina's words made him wonder what the right course was.

"You're stayin' 'ere," Blade said.

"I'm not a boy," Charlie shot back. "Not anymore."

Blade grabbed him by the neck of his shirt and wrenched him onto his toes. "I'm 'bout to lead most of me men on the Tower. It's war, Charlie. I might not come back. Me nor Rip, nor Will… And your sister's lyin' in 'er bed with me daughter, unable to move if anyone takes this chance to attack. You're stayin' 'ere, and if she gets 'urt, I'll thrash you to a bleedin' pulp. You understand me? That's your duty."

Charlie's mouth worked sullenly. "I'm a blue blood."

Lark grabbed his arm. "We'll stay," she promised. "We'll keep an eye on 'em."

Blade nodded and let Charlie go. "Don't disappoint me."

"Good luck," Lark called.

Twenty-five

LORD MATHESON'S MANOR WAS CLOSER THAN Galloway's, in the end.

Leo strode across the deck of the pleasure dirigible, leaning on the rail and eyeing the glittering sprawl of London below. They'd roused Bennett Whitcomb, the pilot, out of his bed at the air dock, and he was white-faced and nauseous behind the wheel. A dozen of Blade's best men and a few of the mechs strolled the deck, staying relatively silent. Weaponry gleamed at their sides.

Mina's glorious red hair whipped behind her in the wind at the prow. She gathered fistfuls of it, knotting it into a loose chignon at the base of her skull. Leo stepped up behind her, plucking the pins from her hand. "Here," he murmured. "Allow me."

Her brandy-brown eyes glanced up at him when he finished. "Thank you."

"You're welcome."

Fire burned out of control in some parts of the city, and the cry of the mob was fierce as they passed over the Theater District. Covent Garden thronged with howling humanists, and he could just make out the tramping gallop of the Trojan cavalry through the narrow streets. People were screaming. His fingers dug into the rail.

"It will be over soon," Mina murmured, resting her hand over his. "We cannot avoid the loss of life, not entirely, but we can make that loss worth it."

A subtle shift of his hand and their fingers laced together. Mina looked down, then squeezed his fingers. Together in this. No matter what happened, he knew they would fight back to back if necessary.

Moonlight gleamed on the Ivory Tower in front of them. "Here we are," he said, steeling his nerves. "Are you ready?"

"Are you?"

Leo slid a hand around the base of her neck and drew her face up to his. The crush of her body against his chest was brief, his lips tingling as he kissed her. Then he forced himself to let go.

"Take the gates!" he roared at the men behind him. They'd all been briefed on the layout and the resistance to expect. "Then we take the Tower!"

"Aye!" a handful of bellows echoed through the air.

Grabbing one of the grappling guns that Kincaid had supplied at the enclaves, Leo climbed onto the rail of the dirigible. Sinking the hooks into the rail, he leaned over the edge as the airship sailed over the high walls surrounding the Tower. Mina echoed him, her expression tight and focused. Leo counted under his breath, listening to the startled cries of the Coldrush Guards below as they realized what was happening.

"Here we are," he said, looking at her. They were near the gatehouse.

Bullets whizzed past. Leo instinctively leaned closer to her, dangling backward out over the airship with his heels on the rail and the grappling hook holding him there.

"Three, two…one!"

Both of them sailed backward, dropping down into the melee at the gates.

❧

Blade's forces spilled through the narrow gates as they opened, a Cyclops smashing a fist into one of the Coldrush Guards as Leo dragged Mina toward the stables. Blade's men and the Nighthawks were a distraction; he and Mina needed to get to the queen.

Rosalind and Lady Peregrine hurried at their heels, along with a force of Nighthawks that were pouring through the south gates. Once inside the Ivory Tower, they'd separate—the Nighthawks to the dungeons to rescue their leaders, and Mina and Leo up toward the throne room.

Fighting their way through the guards, they spilled out into the inner halls of the Ivory Tower.

"This is too easy." Leo frowned. *Nothing good ever came of anything easy.*

"I concur," Rosalind replied. She looked up through the hollow core of the Tower to the top, where the throne room and the atrium lay. "Where are the rest of the guards?"

"Up there," Mina murmured, "surrounding the key to the Echelon's power."

The queen.

"Good luck then." Rosalind ruthlessly primed the

pistol she was carrying. "I'll go rescue my husband and see what we can do to follow you."

She and Perry vanished, leading the Nighthawks.

"Let's hope they're still alive," Mina murmured.

Lynch was a friend, and Garrett too. Leo frowned and led her upward, thighs burning as they ran up the stairs. There was an elevation chamber located at the bottom, but he didn't trust it. Locked inside the brass chamber, they'd be at anyone's mercy.

Reaching the fifth-highest floor, he held out a hand to slow her. If they were going to start encountering guards, here was where they'd find them.

Climbing the stairs on cat-silent feet, he felt her hand slip into his and squeeze it tight. Nervous. For her queen, no doubt. Leo squeezed back. The sounds of fighting broke out below them, hurried shouts and the clash of swords.

And he could hear footsteps coming from above...

A dark figure glided around the corner of the spiral staircase, striding with lethal grace. Light gleamed on the man's pale skin and white hair, and his hand slid down to the hilt of his sword as he stopped in the middle of the staircase.

They both froze.

Caine. The sudden flare of rage blackened Leo's vision, the world springing into stark relief as the darker side of his nature rose. A thousand twisted, conflicting emotions. Guilt, fury, rejection, need...

"What the hell did you do here?" Caine waved a hand, indicating the Tower and the madness outside. "Does this mess belong to you?"

Leo took another step, his body angled between the

duke and Mina. "Stand aside." His hand went to the hilt of his sword.

Caine's eyes narrowed, locking on the way Leo protected Mina. "Fraternizing with the enemy? I thought I taught you better than that."

"The only enemy I see is the one who turned his back on me," Leo spat, stepping closer. "The duchess has proven more loyal than you ever did."

"What the hell did you expect me to do?" Caine snarled. "I swore an oath to uphold my prince's right of power. He said you weren't to be harmed. If I'd had time, I could have argued against the exile...or worked to see you reinstated—"

"He wanted me dead all along," Leo shot back. "And you just sat there."

They stared at each other.

Caine was breathing hard. "No," he said. "I didn't know the consequences. I didn't...expect it."

"You?" Another step forward, fingers curling tight around the hilt of his sword. "The great master of the game? Looks like you were outplayed then, by your own prince." Turning, Leo gestured to Mina, too aware of time passing. The sounds of fighting were growing closer, ringing up the hollow center of the Tower. The Nighthawks, no doubt. "Get out of our way."

Caine's expression tightened. Here were grounds that he understood. "No. I won't let you do this. This is madness! If you take another step, then you *are* committing treason—"

"You're several months too late for that."

The shock on Caine's face... Leo had no time

for this. "Go," he said to Mina. "Go and protect your queen."

"We could take him together." A hand strayed to the sword at her side.

"No, we couldn't," Leo replied softly, and he saw on her face the shock as she realized what he was saying.

He was the only one who knew the extent of Caine's reflexes now. In times past, vampires had slaughtered hundreds before they'd been taken down. Caine had all of their reflexes, their speed, but tempered by cunning and the possession of his senses. He'd be virtually unbeatable, and time was working against them.

Mina couldn't move, her eyes wide and haunted. "Leo?"

"Go," he said, in a softer, knowing voice. "Protect your queen."

"No." She knew exactly what he was saying; he could see it. "No, I'm not going. I'm not—"

"We made these choices. This is war, Mina. I can give you the chance to get to her. Isn't that what you want?" Her hands shook, where they never had before. Leo's voice softened. "I don't regret it. I don't regret a thing. Remember that."

Caine shook his cape back over his shoulder. "Don't be a fool, boy. You're not strong enough to defeat me. Nobody is, not anymore. Don't make me kill you."

❧

"*Kill you…*" The words echoed in Mina's ears.

Leo tugged her hand to his lips. Their eyes met,

his mouth breathing the sweetest of caresses over her knuckles. This…this was the cost of everything she'd set into play. It was too much of a price. She wanted him forever, damn the consequences. "No," she said.

"I finally caught you," he whispered, letting out a harsh laugh as he pulled back. "You're finally starting to see why I could never let you go. I love you, Mina. I love you for everything that you are and that you could be, but I need you to go now and finish what we've both started. Do me proud. Kill that bastard and get the queen out of there."

Everything screamed at her to stay and fight at his side. But as much as she wanted to stay, innocents would die for this—the queen would die—if she didn't finish what she had set in place. The indignity… that she couldn't even tell him how much he meant to her, because at the moment, she couldn't even speak.

Fighting spilled out into the staircase below them, Nighthawks swarming into view as they dueled with the Coldrush Guards. If she wanted any chance at this, she had to go now, before anyone else got to the queen and forced the prince consort into a position he couldn't win from.

"Be strong," Leo said, stepping back and letting go of her hand. "I'll wait for the Nighthawks as much as I can. You know I'll wait for them. And I'll come for you."

If he could.

One last look at Caine, then a scream echoed from above. A woman. Mina's blood ran cold as her head jerked up.

Steel screamed as Leo drew his blade. "Go, Mina."

He stepped in front of her. "Come, Caine. Let us see how well you've taught me."

The moment he attacked, Mina darted forward, slipping past the deadly duke and ducking beneath his sword as he lashed out at her too. Then Leo pushed hard, whipping his blade across Caine's cheek.

"Run!" Leo yelled at her, taking a countering blow across his forearm that he could have dodged. Distracting Caine for her.

No time now for all the things she should have said. Mina started running, lungs burning from the exertion of it.

I love you, her aching heart whispered.

⁓

"Bloody hell, boy. This is foolishness! I don't wish to hurt you!" The sword lashed at Leo's face, whip quick, but Caine pulled away from the blow.

Leo parried. Steel screeched on steel and he was driven back. "Then stand aside."

"You'll destroy everything that we have worked for!"

"I'll create something that you never dreamed of," Leo corrected and lunged.

"With that bitch?"

Leo managed to rake the tip of his blade across Caine's face. "You will speak courteously of my duchess, or not at all."

Caine spat blood, his pale blue eyes reddened with fury. "You bloody fool. She's the one, isn't she? The one you think you'll marry? Do you honestly believe you can trust her? She'll betray you."

Fury fired in Leo's blood. "No, she won't." He drove forward under Caine's arm, smashing his shoulder into his father's ribs. They both went down and Leo rolled, swiftly coming to his feet but staggering on two different levels of stairs. He didn't dare look down. "This is about my mother, isn't it? You think she betrayed you."

He'd never once referred to his mother. That was one lesson he'd learned as a little boy. Caine had beaten him the one time he'd dared ask about her.

The words worked now too. Caine's eyes blazed and he whipped the tip of his sword across Leo's face. Blood splashed against the gleaming white walls and fire flared along Leo's cheek, his lip stinging as the craving virus set to work repairing it.

"Don't you even speak her name!" A roar of fury and Caine drove back Leo, who stumbled down the stairs, trying to keep his feet under the onslaught.

"I damned well will if I want to," Leo spat back, darting to the left and cutting low across Caine's thigh. "She was my bloody mother, damn you." Lunging forward, he trapped Caine's sword between them, shoving him back against the wall. Caine's head cracked on the marble and Leo tried to slide his sword against the bastard's throat, but his hand was trapped too. Somehow he pinned Caine there, his fist curling in the bastard's collar. "*My* mother. And you never let me mention her name. Why? Because you weren't man enough for her? Because she found another man to replace you?"

"You little cur." Caine shoved him back with a strength Leo couldn't match.

He caught himself, fingertips touching the steps as

his father lunged. He blocked the expected blow, but again just barely. Caine didn't bother with finesse, smashing blow upon blow down on Leo's upraised sword. Blood rained from Leo's arms and hands.

Then Caine turned away, kicking at a Nighthawk who ran up the stairs. The man flew back through the air, tumbling head over heels down the marble staircase and crashing into his fellows far below.

Caine turned, baring his teeth. "You will not speak of your mother like that! She was a good woman! The best."

Leo paused.

"Do you think that I didn't know? Who do you think encouraged her to lie with him? You were the child that I engineered. You were mine. I made you. I sculpted you. Mine! My son. Not his!"

"What the hell are you saying?"

"I couldn't give her children." Caine's nostrils flared. "A childhood bout of mumps. I knew it and I still married her, knowing how much she wanted them. She was so furious with me, and then I saw the way Todd looked at her. It was an arrangement, nothing more."

The blood drained out of Leo's face. "*Why?*" he whispered.

"To make her happy," Caine said, his sword lowering. For the first time in his life, he looked uncertain. "Marguerite was my weakness, and I killed her with your birth." His voice roughened. "I killed my Marguerite."

"Then all of this was punishment?" Leo demanded. "Every beating you ever gave me, every time you—"

"Punishment? I made you strong. Clever. I made you a man who could be a duke, the way my own father molded me." Caine laughed roughly. "You want to know about punishment? You should have been raised by that brute."

Leo's sword tip lowered, trailing on the floor. Everything he had ever known about this man he now saw in a new light. "I hated you." And wanted his love—his praise—just as strongly.

"As I hated him," Caine said, tipping his chin up a little proudly. "One day you will thank me."

"You're mad."

"So this is the end of it?" Caine asked. "You'll put down your sword? Surrender?"

Leo looked down at it, spattered with the vampire's blackened blood. "No." He met his father's eyes. "But I will accept yours."

The Nighthawks were nearly upon them. Leo saw Lynch kick Richard Maitland, his old nemesis in the Coldrush Guards, in the face. Lynch was still wearing the same bloody clothes he'd worn that day at court, but he looked none the worse for his time in the cells.

Caine raised his sword, his teeth bared. Seconds dragged out. Caine's gaze jerked to the spill of Nighthawks running up the stairs toward them.

"After all," Leo said, with dawning certainty, "you won't kill me. And not even you can fight off an entire legion of Nighthawks."

"What the hell have you done?"

Leo laughed at that. "I'm overthrowing the prince consort. Haven't you realized yet?"

Leo's sword lowered. Caine stared at it for a moment, looking baffled, then let his own relax. "And do what? Sit on the throne? Do you actually think they'd accept you? Or whatever puppet you put there?"

"We're not putting anyone on the throne. Someone's already sitting on it." He eyed Caine's sword, then took a step forward. It lifted, as if in warning.

"The queen?" Comprehension gleamed in Caine's pale eyes. "She's doing this?"

"And the duchess. You underestimated them, all of us did. They've been running the humanist revolution from the beginning." Another step. Caine's sword pressed into Leo's chest and he pushed against it, their gazes locking—

With a snarl Caine threw the blade away. The sword fell with a clatter on the stairs. "This is insanity!"

"No, this is the only way forward. You know that," Leo replied. "The only madness here is that of the prince consort."

Again their eyes met. Caine looked furious.

"Do you think him any ally of yours? After the other day?"

A vein ticked in the duke's jaw. "We swore... When the prince consort married the princess, we swore to uphold the regency. *I* gave my word."

"He's destroying the city, the people. You have to see that."

Caine's nostrils flared, watching as the Nighthawks clashed with a half-dozen Coldrush Guards that had streamed out of the antechambers to the ballroom.

"The world is changing," Leo said firmly, taking another step. "There is a new future featuring blue bloods, humans, and mechs living as one. You can either be a part of it, or you can be swept away in the wake. Buried, like the rest of the relics from your era."

Thought raced in his father's eyes. "Damn you, this is not easy. He was my brother by blood. You're asking me to break my oath, my word, my *honor*."

"I'm asking you to do the right thing."

In the silence, the sound of fighting grew louder. Something ancient shifted in Caine's eyes. "Tell the queen that I shall expect a seat at her new Council."

Of course. A duke until the very end. "In exchange for what?"

"For information," Caine replied, "and for letting you pass so that you may save her." He knelt against the wall, leather creaking over his thighs, his eyes deadening. "The prince consort has the entire building rigged with explosives. The detonator can be found in the hands of a Falcon named Rigby. You know him as one of the prince consort's attendants, the one with a scar through his left eyebrow."

Hell. "Why would the prince consort do that?"

"Because he's so afraid to lose power that it has maddened him." Caine gave a sad laugh. "Not even Balfour knows what he plans—I overheard the prince speaking to Rigby. They underestimated the strength of my hearing."

"Where?" Leo took another hurried step forward, heat draining from his face. He'd sent Mina into that. "Damn you, where is Rigby?"

"The last I saw of him, he was instructed to watch the massacre from Crowe Tower. The prince consort has a flare gun that he'll fire if things go badly for him." A faint smile twitched the old man's lips. "He's determined that if he can't hold the throne, then he'll take as many of his enemies to the grave as he can."

"And you were just on your way out when I came along. How convenient." Leo's voice dripped scorn.

"I know how this ends, boy." Caine bared his teeth. "The Ivory Tower will fall and there will be no one left with the strength to hold the Empire together except for one."

"You," Leo said. "I'll stop him. You know I will, so why the hell would you tell me this?"

The aging duke sighed and scraped a hand over his face. He looked incredibly tired all of a sudden. "When this is all over," he said, "come to me and ask me again why I do this, but right now, you don't have the time. You either go after your woman and save her life, or you find the man with the detonator."

It was the hardest decision Leo had ever made. He wanted to go to Mina's aid, but how could he trust that Caine wouldn't simply walk away if he sent him after Rigby? And if he sent Nighthawks, would they recognize the Falcon in this melee? The man had been a personal attendant of the prince consort, well away from Nighthawk eyes. Only Leo knew exactly who he was hunting for.

Damn it. His gut clenched. Mina was surprisingly competent, and as far as the prince consort knew, she wasn't involved with this affair. Perhaps she could get close to the queen when others would fail.

"Mina will get the queen away from danger," he said, his voice cool and controlled, where he himself felt anything but. "I'll deal with the Falcon."

Caine picked up his blade and sheathed it.

"Where are you going?"

"Home," Caine replied. "I've had enough of this mess."

"Not yet," Leo found himself saying, stepping directly into Caine's path. "You want a place on the queen's Council? Then you have to earn it. Giving me a piece of information and then scurrying away, just in case this all goes to hell? Not good enough." He shoved his finger in the duke's chest. "Prove yourself. Claim your own damned seat on the Council. Go up and help get the queen out alive, and if you harm one hair on Mina's head, I'll come after you. I swear, by the blood, that I will see you dead, no matter what I have to do."

Caine's eyes narrowed. "Since when do you give the orders, you insolent pup?"

"Since now," Leo snapped. "And I'm no pup, especially not yours."

He thought for a second that Caine would draw his sword again. The duke's gaze flickered to the surge of Nighthawks, and his head lowered in a contemplative bow. "And if a Falcon kills her before I can get there?"

"I'd highly recommend that one doesn't. If she dies, I'll hold you accountable."

The duke stared at him. Something seemed to shift in his eyes, and he slowly nodded. "As you wish."

Leo had made his decision. His heart urged him to go up, to find Mina and protect her—but if he did, then they would both die, together, when the prince consort fired his flare, along with everyone else in this building.

So Leo began running, this time down the stairs. Kicking a pair of Coldrush Guards in the back, he sent them sprawling at the feet of several bloodied Nighthawks. Lynch was one of them, his wife Rosalind at his side.

"Caine and the Duchess of Casavian are going to rescue the queen," he called. "Clear these floors of Coldrush Guards and secure the throne room. Whatever you do, do not present a threat to the prince consort. He has a flare gun to signal a man outside if he feels this has all gone badly."

Lynch strode up the stairs to meet him. "A bomb?"

Leo nodded. "I'm going to deal with the man with the detonator. Give me two of your Nighthawks. He's a Falcon and there could be others."

Lynch snapped his fingers. "Byrnes. Stanton. Follow Barrons and protect him." He nodded at Leo. "Two of the best."

"Let's hope they're good enough," he replied, striding down through the tight pack of Nighthawks and gesturing to the two Lynch had chosen.

Twenty-six

MINA SHOVED BOTH PALMS AGAINST THE DOORS TO THE throne room. They began to part, sliding open with a gasp of air to reveal the throne and the assemblage of people around it.

A dozen pistols were aimed her way. Frightened debutantes and thralls huddled by the enormous marble columns that supported the domed ceiling, with their lords in front of them. Half of the Echelon was here, roused from a ball by the look of them.

Mina strode through the doors. Seven men guarded the dais, armed with differing levels of weaponry. At the side stood another half-dozen Coldrush Guards, grimly keeping their pistols trained on her.

If she showed one hint of fear—or guilt—she'd be dead. The prince consort couldn't know she was involved in this. She was the trick card in the revolutionists' hand.

"Are you insane?" Mina snapped, summoning every bit of arrogance she owned. "Why the devil haven't you gotten Her Highness away from here? The whole bloody Tower is full of Nighthawks."

The prince consort looked like hell. His colorless eyes narrowed and his fingers curled over each arm of the throne, making him seem not quite certain what was going on. "What a surprise to see you, Duchess. The last I heard, you were galloping out of here on one of my Trojan destriers."

"My thanks for attempting a rescue."

His expression told her nothing about whether he was buying this act or not. "Morioch bargained for your return. Unfortunately it was denied."

Liar. Still, she started stripping off her leather gloves with a frown. "Did he?" She didn't dare look at the queen. Emotion was already choking her, and she knew she'd never be able to hide all of it. "I've spent most of the past few days locked in a bloody room while half the city burns."

"Just how, precisely, did you escape?" This came from Balfour, the prince consort's spymaster.

A dangerous man. Mina glanced his way, tucking her gloves behind her belt. "I didn't. The Devil of Whitechapel wanted me where he could see me, considering his home is quite undefended. There was no point in arguing, as he was taking me precisely where I wished to go. I simply knifed his man in the back and took my leave when the opportunity presented itself." She took a step forward and froze as half a dozen pistols lifted. Holding up her hands, she managed her iciest tones. "You think I've taken up with that *rogue*? It seems your senses are leaving you." A quick, frustrated glance behind her. "As evidenced by the unlocked door. Where are all of the guards? What is going on here? You should be escaping."

Not that there was anywhere to go.

The prince consort lifted a hand, lace spilling from his sleeve. Dressed in his finest court attire, with a flute of blud-wein in his fingers, he said: "Leave her be, Balfour. I hardly think the Duchess of Casavian foolish enough to consort with the enemy."

Was that a slur in his voice? "One does have certain standards," she agreed, stepping closer.

Out of the corner of her eye, she could just make out a rumpled pile of yellow silk at his side. The queen, sitting by his feet with her coronation crown on her gleaming brown hair. A glance showed Mina a pale face but no sign of injury. Intense brown eyes locked on her, as if trying to tell her something. Mina looked away swiftly.

"Certain standards," Balfour agreed, his eyes narrowing. "But she's also less than foolish."

"And why the hell would she come back here?" the prince consort demanded, waving another expansive hand. "She has to know she's going to die."

The entire court sprang into a frightened babble.

"Enough!" the prince consort bellowed. "Balfour, shoot the next person who cries out."

The crowd subsided. A woman was sobbing somewhere.

"What do you mean by die?" Mina asked as the prince consort drained his wine.

"Fetch me another," he demanded.

Balfour caught the serving man by the arm as he hurried to attend. "I hardly consider that wise, Your High—"

"Wise?" the prince consort mocked. "I want them

all here, to join my ball." He threw his head back and laughed. "All of them, and not a one to walk free. I'll see them all in hell—"

Mina exchanged a glance with Balfour. He gave a tight shake of his head, just as concerned as she. The rest of the court looked confused, several debutantes whispering worriedly behind their hands. Mina even saw Malloryn in the crowd, a sight that gave her some hope. He was moving nonchalantly through them, circling toward the dais.

"We need to get Her Highness out of here," she tried again. "We can protect her from this crowd of ruffians, perhaps remove her to the safety of—"

"She's not going anywhere without *me*." The prince consort spilled his wine on his sleeve.

The doors slammed open, striking the walls with a thunderous crash. Mina spun, her hand darting to the sword at her hip, and the court behind her gasped.

Caine strode through the double doors, the sound of fighting drifting up the staircase behind him. The sound cut off abruptly as the doors slowly swung shut, but the effect of it was far greater than that. She felt as though somewhere, very near to here, a coffin lid had slammed shut, blocking out all of the light in her world.

Her mouth went dry, her chest seeming to lock tight. She fought to catch a breath, but she couldn't. Not in that moment when the duke's appearance finally gave realization to the outcome that she had feared the most. The one she hadn't allowed herself to think about.

Caine intercepted a glass of blud-wein from the tray

of a hovering drone and strode toward them. "Sorry to miss the celebration." He took a sip of the wine, surveying the court before draining the glass. His eyes locked on Mina for a second, then he tossed the empty glass aside with a smash, blood staining his lips.

"Where have you been?" the prince consort demanded.

Caine laughed a little under his breath. "Discussing the meaning of life with someone."

Her heart wrenched. *No.* As if of its own accord, her hand found the hilt of her sword, her lip curling back in a snarl. "You bastard."

He stopped in his tracks. "Consider, my dear, how wise such an action would be at this current moment."

Time stretched out. Her head was a mess of pain, bleeding around the edges. Her chest pulsed, as if holding a scream inside. She knew that the moment she let herself breathe, it would steal out of her.

But Alexa… She *had* to save the queen, even as her eyes flooded with a heat she couldn't seem to hold back. Only one thing left to fight for now; then she could scream and rail at the world. Then she could let in the enormous, crushing weight of grief.

"Why not?" The prince consort laughed. "A duel! It should give us much amusement in these final moments."

"No, Your Highness—" The queen's whisper.

The sound of a slap echoed in the enormous chambers, dulling even the crowd's buzzing whispers to near-silence. Mina's blood began to boil, her head jerking between the prince consort and Caine. Anger. That was what she could deal with right now.

Mina's fingers curled tighter around her sword. Now…now she just had to get close enough to cut the prince consort down. It didn't matter anymore if she survived it.

Caine abruptly sobered, staring at the prince consort as if the blud-wein had left a foul taste in his mouth. "I think not. I have more important matters to deal with than duels, and I'd rather not get my sword bloodied today." A slow tilt of the head to her.

Despite herself, her gaze dropped. Caine's sword was still sheathed. Black blood had dripped down his thigh from a healed wound, but there was no sign of any other blood on him. Nothing on his clothes suggested he'd fought and killed a person recently.

Her heart gave a little tick in her chest.

Mina's lungs emptied. Was he telling her what she thought he was? Hope was a treacherous bitch, lighting her nerves on fire and threatening to consume her. Their eyes met again, something unreadable in his expression, and then he turned to the prince consort, one hand on his sword as if for balance as he strolled forward.

Where the hell was Leo? She turned to track Caine, licking at her dry lips as he passed her. That precious hope flickered a little. Surely Leo would have followed.

Unless…something had drawn him away. Did she dare hope?

"I do believe Lynch is almost at the last level of the tower," Caine declared. "You're running out of time."

"We're all running out of time." The prince

consort laughed, as if this were the greatest joke he'd ever heard.

Whispers started in the crowd. One of the blue bloods strode for the door, looking uneasy. A bullet ricocheted off the brass, close to his ear, and he jerked his fingers back from the handle.

"Nobody leaves," the prince consort called, his voice becoming deadly serious. "Not until I damned well say so." He gestured to his Falcons. "No more warnings."

"Your Highness." Even Balfour sounded nervous now. "We haven't much time."

The prince consort had somehow found another glass of blud-wein in the confusion. He sipped at it, waving away Balfour's concerns. "I never planned on leaving." Lowering the glass, he glared at his spymaster. "You think I'm going to run? You think…"—this as he stood—"that I'm going to let that filthy cur and the human rabble out there chase *me* from my throne?"

"What would you prefer?" Balfour demanded through gritted teeth. "Have them drag you off it when they come in here? I don't have men enough… not to stop them."

"I'm not stopping them," the prince consort sneered. "Let them come, let them all come." He drew a silver-handled revolver from his belt, waving it in the air. By its look, it had been heavily modified and was probably carrying firebolt bullets. "The more the merrier."

Caine froze.

Of everything happening in the chambers, that alone drew her notice. Mina took a hasty step forward.

The pistol. Caine was watching the pistol like it was a live scorpion. Why? Hardly a threat to him. Firebolts might be enough to rip him in half, if he was slow enough to be stung by one, but the duke's capacity for healing was immeasurable now. Wasn't it?

Or did the prince consort think to use it on the queen? This time she couldn't stop herself from glancing at Alexa. The queen was using the throne to drag herself to her feet as her husband took a step down the stairs of the dais. A heated handprint marred her cheek, her dark eyes wide and weary.

Hold on. Mina took a stealthy half step forward. *I'm going to kill him for you.*

For the first time, she had the means; she had power... Nobody here would care if she stabbed him through his black heart. He was one hairsbreadth away from being destroyed. Alexandra would never have to submit to his brutal touch again.

And Mina could finally let go of her thrice-cursed guilt.

She was almost at Caine's side now. "Get to the queen," he said almost soundlessly. "I'll stop him from firing that bloody pistol."

The queen? How did he—? Mina's gaze sharpened, but Caine was taking bold strides toward the dais. She followed, keeping apace of him with a wary glance. Were they just idle words? Or did he know about the queen's involvement in the revolution? The only way... Her breath caught. Proof that Leo was alive, if she dared believe it.

But why wasn't he here?

Everything happened at once. Lynch and his men

thundered through the doors, just as the prince consort waved a lazy hand and smiled.

"No!" Caine yelled, moving faster than she could see.

The pistol resounded with an enormous flash of light, shattering the nearby window. People gasped and threw themselves to the polished marble floor as light exploded outside like some Chinese firework, burning bright enough to sear the eyes, then sailing down to the ground far below like a dying comet.

And in that moment, flashing against the back of her eyelids every time she blinked, all Mina could see was the queen pulling a narrow dagger from her sleeve and driving it into her husband's throat.

The room erupted. People screamed and ran for the exit, buffeting Lynch and his Nighthawks like flotsam in a current of fear. Mina stumbled aside as one blue blood raced past her, and staggered to her knees beside the dais.

The prince consort was down, blood welling between his fingers from the gaping slash in his throat. Mina crawled forward. "Alexa?" she screamed.

A flash of white caught her eyes. Caine, buried beneath four of the Falcons as he fought to drag the pistol from the prince consort's clenched fingers. Still alive, the prince consort bared his lips in a bloodied rictus as his gaze locked on his wife.

"Kill...the bitch," the prince consort snarled, blood breaking in a bubble on his lips.

Two Falcons remained. Mina threw herself past them, dancing around to place herself between them and the queen, her steel ringing as she drew the sword at her side. "Don't be fools," she snapped. "This is the *queen*! Your queen!"

They hesitated.

For just a second, Mina met the prince consort's almost-colorless blue eyes, seeing in them the shock she'd always dreamed of, and she let herself smile maliciously, let everything she had felt over the past ten years surface on her face. "When you thought you killed Mercury, you were only cutting off the tip of a snake's tail. Mercury was only a decoy. Your wife's decoy."

This was the only revenge she could ever take—to make him realize just how well he'd been played. That this entire revolution was ordered by his wife.

"Kill...her..." He coughed, one hand clapped to the bloodied wound at his throat. "Kill...the duchess..."

This time, when the Falcons looked at her, there was no hesitation.

⟡

Barrons took the stairs like a ghost, whispering up the silent stairwell of Crowe Tower. It was practically abandoned now, except for the rookery at the top where the ravens rested, an enormous room with an open-faced bronze clock facing the Ivory Tower. Dozens of ravens would be in their cages, stirring restlessly with all of the sound outside. Though hardly the best method of communicating now that wireless radio frequency and pneumatic tubes had been invented, receiving a message via raven was something the younger generation had deemed fashionable.

The sort of thing he'd never had time for at their

age. Hell, he felt old. Or perhaps he'd simply been raised as such, knowing that the pressures of a dukedom would rest on his shoulders one day.

In a way, both he and Mina were frighteningly similar.

He thought of her as he paused in front of the door to the rookery. Walking away and leaving her to face her own battles was harder than he'd imagined. Not because he doubted her abilities, but because she had become integral to his life in such a short time. Or perhaps she had slipped her way there in increments over the years as his steadily growing fascination had slowly turned to admiration.

Anything could happen. A stray bullet, a single mistake, the tiniest of oversights. All it would take would be one second to destroy her—to rip his heart out of his chest.

Don't think about it. Not for one second could he allow doubt to distract him. Not with a Falcon to deal with. After all, she wasn't the only one whom a single mistake would see dead.

This was the best place to watch the melee and the Ivory Tower. The Falcon would be within, no doubt. Stanton guarded the staircase below and Byrnes pressed his back against the wall at Leo's side. A quick gesture and both men nodded. Leo eased open the door, letting the stiletto hidden in his sleeve drop hilt first into his hand. A certain kind of coldness came over him, washing away all of the doubt and leaving him centered in a way that he recognized.

"*Go ahead, boy, put aside that hate, that anger,*" Caine's voice whispered in his head. "*Until there is nothing left. Nothing but purpose, nothing but a clear head. You'll thank me for it one day…"*

Of all the ironies… He let his breath release slowly and eased the door wider, catching a glimpse within. A single man clad in black leather stood by the enormous open face of the slowly ticking clock, watching the top of the Ivory Tower as if that were the center of his world.

A whisper of sound was his only warning. Leo blocked a swinging arm, striking out with the stiletto and driving it between a pair of ribs. A man came out of nowhere—from behind the door it seemed—crashing into him and carrying them both to the ground. Leo twisted, locking his arm tight and cupping his thighs around the man's throat. He rolled, taking the fellow with him, a throaty cry ending in the abrupt snap of the Falcon's neck. The sound of scuffling caught Leo's attention. Two other Falcons had cornered Byrnes.

No time to deal with that. The Nighthawk would have to hold his own.

Leo rolled to his feet, bending low as the Falcon by the window turned. An emotionless gaze flickered over the dead guard at his feet, then back again.

"Barrons." The scar through his eyebrow identified him as Rigby, one of the prince consort's body servants, a man so unassuming that Leo had never really paid him much attention. "A rather inconvenient entrance."

"My apologies. I thought about swinging through the clock and perhaps kicking you in the face, but that seemed a ridiculous waste of time and energy." Blade's style, not his. Which was why he was up here in the

3

shadows, while his brother-in-law was flamboyantly burning everything in sight.

"You arrogant bastard—and I use that term in all its derogatory senses. You haven't the faintest idea what is going on, do you?"

"We're winning?" Leo suggested. A grunt sounded behind him, then Stanton joined the fray.

Rigby sidestepped him, tugging a modified pistol from his pocket. One of the current-stimulating devices Mina had explained. Leo stilled, silencing the world around him, letting it all vanish into the shadows as his complete attention focused on the pistol.

"Winning?" Rigby laughed. "It's a trap, you fool!"

Steel-plated cord shot out, the arrow-like prong thundering toward Leo's chest. He sprang forward, rolling under the device and flinging the hidden stiletto at Rigby. Somewhere behind him, a raven gave a throaty scream as the prong tore through its cage and jolted it with current.

"A trap?" he asked, rolling to his feet and planting a boot in the middle of the man's chest. Rigby grunted, wrenching the stiletto out of his arm with a snarl as he fell and rolled. Leo's boot slammed down where his head had been, the man snapping a kick behind him that was insanely fast.

As fast as a blue blood.

Leo backed away. "I see the prince consort has been illegally infecting his nursemaids."

Rigby's eyes narrowed. "And someone has been keeping secrets. You're very good, my lord."

"Caine hired an ex-Falcon to tutor me as a child."

"There are no ex-Falcons. We go to the grave for

our prince." A damning assessment, for it made Rigby a far more dangerous opponent than he'd seemed. A true believer.

"A sentiment not shared by all, it seems."

Taking out a narrow cylinder, Rigby snapped it open with the barest flick of his wrist, turning it into a substantial metal truncheon. It was hardly the type of weapon to inspire fear, but in the hands of a trained professional, far more deadly than any knife.

The violent sounds behind him had stilled. Leo spared the Nighthawks the briefest glance, finding Byrnes kneeling over Stanton and pressing hard on his abdomen.

"Byrnes," he called. Unfortunately there were more lives at stake than Stanton's. "Take his right side."

"Aye, my lord."

With a muttered curse, Rigby shot an anguished look toward the Ivory Tower, then back at the pair of them. "Curse you." He flipped something from his wrist, and a steel shuriken spun through the air. Leo jerked aside, the hot cut of the throwing star slashing along the outside of his thigh.

Rigby threw himself through the open clock, pressing something at his belt. A pair of metal wings tore through his coat, opening up into some sort of segmented gliding device.

Leo ran forward, catching himself on the minute hand. The next thing he knew, an enormous white flash of light erupted in the sky overhead, turning it molten. Rigby's head tracked it, then returned to the ground as he focused on landing safely.

The signal.

Seconds to spare. Leo raked the room for anything to help him, settling on an old winch-and-rope pulley used to close the clock face during inclement weather. "Byrnes!"

The man nodded. Grabbing hold of the rope, Leo ran for the window. Byrnes cut through the rope at the precise moment needed.

The warm summer air lifted Leo for a second, his body arcing out past the ten on the clock, then gravity began to take its revenge. He shot downward, stomach plummeting as the ground rushed up to meet him. Rigby was gliding to a halt at the base of the tower.

Ten feet from the bottom the rope jerked hard in Leo's hands. He gritted his teeth and hung on as he began to swing back toward the tower. Rigby slipped out of the harness of his glider and withdrew something from his coat.

The detonator.

No time to spare. Gauging the distance, Leo let go, plummeting onto the unsuspecting Falcon. They tumbled over each other, the detonator skittering across the ground toward a slim figure in the darkness. An elbow smashed Leo in the face, leaving him no time to look. Grabbing Rigby beneath his arms, he rolled them both until he was on top, grinding the man's face into the cobbles.

His thigh throbbed, blood spilling down his trousers. Leo pinned the bastard, wrenching his gaze toward the detonator. Lark crouched low nearby, as if surprised to see them. Where the hell had she come from? She was supposed to be at the Warren with Charlie, guarding Honoria and the baby.

"Grab it!" Leo yelled. "But be careful with it!"

Rigby smashed his head back into Leo's face. Pain exploded out from behind his nose, leaving him half-blinded as a pair of blows smashed into his ribs. Then he was on his back, trying to shake off the blow. *Damn it.* "Lark! Run!"

Noise was everywhere, filling his head and ringing in his ears, but even over the din he heard the sound of a pistol retorting.

It shocked him out of his pain-induced haze. Lark sprinted toward the gates, and as Leo watched, time seemed to slow down. She jerked, her legs giving way beneath her as red bloomed between her shoulder blades. Like a marionette cut from its strings, she hit the ground, the detonator tumbling from her fingers.

She didn't move.

"*No!*" Charlie appeared out of nowhere, his eyes blackening in a haze of rage as he saw her go down. Driven by his fury and grief, he started running toward the Falcon, fists pumping at his side. Tin Man tried to grab him, but it was too late.

Leo exploded to his feet. The boy wasn't good enough for this… Not ready. *Christ*, he couldn't——

Rigby lifted his pistol again, flicking the hammer back with contemptuous ease. The distance between them narrowed, but Leo knew he wouldn't make it in time.

The pistol barked again, just as Tin Man launched himself at Charlie. They somersaulted out of view as Leo barreled into the Falcon. This time he wasn't going to let anything distract him. A sharp chop of the fist sent the pistol flying.

Blows drove him back, and he swept them aside with his arms and hands, waiting for that one opening.

It came. Smashing a fist into Rigby's throat, he followed up with another to the face when the man staggered, clutching at his neck and gagging. Rigby went down, breathing through broken teeth, and Leo scrambled for the pistol, his thigh almost going out from under him. He couldn't even feel the wound now.

Rigby's body jerked as Leo put a bullet straight through the man's brain. Not even a blue blood could get up from that, but Leo coldly put another into him, just in case. He was starting to feel a little light-headed.

Sound rushed back in upon him with a roar—men cheering in the distance and chanting the national anthem. Fires licked the stone walls that guarded the Ivory Tower from the rest of the world. Dozens of macabre shadows danced gleefully against the backdrop of the flames, a nightmarish tableau his eyes couldn't quite make out.

"*No!* No!" Charlie had Lark in his arms, rocking her gently. Tin Man lay still beside him, his eyes staring blankly at Leo, with half his jaw blown away, where the bullet meant for Charlie had taken him.

"Fix him!" Charlie screamed at him. The boy had a knife out and was trying to cut at his own wrist. "Help me!"

There was no fixing Tin Man. "Don't." Leo's voice came out tight and dry. "You can't… It's too late."

"It's not!" Charlie squeezed blood from his wound into the bloodied hole in Lark's back. A whistling sound came from her chest—still alive, but faintly. The bullet had nicked a lung.

Leo fell to his knees beside the boy. "What are you doing here? Where's Honoria?"

A guilty, furtive look.

"Bloody hell," Leo snapped. "You didn't leave her alone?"

"There's more'n enough men there," Charlie retorted. "The fighting's all here and I'm a blue blood. I can help."

Christ. Blade would tan his hide. "And what about the other Falcon?"

"What Falcon?"

Leo gritted his teeth. "Morioch knew his Falcons' bomb attack on the Warren had failed. Did you never ask yourself how? There's someone else in the rookery ranks that shouldn't be there."

Charlie paled. "But...why didn't anyone tell me?"

"Did they have to?" Leo snapped. "You were given your bloody orders. Keep Honoria and Emmaline safe. Did you think it was a jest?"

Charlie fell silent, a thousand emotions dancing through his eyes. Leo bit off his temper and checked Lark. "*Fuck.*" What a bloody mess.

"Why isn't she healing?" Charlie demanded help-lessly. There was a world of guilt in his blue eyes. "I gave her my blood. That's how Blade healed Rip when he had his throat torn open!"

Leo examined the wound. Lark gasped as he shifted her shoulder. The bullet had gone through her steel-plated over-corset. What the hell kind of bullets were they? Not firebolts, but hard enough to tear through protective armor as if it were nothing.

Blood bubbled on her lips. "It's pierced her all the

way through," Leo said gently. "She'll be bleeding inside. You'll only heal the superficial wounds."

Despair filled his brother's eyes. Then determination. "I can infect her."

Not in time… Not before she bled out. Blade had done so to Rip, but the amount of craving virus in his blood had been abnormally high then. Leo caught Charlie's hand as the boy went to butcher his other wrist. "Here, let me. My CV levels are in the fifties."

A quick slash of his wrist, then he dripped his own blood into Lark's wounds. "Roll her over and let me see the front."

It was worse, as though the bullet had fragmented on its way through her. Leo guided Charlie to hold her head up, then pressed his wrist against her lips. The craving virus would already be infecting her wounds, but the more blood they could get into her…

She couldn't swallow it. Charlie clutched her tightly, rocking her gently no matter how much Leo tried to stop him. A low keening sound was coming from his throat. "What about…Tin Man?"

Leo shook his head.

"Why? Why did he do it? He had to know I'd heal." Charlie stared blankly. "Oh God, this'll kill her. He's her world. If she finds out he's dead…"

Leo didn't have the heart to say she probably wouldn't find out. "Maybe he thought it *might* kill you. You're not invincible, Charlie, and that man was a Falcon, someone who knows how to take down blue bloods."

"It shouldn't be like this." Charlie's voice was broken.

"No, it shouldn't." Tin Man's death had taken far more than just his life; it was also the death of the child that Charlie had still been. He'd never be quite the same after this. Mortality now had meaning for him. Grief had substance. *This was what we tried to shield you from.*

Something that, in the end, none of them had been able to do. Charlie and Lark were both verging on adulthood, but they couldn't see it. Sneaking after the group who'd marched the Cyclops on the Tower had been a romp for them.

But it wasn't a romp; it was war. And people died, including those who probably shouldn't have. All across the courtyard, there were sounds of celebration, but also slumped figures kneeling over the still and bloody forms of their fallen comrades. Leo felt sick. This was the price, and they'd all known they had to pay it, but it was one thing to plot a coup, and quite another to see the results in gruesome detail.

Time was ticking slowly by. Lark's head lolled against Charlie's chest, that dreadful whistling sound echoing in her lungs. Leo sat there beside him, one hand on the lad's shoulder as they waited. He squeezed tightly, feeling the mass of sinew and tendon beneath his grasp, knowing how it felt to realize that he'd been the one responsible for nearly killing someone important to him.

After what seemed like forever, Lark erupted into a hacking cough, blood spattering Charlie's face. Leo grabbed her shoulders and helped Charlie tilt her onto her side as she gagged up copious amounts of semi-congealed blood.

"She's healing," he said in disbelief, wiping her mouth on his sleeve as Charlie eased her against his shoulder. *Bloody hell.*

"Thank you." Charlie hugged her tightly enough to squeeze the breath from her lungs. There were no tears in his eyes, but Leo felt that grateful look like a punch to the gut. One victory among so many other failures.

"She'll need blood," he said. "The moment she can swallow. There's still no guarantee that she'll survive."

"She'll survive," Charlie said fiercely. He stroked the dark hair off her brow, his expression softening as he looked down into her face. "She's stubborn like that."

No need to comment on what Leo saw in the lad's expression. Trouble, that's what it was, but he could completely understand the lure of it. Then he glanced at Tin Man. The fellow would have followed wherever Lark and Charlie went. There'd be a price for this; Charlie just hadn't realized it yet.

Footsteps sounded nearby. Byrnes dragged Stanton across the yard, the unconscious man's arm slung over his shoulder.

"Stay here," Leo murmured to Charlie, finding his feet and pocketing the detonator very carefully. "I need to tell Blade about Honoria. Maybe send Rip back to the Warren to make sure she's safe."

Then it would be time to climb those thousand stairs in the Tower again. Time to find the missing piece of his heart…if she was still alive.

Twenty-seven

MINA WAS PRESSED HARD, DANCING OUT OF THE WAY as the Falcons lunged. Whoever they were, they'd been trained well, using each other's strikes to counter their own until she staggered, the backs of her legs hitting the throne.

Malloryn appeared out of nowhere, deflecting a blow meant for her.

"Thanks." Mina lunged forward, stabbing a Falcon in the thigh as Malloryn parried another blow. For a second they worked together, but then she realized he was trying to shield her with his own body. Mina tripped on his boot, frustrated. *I'm not some pampered princess.* But he'd always been smothering, especially when she'd broken off their affair.

"Behind you!" she yelled.

Balfour slammed a dagger into Malloryn's side. Malloryn gritted his teeth and twisted, slashing his sword across Balfour's throat. The spymaster fell back, clutching at the blade, blood pouring between his fingers. Malloryn tried to go after him, but his leg gave out beneath him and he went down on one knee, holding his side. A Falcon grabbed Balfour by the shoulders and hauled him away as Mina defended her ex-lover.

"Stay down," she snapped at Malloryn, putting herself between him and the two Falcons she'd been fighting.

"Mina!" The queen crawled to her side, her hands still holding the bloodied knife.

"Stay with Malloryn." Mina winced as one of the Falcons nicked her arm. Cool blood splashed down her sleeve, the muscles screaming in her shoulder as she tried to counter the next blow.

A man flew through the air, smashing into one of the Falcons and sending them both tumbling. Caine had thrown him. Mina could barely spare the duke a shocked glance as she met the remaining Falcon's thrust with a quick *prise de fer* of her own. Blood dripped into her palm. Clapping a hand to the wound and panting, she parried another thrust, the jarring force of the steel in her hand ringing up her forearm.

Blood and blazes. Desperation sunk its hooks into her. "Go!" she said to Alexa. "To the Nighthawks!"

"Not without you!" the queen cried, staggering to her feet beside Mina and holding her pathetic little stiletto as if she had some idea how to truly use it.

Blast her. Yet the flush of emotion speared behind Mina's eyes. *We always said we'd do this together.*

Another woman appeared out of nowhere, kicking the Falcon in the back of the knee and driving him to the ground. Mina promptly ran him through, staggering back in relief as the woman—clad in strict black—countered the attack of the two on the ground, whipping her blade across one throat and then spinning low to slash her sword across the back of the other's thigh. A master of the blade.

Lady Peregrine.

The Nighthawks.

Mina's sword tip lowered to the ground and then Alexandra was there, easing her back onto the throne of all things. Mina's fist curled in her queen's sleeve. "Whatever you do, stay with Lady Peregrine."

Lady Peregrine stepped closer, her sword held low and ready as she surveyed the melee. "Are you injured?"

"Nothing serious." Mina's arm was afire now, but at least the bleeding had stopped. Alexandra tore at her skirts, tying a very fashionable bandage of green silk around Mina's upper arm.

"I'm fine," Mina told her, but the queen was crying, endless streams of tears washing her pale face.

Two men faced the entire gathering of Nighthawks who'd surrounded the throne. The rest of the room was emptying, debutantes and thralls having fled in fright.

The prince consort leaned in one of his Falcon's arms, breathing heavily but not dead. Not yet.

"You swore," the prince consort sputtered, blood spraying the fine linen of his cravat. His feet kicked at the ground, as if to get away, but he and the Falcon were trapped against the wall. Nowhere to go. Nowhere to hide. "You swore an oath to me!"

Caine took a threatening step up onto the dais, his sword held low and ready. Emotion burned hotly in his pale blue eyes. "And you spat it in my face."

"Don't do this!" the prince consort said shrilly. "You'll destroy everything we ever worked for!"

"Perhaps...change is coming. It seems inevitable." Sadness flashed through the duke's eyes. "But by the blood I swore to you, I shall see this done myself." His arm lifted. "That much I owe you."

Caine, the only man with the strength to drive that piece of metal through the prince consort's breastplate, sent it straight through the prince consort's heart and into the Falcon holding him upright. They both stiffened, the prince consort's feet drumming helplessly as blood bubbled over his lips.

The duke twisted the blade and then withdrew it with a flick of violet blood across the marble floors. As one, the assembled crowd held their breath.

He turned, tilting his head toward Alexandra, emotionless once more. "Long live the Queen."

Twenty-eight

MINUTES DRAGGED BY. ORDERS. NIGHTHAWKS SETTING up a guard on the queen as Alexandra ordered her husband's body burned. Balfour was missing and Malloryn had sworn to find him, but otherwise, they were in control. Mina caught the queen's sleeve.

"I have to go." Urgency burned through her. "I have to find Barrons."

"Barrons?" Alexandra demanded. "But I need you here. There's so much to do—"

I have done enough. This, at least, was for herself. "I don't know where he is." She flashed a look at Caine. "I don't know if he's still alive, if he's hurt. If he's…" Her voice trailed off.

Lynch knelt beside them, his hand settling over the queen's. "I'll keep her safe," he said to Mina. "The last I saw of him, Barrons was going to find several Falcons who were keeping watch with a detonator. The entire Tower is full of explosives, as I understand. The prince consort meant to see us all dead."

All of the heat washed out of her face. "Leo could be dead then."

"I doubt it. That flare the prince consort fired was meant to be the detonation signal. The very fact that we're still here means Leo is alive."

Or was alive.

The queen gave a wan smile. "I assume this means you have changed your views on marriage?"

Mina gave the queen's hand another squeeze, torn again. "Do you need me...?"

Alexandra reached out and kissed her brow. Her lips were wet with tears. "You have done enough, Mina." The pressure of her lips eased. "Go. Go and find your man. That's a royal decree."

⤜⤛

The smoke was clearing, but still she couldn't find him. Mina shoved through the crowd, pushing past bloodied Nighthawks and some of the ruffians from the rookery. The world sounded strange. Diluted. As if she were traveling through it but no one could see or speak to her.

A tiny sphere of icy cold began to grow in the pit of her stomach, little fingers of it seeping outward, slowly locking through each muscle. There were so many people tromping through the Tower grounds that it made sense she wouldn't find him immediately. Of course it did.

He'll be here. Somewhere.

The cold finally reached her skin, a bone-deep tremble that started from within. *Please. Please let him be alive.* The alternative...she couldn't even think of it.

Not in the yard. She turned toward the other

towers that stood at each corner of the wall. Ravens screamed as they circled Crowe Tower, disturbed out of sleep by the noise and the fires.

A man's form appeared, leaning against the arch that led into Crowe Tower. Mina froze, her lungs tightening in her chest. Not quite believing her eyes. "*Leo*," she whispered, but the word was almost soundless.

As if he heard it, the man looked up, dark eyes locking on her from across the yard, looking at her as if she were the world, *his* whole world. She felt it deep within, her heart finally starting to beat again in her chest—or perhaps it always had been but she could only feel it now. One hesitant step toward him, then she couldn't hold herself back. She broke into a run, darting between men and women alike.

Leo took a step toward her, wincing as he put his right foot down. His arms opened and she ran into them, her body hitting his with a thump, his arms curling around her and crushing her to his chest.

"You weren't there." She gasped. "You weren't there when I looked, and all Lynch could tell me was something about a bomb and a Falcon and—"

"Did you miss me?" His hoarse voice rumbled through her chest. Hands stroking through her hair as he drew back just enough to look at her.

If she could have cried in that moment, she would have. Something shifted in his expression at the sight. A little bit feral, full of need.

"I thought you were dead," she admitted in a small, choked voice. "I thought—"

And he knew. He saw it, his expression hardening. "I wasn't going to die, Mina. Not with everything left unsaid between us. I was always coming back for you. I always will."

"Promise me—"

His mouth met hers, cutting off the words. A hard, fierce kiss that said so much more than words ever could.

Mina melted against him, a whimper in her throat. Then he was dragging her back into the shadows under the arch, his hands relentless as they stroked her back and bottom, cupping her hard against him.

Firelight gilded his face as he drew back just enough to catch his breath, his eyes cast into saturnine pools of darkness. "I'm close to the edge tonight," he said hoarsely, as if she couldn't see the rise of the hunger in his eyes, driven there by strong emotion. She slid her hands into his hair, feeling the unyielding stance of his body. Trying to control himself. *Fair warning.* She didn't care.

Mina fisted her hands in his collar and dragged him against her, her mouth finding his. Their mouths met again, hers just as hungry as his. Reaching out, she shoved blindly at the heavy wooden door, plunging them into the heated darkness inside the tower.

Hard hands bruised her hips, pushing her back against the wall. Leo understood the kiss as consent, biting at her throat and lifting her thighs until they locked around his hips. The heated length of his erection ground against her, and Mina was suddenly desperate for it. Shoving at his coat, his shirt, baring skin to her touch, biting at his throat until he gave a soft groan in the dark.

"Mina... Oh God..." He caught a fistful of her

hair and jerked her mouth back to his, grinding his cock against her sensitive flesh. "I need to be inside you."

She wriggled, trying to undo her buttons. "Bloody Blade. These cursed trousers."

A masculine laugh sounded close to her ear, drawing to a heated purr at the end. "They have their appeal." Hands slid over her hips, his body disengaging just enough for her toes to touch the ground. Leo tugged the leather down over her hips, following with his breath and lips.

A kiss to her navel, trailing lower as he dragged the trousers down over her thighs, trapping her knees together. Mina stilled, a hand trembling in his hair as his breath wet her skin, teeth sinking into the edge of her drawers, then gliding lower until his face nuzzled into the intimate hair between her thighs.

Her heart was pounding fit to tear her chest apart. "*Leo*," she whispered. A single word that meant so much.

Tongue darting between her thighs, he made a sound, half groan, half growl. He dug his fingers into her flesh as he held her legs shut, that wicked tongue stealing into places that made her shudder.

"Blood and glory," she moaned, throwing her head back, aching desperately to part her thighs and let him in. "*Please*."

"Please what?"

Teeth sinking into her lip, she looked down, unable to see him in the dark. But she could feel him, his tongue tracing her clit, those broad shoulders spread before her. "Just let me... *Ah*..." Her head thrashed back, teeth bruising her sensitive lip. "Damn you. Get these trousers off me."

He let her thighs part, just an inch or two, and sucked her clit into his mouth. Hard.

Mina screamed, pushing her knuckles into her mouth, her teeth sinking into them. The pressure built. She threw her head back, driving his face against her body with her hand, not caring in that moment about embarrassment. Just need. Pure, selfish need.

And he gave it to her, kissing her as deeply as he had done her mouth. His tongue darted inside her, then swirled around her clit as if he traced the letters of her name. She couldn't take it anymore. "No... No..."

"Yes," he breathed.

It fractured her. Blew her apart and left her gasping against the wall, one hand fisted in his hair, body racking with violent convulsions that finally ceased as he drew back. God, if she wasn't leaning against something, she'd be a quivering pile on the floor right now, as Leo pressed a gentle kiss against her thigh.

Her whole body trembled. She could feel him slip the hem of her trousers over a boot. Callused hands slid up the back of her legs, cupping her thighs, lifting her easily as he stood and resumed his rightful place between them.

Dazed and floating in a pleasure haze, she slid her hand between them, tugging ruthlessly at the buttons on his own pants, diving that hand inside to cup him as soon as she could. A hiss whispered against her throat, Leo giving a little thrust into her palm. Every muscle in his body tensed. Fingers unsteady, she guided him between her legs, rubbing the slick head of his cock over the wetness there.

Mina moaned as he pushed inside her, sliding her fingernails down his back, raking them into the slick leather of his coat. It clung to his shoulders. She wanted it off, her mouth seeking his and tasting the heat of her own body there. Leo twisted his shoulders, the coat hitting the floor with a meaty slap as he thrust within her. Then his shirt… She couldn't drag it open. There were buttons…bloody buttons… Her mind went blank, filling with him, with the force of those slowly increasing thrusts, the hard rasp of the stone at her back rough against her bottom.

"Mina…Mina…" His mouth was a delicious thing. Bloody hell, he knew how to kiss. "You feel so fucking good. I don't think…" He shuddered, pressing his face against her shoulder as the next thrust took her deep and hard. "I don't think I can—"

"Then don't," she whispered, digging her nails into the hard curve of his arse. His pelvis ground against hers, just holding her there, as if he were trying to push his whole body inside her. Circling his hips just enough so the grind rubbed her sensitive clit, until she was moaning a little with harsh, breathy sounds of need, sounds she'd never heard from her own throat.

Her whole body clenched, locking tightly around his as she came with a sob. Then he was fucking his way into her, pounding her brutally against the wall, one hand outthrust against the stone, the other beneath her arse, holding her there. His body pinned hers, chest pressed against her own as he fucked her in a wild, desperate assault that she knew she'd feel tomorrow.

She had not been the only one who'd felt a little lost tonight. This...this was a claiming. And she encouraged it, let him take everything she had from her and still demand more. Everything that had not been spoken between them—the tension of the past, the fear of the present, and the hope for the future— broke between them. Leo sank both hands into the flesh of her hips as his thrusts became stronger, slower, deeper somehow, bruising in their intensity.

Wrapping her arms around his neck, she clenched everything inside her. It tore a torrent of filthy words from his lips as he swore and quivered, the hot spill of his seed drenching her inside.

He collapsed against her, his breath came in hard pants against her shoulder. His forehead pressed against the wall, the stubble on his cheek brushing against her jaw. He simply held her there, as if he had no plans to ever let her go.

Mina tipped her head back and breathed hard, listening to the pounding of their hearts between them. Sensation was beginning to return. One boot on, the other...lost somewhere. Trousers clinging to her left ankle but not the right. A mess.

She laughed then. Nobody would ever believe this to be her. Bitten and marked, her hair tumbling around her face, body full of the sensation of him. And this *was* her, she realized. A part of her that she'd never, ever allowed to surface, a part that only Leo had ever brought out in her.

Mina pressed her lips against his shoulder, one hand caressing the back of his head. Most of all, the sensation she felt was strangely...tender.

I don't want to let him go. A weakness, she'd once believed. But she didn't feel weak, not at this moment. She felt amazingly strong, like a phoenix bursting from her own scattered ashes, blazing anew. Far from undoing her, he'd been the making of this new, fearless creature that prowled inside her.

He owned her. The most terrifying thing in the world once. But he could only own her if she allowed it, and she held that power in her hands. For the first time, Mina felt as if she were truly seeing the world, realizing that by locking herself away, forcing herself not to let any man in, that...that had been the true weakness.

"You're not alone," she whispered.

His heart rate had been slowing against her. She almost felt it skip a beat as Leo jerked his head up, his half-hard cock moving within her. Mina winced a little.

"What did you say?" A hard demand that she couldn't read.

Old doubt resurfaced, but she refused to let those shadows back in. "I said that you're not alone. The w-way I feel... I was so frightened that you were dead and..." Her voice became a whisper. "I think I love you."

It was hard, in the darkness, when silence fell. Her heart leaped in her chest and Mina froze. For the first time in years she'd dared to bare herself to someone else.

And there was no response. *I'm afraid that I'm standing here alone in this new world...*

Mina pushed him away, yanking her trousers on, her hands rough and trembling, and her mind blank as—

"Mina." Hands caught her arms as she tried to duck past him. "Mina, wait." Leo caught her face in his hands, and then his lips found hers in the dark. Instinct told her to run, but he wouldn't let her, soothing her with the sweetest, most tempting kisses, his hands cupping her face and holding her there as if she were infinitely precious. She hesitated for a fraction of a second, then felt herself softening against him.

Finally he drew back. "You surprised me. I never expected you to...tell me such a thing." Those tender hands rubbed up and down her back, softening the tension from her spine. His voice grew rough. "Maybe because I wanted to hear it from your lips so much." He cleared his throat. "Here. Stand still." He knelt again, a faint shadow in the blackness. Taking her foot, he slipped her boot back on, easing it gently over her calf. She caught only the faintest glimmer of the whites of his eyes, but she knew he was watching her.

"I told you once that you didn't understand my motives," he finally said. "Hell, Mina, I didn't understand them either. I wanted you. I just didn't know what I wanted of you."

"And have you figured it out?"

"I think I'm getting there." Leo pushed himself to his feet, sliding his hands over her hips. "These last few days have cost me everything—power, position, respect...the man that I called a father. Everything that I've spent years working to achieve, all gone. I kept thinking that if there was one thing I couldn't bear to lose, it would be you, and the promise of what I hoped we had, but I didn't know if you felt the same.

"I want what Blade has. What Will has. I want that,

all of that. I want to hold my daughter in my arms and kiss her mother on the cheek. I want a family of my own to make up for the one that I've never had, and when I picture that, it's your face I see. My wife, that's what I want. But most of all, I would like to hear you say those words one more time."

"Say what?" Her heart was starting to beat a little faster now, full of certainty.

"That you love me," he replied, stepping closer, body to body. His hands whispered over her cheeks, tipping her face up to his. "It's the one thing that makes sense in all of this. It's the one thing that makes me feel like I haven't lost anything at all. Or nothing of importance." His lips brushed hers. "Right now, I feel like I've won the world."

Her heart swelled a little in her chest and she rested her hands on his, still shy enough that she was grateful for the darkness. "I love you."

"Again."

"I love you." This time she nipped his lip playfully, wrapping her arms around his neck and drawing him against her.

"Again," he growled.

"Leo!" She slapped his chest and he laughed, then leaned down to plant a toe-curling kiss on her passion-bruised mouth.

"You are the most amazing woman I've ever met." A kiss against her cheek now, breathing the words into her ear. "But now…"

"Now?"

"We'd best be getting back. Or Blade will be taking all of the credit for this, no doubt."

Twenty-nine

Three days later...

LEO PACED THROUGH THE STUDY, HIS HANDS CLASPED behind his back as he waited. The clock ticked steadily in the stuffy silence of the room, and an enormous tiger's head mounted on the wall stared back at him through button eyes. Someone had half drawn the heavy velvet drapes, so that the room seemed even smaller, and he had to avoid several ornate mahogany chairs with their studded red leather seats. The chessboard was set out between two stuffed armchairs, the game frozen in motion, as if merely waiting for its players to return.

He avoided the chess game for a good quarter hour, then stopped in front of it. He'd been in check last he looked, but someone had moved one of his pawns, as if trying to draw out the game.

Devil take him, the bastard was actually withdrawing, offering him a chance to pursue this. Leo frowned, his fingers itching toward his own black knight. He could see the strategy behind it, see how in eight moves he could get himself out of trouble if he did something now.

Except he never had any intention of making that move. He was done with the game and what it represented. Caine could sit here and rot, staring at that chessboard and waiting for him to return so that they could finally resume play. A wait in vain. The only reason he was here was because the queen had requested it of him.

Lips thinning, he turned away, flipping the drapes open to let some bloody light into the room.

The door opened behind him. Leo didn't turn, but he could feel that cool, rational gaze burning over the back of his neck.

"Havers said you had called," Caine said. "Imagine my surprise."

"I'm only here to deliver a message," Leo replied.

A harsh laugh. "Of course. What is it?"

He tugged the envelope from within his coat. "How should I bloody know? The queen asked me to deliver it personally."

Caine broke the seal and read it. "I'm to be reinstated as a councilor. Along with..." His eyebrows shot up into his hairline.

"Mina, Lynch, Malloryn, Rosalind Lynch, Sir Gideon Scott...and the Devil of Whitechapel," Leo added with a nasty smile. "Her Highness feels that more classes require representation on the Council." He bowed. "Now if you'll excuse me?"

"Is that all you came to say?"

Leo paused. "By the way, I'm getting married. You're not invited." With those parting words, he strode toward the door.

"Wait."

Caine's demand echoed through the room. Leo ignored it, his fingertips turning on the brass door handle.

"Damn you, wait!"

Leo arched a brow as if to tell the duke to hurry up.

"I have something for you…and for your fiancée."

Of all the things he'd expected, this was not it. Caine crossed toward the polished walnut writing desk in the corner, hunting through it with an unusual lack of aplomb. He scattered papers and pieces of parchment until he came up with a leather-bound journal. Dusting it off, Caine peered at the cover for a long moment. Not a single change occurred in his expression but Leo wondered what the devil the book was. The gravity with which Caine beheld it…

With a faint sigh, Caine stood, opening the journal to remove a faded photograph. He offered it to Leo.

A young woman stared out at the viewer with wide, luminous eyes, the faintest of smiles curling the edge of her full mouth. A monstrous hat, smothered in ostrich feathers, dominated the picture, but Leo could see that she was pretty, and that the edges of the picture had been handled often enough to show signs of wear. Something cherished then, perhaps.

"For you," Caine said bluntly. "It's of your mother."

Leo's gaze jerked to his. "My—" *Mother.* He hadn't even recognized her. A heavy feeling settled in his chest.

Words were written on the back of it.

For Marguerite… Here's to more stolen waltzes, skating in the park, and lemon-flavored ices.

> *Your friend and admirer,*
> *Corbet Duvall*

"The Duke of Casavian was courting my *mother*?"

Faint contempt flickered in the hooded depths of Caine's eyes. "He wasn't a duke then, just a fool freshly up from Oxford. *I* won her."

Of course he did. Caine rarely failed whenever he set his mind to something. Leo's jaw locked. Was this what had sent the Great Houses of Caine and Casavian into their deadly feud over the years?

"I am not a good man, nor a kindly one. I am what my father made me, as I have tried to make you. A duke. A man of power. Marguerite…for a brief moment in my life, she made of me something else. She made me happy. And when she was gone, so was her light in my life, and all I had left was you.

"It took me a long time to be able to look at you and not see what I had done." The duke toyed with his sleeve. "I know you think I despised her, but the truth is…" His voice roughened. "I shall never forgive myself for what I did to my Marguerite. The doctors said afterward that she wasn't built to accommodate children. I should have left well enough alone."

No. Caine wasn't going to do this to him. Leo steeled himself. "Who wrote that pretty speech?"

To give him his due, the duke didn't try to lie. "Madeline. She seemed to think…" He sighed, then added stiffly, "The sentiment was mine. The words…"

Hers. "You should take care of her. She may be all that you have left someday."

"Leo—"

"Why did you never let me speak her name? Or show me her photographs?" The sleep deprivation, the strict discipline and harsh training as a child…he thought he understood that now, but the rest…

"I did not wish to be reminded of her. I did not wish to show the world my weakness."

An awkward silence reigned between them.

"I am not like you," he told Caine. "No matter how many times you tried to whip me into your shape."

A dignified nod. "You are like her. You always have been. Questioning everything, championing causes that have no financial worth or personal gain. Disobeying me at every turn. She always spoke her mind, arguing that we were too harsh on the human classes…" His voice trailed off. "She would have been proud of what you have become, what you have achieved."

More silence. A glimmer of the mother he had never known.

"Do you think this changes anything?" Leo demanded. In the past few days he'd thought he'd finally found peace with his past—and with the man he called a father. He had Mina now, and his sisters and brother, a family that Caine could not even *begin* to comprehend. He'd even begun to renew his friendship with Malloryn, despite being fairly certain about what had caused the rift between them. Malloryn had wished him well on landing Mina, but there'd been a hint of sadness hidden behind his cynical smile.

"You are my son," Caine said. "No matter what the world says. I have lost her, but I will not lose you, no matter what I must do."

Leo barked a laugh. "You manipulative son of a bitch. You had the chance to prove yourself my father in Council chambers."

"I never…I didn't expect it. I didn't know what to do."

"You didn't know who to choose," Leo corrected icily. "Your loyalties to that bastard, or your ties to me."

"That's not true." This time there was a hint of steel to the words. "I made my choice. I killed my prince and broke my word, for you. Everything that I have ever believed in… Change…change does not sit well with me."

Leo shook his head. Everything that he thought he'd settled within himself in the last few days was thrown into turmoil. In spite of everything, a part of him wanted to believe Caine's words. His own personal weakness. "I've delivered my queen's message. Consider my familial duties finished." He turned and strode toward the door.

"Wait!" Caine shuffled across the carpets, pushing the journal into Leo's hands. "Here! Before you go. Take this! For your…for your fiancée. Perhaps this will explain some matters for her."

Not that there was any choice. Leo's fingers curled around the leather-bound spine. "What is it?"

"An abomination," Caine said. "And a miracle."

Leo flipped the journal open.

Project: Dhampir.
    An initiative undertaken by the Dukes of Lannister, Casavian, and Caine.
    1864.

That caught his attention. More than fifteen years ago. What in blazes had Caine and Casavian been working on together, especially when they'd despised each other?

Spidery scrawl filled the journal. Test notes, tables of subject names, CV levels... Leo flipped through the pages swiftly. "What is this?"

"An undertaking. A means to transmute the effects of the Fade by means of an *elixir vitae*. There was word of it from an ancient Oriental transcript that spoke of the origins of the craving virus."

Leo's heart quickened. "Did it work?"

"Only on seven of the test subjects. And...myself."

Leo's gaze jerked up, interested despite his feelings. Focusing on Caine's silvery hair—not gray with age, so much as faded—and his pale, unblemished skin and eyes. "Who else tried the elixir?"

"Casavian, of course."

Their eyes met.

"What one ventured, the other must as well." The slightest curling of Caine's lip. "Only one of us survived it. In a way, he poisoned himself."

Leo's hands trembled as he kept flipping through the pages. Mina would be devastated, but perhaps this would bring her some peace of mind. The truth behind her father's death.

"And the *elixir vitae*?" he demanded. Honoria's vaccination could reverse the effects of the craving to a point, but what if one could change the fate of all blue bloods? To control their evolution, as Caine had?

"The secret to the elixir...you will find that at the end of the journal."

Leo hurriedly riffled through the pages to the back, where he found an entry written in a less than steady hand.

It has been decided to destroy all records of this project. All of the test subjects are to be executed by Vickers, the Duke of Lannister, and all documents destroyed, after the debacle of Subject X. The testing facility suffered a fire and all that remains of my work is this one journal. I should destroy it, for the elixir is a most dangerous tool in the wrong hands.

However, I cannot bear to see all of my work—of the last fifteen years—turn to ash. Perhaps, if I were a stronger man, I would consign these records to the fire myself, but pride—vanity—compel me to keep some record of such flawed genius.

If you read this, you will know that I have created a creature of such utter perfection that God himself has cursed me for my impudence, and that perhaps, for the first time in my life, I understand the consequences of dabbling in matters best left to the Almighty.

I pray only for redemption now.

With regret,
Dr. Erasmus Cremorne

"It is dangerous knowledge," Caine said softly. "A weapon in the right hands."

And you're placing it in mine. His curiosity was stirred, an itch beneath the skin. Perhaps an inclination inherited from Todd, and Caine, the bastard, knew it. "What happened to the doctor?"

"He hanged himself shortly after writing this appendix. He sent the journal to a compatriot of mine. However, I managed to intercept it in time."

Leo shut the book with a hard slapping sound. "Do you think this can buy my goodwill?"

"Perhaps I think you will know how best to use such knowledge. I have no need of it now."

Eyes narrowing, Leo gave a terse nod. "Thank you." For what it would mean to Mina.

The duke took his seat again, folding into his padded armchair with a stiff kind of grace that made a blue blood seem clumsy. His fingers laced over his middle. "You should continue our chess game. You still have deplorable lack of foresight. I can teach you how to—"

"I'll think about it." He eyed those laced fingers. Left hand over right, the same as his own manner of sitting at times. A disconcerting thought. "And now, I believe I have an appointment at my club."

"Leo?"

Leo jerked the door open, tucking the journal beneath his arm. "We're done here."

"I am proud of what you have achieved. You have done what I could not see was necessary for our country."

The words followed Leo through the doorway, and if he slammed the door a little harder than necessary, nobody was around to see it.

The easiest thing to do would be to walk away and close this chapter of his life. Caine had done little but cause him pain over the years, and nothing about this sudden revelation spoke of any change to that. Caine was—and obviously always had been—a manipulative, cold-hearted bastard. But Leo paused at the bottom of the stairs as the maids rushed forward with his coat, hat, and gloves. ...*I killed her. I killed my Marguerite...* Something had quivered in the duke's voice then. Not the sound or words of a man who'd married for a political match, and if he truly had been raised the way he'd raised Leo, could Leo blame him?

Perhaps his mother's death had more of an impact than Leo could ever realize. Caine had no one else to show him how to live any differently. It was true that Caine did not understand change. He *was* a relic of the past in more ways than one.

The footmen holding the doors open waited impassively as Leo stewed over the matter. He *could* walk away, but a part of him would always wonder. Perhaps now that he understood why the duke was the way he was, they could form some sort of relationship. It would never be the one he'd desired. Never the father he'd always wanted. But maybe he didn't need one now.

"Tell His Grace to move my knight to D5." Taking his top hat, Leo fit it to his head and sauntered down the front steps of Caine House to go find his fiancée.

Epilogue

Six months later...

"I'M NOT QUITE CERTAIN I UNDERSTAND THIS CUSTOM."

Leo slid a hand over the small of his wife's back, the other arm laden with brightly wrapped boxes. Her jacket was a dark aubergine, complete with mink fur around the collar, and a black velvet hat crowned a pile of luxurious red curls. Elegant from top to toe. He'd never had much interest in women's fashion before their marriage, but peeling her out of each luxurious layer was becoming one of his favorite pastimes, particularly discovering what she was wearing beneath. Mina liked silks and lace and naughty little bits of French frippery that she called undergarments.

Leo liked removing them.

"It's a human custom," he replied, holding open the back door to the Warren for her. The scent of baked ham assaulted him, along with something sweet and spicy. "I believe that the Countess of Leverstein brought the traditional customs with her from her homeland. Since the Echelon refused to partake due to the holiday's religious undertones, humans took to it with deliberate enthusiasm."

"Christmas," Mina murmured. "How quaint."

The realm's first official Christmas, something the queen had set in motion to celebrate the passing of her husband's tyranny and help to bring in a New Year. Tomorrow they'd be expected at Balmoral, where the queen was spending the holidays, for a Christmas dinner. Tonight, however, was something he planned on sharing with his own family before the train trip in the morning.

Brushing snowflakes from Mina's back, he stared around the kitchen. Copper pots hung from the ceiling and an enormous stove dominated the hearth. It was like walking into a wall of heat and scent, almost a little like coming home.

Esme entered the kitchen, moving much more slowly than she had before. The froth of bows and silk drapery on her dress somewhat disguised the distinct bulge of her figure, but nothing could hide her brilliant smile and the bright glow of her eyes. Far from struggling with her condition as Honoria had, Esme looked as though it suited her.

"Oh, Barrons," she said, hurrying forward. "And Duchess. Here, let me take those from you."

Leo twisted out of the way. "Absolutely not."

Esme's lips thinned. "I wasn't aware I was suddenly useless."

"'Ardly." Rip's voice echoed in the room as he entered on the heels of his wife. "Leo. Duchess." He nodded. "What are you doin' in 'ere, woman? This is tradition." Taking hold of Esme's shoulders, he turned her about. "Women stay out o' the kitchen today. Blade and I managed not to burn the duck last year, and we can do it again today."

Esme gestured over her shoulder. "Come on in then. Everybody's waiting in the sitting room. I'll just fetch some—"

"You'll sit," Rip growled, steering her through the door. "And let me do the work. Now what were you goin' to fetch?"

The door closed behind them.

Exchanging an amused glance with Mina, Leo helped her out of her jacket. Taking advantage of the opportunity, he curled his arms around her and drew her back against his chest. "That shall be us one day."

"I doubt it." She laughed. "Neither of us can cook."

Leo pressed his mouth against her neck, the vibrancy of her laughter jolting against his lips. It was one of his favorite places to kiss her—the soft skin now warmed by her coat and smelling faintly of the rose soap she used on her hair. His arms softened, his lips lingering there.

"Leo," she warned, tugging free. There was a hint of warmth in her eyes, that melting little expression she got when she was intent on teasing him. "Later."

"Are you going to be my present?"

"If you behave, I might let you unwrap me," she teased, reaching up for her hat.

Watching her undress was almost as enjoyable as doing it himself. Leo set the presents down on the kitchen counter and helped her pluck her hat pins free.

"Do you know," she murmured, glancing up from

beneath her thick, dark lashes, "that a trunk arrived from Madame Peignoir's today?"

"Mmm?" He glanced down into those warm brown eyes, his cock hardening a little. Madame Peignoir was the perpetrator behind most of the flimsy little bits of lace. He could just imagine.

"You should see what I'm wearing under all of this."

"Is this a new way of torturing me?" He tossed her hat aside and stepped closer. He pinned her against the bench, the sleek press of his trousers lost in the swagged velvet skirts she wore. His voice dropped. "Or are you inviting me to do wicked things to my wife in my sister's kitchen?"

"I don't think—"

"Sounds terribly fascinatin'," Blade said, shoving the door open and giving them a bland smile. "But Esme says, 'not in her kitchen,' and some of us 'as preternatural 'earin'." He winked at the duchess.

Molten relaxation washed off her, replaced by her usual upright pose. Leo rubbed the back of his fingers against her cheek, shot her one last amused smile, and then stepped back. *Later*, his eyes told her.

I'll hold you to that, hers replied.

"Blade," he said, nodding at his brother-in-law as he shrugged out of his own greatcoat. "Merry Christmas."

"Sir Henry. The Hero of the Realm." The duchess tipped her own head in a polite nod, her eyes devilish. It wasn't beyond her to provoke her brother-in-law, and she'd recently figured out that the use of his proper name and title made Blade's nose itch a little.

Blade might have taken a great deal of credit for the uprising, but it embarrassed him when people called him the Hero of the Realm in the streets. "Should I curtsy?"

"Duchess," Blade replied, swinging the door open and gesturing through it with an elegant bow. He wasn't above retaliation.

Light and laughter welcomed them into the sitting room where everyone else was gathered. Lena came to her feet with an enormous smile and hurried forward to press a kiss to Leo's cheek. "I thought you two were never going to arrive! We've been waiting all night to distribute the presents!"

Presents. "Damn it, I've left them in the kitchen—"

"I'll get them," Lena replied promptly. She turned toward Mina and took her hands, a little more reserved now. "Duchess."

"Mina, please."

Leo didn't quite watch the exchange, but it made him relax a little when Lena repeated her name, wished her a "Merry Christmas," and then kissed Mina on the cheek. Forgiven, he suspected, but not entirely forgotten, though time would heal that wound.

There was a never-ending barrage of people to greet: Will, looking more relaxed than he'd been in a while; Charlie, who clapped hands with Leo with a weak smile, before glancing at Lark who murmured a hullo to Leo and pointedly ignored Charlie; and then Honoria and the baby. Tin Man's absence from the scene was a hollow blow, and he noticed Charlie shooting Lark hesitant glances as they avoided each other.

Leo arched a brow at Honoria, then gestured to the young pair standing apart. Lark had lost a great deal of weight since Tin Man's death, and he'd heard that she'd had a few choice words to say to Charlie at the funeral. Blade had gone easy on the lad in the end; Lark's grief was punishment enough.

Honoria graced Leo with a sad smile and a little shrug that could have meant anything. "It's good to see you."

"Likewise." Leaning in, he kissed her cheek. "It's been too long."

"I hear Her Highness has been keeping all of you busy."

"One would think she plans to introduce ten years' worth of legal changes in one," he said dryly. "It's keeping Mina on her toes though. The situation suits her."

Honoria snuggled baby Emma against her throat, while Blade watched his wife from across the room. Mina looked a little out of her depth, but she graciously accepted a glass of blud-wein and settled in beside Esme on a sofa by the roaring hearth. "*She* suits you."

"You sound surprised."

"No." A secretive smile. "If anyone was ever to catch your eye, it was going to be someone with a mind of her own. Easy bores you."

Blade sauntered over, leaning in to smother kisses under Emma's jaw. "Easy bores most men. 'Ere, luv. Let me take 'er for a moment and give you a rest."

Honoria reluctantly handed over her daughter, settling Emma's white bonnet more securely on her head. Blade cooed at her, lifting her high in the air as he strolled toward the fireplace. Honoria laughed under her breath. "Not that it has anything to do with playing dirty."

Leo arched a brow, then realized exactly where Blade was heading. Blade handed Mina the baby and leaned against the mantel.

Honoria smiled as they sat, both of them watching their respective partners. "You look well. Content in a way I've never seen you look before."

"I am." It surprised him how much sometimes, and how it was only with such happiness that he'd realized how utterly gray his life had been before.

Blade played peekaboo behind the duchess's shoulder, sending Emma into squeals of delight. Mina eyed him with a certain droll wariness, but that familiar sparkle was in her eyes. Blade's campaign was evidently succeeding.

"He's shameless."

"The Devil of Whitechapel in all his terrifying glory," Leo added. Blade tickled Emma under her chubby chin, sending her jerking backward in Mina's arms. Mina scolded him with a frown, clutching the baby tight against her chest as if she feared dropping her.

"I adore watching him with her," Honor admitted. "I might as well not exist sometimes, except when it comes to nursing. Though I must admit, there's nothing quite like seeing your child in your husband's arms and knowing how much she loves him."

Leo couldn't take his eyes off his wife. Mina pressed her cheek against Emma's. Breathing in the scent of his little niece, he imagined. She'd admitted how much she adored the scent of babies. "Mmmm."

Honoria poked him in the ribs. "Mmm? That almost sounds like you're planning a brood."

"Hardly."

"Leo—"

"I think I'd best rescue her. If you'll excuse me?" he murmured, gracefully dodging the subject.

Crossing the room, he leaned on the back of the sofa and stroked Emma's chin. Her focus on him was absolute, as though he was the most fascinating thing she'd ever seen.

Leaning down, he pressed a kiss against his wife's neck. Mina glanced up, rubbing small circles on Emma's back. The more often they visited, the more comfortable she seemed to be with holding the baby. "I do hope that glow in your eyes isn't pertaining to any particular future plans?"

"No, love. Not yet. I'm quite content to leave it at the practicing stage for now."

A faint blush stained her pale cheeks. Her gaze lingered on Emma for long seconds, utterly unreadable. Then with a sigh, she handed her over to him. Leo lifted his niece up, earning a cuddle. "Hello, my beautiful young lass. Who's your favorite uncle?"

"Uncle Charlie!" Charlie called out from across the room, earning a laugh.

"Yes, well, you're much funnier-looking than me." Being around the lad was growing easier. Indeed, Leo seemed to be the only one Charlie could talk to about his own mistake and the consequences of it.

Warmth washed over Leo from the fireplace. He

settled Emma against his shoulder, then slid an arm around his wife as he sat. Mina rested her cheek against his shoulder, relaxing slowly as Blade excused himself to go help Will and Rip in the kitchen.

"Do you know," Mina murmured, "he's not so bad, after all."

Leo pressed a kiss into her hair. "Making peace with the natives, are we?"

"They're your natives. It stands to reason that I'm going to be around them quite often and should therefore make amends." Her expression softened. "And I like this."

"This?"

"Family. Even when they're not truly related, they're still a family. I like being part of it." Something wistful flashed across her face, and he knew she was thinking of her own brother and parents. A wound, she'd admitted, from which she'd never truly healed.

"I'll remember that the next time you call Caine a crazy, overbearing old bastard." He stroked the smooth skin of her inner arm. "Or complain that Blade's running a blockade against you on the Council."

"Yes, well, he might be in for a little surprise."

"Oh?"

Mina gave him a devilish smile. "He thinks he's winning me over with his daughter. Wait until he arrives in Council chambers next meeting and realizes his little blockade just might be falling to pieces."

"You're making friends then?"

"I'm going to annihilate him." She chuckled. "Not everybody likes this little scheme he has running about the enclaves."

"Rosalind?" The pair of women had been wary allies at first, until both realized they had rather a lot in common. And if Mina had Rosalind on her side, matters dictated that Lynch was possibly not far behind…

"Yes." Mina leaned on his chest, reaching out to coo at Emma. "Blade first, and then your father is going to get his comeuppance at court and I am going to win."

"You do realize that you don't have all of the vote yet."

"I shall. My plans for the enclaves are far superior."

"Of course they are." His wife had the unshakable belief that she was correct in most matters, though at least she was well aware of it. "What if the Council swung in another direction?"

"Nobody likes Caine. They'll vote against him just to block him."

"Perhaps, but Caine's proxy has rather a lot of sway with certain people."

A long, slow silence. Mina looked delighted and sat up straight. "You're accepting his offer."

"Yes, I think I shall." They'd resumed their weekly chess matches—at Mina's request, surprisingly enough—and Caine often had information waiting for Leo on some of the enterprises he was involved in, as if the duke were following his progress. Caine had certainly never given a damn about airships offering commercial trade before.

He caught her fingers and pressed them to his lips. "You do realize this might mean war."

"I know, but I like arguing with you in Council." Leaning closer, she whispered in his ear, "It's exciting."

He understood exactly what she meant.

"Let's say…if you lose the vote, then I get to tie you to the bed and have my wicked way with you."

"That hardly sounds like losing at all."

She smiled. "And if you win…"

That fired his imagination. "I get to return the favor."

Their gazes locked, and he could see the same smile tugging at her lips as he felt on his. "Behave," he said. "I'm holding the baby."

"Do you agree?"

"God, yes."

"Good." Another slow, heated smile. "I love politics, but I must admit, they just became far more fascinating."

Agreed. He looked down at the baby resting her head against his shoulder and tried not to think of the proposition his wife had just put to him. "Later," he whispered in a harsh voice.

"Later," she agreed with a victorious smile.

God, he loved her.

⁕

It was much later.

Leo swung Mina out into the yard behind the Warren, his veins hot with blooded brandy. One glimpse at her eyes, and he saw the same look in them as in his own. No words needed to be said. It had been a long, pleasant evening with far too much blud-wein, laughter, presents…and heated looks shot across the room. Pressing her up against the brick wall, he slid a hand into her hair and tipped her mouth up to his.

A deep, primal kiss, full of possession. Need burned through him like wildfire and he pressed his hips against hers, one hand sliding down to cup her arse through her bustle.

She moaned a little, her fingernails kneading his chest through his coat. "I've been waiting all night for this." The words were breathy, lost under his next assault. They did something to him that he could never quite explain—set loose the raging hunger within him until his vision darkened and he could barely restrain himself from raking his teeth down her neck.

Her gloved hand slid between them, cupping his erection with devastating intent. Something strangled came from his throat, and Leo became lost in the devilish look in her eye.

"Is it later?" He swallowed, hands sliding beneath her jacket and caressing the stiff, boned curve of her stays through her gown. Lips tracing her jaw and the soft curve of her ear, he whispered, "Because I want to fuck you right here."

"Do you?"

"Nice and slowly," he promised.

"Not here," Mina replied, her fingers curling in his collar as she pushed him away from her. The loss of her talented hand from his cock brought another soft groan to his lips. "Take me home and I'll let you do *whatever* you want to me."

Christ. His erection strained painfully hard.

Snowflakes tumbled from the sky, catching on his lashes. Light gleamed through the arch that led out of the yard, a single gaslight hanging from the gilded steam carriage they'd arrived in.

"I've a better idea." Leaning down, he caught her under the legs and swept her up into his arms. "I might just ravish you in the carriage."

"Leo!" She giggled, throwing her head back, one of her glossy curls tumbling wild with abandon.

He liked her like this, all of her defenses stripped away, revealing a woman who was passionate, ambitious, and slightly wicked. The thought that only he ever got to see this side of her made him grin as he heaved her up over his shoulder and strode through the arch.

The footman gave no sign that he saw anything out of the ordinary. Jerking the door open, he stepped aside and Leo lowered his wife slowly onto the prepared step, her body sliding down his in an intimate tease.

"John Coachman?" he called.

"Yes, sir?"

"Take the long way home," Leo instructed, then shut the door behind him and turned to press a kiss against his giggling wife's lips. "Merry Christmas, my love." His hands tugged her coat open, pushing her onto her back on the seat.

Another intimate laugh. "Time for your present."

"Indeed," he replied, bending to press his lips against hers. "What more could any man want?"

Acknowledgments

Huge thanks go to:

My very own hero, Byron, for all the love and laughter, and the way that you're almost more excited about this than I am! To my friends and family, and the local community who have supported me a hundred percent.

To the ELE girls (Kylie Griffin, Nicky Strickland, Jennie Kew, and Dakota Harrison), who bribe me with chocolate, set up our word-count challenges, beta read, and generally create mayhem. You guys rock, and I couldn't do this without you!

To my wonderful editor, Mary Altman, my copy editor Hilary, and all of the staff at Sourcebooks who manage the behind-the-scenes magic, especially my publicists, Danielle Dresser and Amelia Narigon. Mega thanks to Gene Mollica for yet another amazing cover. You had me the moment I saw Mina with that sword!

My agent, Jessica Faust, and the team at BookEnds Literary Agency. Huge thanks as always, for without you, this series wouldn't have begun to breathe!

To Melanie Carter Keary, Sheryl Nyary, and Suzan,

who helped Name That Baby from my newsletter competition!

And, last but not least, to all of my amazing readers, my Facebook fans, and Twitter peeps, the members of ARRA, RWA, and the bloggers who have helped spread the word—thank you all so very much! You've been clamoring for Leo since the beginning, and here he is. I hope it was worth it.

About the Author

Bec McMaster lives in a small town in Victoria, Australia, and grew up with her nose in a book. Following a lifelong love affair with fantasy, she discovered romance and hasn't looked back. A member of RWA, she writes sexy, dark paranormals and adventurous steampunk romances. When not writing, reading, or poring over travel brochures, she loves spending time with her very own hero or daydreaming about new worlds. Visit her website at www.becmcmaster.com or follow her on Twitter @BecMcMaster.